"Ms. Alsobrook has created a timeless emotional tale of love . . . BEYOND FOREVER is . . . a splendid reading experience from beginning to end."

— *The Talisman*

"In BEYOND FOREVER, Rosalyn Alsobrook puts a new twist on the ever popular time-travel romance. Expect the unexpected."

— Robin Lee Hatcher,
bestselling author of *Liberty Blue*

"Rosalyn Alsobrook gives us thrills and chills, humor and romance, and enough twists and turns to keep the reader guessing right to the last page. A super read."

— Susan Wiggs,
bestselling author of *Circle in the Water*

"Rosalyn Alsobrook spins a story of suspense and romance sure to please all her readers . . . a delightfully romantic read."

— *Literary Times*

"Rosalyn Alsobrook's time-traveling BEYOND FOREVER is a story to delight any reader, and its heartwarming conclusion is a balm to the spirit."

— Kasey Michaels, award-
winning author of *The Passion of an Angel*

BEYOND FOREVER

ROSALYN ALSOBROOK

ZEBRA BOOKS
KENSINGTON PUBLISHING CORP.

ZEBRA BOOKS are published by

Kensington Publishing Corp.
850 Third Avenue
New York, NY 10022

Zebra and the Z logo Reg. U.S. Pat. & TM Off.

First Printing: June, 1995

Printed in the United States of America

One

New Orleans
Friday, April 7, 1995

Alisha Sampson refused to slow down. She knew if she did it would give her time to think and thinking was something she did not want to do. Not *today* of all days.

"Where to now?" she asked her friend Roni Belomee, after emerging from the hotel lobby, car keys in hand. They had already visited the Audubon Zoo and the above-ground cemetery where some of her father's ancestors were entombed, and had decided to wait until after dark to ride one of the famous Mississippi riverboats. The full moon that night should make the ride absolutely spectacular.

"Let's head on over to the French Quarter. I'm ready to spend some money," Roni answered, then made a futile grab for Alisha's keys just before they started across the hotel parking lot. "Let me drive." She glanced eagerly at the shimmering red BMW convertible parked well away from the other cars to keep doors from hitting it. The sporty automobile was so new it still had a dealer's tag instead of the usual Texas license plate.

"No, thank you." Alisha lifted the keys high over her head. Since she was seven inches taller than her friend, that action put them well out of reach. "Not after what you did to your own car just last week." She grimaced at the memory.

"But that wasn't my fault." Roni scowled then hurried to keep pace with Alisha's longer strides. "Besides, you know I'd be much more careful with a car like *that*. Why, that beauty had to have cost some major bucks. I still can't believe you bought it."

"You're right, it did cost major bucks, which is why *you* are not driving it." She shot Roni a dubious look, then pressed the door lock release on the tiny remote attached to her keys. "And if that accident wasn't your fault, then why did the officer give you that ticket for excessive speed?"

"Because he was in an incredibly foul mood. After all, I was only going about fifteen miles over the speed limit. Besides, how was I to know that other car was going to come to such a sudden stop?"

"I'd think that the red and white octagonal sign at the corner should have been a good clue," Alisha muttered with a disbelieving shake of her head. She knew the real reason Roni had plowed into the back of that poor man's car. Her attention was on a small throng of half-naked construction workers at the time. "Besides, I've only had this car two weeks. I've barely had a chance to drive it myself."

Roni gave a quick sigh. "Okay, be selfish. See if I care. But what about when we head for home? It's a seven-and-a-half hour drive back to Dallas—especially as slow as you drive. Surely you'll become tired enough in that time to let me take the wheel at least once."

"Oh, give it *up,*" Alisha said, rolling her green eyes. She reached for the door handle. Then more out of habit than because she really meant it, she commented, "You are starting to remind me of Brad."

"Sorry," Roni apologized. Her sulky expression sobered immediately. "I certainly didn't mean to do that. Not when the reason we came to New Orleans this weekend was so we could celebrate your birthday in the city where you were born and at the same time forget all about that bum and the fact that he's actually planning to marry that blond bimbette. And tonight of all nights."

"Yes, happy birthday to me," Alisha remarked bitterly, then forced a smile she did not feel as she opened the car door and slid onto the beige leather seat. "But then what do I care that my dear, sweet husband has decided to get married again on *my* birthday or that they're having a more elaborate wedding than ours."

"*Ex-*husband," Roni corrected, then plopped heavily onto the passenger's seat. "You really have to start getting over him. You've been divorced for six months now, and it is still affecting both your personal life and your work. You'll never make vice president if you don't find some way to get your act back together. And that means I'll never be the secretary to the vice president, which happens to be something I really want."

Alisha's smile dissolved. The hurt washed over her anew. "I know. And I've been trying. It's just not easy."

"I understand that. You loved him. And what's worse, you trusted him. Hey, even I liked Brad. Who would have guessed he was having an affair with that voluptuous little secretary of his? Certainly not me."

"And after five years of what I thought was the world's most perfect marriage," Alisha put in, still finding it hard to believe. "I tried my best to be the perfect wife."

"And look what it got you." Roni sounded just as bitter as Alisha. "Some reward, huh? Just proves you should never make such sacrifices for any man."

Alisha's expression remained grim. "I still don't understand what he sees in her. It's not as if she's knock-down beautiful, and she's certainly not a very bright person. Why, that girl can hardly spell her own name."

Roni's brown eyes rounded with disbelief when she turned to look at Alisha. "Are you kidding? What that blond trollop lacks in looks and brains, she more than makes up for in breasts. Why, you could put the four of ours together and still not have enough to fill the bra of that little gold digger—that is, if she ever wore one."

Alisha glanced down at her own body which, until Trisha Adams had entered Brad's life, had seemed adequate enough. She then looked into the rearview and pushed her long brown hair back from her face. A face which she no longer saw as all that appealing. A face that had not kept her own husband interested—but then in all fairness to herself, it had turned out that faces were not Brad's main interest. "I really don't want to talk about this right now. We came here to forget, remember?"

"And forget we shall," Roni said with a resolute bounce of her short brown curls. "On to the French Quarter. I have some serious money to spend."

"And don't forget you still have a birthday gift to buy," Alisha reminded her, then grinned. "You promised me I could pick it out myself this year. That way I don't end up with a set of tinted drinking glasses with naked men painted on the bottoms like last year."

"I liked them," Roni countered. She fell back onto the soft leather seat with an exaggerated pout, her eyes sparkling at the memory.

By the time Alisha found a parking spot only a few blocks from the French Quarter, Brad Sampson's impending marriage was all but forgotten.

It was a beautiful day for browsing the many shops. The sun shone from a cloudless blue sky, warming the narrow streets just enough to keep

Roni from being uncomfortable in her white shorts, yet not too warm for Alisha, who wore a pair of dark gray pleated slacks with a long-sleeved white silk blouse.

It was also warm enough to prompt a lot of the men strolling along to wear comfortable walking shorts as well, something Roni noted again and again.

"Look at those legs," she commented, nudging Alisha with her elbow for what had to be the twentieth time in as many minutes when she turned to watch a tall, athletic-looking young man pass. His legs muscles rippled beneath lightly tanned skin while he walked. "I'll bet he's like you. I bet he gets out there and jogs almost every day."

"Will you quit that? I told you, we are not here to gape at men," Alisha scolded but turned to look all the same. The truth was, the man's back view wasn't half bad.

"Maybe you're not. But I am. Hey, look over there." Roni poked her elbow into Alisha's side yet again then pointed in another direction. "Talk about a gorgeous hunk of male flesh!"

"You are far too concerned with the way a man looks. Give me an ugly man any day. Ugly men treat women better and can be trusted not to stray. It's the good-looking ones that think they have to go around proving their prowess all the time."

"Yes, and what I wouldn't give to have that one prove his prowess with me," Roni agreed with a wicked grin.

"You're incorrigible."

"That I am," she agreed, then pointed. "Hey, would you look at that!"

Alisha sighed. "I told you I'm not here to gape at men. The last thing I want is to get hooked up with someone new."

"I'm not talking about a man. I'm talking about that little shop over there," she replied, crossing the street to get a closer look. "Look, the sign says it specializes in voodoo."

"Voodoo?" Reluctantly, Alisha followed Roni to the spooky-looking little shop which was wedged in between two larger ones. As they got closer, she noticed a peculiar yet compelling scent drift through the open half of the divided door. Her eyes rounded at the thought of a voodoo shop existing in that day and age.

"Let's go in," Roni urged, clearly excited. When she glanced back and saw the caution pulling at Alisha's face, she narrowed her gaze. "Come on, I dare you."

"I don't know," Alisha said, then chewed cautiously on her lower lip for a moment. She did not like the thought of entering such an evil-looking place. "I think they're closed. It's dark inside."

"Why would the top half of the door be open if they were closed? Besides, the sign says they are open," Roni replied, already on the large step out front. Like so many of the shops along this particular street, the old wooden building stood a good two feet off the ground.

Roni switched her packages and purse to her

left arm so she could open the lower half of the door with her right. Her eyes sparkled with delight when she turned to face Alisha again. "Maybe we can get them to cast some sort of evil spell over Brad's wedding." She grinned. "A spell that turns ol' Brad into a fat little mouse and another that turns his bimbo bride into a hungry alley cat eager for its next meal. What a honeymoon that would make!"

"You're not normal," Alisha stated with a raised eyebrow, although grinning right along with her.

"Neither are you," Roni pointed out, already half inside the store. "Come on, let's have a quick look around. While we are in there, maybe we can talk them into conjuring us up a couple of Mr. Rights. I want mine to be tall, incredibly wealthy, and look just like Patrick Swayze. Of course you'll want yours to look more like Mel Gibson, won't you? You've always been a sucker when it comes to light blue eyes and a devilish grin."

Alisha knew there was no point trying to argue Roni out of going inside and followed grudgingly. An eerie feeling crept over her when they entered and found the shop lighted solely by what sunlight made it through the tall narrow windows and by a vast assortment of odd-shaped candles, some with glass globes to protect their flames and some without. The only electric light was a small unlit lamp that stood beside an antique cash register near the door.

"Great atmosphere, huh?" Roni said in a suddenly hushed voice even though there was only one other person in the shop.

Alisha guessed her to be the proprietress simply from her unusual attire. She wore a long black dress made from layers of gauzy material over which she wore an amazing assortment of colorful wooden beads. She wore so many beads in fact that they clattered when she came forward to greet them.

"My name is Zinita," she said. Her voice was soft and mellow. "May I help you?"

Awestruck by the woman's exotic appearance, Alisha let Roni answer. "We just want to look around if that's all right."

"By all means," the woman responded and offered an elegant sweep of her delicate hand along with a warm smile. "Look all you want. Let me know if you find something that interests you."

While Roni browsed, Alisha's gaze returned to the oddly dressed woman who had walked over to the counter to await their purchases. Zinita was a tall and extremely beautiful dark-skinned woman whom Alisha guessed to be in her mid-to-late thirties. Her long black hair was bound loosely in the back with a shimmering purple scarf, and her long dark eyelashes shaded eyes more amber in color than brown.

Finally Alisha's curiosity got the better of her. "Are you the owner of this shop?"

"Yes, I am Zinita," she repeated and held her head proudly. "A fifth-generation voodoo priestess."

Roni looked up from the scarves she was inspecting on one of the display tables. Her eyes glimmered with mischief. "Are you really?"

"I am."

Roni cut her gaze to Alisha then back to Zinita. "And you can perform magic and cast spells and all that?"

"I can, when there is a need," she said with a noticeable roll to her *r*'s.

"Then cast a spell over my friend here to make her a little more willing to let me drive her new car." Roni grinned to let Alisha know the earlier incident had not been forgotten.

"You joke at my powers?" Zinita arched a perfectly shaped eyebrow. "Perhaps you do not believe in voodoo?"

"To tell you the truth, I'm not even sure what voodoo is," she admitted and picked up the packages she had set aside while looking at the scarves. "But I'm always willing to learn something new."

"Then perhaps you two would like to come into the back room for some spiritual advisement." She gestured toward a door at the back of the shop. Without waiting for a response, she headed immediately in that direction. "It costs only five dollars for the both of you."

Roni's eyes were wide with excitement when she glanced at Alisha. "What do you say we go get our fortunes told? Sounds like a real kick."

"I don't think I want to." Although she wasn't sure why, Alisha did not want to go through that door. Her skin prickled when she watched Zinita pull back the beaded curtain and beckon them forward with a graceful curl of her slender hand.

"Sure you do," Roni insisted in a harsh whisper. "Come on. It'll be fun."

Alisha shook her head. "Why don't you go without me. I'll wait here."

"Quit being such a chicken," Roni replied, then took her by the arm. "Come on. It'll be fun. You'll see. Besides, I'm paying. It's part of your birthday present."

Reluctantly, and knowing Roni would eventually wear down her resistance anyway, Alisha followed the two of them through the door. There they entered a long, narrow hallway draped ceiling to floor with exotic silks. There was just enough light from the front room for Alisha to see the three wooden doors ahead of them. All three were closed and all stood off to the right. Zinita led them to the door farthest away.

There the three entered a small room with two strangely decorated windows. Like the hall, the walls were draped with dark, exotic silks, and the rattan furniture was dark and simple in design.

"Sit here," Zinita said, placing her hands on the backs of two of the four large chairs that faced an even larger chair which sat on a wooden platform.

Several worn tables of different shapes and sizes were placed about the room. Each was littered with an assortment of curious ornaments. There were candles, incense holders, strands of multicolored beads, unusual-shaped bottles, stoneware jars, small bones or bone fragments, feathers, knives, spoons, locks of hair, torn pieces of cloth, old coins, a black scarf, and tiny dolls that looked like they were carved out of either wood or wax. There was also a fat black cat with one gray ear sleeping on a small wall shelf near the door.

"To help me advise you, I will call on the spirit of Imena, my great-grandmother," Zinita explained. As soon as Alisha and Roni had sat down, she headed for the larger chair. "It is she who has the closest alliance with the spirit world."

Because there was a strange pink dust scattered throughout the room, Alisha and Roni both opted to place their bags and purses in their laps while waiting for whatever might happen next. Fortunately, Alisha carried only one sack which she was able to fit inside her small purse, but Roni had four sacks of different sizes in addition to a bulky canvas purse that looked more like an overnight bag. Still, she managed to stack everything on her tiny lap with little problem.

Not knowing what to expect, Alisha and Roni both watched while Zinita settled into the large chair that sat a foot higher than their own. Without explanation, she reached for one of the glass vials that stood on the crowded table nearest her. She drank part of the dark purple liquid inside, then set the vial aside. Resting her arms on the chair, she leaned back and fell quiet for a moment.

With fixed eyes she started to sway from side to side with a slow, easy rhythm. When she spoke again, it was in a deeper voice that carried what sounded to Alisha like a Haitian or maybe a Jamaican accent.

"I am here to advise you."

Thinking it all part of an elaborate act, Alisha and Roni exchanged amused glances but did nothing to interrupt the woman who Alisha noticed had the amazing ability to go quite some time without having to blink. It made her eyes burn just watching.

"I will start my advisement by telling you a little about yourselves," she explained in that same deep, musical voice, although she had yet to look at either of them. "You two are good friends and are both near twenty-five years in age. Neither of you is married at the moment, although one of you has been married at least once in the recent past."

Alisha shook her head at such pitiful revelations. The fact neither of them was presently married was pretty obvious. Neither wore a wedding ring. And when the woman neglected to point out which of them had been married, she realized Zinita was working on odds. In today's world divorce was very common.

Zinita continued. "You two have traveled together to New Orleans from a neighboring state for your own enjoyment and to forget what troubles you, if only for a few days."

Certain that was why many tourists came to

New Orleans and knowing that they both had Texas accents, Alisha was still not impressed.

She and Roni exchanged knowing glances. Anyone could have guessed those facts. But then the woman mentioned something not quite so obvious. "It makes me sad to know that between the two of you, there is but one living parent. A father. There is very little other family for either of you."

Alisha's eyes widened immediately. Her father had died of cancer when she was seventeen and her mother had died in a car accident just two years ago. All she had in the way of family now was her father's Aunt Lila and a few cousins, all who lived in the Dallas area. Roni's father still lived, but her mother had been murdered in her own front yard just over four years ago. She had no brothers or sisters.

Suddenly Zinita had Alisha's full attention as she continued to sway gently from side to side, her dark face still void of expression and her gaze vacant.

"The shorter of you, the one who calls herself by a boy's name, has a reason to be proud. She was plagued with a serious need to drink from the spirits for years, a need that she only recently overcame."

Alisha frowned. That was true, too. After Roni's mother was killed, Roni developed a very serious drinking problem. *That* was not something a stranger would know offhand.

Alisha tensed and leaned forward to listen more carefully.

"The other of you, who rarely drinks at all, was brought up by parents that were not her own. She was adopted by them soon after being abandoned as an infant right here in New Orleans by a frightened sixteen-year-old girl."

Alisha shifted uncomfortably in her seat, aware this woman knew far too much about them. She looked at Roni accusingly, thinking this had to be a setup. She expected to find Roni watching her and grinning wickedly, but instead Roni stared at the woman with round-eyed fascination, looking truly astounded by the woman's knowledge.

Slowly, Zinita rose from her seat. Without glancing at either of them, she stepped down from the small dais and came forward to stand between them.

Still not looking at them, she lifted her arms and, with hands like ice, pressed her palms against their cheeks. Her eyes widened instantly, and she peered curiously toward Alisha. For the first time, she focused.

Alisha was too amazed by what the shopkeeper had said and done thus far to pull away from the woman's icy touch.

"I was wrong," Zinita said. She narrowed her gaze, although she still did not blink. "You were not abandoned at birth as I first thought. You had a very caring, very loving mother who died when you were but thirteen. She gave up too much of her life's blood one cold morning in January while trying to bring an already dead son into her world. That was in the year 1871."

Finally Zinita blinked, but only once, as if ad-

justing to new thoughts. "You were born on the
twenty-first day of December in the year of 1857,
only six squares from where we now sit. You do
not belong to this time." Her amber eyes narrowed when she peered at Alisha more closely.
"Why are you here?"

"I am here because my friend has a very unhealthy curiosity and wanted to see what was inside this shop," Alisha answered, baffled by the
accusing tone in the woman's voice.

"No. That is not true." Zinita lowered her
hands to her sides. "You are here to restore the
past." Her eyes widened again. "You have finally
come back to right the wrong that was done so
many years ago."

"Come back?" Alisha gave Roni a "let's get
out of here" look and was annoyed to see the
fascination in her friend's eyes. Roni was obviously transfixed. "I'm sorry, but I've never been
here before in my life."

The woman, still talking with a Haitian accent, stepped away from them and began rear-
ranging the items on a nearby table. She took
some away and quickly added others.

"The black web can be lifted at last," she told
them as she gathered together a burning candle,
several strings of wooden beads, a necklace
made of what looked like an animal's vertebrae,
a black scarf, and a glass bottle filled with a
dark blue substance. "I can now reverse the mistake done so many years ago and absolve my
family of its dark shadow at last. I can finally
free my realm of that wrongdoing."

She turned to face Alisha again, her eyes again seeing. "I understand that you were in grave danger when you came to me those many years ago, but it was wrong of me to send your soul into the hereafter without first having summoned the spirits for guidance. You looked so frightened that day that I let my heart rule against my head and have had to atone for my foolishness since. You were meant to face your danger, not run from it. A man's life was taken as a result of sending you away. A man who did not deserve to die such a sudden and violent death."

Zinita slipped the black scarf around her neck, where it hung loosely. She then opened the wide-mouthed vial and sprinkled part of the blue powder over Alisha's clothing. Alisha's gaze shot daggers at her friend.

"Don't worry, Alisha," Roni chortled happily. "You don't really look a hundred and thirty years old. At least not to me."

Glowering, Alisha tried to shift the madwoman's focus to Roni. "Don't you want to sprinkle some of that powder over Roni? She looks like she dearly needs to right a few wrongs, too."

Zinita turned her head toward Roni— whose eyes rounded immediately— and nodded.

Again trancelike, Zinita lifted her hands to slip over her head both the scarf and a single strand of wooden beads she wore. She dropped the dark beads, shaped like little bald heads, around Roni's neck and arranged them just so before draping the long silken scarf over Roni's left shoulder.

"This will protect you from what is to come," she said to Roni in a gentle, reassuring voice.

Roni looked down at the beads and scarf curiously while the woman turned her attention back to the items strewn across the table. Quickly, she took another pinch of the thick blue powder between her slender fingers and sprinkled it lightly over the candle flame. Immediately the black candle sputtered and the tiny room filled with a thick cloud of blue acrid smoke that made it hard for Alisha to see or breathe.

Choking on the foul vapors that made her eyes and throat burn, she called to Roni, "I've had enough of this. Let's get out of here." She coughed with such force she could barely push herself out of the chair.

"Me, too," Roni gasped, also choking. "Let's go."

Alisha heard rustling as Roni gathered her packages. But by the time she stood with her purse tucked under her arm, she no longer heard Roni's coughing and realized her friend had already left. Placing a sleeve over her nose to help filter the smoke, she hurried to follow.

Bent with convulsions, Alisha coughed violently even after she had stepped outside and had taken in several large gulps of fresh air.

It was several seconds before she realized that Roni was not there. Glancing first at the tiny shop where both halves of the door now stood wide open, then at the area around her, she looked for her friend and was surprised to see everyone on the street dressed strangely. The women wore odd-looking hats and long cumbersome dresses that touched the ground with heavy folds. The men either had on tight-fitting, square-cut suits with ribbon neckties and button-down shoes or they wore dark work trousers with light shirts held up by suspenders. Even the children, what few there were of them, were dressed in simple, outdated clothing.

She also noticed that while she had been inside, the weather had changed dramatically. The temperature was much cooler than before, and heavy, dark clouds had rolled in, completely blocking the sun.

Carriages and horse-drawn wagons dotted the narrow streets that had earlier been closed to traffic, and many animals ran loose— not only dogs and cats, but chickens, geese, pigs, and goats. One particularly happy-looking gray goat with a white beard stood atop a small pile of garbage that had been dumped right out onto the raised brick sidewalk directly across the street. The shaggy animal was not at all bothered by the countless flies that swarmed around him nor by the large pig that rooted noisily near the bottom.

Annoyed that Roni had yet to come outside, Alisha headed back into the shop to get her. She also wanted to find out why everyone was decked out in such old-fashioned clothing and why there were suddenly so many stray animals and authentic-looking old carriages scattered along the street. Obviously, there was a festival of some sort about to start, but why hadn't anyone mentioned it to them earlier?

When Alisha reentered, a different woman stood near the door. She looked a little like Zinita, only her skin was lighter, more the color of creamed coffee, and her cheekbones were a little higher. She also appeared to be several years older and wore a black silk dress with long colorful sashes that trailed to the ground. Unlike Zinita, who had practically covered herself with beads, this woman wore only one delicate strand that hung to her waist. Because the beautiful woman did not look quite old enough to be Zinita's mother, Alisha decided she must be her sister.

"I need to speak to Zinita," Alisha said firmly. Absently, she brushed some of the blue dust off her clothing with her free hand while she awaited a reply.

"There is no Zinita here," the woman answered with a deep, melodic Haitian accent— much like the one Zinita had used earlier while pretending to be in a voodoo trance.

Alisha scowled and quickly surveyed her surroundings, hoping to catch a glimpse of either Zinita or Roni. Her skin prickled when she noticed that the shop looked suddenly different. Although the room was dark— still lighted by a variety of odd-shaped candles and sweet-scented oil lamps, she noticed that the display tables were suddenly gone as was the cash register and electric lamp that had stood near the door. Someone had obviously made several changes while she and Roni were in that back room. But why?

"Maybe I can be of help to you. My name is Imena," the woman said. Her words were cold and unfriendly.

Alisha's expression hardened. She remembered that Imena was the name Zinita had used for her great-grandmother, not her sister. There was no way this woman was Zinita's great-grandmother. "The only way you can help me is to tell Zinita and my friend Roni to get out here right now. I've had enough. I want to leave."

"I told you. There is no Zinita here."

"I know there is." Angry that this woman would lie to her and eager to prove otherwise, Alisha headed immediately toward the back rooms.

When seconds later she stepped through the same third door she had entered earlier with Roni, she came to an abrupt halt. There was only a tiny bed draped in purple silk and a small black dresser inside. No large rattan chairs. No cluttered tables. No sleeping cat. *And no Roni*.

Alisha's brow furrowed while she studied the changed room. *How'd they do that?* How did these people rearrange a room so quickly? First the front room, and now the back. And where was Roni while they rearranged everything? For that matter, where was Roni now? What sort of prank was this?

As frightened and confused as she was angry, Alisha headed back toward the front of the building to confront Imena.

"Where is the person who came in here with me?" she demanded when she found Imena still there, eyeing her strangely. Her pulse raced with growing fear. "Where is my friend Roni Belomee?" She stiffened to show determination, after coming to a halt only a few feet in front of the woman.

"She is safe in the heart of her mother," the woman answered. She lifted her hand and pointed quietly toward the front door with a long, slender finger. "You must now return to your own time and accept your fate as it was meant to be. Truth for you lies beyond the danger." Her gaze was on something just outside the door.

Alisha was not about to leave there without her friend. "Not until I know what happened to Roni. Where is she? What have you done with her?" Her heart continued its frantic drumming while she shouted out Roni's name several times, finally calling her by her full name, Veronica Louise, something Alisha did only when she was angry or annoyed. Of which she was now both.

Still there was no answer.

Terrified by the silence, she narrowed her gaze and turned to glower at the older woman again. "Is it money you want? Is that it? Money for Roni's return? Money to use your supposed witchcraft to bring her back? Are you and Zinita into extortion? Is that what this is all about? Well, you can forget it. I won't be tricked into paying money for my friend's return, so you might as well save yourself a visit from the police and let her go. Now where is she? What have you done with her?"

Rather than respond to Alisha's accusations, Imena sat down in a tall slender rocking chair near the front door, rested her dark head against the top brace, and closed her eyes. She said nothing else to Alisha.

Determined to get some answers from this vile woman one way or another, Alisha stormed back outside to notify the police. Either those two women returned Roni to her right away, or Alisha would see that they were both arrested for kidnapping and a search made of the place. She would have Roni back one way or another. She just hoped they hadn't harmed her.

Seeing no uniformed policemen on the street and spotting no pay telephones to use to summon help, she headed immediately into the next shop.

"I need to use your phone to call the police," she stated as she passed the threshold. Finding only three people inside the shop, she turned to the person closest to her, a woman about Roni's height who looked to be nearly thirty years old. Alisha gathered by the white apron that she probably worked there.

"You need what?" she asked, glancing up from a long piece of cloth she held, clearly bewildered.

"I need to use your telephone to call 911. It's an emergency."

The woman, dressed similarly to the people outside, looked curiously at a woman who stood behind a long glass counter. "Do you know what she means?"

The second woman, the older of the two, shrugged then looked at a man who sat at a small table sipping coffee and reading an undersized newspaper.

"Raymond, do you have any notion what this young woman is talking about?" She cut her questioning gaze back to Alisha as if finding her quite an oddity.

The man looked to be the oldest of the three, for his skin was deeply wrinkled and his short cropped hair was completely gray. He nodded, then said with a strong Cajun accent. *"Oui,* I dink maybe de lady, she mean one of dem talkin' machines dey have up in de North. I read something about dem in the newspaper not long 'go. People use dem to talk to one another over many miles."

"Talking machines?" the older woman repeated with a raised brow. Her gaze took in Alisha's trousers and blouse while she considered the possibility of what the man had said. "I'm sorry, miss, but we don't have anything like that here."

Alisha found that hard to believe, but decided not to argue the point. She was in too much of a hurry to get help for Roni. "Then where would I find one? I need to call the police."

Aware of how oddly the three looked at her, as if offended by her clothing, she glanced down to see what might be wrong and was reminded that she had chosen to wear a pair of comfortable running shoes instead of the dress pumps her clothes warranted. That was because her feet had started to hurt during all that walking they had done at the cemetery earlier.

She noticed, too, that her trousers and blouse suddenly looked two sizes too large for her. That seemed odd. Having lost at least twelve pounds since the divorce, enough for Roni to comment on how unhealthy she looked, she should have noticed earlier how very baggy her clothing had become. But she hadn't.

Even her Reeboks felt a little loose.

While waiting for someone to give her directions to the nearest telephone, she knelt to retie her shoes and made a mental note to buy some new clothes. Roni was right. She had lost far too much weight during the past few months. She looked like a clown in those clothes.

"There are no telephones here," the woman repeated after a moment. Her eyebrows rose even higher while she watched Alisha hurriedly retie her running shoes. "But if you really have an emergency, there is a bell at the next corner." She pointed in the opposite direction of the voodoo shop. "Go ring it if you have a problem. That's what it's there for."

"A fire alarm?" she asked, thinking that was better than nothing. She would break the glass and someone in authority would come running.

When Alisha stood again, she noticed there was something decidedly wrong with these people, or at least decidedly different. She looked at them curiously. That was when she caught the date that was printed on the small newspaper the man held. *Friday, April 7, 1882.* It also carried the *True Delta* banner.

She must have entered an antique shop, she reasoned, her conclusion based on the items for sale and the employees' garments. The man must be reading a reprint, because the paper looked too new to be one hundred and thirteen years old.

She headed back outside, bent on finding someone more willing to help her or locating the fire alarm they had mentioned. Again she was struck by how different the street looked and how differently the people behaved. It was as if she'd stepped out of that voodoo shop and had entered another world.

An eerie feeling gnawing at her, she asked the very next person she passed what day it was.

"It's Friday," the tall, thin young man with dark brown hair answered promptly. Like so many others he was dressed in a dark brown, square-cut suit with hardly any lapel and no front pocket. His green eyes rounded with surprise when he glanced down and noted Alisha's baggy clothing.

"I know that it's Friday," she replied, annoyed that she had not noticed until now how much her weight loss had affected the fit of her clothing. Had she been *that* absorbed in her problems with Brad? So absorbed she hadn't noticed what her lack of appetite had done to her physically? "But what's the *date*?"

"April 7."

Alisha paused for a moment, glad to hear it was still her birthday when for a moment she had doubted even that. She then drew in a deep breath. "And the year?"

"Why it's 1882, of course." His gaze slid warily across her face.

Alisha's heart froze. *1882?* It couldn't be. She swallowed audibly but said nothing while she fought panic and confusion rising inside her.

First Roni disappeared, and now this. Just what was going on here?

Two

Alisha stared at the young man, dumbfounded. He was undoubtedly mistaken. He had to be. Perhaps he thought she wanted to know the year that was being celebrated in their upcoming festival. Evidently something had happened April 7, 1882, in New Orleans history. Memorable enough to have the entire newspaper for that date reprinted.

Still, something nagged at her. Something that compelled her to question him further. "No. I mean *really*. What year is it right now?"

The young man cocked a dark eyebrow and took a tiny step backward. His hands closed tightly around the small leather satchel he carried. "It's 1882. Has been for over three months now." He wet his lower lip with a quick dart of his tongue and took a second cautionary step backward.

Alisha stared at his round-eyed expression a moment and realized he was serious. This young man truly believed it was 1882. So much so, he thought *she* was strange. But what could she do but doubt him? The date couldn't just suddenly take a tumble like that.

Or could it?

Imena's parting words haunted her while she continued to stare at the young man's wary expression: *"You must now return to your own time and accept your fate as it was meant to be. Truth for you lies beyond the danger."*

What had she meant by that?

At the time, Alisha had discounted the strange words as just part of the act, but now Alisha wondered what Imena had meant by "returning to her own time"? Was it possible that the two voodoo women working together had somehow transported her back through time? Had she really slipped into the year 1882?

No, that was impossible. This was all some sort of elaborate hoax. One that Roni was obviously in on. And probably everyone else at work. Had to be. People simply did not get hurled back through time like that, not even when voodoo was involved.

Still, it had given her pause for thought.

"What's your name?" she asked the young man. She felt a great sense of relief from having realized this was all just one big prank. She refused to believe it could be anything else.

"My name is Anthony. Anthony Allen." He continued to stare at her cautiously but had ceased backing away from her.

Alisha crossed her arms over her purse and tilted her head to one side while she studied him more closely. He certainly looked authentic— from his stiff white collar right down to his button-down boots. "So tell me, Anthony Allen, how much did they pay you to dress like that and then wait around for me to come outside and ask you for the date?"

"Ma'am, I don't have any idea what you're talking about." He swallowed so hard his black string tie bobbed as a result. He cut his troubled gaze to others that walked passed them— others who also had obviously been paid to dress in period costumes and pretend it was 1882. "Why would anyone pay me to do something like that?"

"Because they all got together and decided it was time to do something truly dramatic to jolt me out of my doldrums. They figured I'd been depressed because of my divorce long enough and wanted to find some way to turn me back into my old cheerful self." She smiled, then laughed, pleased that they cared enough to go to that much trouble. What a wonderful and truly unique birthday gift this was. *Everyone* had to have chipped in to help pay for something this elaborate. Why, there were at least two dozen actors on the street in addition to those they had planted inside the neighboring stores. "So how much did they have to pay you to do this— and you are a very good actor by the way."

At having heard the word *divorce*, Anthony's eyes opened farther, and he took yet another cautionary step back. "I am not an actor, ma'am. I help run the telegraph over at Clark's Freight Company. I think you have me confused with somebody else who maybe is an actor. There are sure plenty of them over on Canal Street." While still gripping the satchel he carried with one hand, he reached quickly to touch the brim of his bowler hat with the other. "If you'd excuse me, I have to go. I'm late delivering these messages as it is."

Having said that, he rushed passed her. He looked back only once before he rounded the next corner.

Alisha stared after him, perplexed by such a convincing denial, especially after she had already admitted having figured out the whole scam. It was all so obvious. He *had* to be an actor.

Didn't he?

A chill that had nothing to do with the drop in temperature skittered across her shoulders then darted down her spine just seconds before she spotted an old black man sitting on a doorstep barely half a block away. He was whittling on a large piece of wood and, unlike the others who stared at her openly, seemed completely oblivious to her presence.

Because he was not as elaborately dressed as many of the others— wearing only a pair of plain brown trousers with holes in the knees and a dull white cotton shirt— nor was he trying to attract her attention in any way, she decided he was probably not a part of the complex hoax Roni and the others had set up. She hurried over to speak with him, eager to prove herself right.

"Sir, would you be so kind as to tell me what year it is?" she asked when she was close enough not to have to shout over the clattering carriages and wagons rolling past. She glanced back at the voodoo shop, half expecting to see Roni peering cautiously through the window.

"1882 already," he muttered without bothering to look up from the pile of wood shavings scattered at his bare, worn feet. "Don't seem like it should be, but it is."

"Not you, too," she responded, then disbelievingly shook her head. Even *he* was a plant. What an elaborate scheme her coworkers had executed. They had missed *nothing*.

Impressed by their thoroughness, she headed back to the voodoo shop where she expected to find Roni waiting for her with a "gotcha" grin.

Amazed by such detail, she wondered how Roni had managed to get enough money together to pull off such an incredible hoax—and without her knowing about it.

Roni must have been planning and collecting for this event for weeks to have afforded such detail. Why, they had even thought to have animals brought in and let loose and had hired men with fancy carriages and old-fashioned wagons to travel the street while other actors walked along calling out to them in greeting. It was all so *real*.

"Okay, you can tell Roni I'm back and that enough is enough," Alisha said the moment she stepped back inside and discovered that Roni was not there waiting for her after all.

Imena still sat in the old rocking chair with her head tilted back. Her dark eyes opened slowly, but she did not bother to lift her head or look at Alisha.

"You are not welcome here." Her voice was low and determined while she continued to stare at some fixed point. "Go."

Another foreboding chill wound down Alisha's spine, causing tiny bumps of apprehension to form on her skin. The woman was so eerie.

"Okay. Gladly. Just as soon as you tell Roni the jig is up and that I'm more than ready to strangle her now."

A tiny muscle near the back of Imena's jaw hardened, but other than that, she showed no outward emotion. "You do not understand. You are to leave and not come back until you have faced your dangers."

"Ah, come on. Give it up." Alisha glanced around the room in hopes of spotting her friend, but she saw no one hiding in the flickering shadows. "It's okay to send Roni out here. I promise not to do any grave bodily harm to her."

Imena's dark hands curled around the thin arms of the worn rocker until her light brown knuckles turned almost white. "I told you to leave. I cannot help you solve your problems after all. They are beyond what I can do."

"And I told you I want to see Roni." She shifted her weight worriedly to one leg while she tried to ignore the tiny fear growing inside her. "I've had enough of this."

When Imena's gaze finally met Alisha's, the pure anger glittering in their dark depths caused Alisha to blink hard and jerk her head back.

"If you do not return now and face your danger," Imena warned, "an innocent man will die for the wrong reason and long before he should."

Alisha's face wrenched with confusion. "What are you talking about? What man? What danger? All I want to do is talk to Roni and get out of here."

Imena stood and again pointed toward the open door. A sudden breeze gusted through and billowed both her dark hair and her skirt, causing her to look all the more ominous. "Enough talk. You have no choice. You will stay in this year 1882 until you have found a way to solve your own plight. Once all danger has passed and the problem is resolved, you may return here to me. If little time has lapsed, I will then approach the spirits on your behalf. Only after the danger has passed and all are safe will I seek permission to send you back into the hereafter if that is what you still desire. But you must not take long. There are only so many days my great-granddaughter can hold a place for your spirit. If you do not return with your problem resolved by the full moon, another spirit will be sent to take your place. One who will know nothing about you. That allows you twenty-one days to cleanse yourself of the danger."

The knot that formed in Alisha's chest was so painful it caused her to grimace. Her voice trembled from the weight of her own fear when she spoke again. She did not like this game. "P-please tell Roni I am here and that I want to go."

Imena took a deep breath, held it, then slowly

let it go. "I told you. There is no Roni here. For us, she does not yet exist. Do you not understand? It is now 1882. Your friend Roni will not be born into our world for eighty-eight more years."

"Please." Alisha's body shuddered when she considered the possibility that the woman had told her the truth—that maybe she really had been thrust back into the year 1882. Everything around her certainly pointed toward that being a fact. "Don't do this to me. Please don't."

Imena would not be swayed by Alisha's emotional pleadings. "It cannot be helped. You must stay and face your own danger. You cannot allow an innocent man to die because of an evil you caused. If Zinita could have found you sooner, you would have been returned here long before now. It is as it should be."

"But I have no idea what you are talking about." Her frustration grew. "What is this danger you keep mentioning?"

"That I cannot tell you, for I am not yet sure what the danger is. But what I do know is that the danger is dark and avenging, and I also know that a man who should not will die a violent death if you do not return to face it. You must save the man from such a death if you want to return to the hereafter. You have twenty-one days to do this."

"What innocent man? Can you at least tell me that?" she begged.

"All I know is what the spirits have shown me. A death resulted from my sending you into the hereafter. A death that was to haunt me for the rest of eternity. That death must be undone. You will stay."

Alisha's hands trembled when she jerked open her purse and fumbled for her wallet. She was terrified of being trapped in 1882, even if it was for only twenty-one days. "Please. Don't do this. I have money I can give you."

She thrust the gray suede wallet in Imena's direction. "Here. I have over four hundred dollars in there." She then held up her other arm to reveal her gold wrist watch. "And I have jewelry worth even more than that. You can have it all if you'll just put me back where I was to begin with. I don't want to be in 1882. Not even for a few days."

Imena's expression remained unchanged. "Then you do believe that you have been sent back."

"Yes," she conceded. As unbelievable as it seemed, she had been thrown into another time, the result of what happened in that shop. If only she had listened to her original instincts and stayed away from there. "Yes, I do believe that I'm now in the year 1882. But I don't want to be. Please, take whatever you want from me, just send me back to where I was. Send me back into the year 1995. Before Roni realizes I'm missing and goes completely berserk."

"I told you. I cannot send you back until you have confronted the danger and saved the life that was taken too soon."

"Whose life?" she asked again, frustrated by how vague the woman was. "What danger?"

"Whatever danger that brought you to me in the beginning."

"But I don't know what you are talking about. I don't remember any danger. I don't remember ever having met you before. And I sure don't remember ever having been in the year 1882, which is why I think you are wrong. Besides, how can I face the danger if I don't know what that danger is?"

"It will find you," she said, her tone low and forbidding. "When everyone is safe, come to me and we will talk again." She turned to walk away.

"But I want to talk now," Alisha called after her, her fear so strong it felt like a hard weight crushing her.

"When everyone is safe. Now go."

Angry at the woman for refusing to send her back and puzzled about what to do next, Alisha stormed outside. As incredible as it seemed, until Imena was finally willing to cooperate with her, she was stuck in 1882. What made matters worse, the sky had already started to turn dark and she had nowhere to go. Nowhere to spend the night.

While trying to figure out why it was evening already and what she should do about it, she glanced at her watch and saw that it had been hours since she and Roni had first entered the shop. Even so, it not quite late enough for the day to be turning to night yet. According to her watch, there should be at least one more hour before dusk. But then again, the hour could have changed as easily as the year.

Glancing around in hopes of spotting a clock that might let her know what time it was in the year 1882, she heard a loud, thundering voice in the distance. She turned toward the sound and saw three large men wearing ill-fitting black suits and undersized black caps climbing out of a coach while one pointed in her direction. All three looked angry and determined.

"You're right. That's her," the tallest of the three shouted. "That's the one we're supposed to catch! She's disguised herself in men's clothes. Grab her!"

Suddenly the three started running toward her. One shook a stick of some sort in her direction.

"Don't let her get away again."

Instinct set Alisha's feet into motion. Glad now she had worn her Reeboks instead of her dress pumps, she took off in the opposite direction, running just as fast as possible. With her pulse pounding faster than her feet, she darted in and out of the people who stood along the sidewalk watching the proceedings with stunned amazement.

"Stop her! Somebody stop her!"

Alisha shot first down one street then another, then just before darting down yet a third street, she glanced back to see if she had put any distance between herself and them and was alarmed to find that they were now only a dozen or so yards behind her. Loudly they cursed her unexpected agility.

Aware the quickest of the three was slowly

gaining on her, she tried to run all the faster but couldn't. Her body was giving out on her much more quickly than she would have expected, considering she jogged three to four miles each morning before work. Gasping for breaths that blistered her lungs, she knew she could not continue at that pace much longer. She could never outdistance them.

Panic filled her when she rounded the next corner. For reasons unknown, those men meant to harm her. She had to find place to hide.

It was then she noticed a large wooden box about the size of a steamer trunk tossed haphazardly against the base of an eight-foot brick wall. In a frantic effort to escape the angry men behind her, she decided to use the box to boost herself over the wall. With luck she would be up, over, and out of sight before they rounded that last turn

Throwing her purse over ahead of her, she hurled high but her first effort to scale the wall failed when her arms did not hold her weight as readily as they should. But in a second attempt, Alisha pulled herself up and over. Rolling quickly, she dropped easily to the other side and was not too surprised to find herself crouched in the dark shadows of someone's courtyard. New Orleans was well-known for its elaborate gardens and its many private courtyards.

Straightening, she scanned her surroundings, eager to locate both her purse and the nearest way out of the dark garden, and was startled to

find that she had landed smack in the middle
of a romantic tryst.

Beneath the flickering glow of a single torch
on a padded chaise longue made for two, a very
handsome man with long, wavy brown hair and
startled blue eyes reclined beside a voluptuous
young woman with streaked red hair and intense green eyes. The man wore only a pair of
dark trousers that were open at the waist and
the woman wore nothing at all. Between them
lay Alisha's purse.

Alisha swallowed hard when she realized what
she had interrupted.

"Excuse me," she said between rapid gulps of
air, still breathless from having run so hard. "I-I
didn't mean to— ."

Before she could finish her apology, she heard
deep male voices rising from just the other side
of the garden wall. She paused to listen.

"It's dark, but I think I saw her go over that
wall."

"Well, what we waiting for?" another voice responded, this one carrying strong Cajun accent.
"We have to catch her. The chief will have our
skins if we let her run free again. He says she
got to pay for what she done. Give me push."

Alisha's eyes rounded when she realized she
was not yet safe. She glanced toward the large
white three-story house that formed two sides
of the courtyard and saw that two of the back
doors stood wide open but both were too far
away to do her any good. Judging by the sounds
coming from the other side of the wall, she did

not have enough time to make it safely across the tree-shadowed courtyard and into the house without being seen.

Instead, she looked at the two lovers pleadingly, then slid behind a tall clump of dark green bushes that grew thick in a nearby corner. The branches had barely stopped moving when, seconds later, the men chasing her came over the wall in a tumbling heap.

They recognized the man lying with the naked woman immediately after straightening from their fall. *"Mr. Kincaid.* Excuse us for the intrusion. But a-as you can see, we are policemen and we are chasing after someone we think came over this wall," the leader said.

Carefully, Alisha parted the bushes just enough to allow her to see the men. The torch cast eerie shadows across their faces. Her heart hammered hard and fast while she waited to hear if the two lovers would give her away.

The man called Mr. Kincaid slowly stood, leaving the woman to sit clutching Alisha's leather purse to her breasts, looking very annoyed. It disgusted Alisha that the three did not have the decency to look away and instead stared at the woman openly.

"We were chasing a young woman dressed in men's trousers and white boots, who carried a satchel of money. Did you see her come over your wall?"

"No. The only woman I have invited here tonight is Nicolle— a woman I paid handsomely to be with me," the man replied, then gestured to the woman, who lifted her chin proudly as she gave up all attempts to cover herself with the small purse.

"Are you sure?" The tallest one looked at the others uncomfortably. "I could have sworn I saw her haul herself over that wall not more than a couple of minutes ago."

"Sorry, but even if a woman did come over that wall, I'm afraid I was a little too preoccupied at the time to notice." He crossed his arms over a well-muscled chest and tilted his head. "So tell me, what exactly did the woman in trousers do that has the three of you out looking for her so late?"

Although relieved that the man did not intend to give her position away, Alisha continued to hold her breath while she listened closely. She was eager to know why these men were after her. Was this part of the danger Imena had warned her about?

"Well, for one thing, she cheated the chief's brother out of three thousand dollars in a crooked card game at Beauregard's last night."

"Three thousand dollars?" Kincaid repeated as if not understanding why such a paltry sum would lead to such action.

"I realize that doesn't seem like much to you, Mr. Kincaid," the tall leader said. "And it's not as if the chief's brother can't afford to lose such an amount, because to him that's little more than pocket change. It's the thought of having been done in by such a beautiful and beguiling woman that's got him so riled."

"Which is why we have to catch her," the man who stood closest to the wall explained, then gestured back in the direction they had just come. "And if she not here, then that means she's back along the street somewhere, probably looking for someplace safe to hide all that money." He glanced around as if trying to find something to use to boost himself back over the wall. "Which means we need to be on our way. If Andrea Knight isn't caught soon and that money recovered, there's going to be hell to pay for us all."

"Then why don't you use the front gate so you can be on your way more quickly?" Kincaid suggested and motioned toward a narrow gate that opened into a small carriage lane. The fence that divided the carriage lane from the courtyard was made of lattice, allowing Alisha to watch while they hurried along their way.

Even after they disappeared, Alisha remained hidden, her gaze focused on the area where she last saw them, afraid one of them might find reason to turn back. She was only vaguely aware that the man called Kincaid stood staring in her direction with her purse now clutched loosely in his hands.

"I think it is safe to come out now."

Aware that comment had been directed at her, Alisha parted the bushes and slipped out into the open.

"I want to thank you for not telling them where I was," she said, as she moved closer to them. Even though she was not the person they were looking for, she was grateful to these two for not pointing her out to them. "Especially after I interrupted your evening so unexpectedly like I did."

"I saw no reason to tell those men anything," Kincaid replied, his pale blue gaze sweeping over her, clearly intrigued by the garments she wore. He handed her purse to her. "They are certainly not friends of mine."

Alisha watched while first he refastened his waistband with unnerving slowness, then bent his tall, lean frame over a nearby table and retrieved his wallet. His taut skin gleamed in the torchlight while his long fingers curled around the wallet. Alisha stared at his hands a moment. Never had she met a man who emitted such sensuality. "Well, I still want to thank you for keeping quiet."

"There's no need for that," he said, as he parted the wallet then dipped his long fingers inside. He pulled out an odd-looking piece of paper with dark printing on it, then turned. "Here, Nicky. For your time. Sorry things had to turn out the way they did."

"You want me to go?" The voluptuous redhead looked at the paper and pouted. "But, Rand, I thought you wanted me to stay the night."

"That was before," he said and continued to hold what was obviously money out to her until she finally took it. "The situation has changed in these last few minutes. Now I'd rather you go."

"Don't send her away because of me," Alisha said, feeling guilty to have spoiled the woman's evening. Even though Nicky was a prostitute, it was clear she wanted to stay and see the evening through. And who could blame her? Rand Kincaid was an extremely handsome man, and judging by the looks of his house, if indeed it was his house, he was also a very wealthy man.

A powerful combination to say the least.

"I'll be leaving here in a few minutes," Alisha continued. But first she wanted to give those men enough time to be well on their way. Even though she wasn't the woman they were looking for, she did not want to have to deal with them again. She had enough to worry about at the moment. Like how to convince Imena to return her to 1995.

"I don't think that leaving here would be a good idea. At least not yet," he said, pulling more money out of his wallet and handing it to Nicky.

"What's that for?" she asked, clearly suspicious. "You don't owe me that."

"That is to encourage you to keep quiet about what happened here tonight. I don't want the police coming back and demanding to know why I didn't tell them about my intruder while they were here."

Nicky took the money, then glared at Alisha before slipping off the chair and quickly gathering her clothes. With amazing agility, she slipped into the complicated garments and was dressed again within minutes. She continued to pout while Rand walked her to the nearest door and offered little more than a vague promise to send for her again before he left the city.

Not wanting to intrude on their goodbye, Alisha stood near the chaise longue. She watched while Rand bent to give Nicky a parting kiss on the temple just before the woman disappeared inside. A twinge of jealousy plagued her while she waited for his return. Jealousy because a mere prostitute was being treated nicer by a customer than she herself had been treated by her own husband.

Even across the darkened courtyard where only a dim light glowed through the nearby windows, she could sense Kincaid's animal allure. He was tall and muscular, yet he moved lithely. Because he remained shirtless, she was able to watch the play of muscles across his upper body when he turned and headed in her direction.

She wondered what a man in the 1880s did to stay so ruggedly fit. She also wondered about the thick, dark brown hair that fell in abundance nearly to his shoulders. It was cut shorter around the face than in the back, and at the moment that shorter hair was brushed back into soft waves, allowing her to see every handsome detail of his face.

Was that the way men wore their hair back then? she wondered. If so, she definitely approved. That style, coupled with dark chest hair that trailed down to his taut stomach made him look downright roguish. She also liked the deeply dimpled smile that suddenly appeared and made him even more dangerously attractive. Her heart rate quickened.

"Sorry that took so long," he said as he stepped into the torchlight, allowing her an even better glimpse of his amazing physique and his deeply tanned skin. "But I had a hard time explaining matters to Nicky."

"I can imagine," she said and shifted nervously beneath his glittering gaze. She realized her awkward reaction was because she found his deep smile so alluring. "I doubt that every night a woman comes tumbling over your garden wall."

"Especially one dressed in men's clothing and in such a wild state of panic," he agreed with a quick glance down. His eyes sparkled with curiosity. "I suppose the safest thing would be for you to stay the night here."

"But I can't," she argued, then realized how foolish that was considering she had nowhere else to go. It would be far better to stay there in his relatively safe company than head back out into the streets of a city she no longer recognized and chance those same policemen finding her again.

"You can't what?" Rand asked, clearly ready to challenge whatever arguments she intended to offer.

"I can't possibly say no to such a generous offer," she continued, then smiled sweetly as she set her purse aside to indicate her decision to stay. Suddenly she wished she had a mirror. She could just imagine what she looked like after having scrambled over that wall. "That is if you are sure I'll be no trouble."

Rand chuckled. "Miss, I have a very strong feeling that letting you stay here is going to lead to nothing *but* trouble." He studied her more closely. "But apparently that's a risk I'm willing to take."

Three

Rand stared at Alisha for several seconds as if expecting a reply. But when all she did was stare back at him with those big, round, questioning brown eyes, he finally broke his gaze and gestured toward a silver serving tray on which sat a frosted bottle with no label, a footed silver pitcher, and two slender glasses. "You look thirsty. Would you like some wine?"

Alisha cut her gaze to the serving tray, aware he was right. She was thirsty from having to run from those three men. She reached up to wipe away some of the perspiration that had formed across her forehead before it trickled into her eyes. "No, I'm not all that fond of wine, but a glass of water would be nice."

"Then water it is," he said and moved quickly to the small table where the serving tray waited.

The torchlight cast a soft amber glow across his bare shoulders as he bent forward and filled one glass with water and the other with wine.

Alisha crossed her arms to ward off the chill of the coming night and tried not to notice the man's body.

"Here you go." His strong arms rippled with movement when he handed her glass to her.

Eager for that first gulp, Alisha nodded thank you, but then grimaced. The water was cool but tasted murky like it had been pumped directly from a lake or more likely from a shallow well. Rather than chance getting sick from what was obviously untreated water, she immediately handed the glass back to Rand. "I've changed my mind. I think I'd rather have the wine."

Rand took the glass and tossed the remaining water into a nearby flower bed, then refilled it with dark wine.

"So tell me," he said as he handed her the wine, "why did you cheat the chief's brother out of three thousand dollars? Didn't you know the trouble that would get you?"

"I didn't do it," she told him simply, then paused to take a first long sip of wine. Although the liquid was more tart than she would have liked, at least it was cool and wet, and had to be safer to drink than the water. "My name is not Andrea Knight. Those men have me confused with someone else."

Rand dipped his gaze. "Then why the disguise?"

"It's not a disguise." Alisha started to tell him that the clothes were hers but then realized there was no logical reason for a woman to be dressed in casual slacks during the year 1882. It simply was not done.

Rather than try to convince him that she was actually a refugee from another century when she was having a hard enough time accepting that information herself, she quickly conjured what she hoped was a reasonable lie. "The truth is that I fell earlier while being chased by those same men and tore most of my dress away. Rather than try to make my way back home like that, I stole these clothes off a wash line and put them on." Then aware that that would make her guilty of a minor theft, she quickly added, "Of course I left enough money behind to pay for them."

One dark eyebrow arched sharply. It was obvious he did not quite buy that explanation. "Then you didn't put those clothes on as a clever way to disguise yourself from those policemen?" He tilted his head to one side as if that might help him better gauge the truth. "And you are not the woman who cheated Jeremy Miller out of three thousand dollars in a public gambling house?"

"No. I'm not. And I don't know why they think I am, unless maybe I look like her, which I suppose is possible."

"Then you don't have three thousand dollars inside that little satchel over there?" He nodded toward her purse which still lay on a small wrought-iron table.

"Go look for yourself if you don't believe me," she said, though she hoped he would not. She knew she would have a hard time explaining some of the items he would find there, like the solar-powered pocket calculator or the lighted notepad.

Rand considered the offer a moment, then

nodded in agreement. "You're right. There's no money in there. Only a fool would carry that kind of cash with her in this city."

"And I'm no fool. But I'm also not Andrea Knight. My name is Alisha Sampson."

He continued to study her face closely. "If that's true, why did you run from those men?"

"Because it was obvious they were after me for some reason, and until I overheard them telling you about the gambling incident, I had no idea why. I didn't even know they were policemen until I heard them identify themselves to you."

"You couldn't see their uniforms?" he asked skeptically.

"I didn't take the time to really look at what they had on," she admitted. "I was too busy running."

He studied her a moment longer, then shrugged. "I hope for your sake you're telling the truth as it is well-known that both the chief and his brother have strong financial ties with the underworld and could as easily have you killed and be done with it as they could make you spend the rest of your life rotting in jail."

"The underworld?"

"Yes, but then it's really not all that unusual for them to have such connections. More than half the policemen and almost all of our city officials are every bit as corrupt. Truth is, money can buy you just about anything you want in this city. But if you are telling me the truth, you don't have to worry about any of that."

"I *am* telling you the truth," she insisted, resenting the doubt still evident in his voice. "I've never even been inside a gambling house much less tried to cheat a man out of his money."

"Then your life and your virtue are not really in that much danger are they? All you have to do is find out exactly when the incident took place and prove you were somewhere else."

Alisha frowned, wondering how she could possibly do that. Her alibi was that she was in another century at the time. "What has my virtue to do with this?"

Rand's eyes rounded as if unable to believe such innocence. "Don't you know what happens to beautiful women like you when they are thrown into New Orlean's jails?"

Alisha's stomach knotted with immediate apprehension despite the unexpected compliment. She wasn't so sure she wanted to hear what happened to them. "No, what?"

"Well, let's just say she's fair prey to any man who happens to be there."

"All the more reason not to let them get their hands on me," she said, more frightened than ever. So frightened, she felt both queasy and lightheaded. Or were those merely aftereffects of having gone through such an unexpected time change? "Can we please talk about something else?"

Rand shrugged, then shifted his weight to one leg. He looked at her questioningly. "What do you want to talk about?"

She paused, not knowing what they *could* talk

about. They had nothing in common. Not even the time period in which they were born

"How about what you do for a living? It's obvious you are not a poor man." She gestured toward the opulent three-story house and its inner courtyard that together took up over half a city block. Handsome *and* quite rich. Roni would be beside herself.

"No, I am not a poor man," he agreed, then turned to look at his own house as if studying the white painted brick with its stark black trim for the first time. "And if by what I do for a living you mean what is my livelihood, I have a large sugar cane plantation just a few miles upriver that has proved very profitable through the years. I also own a shipping company right here in New Orleans. I'm Rand Kincaid."

He looked at her as if he expected her to recognize the name. His wealth probably made him an important man in New Orleans. She remembered how quickly the police had recognized him.

"Pleased to meet you," she said and wondered if she should offer her hand. Did women shake hands back in the 1880s? Or would that make her seem even more odd?

Rand studied her a moment longer, then asked, "The name isn't familiar to you?"

"No, but then I haven't been in New Orleans very long," she answered honestly.

Rand continued to study her, but made no further comment.

Feeling awkward at having those startling blue

eyes staring at her so intently, she looked again at his home. "Do you live alone here?" she asked.

Surely not. This house was large enough for a family of ten.

"Alone? No. I have several servants who live on the third floor and also off of the kitchen. But if you are wondering if I have a wife, no, I don't. Nor are my parents living. I lost my father and my older brother near the end of the War Between the States. They were blockade runners. And I lost my mother to yellow fever later, in 1874, when I was twenty-two and only two years out of college. Shirley was only twenty at the time and had just lost that first baby." When he saw her questioning expression, he explained, "Shirley is my widowed sister. She and my four-year-old nephew, Shawn, live in the house on the plantation and have since her husband died from being trampled by a horse three years ago. She helps oversee matters there."

Having always been afraid of horses, Alisha cringed at the thought. "And you live here?" She did some quick mental arithmetic and concluded that Rand was twenty-nine years old. Four years older than older than she.

"Sometimes here. Sometimes I live there. I pretty well divide my time between the plantation and the shipping company. Both are important to me." He paused a moment, then asked, "And you? Are you married?"

"I was," she admitted, but when she remembered the reaction she had gotten the last time she had mentioned the word *divorce*, she did not elaborate.

"Oh, then you are a widow," he surmised. "Do you work anywhere?"

"Yes," she answered before she realized he would have a hard time understanding just what it was she did. Computer analysts did not exist in 1882. Nor did computers, for that matter. The closest things they had in the 1880s were adding machines, and even they were crude.

Because of that lack of technology, she decided to keep her answers vague. She knew the more lies she told the more lies she would have to remember. Convincing him that she had been abducted from another century was out of the question: he would think her deranged.

"I work in an office. Or at least I did until last week." Now she wasn't so sure. If she did not find some way to convince Imena to return her to the twentieth century right away, she just might lose that job. Taking an unannounced three-week vacation would not sit well with her employer. By not being able to phone in and explain why she was not there, she risked losing it all, including the promotion. If only there was a way to send a message forward in time. "It may not sound like much, but at least it's honest work."

Rand fell silent a moment, then without explanation headed toward the house with long, easy strides. When he realized she had not followed, he signaled for her to do so. He waited until she was beside him before he shouted, "Millicent!"

Seconds later, an older woman about the same height and weight as Alisha with graying blond hair poking out from beneath a gathered white cap appeared in the doorway farthest to the left. She wore a long black dress with a gathered waist and a starched white apron. She smiled pleasantly.

"You wanted me?" she asked as she reached into her apron pocket and took out a small box of wooden matches. Without being told to do so, she lit a nearby lantern so she could see Rand better. A startled expression crossed her face when she caught sight of Alisha. Obviously the housekeeper was no more used to seeing a woman in trousers than Rand.

"Yes, I want you to bring me one of your dresses." He offered no explanation. "Bring one that has been freshly laundered."

"Will you be wanting an apron, too?"

"No, just a dress," he replied. "And a pair of shoes if you have extra. I'll pay you for them."

When Millicent returned only a few minutes later with a long black garment draped over her arm and a pair of stiff button-up black boots in her hand, Rand immediately took them from her and held them out to Alisha.

"I don't know if the shoes will fit, but the dress should. Of all the servants, Millicent is probably closest to your size. You can change in the summer kitchen since it isn't being used just

yet and I have no bedrooms prepared for guests
at the moment."

He gestured toward a small white-brick building surrounded by drooping shade trees that
stood separate from the rest of the house. Turning back to Millicent, he said, "This is Alisha
Sampson. She is to be my house guest for the
night. Have Faye make ready one of the guest
rooms on the second floor."

Millicent looked at Alisha questioningly, but
turned to do as told without further comment.

"There, that should take care of everything,"
Rand said, reaching for the lantern Millicent
had just lighted and lifting it off its catch. "Because I'd expected Nicky to be here for supper,
there should already be an extra place set at the
table."

He started to hand the lantern to Alisha, but
when he realized her hands were full with the
dress and the boots, he carried the light for her.

As he led the way, Alisha could not help but
notice that when he walked, each step affected
only the lower half of his body. His shoulders
and head remained perfectly still while his hips
and legs absorbed all movement. It reminded
Alisha of watching a sleek cat steal through the
darkness.

When they entered the small kitchen, he lit
one of the small wall lamps near the door, then
placed the lantern he carried on a nearby table.
"I'll be outside if you need me, he said, then
left.

She did her best to hurry. It was not easy,

slipping into a garment that had enough material to cover a small car. After she finally found her way inside the dress and had fastened all of the twenty or so buttons that ran down the back as well as the eight that ran the length of each long cuff, she sat on a small wooden stool and tried on the boots. They were far too large and far too uncomfortable to consider wearing even for the one night. Quickly she changed back into her Reeboks, knowing the skirt was long enough to hide the shoes.

Standing again, she quickly dropped the heavy skirt back in place. Since there was no mirror, she twisted from side to side, checking to make sure the skirts lay properly. When she did, her dark hair fell forward, but she quickly tossed it back out of her way. She frowned. Her hair felt longer than she had expected, though only by a few inches. Even so, the difference was noticeable.

Glancing down, she saw how much darker her hair looked in the soft lantern light. Holding the ends out in front of her, she tried to remember the last time she'd had her hair trimmed and was again reminded that she had not paid much attention to herself recently. She had no one but herself to blame for such personal neglect. She had let what happened with Brad affect her far too deeply and for far too long.

Roni was right. It was time to get over what had happened during the past year. Time to push those bitter emotions aside and get on with her life. And just as soon as she could find her way back to 1995, she would do just that. She would put all thoughts of Brad and his upsetting marriage behind her and concentrate again on herself. She would do far more to pamper herself than merely buy a sporty new car. She would get out and meet new people. Make new friends. She would finally get on with her life.

But first she had to convince Imena to send her back. Reminded of the seriousness of her situation, her stomach knotted again.

What if tomorrow when she returned to talk with Imena more calmly the woman still refused to send her back? What if Imena still claimed she had some sort of unknown problem to solve first. What would happen then? Would she be forced to stay back in these olden times for three weeks just to appease a woman she didn't even know? And what about poor Roni? She had to be beside herself with worry by now. It was not every day one's best friend vanished into thin air like that.

Alisha chewed on her lower lip while she wondered about Roni. Would her friend be as worried as she herself had been when she thought it was Roni who had disappeared? Or would Imena be able to put her back at the very same moment she'd taken her? If that was the case, then Roni would never know. But chances were that 1995 was continuing without her.

She pulled back the black cuff and looked at her watch. It had been two hours since she'd been abducted. Had Roni contacted the police yet? Were they out looking for her by now? Or

were they saying that twenty-four hours had to
pass first, a statement that was sure to make
Roni absolutely hostile.

And what about her new car? What would happen to it? Would the police eventually haul it in
for having been left on the street too long, or
would Roni remember that extra keys were in
their hotel room. Alisha hoped Roni had the presence of mind to take the car back to the hotel.
No telling what damage would be done to it while
parked in an impound lot or, worse yet, left on
the street. Surely Roni would not let that happen.
Surely she would remember the extra keys.

Despite her fear, Alisha smiled. Roni would
finally have a chance to drive the new car, although maybe not under the circumstances she
had hoped.

Aware that she should return to Rand, Alisha
reached over to pick up the lantern. When she
did, she noticed how difficult it was for her to
move in the cumbersome dress. Because what
few darts there were had been placed in all the
wrong places, the heavy garment allowed for
very little motion. She was glad she only had to
wear the dress that one night. She would hate
to wear that sort of clothing permanently.

She stepped outside, carrying her modern
clothes folded neatly. She knew she would want
to put them back on that following morning before she returned to the voodoo shop to ask
again to be sent back to 1995. Suddenly showing
back up wearing the antiquated dress instead of
her slacks would be too hard to explain.

She had already decided it would be pointless if not downright foolish to try to make anyone in 1995 believe where she had been these past few hours. Everyone might decide she'd gone off the deep end, and have her committed.

But how else could she explain her temporary absence when asked where she'd been? She supposed she could make up some wild story about having been kidnapped by a gang of hoodlums. She could claim that she never actually got to see them because they had covered her face, which would also explain not knowing where she had been taken. That would be far easier for everyone to believe than the truth. But then she would end up wasting the police department's time by having given a false report. They would be out searching for a gang of hoodlums that did not exist. She did not want that either.

Still puzzled over how she should handle her return after she finally managed to convince Imena to send her back, she was greeted with a wide, appreciative smile from Rand as she appeared in the doorway.

Knowing there was very little she could do about her odd situation at the moment, she temporarily set aside her strange problems to concentrate on how truly handsome this man was and how truly pleased he seemed by her appearance.

"I see the dress fits," he said, as he took the lantern from her with his left hand and held his right hand out to help her down the three small steps.

Feeling uncharacteristically timid at such a gallant gesture and also because he had not yet put on a shirt, Alisha hesitated before shifting her folded clothes to her right arm so she could rest her left hand in his. When she did, she felt an unexpected jolt to her senses, one that set her heart to racing and put her body on alert. *This man was so virile he was downright dangerous.*

"Th-the boots did not fit," she said, trying to recover from her reaction to his touch without actually pulling her hand away from his. She did not want to chance insulting him in any way. He had been too kind. "I didn't know what to do with them so I left them inside, near the door."

"I'll tell Millicent where they are," he assured her.

He watched approvingly while she moved as gracefully as the awkward dress would allow down the three planked steps and onto the brick path.

"I-I left the wall lamp burning so someone could find them," she said in a strained effort to keep a conversation going. She was afraid that if they ever stopped talking she would end up gawking at him like a young girl. "I hope that was all right."

"That's fine. I'll have Millicent take care of it," he said, then gestured toward the grouping of wrought-iron lawn furniture with the lantern while he gently tugged on her left arm with the other. "It should be awhile yet before the food is ready. Why don't we sit?"

Still aware of Rand's touch, Alisha followed

him. In addition to the double chaise, the grouping included several small tables, a number of chairs, and a small love seat. Her eyes widened when at first it looked as if he planned for them to sit on the double chaise, but she relaxed when he led her beyond to two tall wrought-iron seats supplied with thick cushions.

He waited until she had seated herself before releasing her hand and moving to the other chair. No sooner had Alisha placed her clothes on the table next to her, the same one that held her purse, and had smoothed her skirts than a woman appeared in a different doorway and called out to them that supper was ready. Like Millicent, the woman wore a long black dress with a white bibbed apron and a white cotton cap shaped something like a shower cap. But unlike Millicent, this woman was much younger and larger. Alisha decided the tall woman had to weigh in at nearly two-hundred pounds.

"Thank you, Caroline," Rand called back to her. Because he had not yet sat down, he immediately turned to Alisha again and held out his hand. "Looks like I was wrong. Supper is ready."

Remembering the effect his touch had had on her just seconds earlier, Alisha stared at his hand a moment before finally putting her own hand there. As expected, a warm, tingling sensation developed in her fingers, then spread quickly through her body, making her all the more aware of him as a man—a man destined not to be a part of her life. Sadly, she wondered if she would remember him once she returned to 1995. She certainly hoped so.

"I hope you like your Creole shrimp spicy because that's the only way Jolie knows how to cook it," Rand said as he guided her toward the house. "Spicy enough to make your tongue curl and your eyes water."

"Millicent, Caroline, Jolie—" Alisha repeated, her brow drawn questioningly while she walked side Rand. "How many house servants do you have?"

"Just four," he answered as if that should be considered a low number. "But then they only have to cook and clean for me. And I'm not here all that much. Even when I'm staying in the city, I'm usually out of the house."

Alisha looked at him curiously. It sounded to her like all four were live-in maids. She wondered what they did with their extra time, because although the house was large, it was not *that* large. Two live-ins should be able to take care of a place that size with time to spare. But then she remembered these women did not have any of the modern conveniences she was used to using. No vacuums, no microwaves, no dishwashers, no permanent press fabrics, no food processors or blenders, and certainly no automatic washers and dryers. Why, they probably even had to chip their own ice and scrub pans that had no Teflon coating. Well, no wonder it took four women to take care of that one house.

Rand continued, "And in addition to Millicent, Caroline, Jolie, and Faye, there's William,

Jolie's husband. He helps by seeing to some of my personal belongings and to the general upkeep of the house while I'm not here."

When they reached the door, he set the lantern on a hook, then paused to grab up a shirt that had been casually tossed across a white statue of a naked man and woman locked in a passionate embrace.

Alisha pretended to study the piece of art while Rand slipped easily into his shirt. But what she really did was watch him. She watched the way his taut stomach muscles rippled when he lifted his arms to swing the shirt around behind him. She tried to repress her strong physical reaction but found that impossible to do. While he slowly fastened the tiny buttons with his long fingers, she felt a strange combination of both fascination and discomfort.

"Hope you are hungry," he said when he looked up from having buttoned the lower half of his shirt. "Jolie always makes enough to feed a crew."

I'm starved," she answered truthfully. Because she and Roni had intended to be veritable gluttons during the dinner buffet served on the riverboat they'd planned to ride that night, they had opted to skip lunch. She had not eaten since breakfast— of which she became painfully aware when they stepped inside and the rich aroma of food caught her.

"Good." He paused to make sure the spring had pulled the screen door shut.

Alisha took in the spacious surroundings, not

too surprised by the grandeur. From where they stood at the end of a wide, lamp-lit hallway, she counted four large doors, three of which stood open. At the far end of the hall, an open area led to three other corridors. In the center of that same space, to the left, stood a wide, mahogany staircase flanked by two huge white-marble urns. Above the staircase a huge chandelier dripped with crystal.

In the corridor in which they stood, several large paintings hung in magnificent frames just above eye level. There was also a gray and white Oriental rug that ran the length of the gleaming hardwood floor up to and beyond the stairs, and hand-carved tables had been placed along the walls. On the tables stood various appointments made of silver or porcelain, or both.

Although Rand's house was a showplace from its tall sculpted ceilings to its mahogany floors, there was still a certain warmth to it, a feeling of home.

"The dining room is this way," he said with a quick wave of his arm. He placed his hand at her waist, where he gently guided her toward the nearest door to the right. Awareness again shot through Alisha.

Once inside the elegant room, she noticed that beneath two more gigantic chandeliers similar to the one in the grand hall was a table long enough to serve sixteen. At the far end were two place settings.

After sitting in the chair Rand had pulled out for her and while waiting for him to be seated at the head, she noticed that her place was set differently than expected. All the silverware had been placed horizontally at the head of the plate rather than vertically on either side, and a heavy cloth napkin lay folded in the center of the plate. The water glass sat to the right of the plate, where Alisha was used to finding her silverware, and a wineglass sat to the left.

When she studied the silverware more closely, she noticed that in addition to the usual fork, knife, and tablespoon, there was a second spoon, this one very long and very tiny. It was so small that she wondered what possible use it could have and decided to wait and see how Rand used his before bothering to touch hers.

While placing her napkin in her lap, she looked again at Rand, eager to find out what would happen next, for this was an adventure. Her gaze met his, and they studied each other silently in the sparkling candlelight.

As Alisha drank in his strong handsomeness, she barely noticed when a large black woman dressed like the other servants suddenly appeared across the room. The large silver tray she carried held several steaming tureens.

Smiling, she set the heavy tray on a small table just behind Rand, then ladled food onto their plates.

Alisha's body trembled with anticipation at the sight and smell of the food, and she could hardly wait to dip her fork into it but forced herself to wait until Rand, too, had been served.

When she was finally able to put that first

forkful of shrimp Creole into her mouth, it
turned out to be just as spicy and just as delicious as she had expected. It took all the restraint she had to eat slowly.

"Do you like it?" Rand asked only seconds
after the servant had swept from the room, her
longs skirts swishing behind her. He watched
Alisha closely while awaiting her answer, as if
worried the cuisine might not be to her liking.

"Mmmmmm," Alisha responded with an appreciative nod, having a large bite into her
mouth. Quickly, she chewed and swallowed. "It
is delicious."

"Good. I was worried you might not like it.
Not everyone likes their food as spicy as I do."

"I love it," she admitted. Aware he had yet to
touch his food, she asked, "Aren't you going to
eat?"

Rand blinked as if surprised by that question,
then shrugged. This movement caused his shirt
to gap open at the top, where he had left several
buttons undone, revealing dark chest hair. She
valiantly tried to ignore this. "Of course. I was
just waiting to make sure you liked the food."
Having said that, he reached for a small bowl
that held either sugar or salt, and dipped the
tiny spoon Alisha had wondered about into the
crystals. With the spoon half-filled, he then
lightly sprinkled the contents over his food.

Aware that this was their answer to salt shak-
ers, Alisha did likewise.

As Rand began eating, a loud, metallic knock
sounded somewhere in the distance. A few min-

utes later, a tall, lanky black man appeared just
inside the door. Like everyone else, he too was
dressed in black, but wore a bright red bandanna tied around his dark hair.

"Mr. Rand, there be three policemen at the
door wantin' to talk with you," he said with a
slight Cajun accent as he came farther into the
room. He looked more annoyed than worried.
"They say it be important. They say something
about havin' been here before and somethin'
about not believin' what you told them."

Alisha's stomach knotted when she looked at
Rand. The policemen were back looking for her.

He frowned as he pushed his chair back. His
blue eyes glittered with irritation. "I'll go see
what they want. You wait right here."

Alisha's pulse raced as she watched him follow
the servant out of the room with long, determined strides. She tried to decide what to do
next. Taking a deep, calming breath, she pushed
her chair back and went to the dining-room
door, where she stood listening.

When she heard nothing, she peered cautiously into the hallway and discovered no one
within sight.

Aware the men must be at the front door, she
slipped quietly into the hall and followed as far
as the corner nearest the stairs. There she listened again and off to the left heard Rand's
voice say casually, "Well, gents, did you ever find
that woman you were after?"

"No, but we have it on good word that she
did indeed go over your garden wall like I

thought," came a stern response. "You had to have seen her."

Alisha closed her eyes against a twisting stab of fear while she waited to hear Rand's response.

"Well, as I said before, I was a little too preoccupied at the time," Rand replied. "But if you'd like to go back out into the garden and have another look around, please feel welcome to do just that. Here, I'll show you the way."

Alisha's heart slammed hard against her chest when she realized they were probably headed in her direction. Afraid the policemen might see her, she picked up her heavy skirts and darted back into the dining room. Quickly, she ripped the netting out of one of the windows and without knowing where she was or where she was headed she escaped into the night.

Four

As the garden torch had burned down and the lantern had been extinguished by a servant, Alisha could barely make out her surroundings when she first dropped onto the ground.

After establishing where she had landed— not far from the door where they had entered— her first thought was to make a quick dash across the courtyard to grab her purse and clothes but realized she might not have time for that. The policemen were being led outside at that very moment.

Spotting a small wooden gate a few yards to her left, she decided to forget the purse and clothes, at least for now, and head for the gate. With her heart still pounding rapidly, she made a wild dash for freedom.

After closing the gate behind her, she found herself not on a street as she had assumed she would be, but inside a shaded lane of some sort, a lane just wide enough for a small car— or rather a small carriage to pass.

From what she could see in the darkness, the lane was formed on one side by a six-foot-tall, vine-covered brick wall and on the other side by the garden wall she had just slipped through and farther down by the house itself. Except for several small splashes of light that spilled from Rand's house to her left, the lane was dark and the shadows still.

Frowning, she quickly glanced both directions. It was too dark to really tell what lay off in the distance, but that did not really matter. What mattered was that she needed to get away from the house as fast as possible. She could not risk standing still.

Praying she was picking the quickest route to safety, she twisted the heavy black skirts up so she would need only one hand to hold them, then took off running to the right.

When the dark shape of what looked like a small carriage house and stable came into view, she sped up. She hoped to find a back way out— one that would lead directly onto the street or into an alley. But to her mounting panic, when she tried to lift the heavy metal bar that held the huge double doors in place, it refused to budge. It was then she noticed a large padlock holding it down.

Horrified, she heard men's voices coming from the other side of the garden wall. They were already outside looking for her. It was only a matter of minutes before they decided to check what lay beyond the different gates. She ran farther on.

Guided by what little light there was, she hurried toward what turned out to be a massive ironwork gate. Through the scrolled bars, she saw the outline of a black carriage pulled by two horses plodding past and realized she finally had a way out. Prepared to climb over the carriage gate, even in her long dress, she ran toward it. When she got closer, though, she noticed a small pedestrian gate off to one side and headed for it, instead.

Relieved to find the smaller gate unlocked, she quickly threw it open, smoothed her skirts down so she would not attract unwanted attention, then hurried out into the street. She did not make it ten feet before she noticed two more policemen standing near a pair of saddled horses tied to the side of a tall black wagon.

The two spotted her immediately.

"Ain't that her?" the closest one asked, quickly nudging the other into action.

"Looks like her to me," the larger one responded, already reaching for one of the horse's reins. "Let's get her."

Alisha's heart jumped to her throat. Remembering what Rand had said about women who ended up inside the local jail, and not certain she could convince them she was not who they thought she was, she snatched her skirts back up and ran as hard and as fast as she could.

Just before she rounded the corner that carried her from a residential street onto a commercial one, she glanced back to see how much distance stretched between her and the two policemen. She noticed that only one had given chase on foot. The other had climbed onto the

back of one of the horses and was already pulling away from the wagon.

Aware she was no match for a horse and seeing that there was no one else around to help
her, her one hope was to find a place to hide.
Spotting a small alley only half a block away, she
prayed it would yield her a safe place and darted
quickly into the darkness.

To her horror, the alley turned out to be not
only empty of any crates or boxes but also a
dead end with only two doors in sight. She
prayed she would find one of them unlocked.

With her entire body trembling, she ran toward the first door and found that not only was
it locked, it was boarded shut. Immediately she
ran on toward the next door, this one at the very
end of the alley.

But by that time, the man on the horse had
spotted her and entered the alley, too. With her
heart pounding harder and harder, she tried the
second door and found that it, too, was locked.

"Here she is, George!" he shouted. "We've
got her now. Hurry up." He pulled his horse to
a halt about halfway into the alley and waited
for the man on foot to catch up with him.

Alisha turned to face the rider, wondering
what he would do if she dared try to dart past
him. But when the other man appeared inside
the entrance only seconds later, she knew any
attempt to rush by them would prove futile. She
pounded on the door instead. She could not let
them take her to jail.

"That won't do you no good," the dark

shadow on the horse said as he slowly nudged the animal closer. "That's the back door to the Merchant's Bank. Nobody's there this time of night."

Alisha's heart hammered with brutal force while she watched the horse come ever closer. She had to do something. But what? She certainly couldn't scale a brick building. Her only choice was to make one last run for the street.

Pulling in a deep breath, she tightened her hold on her skirt and bolted suddenly toward the entrance of the alley. To her amazement she made it by the man on the horse with little problem but was not so lucky with the second man. Rather than chance her slipping by him, too, he tackled her, slamming her to the ground.

Although Alisha's breath was knocked out of her, she fought with her assailant as best she could, but not only did he have her pinned against the packed earth by her arms, he had her heavy skirt trapped beneath his knees. There was no escaping him.

"I'm not who you think I am," she said when she was finally able to draw her next breath. She tried to ignore the pain in her arms and shoulders while she continued her struggle to free her hands at least. "I'm not Andrea Knight."

"And I'm not Officer Gray, either," the man lying on top of her said through tightly gritted teeth. "And this here ain't Officer Butler."

"But really I'm not Andrea," she said again. "My name is Alisha Sampson. For some reason you have me confused with the woman you're really after.''

"Sure we do," he commented. His shadowed face hovered just inches above hers while he continued to keep tight hold of her arms. Without lessening his grip, he shouted over his shoulder to the rider, "Heath, aren't you plannin' to help me here?''

"What's the matter?" the rider asked, clearly amused by the struggle below. "Can't you handle her alone? She too much woman for you?''

"Ah, shut your trap and get down here. We don't got all night. If we don't get on back, the others are going to wonder what happened to us.''

"Well, since you can't handle her alone," he responded, already swinging one leg over the saddle. He dropped to the ground with a thud. "I guess I have no choice. Here, let me show you how to handle a hellcat like that one.''

Alisha fought a moment longer, but when she realized she had two of them to contend with and that one of them was the size of a small mountain, she finally gave up her struggles completely. She decided it would be better to conserve her energy should a better chance to escape arise.

When she finally quit fighting, the man on top of her let go of her arms and sat upright, but his legs still straddled her hips. In the darkness she could not make out his face, but then she did not really want to.

He waited until the other man had bent and

taken hold of one of her wrists before finally stepping away.

"You going to come peaceful like, or do we have to drag you kicking and screaming?" the second man asked. When he did, the rancid stench of stale whisky and old sweat washed over her, forcing her to turn away.

"I'll go peacefully," she answered, still determined to save what was left of her energy for a more appropriate opportunity. "Let go of me so I can get up."

He snorted, than tightened his meaty hold around her tiny wrist. "I don't think that would be a wise thing to do considering you've already managed to escape us once." He pulled her to her feet with a painful jerk. "And let me tell you, we got yelled at plenty for letting you get away from us like that. That ain't going to happen again."

"Then you've seen Andrea Knight personally?" she asked, suddenly hopeful. She looked at the larger man, but the shadows in the alley were too dark for her to see his face or vice versa. "You've seen her up close?"

"You know we have," he responded. While he continued to hold her wrist painfully, he gave her a hard shove with his free hand to start her toward the entrance. He stayed directly behind her. "We all got a real good long look at you before you suddenly kicked our buddy in the shin and took off running like you did. Danged if you didn't nearly break old Glenn's leg."

"But I told you. That wasn't me. I'm not Andrea Knight. And when we get out into a better light, you'll finally be able to see that for yourself."

"Sure I will," he muttered. He gave her another sharp shove before he called back over his shoulder, "George, grab that horse." He turned his attention back to her. "Move faster, will you?"

Eager for them to see their mistake so she would be allowed to return to Rand's house, Alisha did exactly that. She walked quickly out into the street, headed toward the nearest street lamp, when suddenly he gave her arm another painful jerk.

"Not that way, woman. This way. Back toward the wagon."

"But I want you to take a look at my face. I want you to see that I'm telling you the truth. That I'm not Andrea Knight. How do you think it will look to the other men when you two go to all the trouble of bringing back the wrong woman?"

She had obviously given her captor pause for thought because he slowed for a moment then abruptly changed directions.

"Okay. Let's have a look at you then. Let's see if you really are someone else or if you're just pulling another one of your tricks."

Alisha felt weak with relief while she allowed him to drag her back toward the street lamp. Finally she could bring an end to this lunacy. Finally she could turn her attention to what mattered— getting back to 1995.

She waited until they had neared the sputtering gas lamp and he had spun her around to face him, before smiling with relief. "See, I told you. I'm not Andrea Knight."

His eyes narrowed instantly. He spun her back around before she could even get a good look at him.

"I don't know what you are trying to pull here, but you sure as hell *are* Andrea Knight." He jerked her arm again, this time with such twisting force it caused a wrenching pain in her shoulder. "Now get going."

"But I'm not Andrea Knight," she tried again, unable to believe that even after having had a closer look at her they still thought she was the woman they were after. Her fear returned, more intense than ever. "I'm Alisha Sampson. I'm not even from around here," she explained, knowing *that* was an understatement. She wasn't even from this time period, but she knew better than to try to convince them of that fact. They were having a hard enough time believing her.

"I said get going," he repeated angrily and jerked her arm again, but this time it was the other man who gave her a hard shove, for he, too, had followed her over to the light and decided she really was Andrea Knight.

"But you are making a mistake," she tried again. She looked pleadingly over her shoulder but was unable to make eye contact with either man. "A terrible mistake."

"No, *you* are the one making a mistake," the man still holding her arm stated. He continued to propel her forward along the nearly deserted street back in the direction they had come. "Your mistake was thinking you could talk us into believing you are someone you're not when you know as well as we do that you are who you are."

Alisha was temporarily lost to the illogic of that statement when they rounded the corner that put them only a block from Rand's house. The man leading the horse rushed ahead. While still holding the reins, he tossed open the back door of the black box-shaped wagon where they had stood waiting for the others only a few minutes earlier.

It was not until she saw the iron-barred door and the dark chamber inside that she realized the wagon was a prison cart and that they intended to put her inside it. Horrified, she started to fight again— harder than ever.

The man holding the horse dropped the reins to help wrestle her into the wagon. Together they managed to lock her safely inside, though they both ended up out of breath for their efforts.

Alisha sat on the floor of the compartment, staring through the crossed bars at the two men, stunned. She could not believe what had happened to her. It was hard enough to believe she was in another time period but even harder to believe that she had just been mistaken for someone else and had been ruthlessly tossed into a foul-smelling cubicle with no possible way of escape. There was only the one door and one small window, and both were secured by iron bars and heavy padlocks.

"George, get on in there and tell them we got her in the wagon," Heath, the meaty one, said. He paused to light one of the two smoke-stained lanterns that hung from small metal grapples just outside the door. "I'll stay here and make sure the slippery little wench doesn't find some new way to escape."

As the lantern light entered the wagon, Alisha was allowed her first glimpse of her surroundings. Her stomach wrenched when she saw the reason for the sickening odor. The floor where she sat was splattered with brown patches of tobacco and dried blood, and the walls around her were stained with splashes of urine and what looked like it might have been vomit. Other than a horde of flies buzzing about, there was only one narrow bench inside the cart and a half-dozen leather straps attached to the walls.

Aware now that she sat in filth, she hurriedly climbed up onto the bench where she waited for what might happen next— far too afraid to try to second-guess what that might be. Nothing that had happened thus far made any sense to her, and she now wondered if it ever would.

Moments later, after the shorter man called George had gone off to inform the others, Heath peered angrily into the wagon, his ugly features webbed by the grid bars that shaped the iron door. Because of the lantern over his shoulder, Alisha got a good look at her captor and was repulsed by what she saw.

Although the right half of his face remained shadowed, she saw enough to know he had a large, round face with shaggy black eyebrows and a wide, bulbous nose set between narrowed dark eyes. Thick lips protruded from a dirty, matted beard to form a hideous sneer. Above that, across his upper left cheek, rising from his beardline, was a craggy pink scar that slashed upward and barely missed the outer corner of his eye. Alisha decided the man looked more like a street thug than a city policeman.

"Comfortable in there?" he asked sarcastically while he studied her closely. His sneer widened to reveal the not-too-surprising fact that he had not bothered to brush what few teeth he had in quite some time.

"No," she answered, then met his gaze with a defiant lift of her chin. "And you won't be comfortable out there for long. Not after it is revealed that I am not Andrea Knight and that you are the one who has to answer to the fact that I've been so badly mistreated."

Rather than discuss the matter further, the large ugly man merely rolled his grotesque eyes and turned his back to her. Within minutes, the other policemen clamored out of the house, eager to see if it was true— eager to see if George and Heath had really captured Andrea Knight and had her already locked away inside the wagon.

To further Alisha's concern, more men like the first peered through the door, all looking more like heinous criminals than policemen, and all smiling proudly as if they had each personally put her there.

Satisfied they had the woman they sought at last, two of the six policemen climbed onto a small rail attached to the back of the wagon where they stood staring down at her with lurid smirks while two sat at the head of the wagon and two followed on horses closely behind.

Alisha sat stiffly on the bench pretending not to notice the flies swarming around her or the degrading way the men in the back looked at her. All the while though, her stomach churned from what Rand Kincaid had said about the plight of women in jail.

Renewed fear washed over her. Apparently these men hoped to participate in whatever was in store for her. She shuddered and closed her eyes for a moment in an effort to steady her nerves. Surely Rand had exaggerated. Surely these men would not take advantage of her.

"Sure do wish I was Chief Miller's brother," one of the men on horseback said. "I'd sure like to be the one teaching that little hellcat a lesson. George said it took both of them just to get her in there. Can you imagine how many men it will take to bed her?"

Alisha pretended she neither heard nor saw them. Instead, she stared determinedly at a large brown spot on the wall in front of her while she tried to think of some way out of this dilemma. She knew it was important to keep her wits about her, especially now that she was already in their clutches with no foreseeable means of escape.

"I wish I was him, too," agreed one of the men hanging on to the back of the wagon, knowing full well his words reached her ears. "Just think of what all a woman would have to do to make up for cheating a man out of three thousand dollars. Makes me itch just thinking about it."

The others laughed. "Don't it though."

Alisha's blood ran ice-cold.

"Take heart, old man. I know we was told no one was to touch her until the chief's brother was finally through with her, but nothing was ever said about what happens after that. Could be we'll all get a turn with her before this is over."

"Just remember Moore has to go last. He's still got all them sores from that mulatto he bedded last month. Besides, he's the one who let her get away in the first place."

Alisha pressed her eyes shut. Her whole body trembled while she tried to figure out some way to convince these men of the truth. She was *not* Andrea Knight. Somebody somewhere had to know that, but who?

Her one hope now lay with the chief's brother. Certainly he would set her free.

"I can't wait for the chief to hear the news," someone else said. "Maybe I should ride on over to Miss Jennifer's and tell him we've got her and are headed to jail."

Several muttered agreement, and seconds later one of the men on horseback pulled away. She knew that left five officers to guard her. She shook her head dismally. Five to one. She didn't stand a chance of escape.

She rode on in dismal silence. She wondered what the chances were that the chief's brother would be waiting for them when they arrived at the jail, or would she have to wait until he could be brought there before proving her innocence? Although she wasn't looking forward to meeting a man Rand had described as being corrupt and having some sort of link with the underworld, she hoped he would already be there when they arrived. She didn't think she could go on much longer not knowing her fate, not knowing if they would free her or keep her.

Her body shuddered violently when she realized they just might keep her. Not only did that mean she continued to run the risk of being prey to any man at the jail, she could miss the three-week deadline Imena had given her.

It was then she realized that this must be the danger Imena had mentioned. This must be what she had to face in order to save some unknown man's life, but why? Why did she have to suffer like that? Why not someone else?

With those thoughts still mulling about in her mind, she sat back and wondered if being hauled in might not be a good thing after all. Perhaps by being taken in and found innocent, she was unwittingly accomplishing her task.

But what if they didn't let her go in time to be sent back? What if instead they kept her longer than three weeks? Would that leave her stuck in the past forever? Surely not. Surely there would still be some way to send her back even after the three weeks had passed. Maybe by using that same blue power that had transported her there to begin with.

With her pulse throbbing, the wagon clattered to a sudden stop. Seconds later, the heavy door squealed open. The time had come to face her accuser.

Alisha did not wait for an order to climb out of the stench-filled wagon. She immediately headed for the opening and was already climbing down when suddenly one of them grabbed her by her hair and yanked her the rest of the way out.

"Hurry up, woman. We don't have all day."

Alisha tried to see which man had her, but her attempt to look back brought another sharp jerk on her hair. She cried out with pain.

"Let go of me," she wailed. She saw no reason for them to treat her in such a way. She had made no attempt to escape.

"Not till we get you inside and find out just what we are to do with you."

Alisha gritted her teeth against the pain while she was dragged by the hair into a nearby building. The man pulled with such force, it felt as if her whole scalp would tear loose. Finally, once inside the building, whoever had her hair abruptly let go, and she was allowed to collapse on the dirt-covered floor. Dazed, she reached for her scalp and felt droplets of blood near her hairline.

"Oh, yes, that's her all right," someone stand-

ing off to the side said. "I'd recognize that
beauty anywhere. The chief is certainly going to
be glad to have her back. Where'd you find
her?"

Wondering who had spoken, she glanced up
and saw a man with his pant leg torn away and
a large cloth bandage around his left leg staring
angrily down at her. He was tall and burly and
had not brushed his black hair nor had shaven
his ragged beard in what looked to be days.
From where she sat crumpled on the floor, he
looked like the very devil himself.

"Gray and Butler caught her in the alley behind the Merchant's Bank."

"Good. Take any jewelry she has, then toss
her back in that same cell until the chief gets
here, and don't none of you stay around long
enough for her to trick you into letting your
guard down like she did with me. She's a crafty
one."

Before Alisha could form the words necessary
to plead her case, someone again grabbed her
by the hair and forced her to walk ahead of him
toward a nearby hallway. While she stumbled
ahead, someone reached up and snatched her
necklace from her while someone else noticed
the watch on her wrist and took that. Once inside a dimly lit corridor that smelled of mildew,
urine, and sweat, she was pulled to an abrupt
halt in front of a small, dank cell and shoved
her inside.

The door clanked shut and she was left alone
inside a hot, damp jail cell that stank even worse

than the wagon had. Only instead of a narrow bench, this room had a small cot with a torn mattress, a metal bucket of some sort, and a wooden stool. The floors were laid with uneven boards and the walls of unpainted brick with names, initials, and foul language scratched in nearly every stone. Alisha sank helplessly onto the stool.

Off in the distance she heard the deep, grating sound of a man moaning, but because her cell faced a solid wall, she saw none of the other prisoners, which to her was just as well. It was enough that she had to sit and watch the matted gray rats that scurried in and out of her cell.

Five

For the next hour Alisha sat in the damp, dim, rat-infested cell that smelled of mildew and human waste, waiting for the police chief or his brother to appear. She blocked out the annoying sound of water dripping in the distance and fanned her heavy skirts to help stir the unmoving air while she thought through her situation better.

Hers was clearly a case of mistaken identity. She was not who these men thought she was; but how could she possibly go about proving that to them? How could she convince them of such a simple truth when they were so determined to believe otherwise?

What she needed to do was find someone who could positively identify her as Alisha Sampson, but there was only one person in 1882 who even knew her: Imena. Imena was the only one who knew she was not Andrea Knight.

Alisha stopped fanning her skirts long enough to dab at the perspiration on her forehead with a torn sleeve. She wondered if she should have the voodoo priestess summoned to speak on her behalf. But would that do any good? Would these men believe someone like Imena? Would they believe a woman who made a living out of practicing magic? Would they believe that Imena had somehow brought her there from a future time period because she held an odd notion that Alisha was originally from the past?

Probably not.

It was hard enough for herself to believe such a thing could really happen and *she* was the one it had happened to. It would be far more prudent to wait until all other avenues had been tried before attempting to convince anyone she was a time traveler from 1995.

Alisha was drawn from her thoughts by the rapid sound of wooden boot heels clicking against the stone floor. Hoping it was someone coming to talk to her at last, she turned to face the sound.

A moment later, a man approached the door wearing what she now recognized to be a policeman's uniform. He was tall and skinny with slick black hair but was too busy looking over his shoulder for her to get a good look at his face.

When he finally did turn to peer at her through the thick iron rods that separated them, she was not surprised to see yet another seedy-looking face. Like many of the others, he was dirty, ugly, and unshaven. It made her wonder if Rand Kincaid was the only man in that century who cared about his appearance.

"Come here," he called in a hushed voice.

He stretched his neck and quickly looked both ways again, then slipped his hand into his coat pocket and came out with a large rusted key. He held it up so she could see what it was, then quickly unlocked the door.

When she did not immediately come forward, his dark eyes narrowed.

"Don't ya want out of there?" he demanded with an angry hiss. "You are Miss Sampson, aren't ya?"

Alisha's eyes widened upon hearing her real name. Evidently someone somewhere believed her. "Yes! Yes, I am."

She rose from the stool and hurried forward, not bothering to lift her now ragged and filthy skirts off the damp floor. "Who are you?"

"Don't matter who I am," he cautioned, then opened the door halfway. A trio of fat, brown water bugs leaped from the bars and scurried off under the bed. "Just get the hell out of here while ya got the chance. There's a carriage waitin' for ya in the back alley." He pointed off in the direction he had just come.

Alisha looked at him a moment, confused. She wondered why there would be a carriage waiting for her and why would it be parked out back instead of in the front, but wasted no time in complying. Not when the alternative was to stay in that rat-infested cell waiting for "Chief Miller to have first crack at showing her what happens to anyone who crosses his brother."

With renewed hope, she lifted her skirts to keep from stumbling while she hurried down the narrow hall toward the only door that did not lead into another cell.

When she came closer to the solid door, she felt a sudden rush of excitement, for the door stood open half an inch. For some reason, the skinny man with the key was giving her this very real chance at freedom.

Wasting no time, she tugged on the heavy door until it opened wide enough for her to pass through, then she quietly closed it shut again. Though the only light was from the nearby street, she could tell that she had just entered a large alley and, as promised, at the far end of that alley sat a small open carriage waiting for her. Because it had been backed into the alley so that it faced the street, she could not tell who the driver was.

Unsure if the vehicle carried friend or foe, for she really had neither at the moment, she quickly glanced in the other direction to see if there might be another way out of there. But like before, the alley was a dead end. There was only one direction to go. Unless of course she wanted to return to the jail cell.

Drawing a deep breath to steady a rapidly pounding heart and bolster her courage, she quietly started toward the alley entrance. She hoped to slip by the carriage.

It was not until she realized that Rand was the driver did she begin to relax. "Hurry," he encouraged needlessly. "Get in."

The black carriage took off even before she sank onto the seat beside him.

"How did you manage to get me out of there?" she asked after she had settled into place. "I was starting to think I'd have to spend the night there."

Putting her hands out for balance, she turned to look at him. As they entered the street, the shadows moved away from his face, revealing a deeply concerned expression. Her senses leaped at the visual reminder of just how truly handsome he was. She also remembered what he looked like without the shirt and lightweight summer coat he now wore.

"I told you," he responded in his deep, comforting voice. The breeze created by the brisk movement of the carriage tugged at his soft hair while the reflection of a nearby gaslight passed with crystal clarity across his blue eyes. "Money can buy just about anything in this city."

Alisha smiled. "I'm certainly glad of that."

Thinking her danger over at last, she plopped her head wearily against the back of the cool leather seat and sighed audibly. "Thank you for getting me out of there. I realize you didn't have to."

"Don't thank me too soon," he cautioned. "All I did was bribe one policeman. Chief Miller will have his men out looking for you again just as soon as he realizes you've escaped."

Because they traveled at such a rapid clip, he returned his gaze forward. There was not much traffic on the street at that hour, but there were several wash holes, pieces of garbage, and loose rocks to be avoided. "The chief and I don't get along very well, so I didn't even bother trying to buy him off. Besides he's not a man to be trusted even when bribed."

A renewed feeling of dread washed over Alisha. She crossed her arms protectively. "So I'm not completely safe from all this yet?"

"No. That's why I've decided to take you straight to your father's. He may know of a safe place to send you until all this finally blows over."

"My *father's?*" she asked and sat erect again, perplexed. Even in 1995 she had no father. He had died of cancer when she was only seventeen. "How can you do that?"

"Well, I can't very well take you back to my house," he said, clearly annoyed that she dared question his help. "That will be the first place they look for you."

"But my father's dead." Or rather, he wasn't even born yet.

Rand's expression hardened while he continued to study the road ahead. Soft shadows rolled across his lean, angry features, making Alisha wonder what she had said to provoke such wrath.

"Quit pretending, Andrea," he said, his voice edged with impatience. "I know who you are and I know the real reason you ran from my house. I've seen you at Beauregard's myself. It's hard not to notice beauty like yours, which is undoubtedly why Beau hired you to begin with. Also, I think I should tell you that I played cards with your father there just last week, which means I know for a fact that he is still very much alive, though he doesn't really deserve to be. Not when you consider some of the people he owes money to."

He glanced at her again, this time with a strange, dark glimmer in his eyes. "But I think I just figured out a way for that old man to get out from under the debt he owes me." His blue eyes raked over her boldly. "Looks like he won't have to come up with that six thousand dollars after all."

"I'm not Andrea Knight," she protested, angry that now even Rand did not believe her. "I don't know why everyone keeps insisting that I am."

Rand studied her a moment longer. "Then you're about to have a chance to prove that fact, aren't you?"

He returned his gaze to the road ahead.

"How?"

He let out an annoyed breath. "I figure Thomas Knight ought to know his own daughter, don't you? If old Tom can look me directly in the eye and tell me that you are not Andrea, then I'll believe it. The man may be a lousy card player, but he's always been an honest one. At least when playing with me." He glanced at her scornfully. "Too bad the same can't be said for his only child."

Aware that Rand was right about a man knowing his own daughter, Alisha agreed to go with him. She would gladly meet Thomas Knight so that this nightmare could be over. Or at least a part of it. Granted, she would still have the very real problem of being stuck in the wrong century, but at least she could better concentrate on finding a solution after she had the other matter resolved.

Now that she realized Rand was actually doing her a favor, Alisha sat back and quietly watched the brightly painted buildings with their fancy ironwork embellishments pass by them while Rand took first one street then another before eventually entering a more disreputable-looking part of the city.

"Just exactly where does Thomas Knight live?" she asked, glancing at the shabby buildings and littered sidewalks.

Rand's expression grew more impatient. "Over Beauregard's."

Alisha's eyes widened. "The same gambling house where the police chief's brother was cheated out of all that money?"

"Yes, the same gambling house and saloon where you have worked as a card dealer since long before I ever stumbled in there."

Narrowing her eyes, Alisha started to argue, but realized that until Rand talked to Andrea's father and learned the truth, he would not accept a word she said. Annoyed, she returned her gaze to the buildings they passed, noticing that the farther they traveled, the more people there were milling about and the more carriages and horses were tied to posts. In the distance, old-time piano music clattered above a din of male voices, punctuated occasionally by the peal of female laughter or the shattering of glass.

While she observed the many drunk and stumbling men and gaudy women lingering around the brightly lit buildings, three loud gunshots sounded from somewhere just behind them.

Startled, Rand's horse reared, then bolted. The sudden lurch sent Alisha's head back with a snap.

"Damn," Rand cursed under his breath. He leaned forward and pulled back hard on the reins in an attempt to regain control of the animal. "Whoa, Rebel. Whoa, boy."

Alisha tried to steady herself by holding onto the side. Staring helplessly at the people hurrying to get out of their way, she prayed they would not hit anyone. She was ignorant of her own danger until the carriage struck a deep rut at such a speed it shattered the wheel. Suddenly airborne, she made a wild attempt to grab hold of the door molding but missed by inches.

When she closed her eyes and braced for the impact, she heard Rand's panicked voice shout, "Andrea!" After hitting the ground, she heard a loud splintering crash, and the back of her head slammed against something hard. An explosion of white light burst in the darkness, then there was nothing.

"Andrea? Andrea, are you all right?"

The vaguely familiar male voice sounded from somewhere in the foggy distance and pulled at Alisha from the aching darkness that engulfed her.

"Andrea, please, can you hear me? Wake up.

Try to open your eyes. Somebody go get a doctor. Look at her. She's bleeding."

Alisha tried to respond to the frightened voice, if for no other reason than to explain yet again that she was not Andrea Knight. But despite her effort, all she could summon was a deep, throaty moan. The words would not push past her lips. It was as if there was no longer a solid connection between her brain and her mouth. Or her brain and any other part of her body, for that matter.

Finally, she forced her eyes. She could tell that someone hovered over her, probably the same person who gently cradled her head; but she did not have the strength to keep her eyes open long enough to focus and let her lids fall shut again.

She was in pain but could not quite pinpoint where she hurt. Nor could she remember what had happened to cause such pain. Even so, she could tell by the cold, rough surface beneath her that she lay on the ground somewhere. But what had happened to put her there? And what had happened to cause her such pain?

Again Alisha forced her eyes open and tried to focus on the face bent so close to hers, but her vision was too blurred, the shadows too dark, and her pain too great. Slowly she closed her eyes again and heard someone with a heavy French accent say something about getting her father; seconds later she gave herself to the beckoning darkness.

* * *

When Alisha regained consciousness a second time, the sensation of lying on the cold, hard ground was gone and in its place was the feeling of being wrapped in softness and warmth. The pain of before was reduced to a dull, nagging throb at the back of her head.

Curious to know where she was and hoping to find herself back in the twentieth century, she forced her eyes open. Although her vision was decidedly better, everything still looked a little hazy, and her head felt extremely groggy.

Frustrated by her inability to focus, she blinked several times to clear her sight. Blinking helped, but still it was as if she looked at the world through a thin mist. A mist that not only hampered her vision but also muddled her thoughts. It made her feel as if she floated in a gray cloud. Even so, she could hold her concentration well enough to discern that she lay in a room with tall ceilings, light-colored walls, and dark furniture.

Squinting to have a clearer look, she studied first the tall, rounded bedpost, then the dresser, and finally a small wooden vanity. She was disappointed to find that everything looked to be from the nineteenth century. Nothing looked modern.

An eerie feeling crept over her while she continued to study the outdated surroundings. Although certain she had never been in that room before, the furniture and the many items scattered about the room and across the fireplace mantel looked oddly familiar. Even the bedspread and the lace curtains with tiny pink ribbons woven throughout looked familiar.

Frowning, she tried to figure out why she felt so at peace with everything in that room, but she was far too groggy to keep hold of any one thought for long. For a moment she wondered if she might still be asleep but realized she had to be awake when she heard a horse's whinny outside her window and low voices in another room— male voices. But they were too low and faraway for her to make out any actual words. Looking about, she noticed the door to her bedroom was ajar.

Listening intently, she heard footsteps recede and a door close. A moment later a different set of footsteps were heard, these coming in her direction. Curious, she stared at the door, waiting. As she focused, her vision became almost clear again, even though her thoughts were still a bit muddled.

Thinking herself better, she tried to sit up, but when she attempted to push herself into a seated position, she felt such a sharp pain in her right shoulder, she fell immediately back onto the pillows. Her eyes closed against the intense pain, and she tried to remember its cause.

She recalled being in a carriage with a man named Rand Kincaid on their way to see another man named Thomas Knight. She also remembered the gunshots that frightened the horse, but she could not remember exactly what happened after that. There was a vision of someone hovering over her while she lay on the ground and the memory of an intense, all-enveloping pain, but even that was vague.

Frustrated, she opened her eyes again and stared intently at the ceiling while she tried hard to remember the rest. There had to have been an accident, but what kind of accident? Did they hit another carriage head-on, or did the horse, in a state of panic, run them into a wall? If so, was Rand Kincaid hurt, too?

Her heart ached at the thought.

"Well, I see you are finally awake," an unfamiliar voice said.

Forgetting her injuries for the moment, she turned her head and tried to sit up again. A second burst of pain pierced her shoulder while an even stronger pain shot through the back of her head. Lifting her hand, she gingerly touched the spot where the pain seemed the greatest and found a large, tender knot bulging near the base of her skull.

"How do you feel?" asked the tall, lean man with shaggy white hair and weathered face as he came to stand beside her. His eyes formed deep creases at the corners when he smiled down at her.

When she noticed what a friendly, caring smile it was— the sort that reached right into the depths of his brown eyes— Alisha knew she had nothing to fear from this man. If anything, his being there made her feel calmer.

"Or is that a stupid question?" he continued and bent to have a closer look at something on the side of her face.

When he did, she noticed his broadcloth trousers and cotton shirt smelled of woodsmoke and bacon. Suddenly she was hungry, though she was not sure she wanted to put anything into her stomach just yet. For some reason, she felt a little queasy.

Curious to find out why her face held his attention, she moved her hand to touch the area and grimaced when she discovered that part of her temple had been scraped away. She wondered what other injuries she would discover.

"Hurts, huh?" He nodded.

"Where am I?" she asked in a voice so raspy it sounded foreign even to her.

His warm smile was quickly replaced with a look of deep concern. "What do you mean where are you? Don't you recognize your own bedroom?" His thick white eyebrows knitted together.

"This is not my bedroom," she said. "I have never been here before."

"Sure you have," he said, then sat gingerly on the side of her bed so he could look at her better.

When he did, she noticed a swollen bruise with a jagged cut on the side of his head not far from his left eye. She also noticed that behind his concerned expression lay a certain sadness, or was it despair that darkened his eyes? Although she had no idea why she should, she suddenly felt very sorry for him.

"Don't you remember?" He took her left hand in his and patted it gently.

There was such comfort in his touch. And there was such true caring in his eyes— eyes that reminded her of someone close to her, but she couldn't quite figure out whom. It was like her feeling about the room: he was familiar in a vague sort of way, though she knew she had never seen him before.

"No. But that's because there is nothing to remember," she said, too weary and befuddled to argue. Besides, in time everyone would know the truth. "Where's Rand?"

His eyebrows arched. "You don't remember your own bedroom, yet you remember the man who brought you here? A man you hardly know and yet you call him by his given name?"

"Yes, where is he? I want to talk to him." She also wanted to make sure he was all right. Not being able to remember clearly, she worried he might be hurt, too. Or worse. She shuddered at the thought.

"He just left. Stopped by here to see if Doc Owen had been by again this morning and to find out if you'd come awake yet. He seemed plenty concerned over your welfare."

"This *morning?*" She blinked. She glanced at the windows and realized daylight lay beyond. "How long was I unconscious?"

A ship's horn sounded in the distance as the man squinted at a small, white ceramic clock on the mantel. They must be somewhere close to the water, she thought.

"Let's see, it was nearly ten o'clock when they first brought you up here," he muttered, more to himself than to her. His heavy eyebrows notched while he figured out the hours. "And it's after one o'clock now. Looks like you've been out just over fifteen hours, but then the doctor said you probably would. He gave you a pretty stout dose of laudanum to get you through the night. Gave me more to give you this afternoon when you finally came awake. You ready for some more?"

"No." She was having a hard enough time concentrating. Besides, she knew laudanum contained opium, which was strongly addictive. She'd rather suffer the pain than risk getting hooked.

"You sure?" Doc Owen said that knot on the back of your head was going to hurt something fierce for at least a couple more days." He gestured toward a small dark blue bottle that sat on her bedside table. "And since there's the very real possibility we are going to have to move you on out of here before tomorrow, he gave me enough to last you awhile. Also told me to keep cool cloths on that bump on the back of your head."

"How'd I get the knot? Did Rand say?"

He reached up and scratched his head while his concerned expression deepened. "You don't remember your own bedroom, but you do remember the man who stole you out of jail for the simple reason he couldn't stand the thought of you being there, but you don't remember the accident. What else don't you remember?"

"How I got here for one thing," she said, too tired to try again to explain that the reason she did not remember the bedroom was because she had never been there before. Or maybe it was not fatigue that kept her from finding enough strength to state the truth. Maybe it was the opium she had been given. But whatever the reason, she could hardly keep her eyes open, much less her rambling thoughts in order.

"Rand and Beau carried you up here," he explained, still frowning. "You were unconscious and bleeding real bad at the time."

"Beau?" the name was familiar, but like the room, she had no idea why it would be. She did not know anyone named Beau. She peered up at him questioningly.

"Your boss." His grip around her hand tightened. "You do remember your boss, don't you? You've worked for him for nearly seven years now. Ever since you were sixteen. Surely you remember him."

"Sixteen? I went to work in a gambling house at the age of sixteen?" she asked, too stunned to realize that inadvertently she had the same as admitted she was Andrea.

"Had to," he explained and looked away briefly. "We needed the money and you were the only one he wanted to hire. He didn't want me because of my— problem."

Aware the man was obviously linked to Andrea Knight in some way, she studied him a moment, then asked, "And who are you?"

His eyes rounded with instant hurt. "You don't remember me? Your own father?"

"No, you are not my father. Why would you even say— "

He cut her off mid-sentence. "Andrea, just what *do* you remember?"

She fought the gray fog trying to close in around her thoughts. "Just that my name is not Andrea and that I've never been here before in my life." Vaguely, she was aware that her words had come out slurred and that her tongue felt very heavy and thick. "I couldn't have been here before. I'm not even from this century." She shut her eyes to rest them and for a moment saw tiny blue spots drifting in the darkness. "I don't belong here."

"That's the laudanum making you say such wild things," he assured her and patted her hand gently. He bent forward to make sure she heard him. "It has a way of doing that to some people. It makes them say strange things. I think maybe I should get on out of here and let you have some more rest. Doc said that's what you needed most and Beau said that's what you will have. Considering your situation, he doesn't expect you back at work anytime soon. He's already replaced you with Sheila but will gladly put you back to work just as soon as we get this other matter cleared up."

"No. No. It's the truth," she tried to explain but could not hold on to consciousness much longer. "My . . . name . . . isss . . ." Before she could finish the sentence, she was asleep again.

Six

When Alisha awoke again, her vision was sharp and her thoughts not nearly as muddled as before. Although her memory of waking earlier was not all that clear, she did remember talking to a weathered old man who had tried to convince her he was her father. She glanced around to see if he was still in the room and was relieved to find he was not.

She was alone and the bedroom door was closed. That gave her the time she needed to think through everything that had happened to her since she had been yanked back to 1882. It also gave her time to decide what her next course of action should be.

Remembering her injured right shoulder, she rolled onto her left shoulder, then propped herself on her elbow so she could get a better look at her surroundings. The bedroom was clean and neat— mostly white, though accented heavily with browns and pinks. The dark wood furniture around her looked plain but sturdy.

Against the wall to the left of the bed, which she now faced, stood a tall chest of drawers and a rectangular wardrobe with a narrow mirror on one of the two doors. Between the chest and cabinet were two large guillotine windows below which stood a tall porcelain bucket. Toward the foot of the bed, beside the closed door was a small vanity with an oval mirror. Against the wall behind her she remembered was a fireplace, a large dark green steamer trunk, and a straight ladder-back chair. At the head of the bed sat a cluttered nightstand on one side of her and another guillotine window on the other.

The room was about as large as the master bedroom in her apartment, though the ceilings were much taller. And like in her own bedroom, the walls, ceilings, curtains, and bedspread were mostly white and the floor and trim were the same shade of dark brown as the furniture. It was odd that she and Andrea Knight should have such similar tastes.

But there were differences, too. Unlike in her apartment, which except for the kitchen was completely carpeted, the floor here was wooden and bare with only a small pink-and-white braided rug near the vanity. Also unlike her apartment, the deep rumble of male voices drifted from below, accompanied by the light sound of piano music.

Remembering that Rand said Andrea and her father lived over a gambling house and saloon, she thought little of the noise and turned her attention back to the twelve-foot walls surrounding her. She studied the two paintings of the ocean, the four wooden sconces with candles, and the three sooty gaslamps, two of which were lit.

Thinking it odd to burn lamps during the day, she looked at the shelf clock and was surprised to see that it was nearly eight o'clock. She again looked at the lace-covered windows and noticed that this time darkness lay beyond. It was hard for her to believe that almost seven hours had passed since the last time she remembered being awake.

Suddenly realizing she wore a nightgown, she tossed back the covers to have a better look at it. The thin white cotton gown clung to her curves in such a provocative way that it made her body look more shapely than it actually was. Her underclothes were missing, too.

Alisha blinked. Who had changed her clothes? The old man who claimed to be her father? Or Rand? Or someone else entirely? Perhaps Andrea had a mother. She certainly hoped so because the thought of Rand Kincaid undressing her while she lay unconscious was very discomfiting. As was the thought of having her clothes removed by some old man who had proved quite willing to lie about who she really was.

Eager to find out what had become of her clothes, she scanned the room again and noticed what looked like a white satin robe lying neatly folded on the small stool in front of the vanity. Beneath the stool was a pair of pink slippers. She saw nothing else in the way of clothing.

Wondering what they had done with her clothes and what they had thought of the strange-looking undergarments and shoes she wore, she gently pushed herself into a seated position. She did that without putting any pressure on her right shoulder, but even so the shooting pain returned, though not nearly as severe as it had been earlier. The pain along back of her head had diminished to such a dull, even throb it was more an annoyance than anything else.

After discovering she had the strength to sit unaided, she decided to try to stand. Gingerly, she eased her bare feet onto the cold, wooden floor and, while steadying herself with her hands, stood perfectly still for several seconds. When that did not bring on the dizziness she thought it might, she let go of the bed and took several cautious steps toward the stool. Her legs felt weak and her hands trembled slightly, but she had little problem crossing the floor.

It was not until she had unfolded the robe and tied it around herself that the first wave of lightheadedness struck her. Rather than try to make it all the way back to the bed, she sat down on the stool, then leaned forward toward the vanity and lowered her head to her knees.

After several seconds the reeling sensation finally passed. Slowly, she lifted her head again. When she did, she caught a glimpse of someone in the mirror above the vanity. Looking again, she saw it was a woman she had not noticed before.

Dumbfounded, she looked away to see who else was in the room and was perplexed to find herself still alone. Yet when she returned her gaze to the mirror, the woman was there. Instead of seeing her own reflection, that of a young woman with light green eyes and light brown hair that fell in soft waves just past the shoulders, she saw the reflection of a young woman with almond-shaped brown eyes and thick dark brown hair that fell in wild curls nearly to the middle of her back.

Again deciding there had to be someone else in the room, she quickly gave a second look around. A spooky feeling washed over her when, again, she found no one else there. She was the only person in the room and yet her reflection did not appear in the mirror at all.

Baffled, she looked down to prove to herself that she was in no way the woman reflected before her—even though she remembered thinking her hair was a little longer than usual when she had changed clothes inside Rand's summer kitchen. Her breath caught deep in her throat when she discovered that the hair falling down over her uninjured shoulder was not only longer, it was also a lot darker. Especially in the bright lamplight.

Her heart drummed a frantic rhythm while she tried to figure out why her hair looked so different. Had traveling through time changed it in some way? Or was the hair really hers?

Although she did not feel like she had on a wig, she gave the hair that fell over her shoulder a sharp pull. The responding tug at her scalp assured her that the hair was indeed hers.

Forgetting all about the nagging pain in her

shoulder and head, she leaned closer to the mirror and saw that the image before her had done likewise. When she lifted her hand to feel her face to see if she really did have that slender, upturned nose and those strong cheekbones, the image did, too. It blinked when she blinked and frowned when she frowned.

The image had to be hers, but it couldn't be. The woman staring back at her was *too* different— much prettier in an exotic sort of way, despite the small, reddened abrasion near her right temple.

Leaning closer, she turned her head in different angles and noticed that her skin was lighter. She also noticed that not only were her cheekbones higher, the almond-shaped brown eyes that peered so questioningly at her were surrounded by the longest, darkest eyelashes she had ever seen. Thinking them false, she batted them several times, then twisted her mouth perplexedly when she discovered they were hers.

Still baffled, she glanced down to see if there were any differences in her body. That was when she realized that it was not the way the gown clung to her that made her look shapelier. She really was shapelier. She lifted the scoop-necked, cotton gown away from her body to peer beneath and blinked disbelievingly at what she saw. Frowning, she felt her breasts, then her arms, and found that her muscle tone was different, too. She was much softer than before and looked like she could possibly be several inches shorter.

She was definitely not herself.

While she continued to stare down at the rounder, softer body, she remembered how loose her clothing had felt shortly after she entered the new time period and realized now that that had nothing to do with any weight she had lost. Her clothing had felt baggier because, except for her breasts, which were somewhat larger, she was an altogether smaller person.

Her forehead notched while she tried to figure out why she suddenly looked so different. Had she, at the same time she had entered a new century, also entered a new body? But how could something like that happen? And whose body had she entered? Andrea's?

Her eyes widened when she realized that was what had happened. That was why almost everyone she had met thus far had proved so unfailingly determined to believe she was Andrea Knight. Because she had somehow taken over Andrea's body when she'd moved into this century.

But if that was so, if she had somehow been shoved into another's body, where was the real Andrea? She blinked at that last thought and wondered if Andrea was still in there with her, or had Andrea been sent into the future to take possession of her body in a sort of temporary trade-off?

Or was this happening at all?

Staring again at the unfamiliar image, she wondered if she might have thoroughly lost her mind. Or could it be she was merely hallucinating because of the strong drug she had been given after the accident?

Alisha's shoulders sagged with relief. That had to be it. She was hallucinating. None of what had happened during the past few minutes was real. It was all a drug-induced dream brought about by the opium and the belief of those around her. The opium had caused her to accept what she knew was not true.

Believing none of it real, she stood to have a better look at the beautiful image she had conjured for herself, but was immediately taken by a second wave of dizziness.

Thinking it would be best to lie down until both the dizziness and the hallucination had passed, she quickly returned to the bed.

After easing gently back under the soft linens, she lay staring idly at the white ceiling overhead. She tried not to dwell on what she had just experienced, knowing now that none of it was real. Instead, she focused on her diminishing pain, aware that it was mild enough now that two Tylenols would probably knock what was left of it on out. If only she still had her purse. She had a whole bottle of Tylenol in there.

She wondered then what had become of her purse and her original clothes. Were they still out in Rand's garden or had someone taken them inside for safekeeping. Or had they been purloined by one of the staff?

Drowsy again, probably from the drug still lingering in her system, she slowly drifted back to sleep.

* * *

The soft click of a door opening brought Alisha awake again. Groggily, she turned and saw the side of a man dressed in dark clothing. He stood blocking the narrow doorway while talking to someone just out of her sight. Because of the man's lean build and his long brown hair, she knew immediately it was Rand.

She blinked to clear her thoughts, then quickly lifted her left hand to make sure her hair was not a jumbled mess and was surprised that although it felt as if someone had brushed it, her hair still felt longer and thicker than it should. Glancing down, she noticed that it was also still a shade darker and that she still had the same shorter, rounder body she'd had before— *the sort of body most men lusted after.* It was a body that would make even Brad's new wife envious, because she was well proportioned all over, not in just the one area. All it needed was a little toning so that it wasn't quite so soft, but even that was not much of a problem.

It was obvious to Alisha that she was still hallucinating because of all that opium she had been given— only this time Rand was to be included in the dream.

Well, that should certainly make this more interesting, she thought with an inward smile while she studied the muscular physique inside the door. Maybe there was something good to be said about taking mind-altering drugs, after all.

"So, you are awake," Rand said after he finally turned and noticed her eyes open.

Ah, so the hallucination speaks.

"Not really," she replied, thinking that as appropriate an answer to a hallucination as any. She gazed contentedly at him while he entered the room, thinking him good dream material. "What are you doing here?"

"I came by to see if you were any better," he said, entering the room. "That was one nasty bump you took." On his way across the room, he grabbed up the only real chair and brought it with him to the side of her bed.

"I know," she agreed and grimaced when she reached up to touch the small bump at the back of her head. Why did pain have to be a part of this particular hallucination? It didn't seem quite fair to have to balance the good with the bad when it was her own mind creating it.

"I see you've stopped bleeding," he continued. He studied her closely from a few feet away. "I'm glad of that."

While Alisha continued to gaze at Rand's rakishly handsome face, she wondered why he had no bruises or bumps, then remembered this was all just an hallucination, which meant he would not necessarily show any injuries. "But I see you came away from the accident okay."

"I bruised the side of my leg, but that's about it," he admitted, then placed the chair so that he could straddle it and rest his arms on the back. "I managed to jump clear of the carriage before it hit the ground."

"I guess I should thank you for bringing me up here and making sure I was cared for."

He nodded, then smiled. An invisible current shot through Alisha which was so strong and invigorating it made her wonder if his being there might not be real. The thought that this might *not* be a hallucination, after all, made her heart race with sudden caution.

"I guess by now you're finally willing to admit that you really are Andrea Knight and not this Alisha Sampson you claimed to be," Rand said. He turned as Thomas came to stand quietly just inside the room.

Alisha saw how uncomfortable Andrea's father looked to have Rand there in his home and realized that was probably because of all the gambling money Rand claimed Thomas owed him.

"Not at all," she said. "I really am Alisha Sampson. I only look like Andrea Knight."

"Now, Andrea, there really is no reason to lie anymore," Rand said as if talking with a small child. He reached forward to take her hand in his, much like Thomas had that afternoon.

When he did it, her senses jolted. Suddenly she knew that everything happening around her was real and not part of some dream brought on by the opium.

Reluctantly, she glanced down at hands that were still not hers. The time had come to accept the startling fact that not only was she in a different time period, she occupied someone else's body as well.

Alisha gazed again at Rand, unblinking, while

she allowed that realization to sink in further. His expression hardened. "You more than just look like Andrea Knight and you know it. Just what is it you hope to gain by continuing this lie?"

"I'm not lying. And I am not Andrea Knight." She looked at Thomas pleadingly. He had to know she was telling the truth. Even if the body was the same, he had to notice how differently she behaved. He had to know *something* was changed. "I never met either of you before this weekend."

"See?" Thomas put in and took several timid steps forward. "I told you that either that rap on the head or the laudanum has affected her memory. She doesn't remember who she is."

Rand's scowl deepened. He looked at Alisha accusingly. "Her memory loss has nothing to do with her injury or the drug. She was putting on this little act long before the accident happened."

"It's not an act. It's the truth," she said, angered by his unwillingness to believe her. Forgetting her fear that everyone might think she was nuts, she explained quickly, "My name really is Alisha Sampson. I'm a computer analyst from the twentieth century. This is not my bedroom and this is not my bed. This is not even my body. It belongs to someone else. My guess is that it belongs to this Andrea Knight everyone keeps talking about."

Thomas shook his head. "See? Her thinking's been affected. She's confused about who she is. Too much of her memory has been lost."

A muscle in Rand's jaw worked furiously while he continued to study Alisha through slightly lowered eyelashes. "If that's true, if it's her memory that's so affected, then how did she remember me, which she obviously does, and how did she remember the name she used on me last night? If her memory was so badly damaged, how'd she ever remember the name Alisha Sampson?"

"She didn't have to. *You* spoke the name first," he pointed out. "As for why it is she remembers you so well and not me, I don't know. After all, I'm her father. I've been with her all of her life." He looked at her sadly.

"Oh, she remembers you all right. She's just *pretending* not to know you," Rand replied, frowning while he divided his attention between the two.

"But why would she pretend something like that? I'm her father. Her only living family. I'm the reason she tried to cheat Jeremy Miller out of that three thousand dollars."

Alisha had opened her mouth to clarify the fact that she was not a card cheat but decided against interrupting just yet. She was learning much about Andrea, whose body she was in, and would rather listen than argue.

Rand turned to face Thomas squarely. "What did you have to do with her cheating Miller out of that money? Did you put her up to it?"

Thomas shook his head adamantly. "No. If I'd known what she planned to do, I would have stopped her right away. I would have explained that cheating at cards was breaking the law and would be the wrong way to handle the problem. Why, in the thirty-five-plus years that I've been gambling, I never once cheated." He lifted his chin proudly. "I might be a loser and a drunk, but I'm not a cheat, and I would never encourage my own daughter to be a cheat."

Rand glanced at Alisha before returning his questioning gaze to Thomas. "Then why did she do it?"

Thomas blinked several times to stop a sudden rush of tears, then slumped his skinny shoulders. "Partly because of all the money she found out I owe. And partly because of this." He pointed to his battered eye. Although the bruise had faded considerably, the cut was still there. "You aren't the only man I owe money to."

"How much do you owe?" Alisha asked, forgetting she planned only to listen. For some reason she felt sorry for this gentle old man and wanted to know just how much trouble he faced.

Thomas glanced away for a moment as if hesitant to answer, then met her gaze forthright. "I won't lie to you, Andrea. At the moment I owe over eleven thousand dollars to three different people. I owe six thousand to Mr. Kincaid here, a thousand to Gil Platt, the fancy riverboat gambler, in addition to the forty-two hundred you know about that I owe to Frank Potter."

"Frank Potter?" Rand interrupted, having recognized the name. "You owe money to Frank Potter? The same Frank Potter who's connected to the underworld?"

Thomas nodded sadly, then pointed to his eye again. "That's where I got this. He sent a couple of his thugs around to convince me to pay up what I owe. They told me Potter would have me killed if I didn't come up with the money by the end of May."

His expression was regretful when he looked again at Alisha. "And when Andrea saw the bruises and cuts on my face and arms and found out how I got them, she vowed to find some way to get that money for me. She couldn't stand the thought of those men coming here to hurt me again."

Rand shook his head as if he found the story hard to accept. "She vowed to go out and get all eleven thousand dollars herself? Just like that?"

"No. She only knew about the money I owed Potter. She didn't know about the other seven thousand, and I sure didn't have the heart to tell her. She thought she would be getting me out of trouble altogether if she could just find some way to get her hands on forty-two hundred."

When Rand looked at Alisha again, the hard lines of his face had softened. "So that's why you did it. To try to save your father's life."

Alisha felt a warm glow when she noticed the admiring way Rand looked at her and decided it would not be worth her while to argue with him.

"She did it out of the love she has for a worthless old man who doesn't deserve it," Thomas

said. He blinked, then looked away. "She should
have known she'd get caught."

Rand thought for a moment. "So what happened to all the money? What happened to the
three thousand dollars she swindled?"

Thomas looked at Alisha questioningly.

Her eyes widened. "Don't look at me. I don't
have it."

Thomas let out a heavy sigh and shook his
head. "I guess she doesn't remember that either.
All I know is that she still had it with her when
she first took off running from the police. She
had it stuffed into a secret pocket she had sewn
into the side of her drawers where she sometimes
kept a small derringer when working downstairs." He shrugged. "I have no idea what she
did with it after that, but I do know she didn't
have it on her when you brought her here. When
Ruby undressed her earlier, she didn't have on
her usual drawers. Just some sort of lacy strap
with leg holes."

He looked at Alisha disapprovingly but did
not question her about it. "She wore another
strip of lace in place of her camisole." He shook
his head as if unable to believe women's fashion
had reached that level. "Probably something
new those Frenchmen came up with to help
fight the heat of summer. She's always been fascinated by whatever the French wear."

Alisha felt a strong rush of relief to discover
that neither the old man nor Rand had been
the one to undress her. Even though she was in
someone else's body at the moment, she did not

like the thought of a strange man undressing her while she was unconscious. "Who is this Ruby and what did she do with my clothes?" She ignored the annoyed huff that came from Rand. She was past caring if he believed her or not.

Thomas's forehead drew into another perplexed frown. "You don't remember Ruby either? She's been almost like a mother to you for six or seven years and you don't remember her either?" He paused a minute, then explained, "Ruby Brooks is a good friend of ours who works downstairs with you, only instead of sitting at the tables dealing cards like you do, she serves drinks and tobacco to the men."

A glimmer of what had to be affection lit his brown eyes when he added," She may be a good fifteen years older than the rest of you girls, but she's still quite a looker and can still turn an honest dollar."

Alisha smiled when she realized there was more between Ruby and Thomas than friendship. "And what about my clothes?"

"Ruby took them with her to wash and mend. Your dress was torn in four different places. She said it would take her a couple of days to mend it back good as new. But then you have that whole wardrobe full of clothes. One black dress shouldn't matter all that much."

He gestured toward the tall wardrobe, then stepped over and flung the doors back so she could see the colorful clothing inside. Most of it hung from large brass hooks that lined the inside, but some lay folded at the bottom. "You also have all those drawers filled with clothes."

He turned at Rand. "She's always had a hankering for new clothes, which is why she's probably always been one of the best-dressed women at Beau's. Ruby's always felt a little jealous of that," he admitted, but quickly added, "but not jealous enough to steal that money so she could go out and buy herself some of her own. No, sir, Andrea did not have that money on her when you brought her here."

Rand thought about that for a moment, then turned to Alisha with a stern expression. "I know you think you are helping your father, but you can't keep that money. You have to return it. It might not save you from going to jail, but returning it should keep you alive. You don't know these people like I do. Jeremy Miller is very much like Frank Potter. They are connected to the same group of people. If you don't return that money, you could end up just as dead as they have threatened to make your father."

He paused a moment, then quietly added, "Andrea, if you're worried about what will happen to you in jail, maybe I can help keep you out of harm by placing a little protection money in the right hands. I'd be willing to do that if you'd just quit acting like a fool and return Miller's money."

Alisha curled her hands into fists, then pressed them together in a very real effort to keep from shaking in rage. She had reached her limit with these people. "I told you. I'm *not* Andrea Knight and I have no idea where that money might be. When I suddenly found myself wandering around in this body, I still had on my own clothes, so I had no access to the woman's drawers. I don't know how or why it is my clothes made the trip with me and yet not my body, but it's true."

"That's ridiculous," Rand said with a disgusted shake of his head. "How can you expect us to believe a story like that?"

Alisha's eyes narrowed. "Frankly, I don't care what you believe. Just quit hounding me about money I never even knew existed before now."

Rand compressed his lips against clenched teeth. "Why do you keep pretending you don't remember who you are— that you are someone else? Do you think that will help get you out of the trouble you're in with the police?"

Alisha met his intense gaze with one of her own. What did it take to convince these people? "I'm not pretending. I'm merely stating the truth. I am *not* Andrea Knight. I'm Alisha Sampson forced into being Andrea Knight, though I have no idea why. If you don't believe me, why don't you look up some voodoo woman named Imena and ask her who I really am? Her shop should be only six or eight blocks from here, though I'm not really sure. But maybe *she* could explain everything to you in a way that will make you understand that I'm not really Andrea. I'm Alisha."

Rand drew in an irritated breath, held it a moment, then slowly released it. "How can you continue with this farce when your own father has already identified you."

Alisha was so angry with his refusal to accept the truth, she clenched her fists until her fingernails dug deep trenches into her palms. It was that pain that kept her from screaming her next words. "He is *not* my father. I wish you would quit trying to convince me that he is."

Upon hearing the animosity in her voice, Thomas closed his eyes and turned away, his shoulders hunched in anguish. "Maybe the reason she doesn't remember is because she doesn't want to remember. Maybe she is so ashamed of what I have done that deep down her mind *wants* her to believe she's someone else. She wants to believe she's someone with a father who doesn't drink too much and gamble away more money than they'll ever see in a lifetime."

"No," she responded quickly. She had not meant to hurt Thomas. He looked like he'd suffered enough in life already. "It has nothing to do with you."

"Yes, it does," he replied, his voice strained. "You are ashamed of me, and I don't blame you. I've made your life miserable. I've made both our lives miserable. If it weren't for you having to take care of me all the time, you'd be off married and living a normal life. Instead, you have very few friends and no prospects for a husband whatsoever. You're too busy working at Beauregard's to get out and meet anyone worth marrying." Without looking back at her, he hurried out of the room, his shoulders shaking visibly with remorse.

Rand looked at her with fury-darkened features. "How could you do that to the old man?"

Rand asked, clearly disgusted. "How could you hurt your own father like that?"

Alisha ran a trembling hand over her cheek. The strain was becoming too much for her. The dull, throbbing pain at the back of her head was now sharp and grasping, and had spread all the way to the front. "I told you. He's not my father."

Rand stared at her a moment longer, then threw up his hands. "Fine. Have it your way. You're not Andrea Knight. You're Alisha Sampson. But just keep in mind that while continuing this little charade you are breaking that poor man's heart."

He then stood so abruptly, the chair he straddled toppled sideways and clattered to the floor. He made no effort to set it upright. "And don't think for a minute that this pretense will save you from the police. They won't care who you say you are. And don't think it will save you from me."

Having stated that, he turned and stalked angrily out of the room, leaving Alisha to stare after him, pondering that last statement. Why did she need saving from *him?* What possible danger could he pose for her?

Although she did not know the answer, a cold, nagging fear curled slowly into her heart.

Seven

Early the next morning Rand appeared at Thomas's door. He waited impatiently in the darkened hall just outside Alisha's bedroom door while Thomas went inside to make sure she was awake. Having heard her tossing and moaning most of the night, Thomas was not sure she had gotten a good night's rest, which was why he could not understand her continued refusal to take any more of the medicine Dr. Owen had left for her.

"Andrea," he called to her gently when he found her lying on her side with her eyes closed, still asleep. He reached out to place his hand on her shoulder. "Andrea, Pumpkin, you have to wake up. Mr. Kincaid is here again and wants to talk to you."

Because most of the opium had finally worked its way out of Alisha's system and because she had slept intermittently for nearly thirty-six hours straight, she came easily awake and glanced up at him questioningly.

Thomas looked apologetic as he said, "He came by to tell us that you're still safe here for the moment. Because of all the blood that was on your face after the accident, very few people got a good look at who you were. Rand has told everyone that you were a woman he'd picked up for an evening's pleasure and that he carried you up here because he had already paid me for the use of my bedroom and didn't know where else to take you."

He paused to place more pillows behind her so she could sit. "He also told them that when it turned out you were not as injured as first thought, he went ahead and had his night of pleasure, then sent you on your way. Since Beau, Ruby, and Doc Owen are the only people who know the truth, he has talked them into going along with that same story. They agreed since they realize the danger you are in."

Alisha's stomach knotted at the unexpected reminder of her peril. She remembered only too well how cruelly the police had treated her. It was then that Rand entered the room.

She looked at his dark expression, puzzled, then asked in a low voice so only Thomas could hear. "Why would he do that when it's obvious he's still very angry at me?"

Thomas shrugged, then glanced at Rand. "I suppose for the same reason he paid your way out of that jail last night. I guess he is just one of those men who has a soft spot for beautiful women, or maybe he feels guilty because the police caught up with you after he'd convinced you you'd be safe in his house. Either way, his plan might buy me enough time to try and contact my cousin in Texas to see if he'll let you come stay with him for a while. You should be safe there. I'd go, too, but that would only add to the number of people trying to find you because they'd also be trying to find me. This way only Miller and his men will be hunting for you."

Alisha's eyebrows arched at such an unexpected reference to her beauty. She then remembered the image in the mirror. Although she had been pretty enough back when she was in her own body, now she was breathtakingly beautiful, even with the many scrapes and bruises.

Both pleased and discomfited by that fact, she looked again at Rand. She noticed he was freshly shaved and had changed into a pair of black trousers and a crisp, blue linen shirt that fit his muscular frame very well. He stood very still with his hands behind his back.

"I suppose I should thank you for going to so much trouble for me," she said in a voice loud enough for him to hear. She did not know how to respond to someone who had done something that nice, yet at the same time looked as if he could at any moment strangle her with his own hands.

"Yes, you should," he said curtly.

He neared the bed, and she cautiously pulled the sheet to her chin as if that might protect her from his burning gaze. He then brought his hands around, revealing her purse. His blue eyes glinted when he tossed it down beside her.

"There. You left that at my house. I thought you might want it back."

Relieved to have her purse again, Alisha

picked it up and unsnapped the main compartment. "Is everything still there?" she asked even before she peered inside.

"I wouldn't know," Rand stated, his lean jaw thrust forward. "But if you do find something missing, I'm not the one who took it. I never even opened the thing. And I really doubt anyone else did either. It was still in the same spot this morning where you left it last night."

Alisha breathed a sigh of relief, glad he had not bothered to look inside. She was not up to explaining some of what he would find inside, even though it might substantiate her claim to be from another time period. Still, she scrambled through the purse's contents and decided that Rand had told her the truth.

"Now, if by some chance, you happen to have three thousand dollars hidden away in there, I think it would be wise to turn it over to your father so he and I can carry it to the police for you." When she suddenly shot him a sharp look, he quickly held up his hands. "Oh, I forgot. You still have no memory of this man being your father, do you?" he said, his voice rimmed with sarcasm.

Rather than hurt Thomas by again angrily disclaiming his fatherhood, she merely nodded to affirm the statement, then met Rand's gaze with one that let him know her annoyance. "That's right. I have no memory of this nice man being my father. So sue me."

Rand blinked, as if trying to figure out how a lawsuit could result from any of this, then went on with what he had to say. "I think you should know that I searched the summer kitchen this morning. I thought you might have hidden the money in there while you were changing clothes. I didn't find anything, but then I was in a hurry and could have overlooked it. I'll search again later, this time more carefully."

"Search all you want," she told him, too tired of being doubted to care what he did or how much time he spent doing it. She refused to be bullied by the likes of him. "I've had nothing to do with that money."

"I wish you'd leave her be about that," Thomas injected in ready defense of his daughter. "It seems pretty clear that as a result of that accident she has lost a large part of her memory."

Rand let out an annoyed breath, then narrowed his gaze until his eyes looked like shards of blue steel. "Just because she has you fooled doesn't mean she has me fooled. I happen to see right through her little charade." He glowered at Alisha. "And if she would just stop all this pretending, then perhaps I would feel more like helping her."

Thomas cocked his head, clearly interested. "Helping her? How?"

"By seeing that she gets treated decently while she is in jail awaiting trial for having cheated Jeremy Miller out of all that money and by seeing she gets a lenient judge for that trial. Or if she doesn't want to go that route, if she's still determined to keep that money so you can use it to pay off some of your debt, then I could help out by seeing that she arrives safely at your cousin's house."

"You'd do that for her?" he asked, clearly wondering why. He ran his hand over his stubbled chin.

"Only if she decides to climb down from that high horse of hers and admit the truth to me. I won't help her as long as she keeps lying to me like that."

"I've already told you the truth," Alisha said, clenching her hands. Although she understood why it was so hard for them to believe such an odd story, she was not accustomed to having her word so blatantly questioned. "I don't know what happened to that money. If I did, I would gladly give it to Thomas so he could use it however he saw fit. *I* certainly don't need it. If all goes well, I won't be around long enough to spend it anyway."

"Why do you say that?" Thomas asked, clearly worried by that last statement. "You aren't planning to do something foolish like run away before I have time to hear back from Cousin Lawrence, are you? Where would you go?"

"You wouldn't believe me even if I told you," she muttered, then decided not to bother. It was clear they had already made up their minds about her. One believed she suffered from amnesia and the other thought she was running some sort of scam. Hearing the truth would only reinforce what they already believed.

"Don't worry," Rand put in. His blue eyes narrowed slightly. "She's not going anywhere.

She knows there's too much danger for that. She knows that every policeman in this city has been told to watch for her. She doesn't dare step foot outside this apartment."

Tiny bumps of apprehension rose on Alisha's neck and arms when she realized Rand was right. It *was* dangerous for her to be out on the street right now, very dangerous. But danger or no danger, she could not stay there. She had to try to find her way back to Imena's so she could convince the woman to return her to the future where she belonged. She certainly couldn't stay where she was.

"But how safe is she here?" Thomas asked, thinking ahead to other possibilities. "What if the police come here looking for her again like they did two days ago?"

"Then she takes off out that window just like she did mine," he said, gesturing to the window closest to the outside stairs. "Or if she has time, she hurries down the back steps into Beau's storage room where there are a number of places for her to hide. She has turned out to be very good at that sort of thing. But then I doubt it'll ever come to that. As soon as the police have come to my house and searched it again, we can move her there for awhile. The trick will be to stay one step behind them."

Thomas smiled appreciatively, then looked puzzled. "Why are you doing all this for us? Especially when I owe you all that money you now know I won't be able to repay for quite some time— if ever."

"Because I think I've already figured out a way for you to repay every penny," he said. He stared at Alisha in such a way it caused her heart to skip a beat.

Thomas looked at Rand questioningly. "You have? How?"

"I'll let you know later," Rand said, unwilling to reveal his plan just yet. "After the police have satisfied themselves by having searched my house completely and it is safe for her to go there."

Thomas's puzzled expression deepened, but he did not question him further. Instead, he smiled again, this time at Alisha. "Well, if looks as if you have very little to worry about, at least for now. If you do hear the police come tromping up those stairs," he gestured toward the open window beside her bed with a slight nod, "then you take off down the other stairs like Mr. Kincaid said. If you can't find a place to hide down there, then unlatch the back door take off into the alley. There are lots of places to hide out there."

"Where are the other stairs?" she asked, thinking that might be good to know even if the police did not come there looking for her. She would need a safe way out of there when she finally felt up to confronting Imena again.

Rand let out a loud, exasperated breath. "You really are determined to play this for all its worth, aren't you?"

Thomas gave Rand a sharp look. "Why can't

you believe that she's not playacting? That she really has lost part of her memory?"

But before Rand could answer, Thomas turned again to Alisha. "The stairs are on the far side of the small room that is just across the hall from this one. You just open the door and there they are. They lead directly down into Beau's storage room, which is usually piled high with whiskey barrels and crates. There are also two doors down there. The one to the left would take you directly behind the bar in the main gaming room. The one to the right leads into an alley that leads into that one." Again he gestured toward the window beside her bed. "And that alley leads right out into the street."

Alisha quickly stored all that information away for future use. "And how do I get to the steps outside the window?"

"The door at the far end of the hall. This is not a big apartment. There are only four rooms and one hall."

Glad to finally have some information concerning the apartment in which she lay, and slowly realizing the pressure growing beneath her abdomen, she asked, "And which of those four rooms is the restroom?"

He looked at her a moment as if trying to figure out what she meant. "You rest right here."

"No, I mean where is the bathroom?"

He reached up to scratch his head. "But you don't need a bath. Ruby took care of all that while she was changing your clothes.

"No, not for bathing—for *relieving* myself," she said for lack of a better way of stating it.

"*Oh*, you mean a privy," he said, smiling. "We don't have one. All we got is that pot." He gestured toward the odd-shaped porcelain bucket that sat on the floor between the chest of drawers and the clothes cabinet.

"That?" Alisha eyed the jar with uncertainty. "I'm supposed to sit on that?"

"Well, no, you don't actually sit on it," Thomas started to explain but was interrupted curtly by Rand.

"I think I've had about enough of this nonsense." He shook his head disgustedly. "I have far too much to do today to stand here listening to her try to convince you she doesn't even know what a chamber pot is, much less how to use it. I'm leaving." He took several steps then paused in the doorway. "But I will stop back here late this afternoon to see if Andrea's feeling any better." He tilted his head. A meaningful look glittered in his blue eyes. "I hope by then that that damaged memory of hers will finally be on the mend."

Thomas waited until Rand's heavy footsteps sounded on the wooden steps outside her window. "Strange man, that one. One minute he does all he can to help us and the next he's stalking out of here as if we've purposely done something to offend him."

"That's because he doesn't believe me when I try to explain to him that I'm not your daughter," she said with an annoyed scowl, then looked at Thomas questioningly. "But then you don't believe me either, do you?"

"I believe that you believe it," he said softly. He bent forward to brush her dark hair gently away from her face with his weathered fingertips, then pressed a warm kiss on an uninjured portion of her forehead. "And I also believe that in time your memory will start coming back to you. I just hope that happens before you have to leave here. I'd hate for you to go before finally remembering who you are and how very much I love you."

Alisha smiled despite the fact she had yet to gain headway with either Rand or Thomas. "I can see that you love me— or rather that you love the person you think I am. If it weren't for the very serious trouble you and Andrea seem to be in at the moment, I'd say that she was really a very lucky girl."

At least her father was still alive, she thought sadly, then quickly pushed aside the aching memory of her own father's death. How dearly she still missed her parents, though her father had been dead for eight years and her mother for two.

"Thank you," Thomas replied, then tilted his head to one side. "I think."

Alisha laughed at the playful confusion marring his aged face. She truly liked Thomas Knight, despite his obvious flaws. "And you're quite welcome. I think."

Thomas chuckled. "So, are you feeling up to any breakfast?"

Alisha thought about that. Even though she knew she had not eaten anything in over two days, she really was not all that hungry. Still, she knew she needed to eat to gain back her strength.

"Yes."

"Good. I'll go make some biscuits and bring them to you," he said and headed for the door. "Meanwhile, you catch yourself some more sleep. The doctor is supposed to come by this afternoon to check on you, and I want him to find you much better. I want him to know that I've been right here taking good care of you."

Although Alisha dearly hoped to be out of there come afternoon, she did not mention that to Thomas before he left the room. If he knew her plans, he would do what he could to stop her. He might even try locking her in, and that would never do. She had to leave for Imena's shop as soon as was humanly possible. She had already been in 1882 a lot longer than she'd wanted.

With plans to slip out shortly after she had eaten something, Alisha flung back the sheets and tossed her legs over the side of the bed. She waited a moment, then slid to the floor. Although her legs felt a little shaky, probably from not having eaten in those two days, she was much stronger than before and this time made it all the way to the window without as much as a dizzy spell.

Curious to get a look at the alley Thomas had mentioned, she pulled back the curtain and peered though the netting. A set of narrow, steep, planked steps were attached to the side of the building. They looked just wide enough for one person to pass. They reminded her of the old stairs that led up to Doc Adam's office in the old television series "Gunsmoke."

Glancing up, she noticed another set of stairs attached to the building across the alley, only that staircase had wet clothing hanging from the banister.

Wanting to get a better idea of her location and what to expect when she finally left there, she pushed the window netting aside and stuck her head out far enough to peer in the direction of the street. Not far beyond the alley's entrance, she noticed three scrawny dogs scratching through a small pile of garbage and beyond that a young boy running barefoot from one side of the street to the other. Behind him, in the small area of the street she could see from her window, a man wearing a dark coat pulled an empty wagon to a stop in front of what looked to be a leather store where he called out to someone inside.

In the distance she heard the sharp bellow of a steam engine and the loud clanging of a ship's bell and realized that although she was not sure where she was, she was not too far from the main docks.

Wanting to see more of the street than that particular view provided, she tugged the netting back into place then hurried to peer out the other two windows. From there she saw several more businesses along the rutted street, but very few of them looked to be open.

Aware it was after nine o'clock, she wondered why so many doors remained closed, then realized it was Sunday. The saloons and gaming houses that lined the street were obviously forbidden to open on Sundays, or at least on Sunday mornings—and even if they were allowed to open, the patrons probably were still too hung over from their drunken revelry of the night before to be out and about yet.

Glad for the quiet, Alisha studied the street a moment longer, still in awe of the fact that she really was in the year 1882. After awhile she returned to her bed to await breakfast. Lying there with nothing to do but wait gave her a chance to think more about her plight, a chance to try to figure out why she had been sent back in time and why she had been placed in some stranger's body. She wondered why Imena had not mentioned that she would not have the same body while in 1882. Why hadn't she warned her that she would instead possess the body of someone named Andrea Knight?

She frowned and wondered what else Imena had neglected to tell her, then remembered the untold danger Imena had warned she would face and realized she had meant Andrea's danger. For some reason Imena wanted her to take Andrea's place during this time. But why? What could the woman possibly hope to accomplish by doing something so bizarre? And why would she choose her of all people?

Something else that bothered Alisha was not knowing how she could have possibly been transported into a different time period and into a different body and yet ended up having on the same clothes as before? How was it her clothing had made it back into time and yet her body had not?

Her frown deepened. She next wondered what had become of her own body. Did Imena have Andrea trade places with her? If that was so, she hoped Andrea was taking better care of Alisha's body than she was Andrea's. She glanced down at the scratches and bruises on Andrea's hand, then touched the tender spot at the back of her head and could imagine her own body having suffered a similar fate.

Although she hated the thought, she could see Andrea panicking and doing something foolish after finally realizing she was no longer inside her own body much less her own time period. Even if she did not panic, she could still do something unwittingly dangerous, like step out into the street, not understanding the perils of modern traffic.

That thought gave her another reason to hurry back to Imena's. She needed to convince the woman to switch them back before Andrea did something to hurt herself. She would be living in a world far too modern for a woman from the 1880s to cope.

More determined than ever to leave there just as soon as she had eaten and Thomas had left her alone again, Alisha headed to the wardrobe to find something suitable to wear. She looked through the colorful clothing that hung inside and finally decided on a lavender cotton dress with a white collar, white cuffs, and white lace set into the bodice.

When she pulled the dress out and draped it over her arm to have a closer look, she noticed the skirt was badly wrinkled at the bottom. Having no iron to press the hem smooth, she stepped back and gave the garment a good, hard shake. When she did, a fresh spasm of pain pierced her injured shoulder.

Angry with herself for having forgotten her injury so easily, she laid the dress across the foot of her bed and headed to her purse for a couple of Tylenol. She took the caplets with a few sips of the foul-tasting water Thomas had left by her bed earlier.

Knowing she wasn't planning to leave until after she had eaten, rather than try to get dressed while her shoulder still hurt from having shaken the dress, she eased back into bed to wait for the sudden soreness to ease.

The next thing Alisha knew, Thomas was waking her again, this time carrying a plate filled with steaming-hot homemade biscuits and a small jar of what looked like orange marmalade.

He set the plate on the table beside the bed, then frowned with fatherly annoyance when he noticed that she had laid one of her dresses out.

"There's not much point in you getting dressed until after the doctor's been here to see you," he said, already putting the dress away. "He's going to want to listen to your heart and to have another look at those bruises on your back. And even then, he might not give you permission to get up."

Rather than argue with him, she wriggled into a seated position and rested the plate he had just brought her in her lap. Eagerly, she broke open one of the half-dozen fat biscuits and breathed in deeply the tantalizing aroma. Although orange marmalade was never a favorite of hers, she spooned a liberal helping inside and bit deep into the fluffy white mound. The bread was so delicious and the marmalade so tangy sweet, she pressed her eyes shut and moaned softly her appreciation.

"Good?" he asked and looked back as he closed the cabinet doors.

Alisha answered by offering a brisk nod before she took an enormous second bite, then a third, and finished it with her fourth bite. She had not realized just how hungry she was until she had actually tasted the food. Now she knew she was ravenous.

Because Alisha had not eaten in days, or perhaps because Andrea's stomach just did not hold as much in one sitting as her own had, Alisha started to feel full after just three biscuits but managed to put away five of the six before finally setting her plate aside.

"Aren't you going to eat that last one?" Thomas asked, having returned to the side of her bed. When it was apparent she was not, he reached over, tore it in half, then ate both halves himself.

It was not until she had rested her head

against the pillows again, so stuffed she could hardly move, that she realized Thomas had changed clothes. Instead of the pair of plain brown trousers and the white shirt he had worn earlier, he now wore an oversized black suit with a rumpled gray shirt beneath. Although he still had on the same scuffed work boots as before, it was obvious he had taken a wet brush to them, for much of the grime from earlier was removed. He had even shaved the white stubble off his chin and slicked down his heavy eyebrows.

"Where are you headed?" she asked, believing it a stroke of good luck that he apparently had plans. She would not have to answer any annoying questions when she again climbed out of that bed, dressed, then headed out.

"To church," he said, then grinned dimple deep. "I know. I know. The ceiling is probably going to cave in on me, but I thought I might try to talk Mr. Philen into letting me do a little work for him again, and what better place to ask than in church? It's obvious you aren't going to be able to work for awhile, not with the police looking for you in every nook and cranny, and Beau doesn't need me to do more than sweep up in the mornings, and still pays me in food only for that work. So I thought I might try to get back on with Mr. Philen for awhile and see if I can't pull together a little of that money I owe Potter myself." He straightened his shoulders as if very proud of himself for having come to that decision.

Not knowing who Mr. Philen was or what sort

of work the man offered, and at that point not really caring just so long as asking for the job got Thomas out of the house for awhile, she nodded and smiled. "I hope he says yes. How long will you be gone?"

Thomas wrinkled his eyes and glanced at the clock as if hard to see that far. "About an hour, I guess. But don't worry. I'll be back long before Doc Owen comes by to see about you, and I'll be sure and lock the door behind me so the police can't go slipping in on you while I'm gone and you're asleep."

Alisha worried that by locking the police out, he might also be locking her in. "That won't be necessary. I'm not sleepy anymore, so I'm sure I'd hear them if they came clamoring up those stairs." Which was true. She would not be falling asleep again that day. Her heart hammered at far too rapid a rate to let her doze off again even if she wanted. What was to happen during these next few hours was far too important.

"You probably would hear them, but I still don't want to take any chances," he said and bent forward to pat her hand lovingly. "Not with my girl. Especially when there's no one downstairs right now to come running should you call for help."

Aware there would be no talking him out of his protective precautions, and at the same time remembering that there was supposed to be a second stairway in the room across the hall, and knowing an inside stairway might provide her more protection from prying eyes, she finally relented.

"Okay, lock the door if you want, but don't you dare worry about me the entire time you are gone," she said, then felt a stab of guilt for what she was about to do. Poor man, when he returned from doing what he obviously considered such a noble deed, he would discover the young woman he believed to be his daughter gone from her bed. She just hoped that Imena would be quick in changing them back so Andrea could hurry home before Thomas had too much time to worry about what had happened to her.

When it then dawned on Alisha that Andrea might not make it back home, her feelings of guilt deepened. It was quite possible Andrea would be intercepted by the police before making it all the way back there. But there was not much Alisha could do about that. The police search was Andrea's problem to begin with— *not hers*.

"No matter what happens, you are not to worry about **me**," she continued, hoping her reassurances would keep him from panicking too soon. "I'm a strong woman. I'll be fine."

"Can't help the worrying," he told her. Yet another fatherly smile stretched across his worn features when he took the empty plate from her. "It happens to be my calling to worry about you. It's the one thing I do very well. That's why I don't want you opening that door for anyone while I'm gone. It's clear you don't remember who all we can consider friends and who we can't. Promise me you won't open that door to anyone.''

"I promise," she vowed, knowing she did not plan to stay there long enough to let anyone in. Just as soon as he had left, she was out of there. "I won't open that door for anyone."

A smile lingered on Thomas's clean shaven face. After he checked to make sure her pitcher had water and that her chamber pot did not need emptying again, he left with the empty plate. As soon as Alisha heard his footsteps outside her window, she hurried to take the lavender dress back out. She knew he would be gone only a little while. She had no time to squander.

Because her panties and bra had not yet been returned to her, she quickly searched the drawers and wardrobe for something to wear underneath the dress and finally came out with a pair of baggy white underdrawers like those she had seen worn in those old Western movies Roni liked to watch.

Thinking the bulky garment better than nothing, she pulled the drawers up over her legs and quickly tied them into place. She then pulled off the nightgown and replaced it with a thin cotton camisole she had also found. Because of the heat and her grave need to hurry, she decided against putting on any of the floor-length petticoats she had come across or the corset, and pulled the bulky dress on directly over the drawers and camisole.

As soon as she had the skirts smoothed, she sat in the chair Rand had left standing near her

bed to pull on a pair of white stockings she had
found that were shaped a little like hose but
looked more like thin socks. Because her Reeboks were also nowhere in sight, she slipped her
cotton-clad feet into a pair of black boots that
turned out to be a lot more comfortable than
they looked.

When she finished tying everything that
looked like it needed to be tied and hooking
everything that looked as if it needed to be
hooked, she stepped over to the mirror to study
the results of her strange costume.

Again she was startled by how truly beautiful
she looked— or rather how beautiful Andrea
Knight looked— with those large almond-shaped
brown eyes and that long, shimmering dark
brown hair. Even uncombed, the thick curls
swirled around her sculptured face becomingly.

If only *I* could look that good after lying in
bed for nearly two days, she thought with a wry
frown, knowing her own hair would be a ratted
mess by now, probably because her own hair was
so much thinner than Andrea's.

Even though she felt she already looked pre-
sentable, Alisha decided to brush Andrea's
hair. Remembering that her purse had been
returned, she opened it, found her hairbrush
and makeup, then returned to the mirror. Although she decided against any makeup after
she realized just how flawless Andrea's skin
was, she quickly worked the hairbrush through
what tangles there were, then bound the shimmering mass away from her face with a dark

purple ribbon she'd found inside one of the vanity drawers.

Pausing a moment to study the beauty before her, she wondered what Andrea's life must be like. Being *that* attractive *and* unmarried, she had to have the men of this city groveling at her feet. Alisha sighed at the thought of what that had to be like. If only *she* could get even one man to wallow at her feet. Then maybe it would not hurt so much to have lost Brad.

She smiled at the titillating thought of what it would be like to have someone like Rand Kincaid be the one doing all the wallowing. Not only would having a man that incredibly handsome and that sure of himself brazenly pursuing her affections irritate the hell out of Brad, just knowing he had been so quickly replaced by someone far more attractive and manly than he ever hoped to be would kill him. Roni would also be eaten alive by envy. Roni, who rated men by their looks and money alone.

Too bad I can't take Rand back with me, she thought, unaware her smile had turned wistful. Not only would having a man like that do wonders for my trampled self-esteem, he'd have dear Brad eating his heart out.

But when she realized the impossibility of that fantasy, her smile flattened. Not only would Rand be out of place in her century and therefore not the same confident man he was now, he could never be interested in someone like her. They were far too different and, besides, he already thought her both a liar and a cheat.

Feeling unaccountably disheartened by that last thought, she took one last look in the mirror, decided everything was in place, then returned the hairbrush and the bottle of makeup to her purse.

Finally she tucked the purse up under her arm and went in search of the inside stairway that would allow her to slip downstairs unnoticed. Quietly, she entered the small bedroom directly across the hall. Inside she found a clutter of boxes, crates, and old pieces of broken furniture, but she did not see the promised stairs. It was not until she was about to leave and go try climbing out one of the windows nearest the outside stairs that she noticed what looked like a trapdoor cut into the floor.

Moving a heavy box that overlapped one corner, she lifted the cover gently and discovered what was little more than a slanted ladder underneath. The ladder led down into a room so dark she could barely make out the shapes of the crates and barrels stacked below.

She paused to listen for sounds that might indicate someone down there, and when she heard nothing, she wadded up her skirts and carefully made her way down the rickety steps. Her only light came through one small, unwashed window high off the floor.

Like Thomas had told her, there were two doors for her to choose from downstairs. The one to the left looked to be a swinging door of some sort designed to accommodate carrying large items in and out. The door to her right, only a few feet away from the only window, was a larger, stronger door— clearly the door that would take her outside.

Seeing no evidence of a lock, only a large security bar which she could easily lift, Alisha's heart hammered wildly at the realization she would soon be on her way to Imena's shop. With the corner of her lower lip caught lightly between her teeth, she hurried to the door, lifted the heavy bar, then stepped quickly outside.

Because it was nearing noon, sunlight flooded the alley, causing her to squint a moment to help her eyes adjust to the sudden change in light. As soon as she could see clearly enough, she headed for the corner where she knew the adjacent alley awaited, the one she had seen from her room that emptied into the nearly deserted street in front of Beauregard's.

It was not until she had already rounded the corner and was nearly to the narrow stairs that led to the Knights' apartment that she first heard the heavy footsteps.

Her heart froze at the realization.

Someone was coming.

Eight

"What do you mean you can't find her anywhere?" Chief Clay Miller asked, then yanked his hat off his balding head and flung it carelessly on top of his cluttered desk. "You men had all day and night yesterday to find out what happened to her. Weren't you listening when I told you I wanted that woman back in my jail by this morning? Don't you understand that it is dangerous for all of us to allow her to continue roaming the streets like she is?"

"Yes, sir, we know you want her back and we know how important it is we find her." Heath Butler glanced nervously at his partner, George Gray, who stood rail-stiff at his side. Neither man liked facing the chief when he was that angry. "And I swear to you, we've been looking for her all over this city, but no one has seen her. No one knows what happened to her."

"No one?" Chief Miller asked. Clearly he did not believe that. He looked at Butler with a raised eyebrow. "Are you trying to tell me that she just *vanished* into thin air?"

"Well, no, sir. Of course not. But we have been looking for her everywhere. And not just me and George. All of us have been looking for her."

"How hard?" The chief asked, then leaned forward, pressing both hands flat on his desk. "Have you been back by Kincaid's house to search like I suggested? If so, why haven't I been told? And what about that rathole where her father lives? Have you been by there again? What did he have to say about her having escaped from us yet again? Did he seem at all surprised? Did he seem like he might have been the one who paid to have that cell door left open? And has anyone figured out yet just who it was who left that door open?"

"Well, no, we don't really know who did it, but I can promise you it wasn't me or George," Butler stated, then looked away while he rubbed the jagged scar near his left eye with a dirty fingernail. For some reason that scar always itched whenever there was trouble to be had. "And, no, we haven't searched either of those two places yet. But there's good reasons for that."

"Oh, pray tell," Chief Miller replied sarcastically. He moved around his desk to stand directly in front of the larger of the two men he had put in charge of recapturing Andrea Knight, mainly because they were the ones who had managed to recapture her the first time. "So you have good reasons for not checking out the two most likely places for her to be, do you, Butler? And what reasons might those be?"

The larger officer swallowed so hard his

Adam's apple quivered then bobbed twice. He knew only too well what became of those who hampered either of the Miller brothers. He hurried to explain. "Well, sir, for one thing, Mr. Kincaid ain't been home. We've tried there several times, but each time that uppity nigger of his tells us the man ain't home and he won't let us go in and have a look around until he is."

Chief Miller threw up his hands. "What do you mean he won't *let* you in?" he demanded, so angry now that the veins in his neck stood out like small blue cords. "And why do you have to wait to be *let* in? If I recall correctly, you are probably twice the size of that black monkey." He was so angry now, his massive body vibrated when he shouted. "What's to keep you from simply pushing him aside and searching the place anyway?"

Butler cringed, then blinked. He halfway expected his boss to strike him.

"But we're talking about Randall Kincaid's home," he reminded him. "He's one of the wealthiest, most respected men around these parts. He could cause us some real trouble if he wanted to. I didn't think you'd want us to cross somebody like that unless we had to."

"I don't care who he is or how much trouble you think he can cause," Miller sneered. "He has far too many principles for one man, and because he does, I can cause him a lot more aggravation than he can ever cause me. Besides, if it turns out she's there, you should be able to get her out of there so we can do what we

want with her long before he can gather enough
forces to cause us harm. *I want that woman.* I
promised to turn her over to my brother."

"Then I'll put a few men together and head
over to Kincaid's right away to see if she's there,
although I don't rightly think she will be. I think
it was just a coincidence that we caught her coming out of his gate that last time. I think to her
his garden was just someplace to hide until she
thought it safe to head out again. After all, we
were chasing her blindly down the street when
suddenly she decided to jump over that wall. It
wasn't as if she planned to do that."

"It very well may be that her being there was
just a coincidence," Miller admitted, his voice
strained with anger. "But then again it might
not be. Beautiful women flock to Kincaid like
mindless geese. It could be that Andrea Knight
is one of his mistresses and he's willing to protect her by giving her a place to hide. He might
be protecting her father, too. Why haven't you
searched his place?"

"Oh, but we *are* looking there," Butler offered. His grim expression brightened suddenly.
"Andrew and Kevin are headed over there right
now to see if that's where she could be. Even
though I really don't think we'll find her there
either— it being her own home and such an obvious place for us to search— I did tell them to
go over there and have a look. They should be
back with a report of what they found in about
an hour. Meanwhile, George and I will see if
we can find a couple of others and head on over

to Kincaid's and have a look there whether that darky wants us to or not."

"Good. I'll want to hear all about what you find over there, too," Miller said, then returned to the far side of his desk where he plopped heavily into a squeaking chair. "Meanwhile, keep talking with anyone who might know her. It's pretty obvious that someone, somewhere is hiding her. I want to know who that someone is."

"If that's true, if it turns out someone is hiding her, you want us to bring that person back with us, too?"

"Not necessarily," he answered with a gruff scowl. "I really don't care what you do to whoever proved foolish enough to help her. Kill the bloody bastard if you want, but I still want *her* brought in here and I want her pretty much unharmed." A sinister smile lifted the corners of his mouth. "My brother has big plans for that little filly. Plans that will assure she never cheats him or anyone else at cards again. He'll also make sure that she never reveals to anyone whatever he may have told her that night."

The chief shook his head with annoyance. "My little brother needs to learn to hold his tongue better when he's been drinking. Either that or give up the spirits all together. We can't keep killing people just because he may have told them too much about our operations when he's stinking drunk. If enough gets out, that new mayor of ours might start to get suspicious, and we sure don't want that. There's already talk of him getting together some sort of vigilante committee to take care of the likes of us."

"What exactly did your brother tell her?"

"He thinks he mentioned the guns and the opium we have stored in that old warehouse down by the docks. He won't know for sure what he said until he's talked to her. But even if it turns out he didn't mention the confiscated goods to her, she's a dead woman. That's why we need to get her on in here whether she knows about us or not. He'll still want to make her pay for having cheated him out of that money."

Chief Miller's evil smile widened when he thought more about that. "Might even let a few of you have a bit of pleasure with her before we kill her. He'll probably let whoever brings her back be the second to enjoy her." His expression quickly turned serious again when he then added, "But first we have to get out there and find the little hellion. And find her you will!"

The footsteps that clapped against the main sidewalk sounded as if they might be only a few dozen yards away. Afraid that whoever it was might be headed for the alley, Alisha quickly scanned her surroundings for a place to hide. When she found nothing tall enough or wide enough nearby, she ducked back around the corner where she had just come.

With her heart pounding savagely beneath her breast, she pressed herself against the sun-warmed wall and listened carefully while the footsteps grew ever louder.

It was obvious by the rapid clack of boot leather against damp bricks that at least two people had just entered the main alley and were headed in her direction. Knowing they would find her if she stayed where she was, she looked around for another way out and realized that like so many others, this alley had only the one outlet.

Knowing that her only chance to escape notice was to go back inside the same door she had just left, Alisha had started to move quietly toward the opening when she realized that the sound of the footsteps had changed. She paused to listen more carefully and realized that whoever had entered the side alley was not headed on around to the back alley after all. She could tell by the clunk of boots against wood that they had started up one of the two sets of stairs instead.

She closed her eyes and tried to determine which of the two stairs they had taken but there was no way for her to know. She quickly opened them again when she heard a loud knock followed by the gruff sound of a male voice. "Open up."

There was only a few seconds' hesitation before she heard the splintering crack of wood. A door had been kicked in. Whoever was out there did not intend to wait.

With her hand pressed firmly against her throbbing heart, Alisha heard several crashes and thuds. She cut her gaze to the windows above her where the sounds came.

Aware that they had entered the same apartment she had just left and knowing she did not dare go back inside now for fear they would soon discover the trapdoor she had left open, she headed again toward the side alley, keeping close to the wall so she could not be easily seen from above.

She expected to find the side alley now empty, but when she ducked her head around the corner to make sure, she was panicked to see a man still standing at the top of the steps, facing the street. She recognized him as a policeman by the dark uniform he wore and by the large pistol he held ready in his hand.

Knowing that at least one other policeman was already inside the apartment tearing it apart and would soon discover the trapdoor, she had no idea what to do next or where to go. One thing was certain though, she could not stay there. She could not stand out in the middle of the sunny alley waiting for their search to lead them to her. She had to hide.

With trembling hands, she studied the possibilities, which were few, then finally slipped behind a stack of empty crates near the closed end of the alley where she had to crouch not to be seen. The crates were so loosely constructed she had a partial view of the door that led into Beauregard's storage room and the tiny window beside it through the uneven gaps.

Eventually the policeman inside stuck his head

out the door, looked in both directions, then shouted to his partner around the corner, "If she was here, and it looks like she might have been at one time, I think she probably escaped out this back door long before we got there. Whoever let her escape that second time must have somehow tipped her off that we were coming."

Rather than retrace his steps inside, he stepped out that same door. In each hand he carried a large bottle of liquor. He quickly rounded the corner to the side alley.

Although Alisha could no longer see the man, she could hear him for he continued to shout. "But as it turns out, the search for her wasn't a total loss. Look what I found."

Alisha let out a sigh of relief when she realized they did not intend to search the alley for her. Gratefully, she fell back against the wall and waited for what would happen next.

"Ooooeee, dat sure do look like it be fine whiskey to me," the man at the top of the stairs responded with a brisk Cajun accent. "Here, let me have one of dose."

Alisha closed her eyes and listened. To her dismay, rather than leave, they agreed to rest a moment on the bottom steps and partake of their bounty, leaving her trapped in the hot, stifling alley.

While she fanned her skirts to help stir the unbearable heat, her pounding heart ticked away each vital second. If only those men would realize the precious time they were wasting and go away. She wanted now more than ever to find her way back to Imena's little shop and demand the priestess send her back. She did not belong in 1882.

But the men did not leave, and all too soon she heard the footsteps of someone else entering the alley. Her heart plummeted when she recognized Thomas's apprehensive voice calling out to the other two. Her chance to leave there unnoticed was gone.

"What are you men doing here?"

"Why?" came the slurred response. "What'zit matter to you what we're doin' here? You ain't the owner of this place. I know Beauregard and you ain't him."

"No, but I live at the top of those stairs you're sitting on."

"You're Thomas Knight?"

There was a moment's hesitation. "Yes, I am. How do you know me?"

"I don't. But I sure know your apartment." He chuckled, clearly pleased by what he had done. "I just tore the hell out of it while up there looking for your daughter. Left it in real bad shape."

Having heard the thuds and crashes, Alisha did not doubt that he had done just that.

"But why would you do something like that when everyone knows that Andrea doesn't live with me anymore?"

"Oh? And just where does she live?"

"I really don't know. And what's more, the way that foolish girl has been behaving lately, I really don't care. I did not raise my daughter to be a card cheat."

"Is that so?"

Alisha knew by the policeman's cocky tone that he had not readily accepted Thomas's words.

"Of course it's so." Thomas sounded insulted that the policeman had questioned his honesty. "And it's also why she's no longer welcome in my home."

"You threw her out?" This time the policeman sounded more curious than doubtful.

"Of course I did. Wouldn't you if she were your daughter?"

"Maybe. But even so, we were told to search your place for her and search it I did," he explained.

"And you didn't find her, did you?"

There was a short pause, as if the man wanted to consider the question before answering it. "Well, no, I didn't. But I did find plenty of her clothes up there. How you explain *that*?"

"Easy. After what she did, I refused to let her go inside and get them and I would not go gather them for her. Her bedroom is exactly the way she left it the afternoon before she cheated that rich man out of all that money. I refuse to even go in there. Not even to make her bed. I don't want to be reminded of her."

Alisha smiled at how convincing Thomas sounded and could just see the indignant look on his weathered face.

The officer responded with a snort. "Well, I

don't think her bedroom will be reminding you
of her anymore. Not after what all I just did to
it. Fact is, it should hardly remind you of a bedroom at all."

Because of his smugness, Alisha's anger rose
to match the stifling heat outside, and it took
considerable restraint not to march right around
that corner and tell the arrogant drunk just what
she thought of him and his destruction. Glowering from her still-crouched position behind
the crates, she waited to hear Thomas's angry
response. But instead, a long silence ensued.

The policeman spoke again, this time somewhat less amused. "I suppose you want by."

"If you don't mind." Thomas's words were
now punctuated with an undertone of anger.

There was another lengthy pause before the
policeman finally responded, "No, we don't
mind, do we, Andrew? We need to be on our
way anyhow. The chief is waiting for us to come
tell him what we found here."

"You mean besides the whiskey?" Thomas
ventured.

"What whish-key?" he asked.

"The whiskey you two happen to have behind
your backs. The whiskey I won't bother to tell
anyone about if you'll just go away now and
leave me alone. I've had a bad day. I'm in no
mood for company."

"Oh, *that* whish-key. It's so blamed hot out
here today. Our throats got a little parched."

Alisha could certainly understand that. Because of the heat and the stifling humidity, her clothes were soaked with perspiration.

"Only drank enough to wet our thirst."

Alisha next heard the sound of shuffling feet as the drunken men stumbled to the street. She waited until she heard no sound at all coming from the side alley before venturing out into the open.

Feeling a little weak from having crouched in the heat too long, yet still hoping to make good her getaway, she headed immediately toward the side alley but only made it halfway before a sudden wave of dizziness forced her to look for a place to sit.

Spotting an upended keg near the still-open back door, she moved toward it. Before she actually sat down, though, Thomas appeared from around the corner and hurried in her direction.

"They're gone now," he assured her, then steered her gently inside.

Too weakened by the heat to make it very far on foot and not knowing just how far it might be to Imena's shop or how long it would take her to locate it, Alisha allowed Thomas to guide her to a small wooden chair just inside the door. There she rested long enough to gather the strength she needed to go back upstairs.

As expected, the apartment was a shambles, especially Andrea's bedroom. Furniture, clothing, and personal possessions had been flung everywhere.

"I know it is hard to imagine, but one good thing may have come from all this," Thomas said as he cleared the debris off her bed and put the pillows back where they belonged so she could lie down.

"What's that?" she asked, wondering how he could think of anything positive while viewing such a senseless mess.

"You are probably safe here now— or at least for the next few days. It should be that long before they run out of other places to look and come back to search this one again," he answered. Taking her purse from her, he looked at it and her clothing questioningly. "Why are you dressed? I thought we agreed you should stay in your nightdress at least until after the doctor came."

Alisha quickly searched her throbbing head for a reasonable answer. She glanced at the inviting bed. "I had time to think more about what all might happen while you were gone. I knew that the police could come at any time to search this place, leaving me no choice but to escape out into the alley. I did not think it would be wise to be caught out there wearing only my nightclothes. Not in *this* neighborhood."

Thomas pursed his mouth for a moment, then nodded his agreement. "I hadn't thought about that."

"I hadn't either until after you left. It was then I decided to go ahead and get dressed, and it's a good thing I did." Weakened by the pain that now slashed across the base of her skull, she did not wait for him to straighten out her covers before crawling across the mattress and lying down. She could hardly wait for Thomas to leave the room so she could open her purse and dig out a couple more painkillers. It had been over four hours since she had taken the last two. "When is the doctor going to be here?"

Surely Thomas would go to the door to greet the man when he came.

"I expect him anytime," he answered, then gently stroked her flushed cheek with his cool palm. Aware she was still sweating from having been in the sun, he went to the closest window and opened it all the way. "But we don't have to wait for him to get here to do something about your pain. I still have the laudanum he left for you. All I need to do is mix it with water."

Alisha considered that for a moment. The offer was certainly tempting, but she had to keep her thoughts clear if she was ever to get out of there. She already had lost nearly two days as a result of having taken the drug earlier. "No, I'm not in that much pain. All I really need is a little more rest," she assured him, then drooped her eyelids to make him believe that was exactly what she needed. "Why don't you go on into the other room to wait for him so I can nap?"

Thomas left the room immediately and within seconds, Alisha was fumbling inside her purse for the white plastic bottle. Quickly she downed two more caplets, then put the bottle back into the purse before returning it to the table. Thank goodness her purse had made the trip back in time with her. She would hate to have to face such pain with no medicine at all.

Disappointed that her attempt to leave had failed, she lowered herself back on the pillows, pulled her skirts up to let the cool air brush against her damp skin, then closed her eyes to wait for the pounding at the back of her head to abate. It was nearly two hours later that she awoke to find Thomas and the doctor standing over her bed. Because she had not expected to fall asleep, it took her a moment to gather her thoughts again.

The first thing she noticed was that her skirts had been pulled back down to her ankles and that the earlier pain was gone. She moved her head from side to side to test the effect of the caplets and discovered only a slight tenderness near the injury itself.

"Thomas, I don't think you realize just how lucky this young lady was not to have been injured any worse than she was," the doctor told Thomas in a deep, reassuring voice, then smiled.

Alisha stared at the pleasant smile curiously. Like Thomas, the doctor was an older man with graying hair and thick bushy eyebrows, but unlike Thomas, who was a rather frail man, the doctor was tall, dark-complexioned and strapping.

"Hello there, young lady," he said in a tone as light and as cheerful as his smile when he realized she was not only awake but staring at him. "I'm Doc Owen, remember me?"

Still confused from being so suddenly awakened, Alisha shook her head, then blinked several times to bring her thoughts into sharper focus. "No, I'm sorry, I don't. I don't think I was awake the first time you were here." Although he did remind her of someone, she just wasn't sure who.

"The first time?" He pulled his thick eyebrows together and glanced at Thomas, then back at her. His smile melted into a look of professional concern. "You don't remember me from the many other times I've been here?"

Again she shook her head, glad that such movement had yet to bring back any of her pain.

The doctor's expression deepened. "Don't you remember when you had that fever two summers ago and I had to come by at least a dozen times to make sure you were being kept cool and taking your medicine?"

She shook her head again.

His gaze narrowed further. "What about the time those two men got into a brawl at your table and you got that piece of broken glass in your hand? It caught in such a way I had to come over later and remove it. Don't you remember that?"

"I'm sorry, doctor, but I don't remember because I can't remember," she told him, even though she already knew what his reaction would be to what she had to tell him. Like everyone else, he would not believe her. "I was not here for any of that."

He gazed questioningly at Thomas. "What does she mean she was not here?"

Thomas looked at her sadly. "Andrea had

some very strange dreams after taking the laudanum, and for some reason she thinks they were true. I guess because she no longer remembers her own past to know the difference, she has decided that what took place in those dreams was real. Ever since she came to she's been trying to convince me she's somebody else. It seems she's taken to a name Rand Kincaid mentioned right after she first woke up."

"My believing I'm someone else has nothing to do with the laudanum or with Rand Kincaid. I really am Alisha Sampson— or at least *part* of me is." Her expression revealed how truly perplexed she was to be caught in such an odd situation.

"See?" Thomas shook his head. "Kincaid thinks she's just pretending because she thinks it will help her get out of the trouble she's in with the police somehow, but I can tell that's not true by the way she looks at me. She really doesn't remember who I am."

He looked at the doctor with such doleful brown eyes it made Alisha wish she could reach out and console him somehow. He was such a nice old man.

"She doesn't even try to remember," he continued. "Maybe because deep down, she doesn't *want* to remember. I don't know."

The doctor turned her head slightly, then leaned over to examine the small injury at the base of her skull. "Could be she hit her head a lot harder than I first thought." He prodded the tender spot gently with his fingertips, causing Alisha to wince. "The outside swelling is pretty much gone, but that doesn't mean that there isn't still some inside swelling."

"Inside swelling?" Thomas repeated apprehensively.

Dr. Owen nodded, then turned his attention to her other injuries. "It's possible. And if there is, that could explain why she's having so much trouble remembering who she is. The swelling could be pushing against some essential part of her brain."

"Is that dangerous?"

"It can be. But in this case I don't think so because she is alert otherwise." He lifted her chin to study her pupils. "Chances are once the swelling inside finally goes down, her memory will eventually return, and when it does, she'll forget all about this nonsense of thinking she is someone else. When she has something real to compare with, she'll realize the other was just part of a hallucination brought on by the medication."

If only it were a hallucination Alisha thought dismally. But it wasn't a hallucination. This was all real. *Too* real.

"You are wrong. Knowing who I am has nothing to do with the medication you gave me," Alisha argued, but then decided to further the dispute would not be worth the effort. This was a man of medicine. A man who lived by logic and reason. Not a person who could be easily convinced that she was the hapless victim of magic, that although the body might still be Andrea's, there was someone else inside. Someone who did not want to be there. "And I wish you two would quit talking about me as if I'm not even here."

"I'm sorry," Dr. Owen responded, duly chastised. "But I wanted to reassure your father. And I also want to warn him against sending you to Texas like he plans. The trip, whether by ship or land, would only aggravate your injuries and prolong your memory loss."

"How'd you know about that?" Thomas asked, looking both startled and worried. "No one knows about that but us."

"Obviously Rand Kincaid does. He's the one who told me. You see he, too, is worried about how such a trip might affect her health."

Alisha arched an eyebrow. Why would Rand care so much about her health? He thought her a liar and a cheat. "He told you that?"

"Yes, he did. And I agree with him. The trip would be hard on you. What your father needs to do is find someplace much closer for you to stay, somewhere where he can slip away and come see you occasionally. I think that being around familiar places and seeing familiar people from time to time will eventually help you to remember."

Thomas intervened. "But there's nowhere I can send her that's close by. I don't have any relatives living closer than Texas."

The doctor paused a moment. "It doesn't have to be relatives. Find a friend who will take her in, or use whatever money you've got to pay someone you can trust to keep her. I really don't think she should have to make that trip. At least not for a while."

"But I'll need most of what little money we have to pay you," Thomas pointed out.

"No, you won't. I've already been paid. By Mr. Kincaid. He paid me yesterday when he came by to explain why it was so important for everyone to keep her whereabouts a secret. Paid me generously, as a matter of fact. You use your money to help Andrea find someplace safe to stay until the swelling is down and her memory has returned. Then, if the police are still after her and she's still willing to go, you can send her on to Texas."

"I'll see what I can do," Thomas said, looking doubtful. "How long do you think it will be before her memory finally starts to return?"

Until I can get to Imena's shop and convince her to switch us back, Alisha thought wryly.

"I don't really know," the doctor answered honestly. "I haven't dealt with too many cases of amnesia. Sometimes something happens to jog the memory right away and other times the memory loss lasts for weeks, even months."

Alisha frowned, knowing if she could just get her strength back and find some way to get safely to Imena's, the memory loss would prove very short-lived.

There was no rational reason for her to have to stay in Andrea's body any longer than she already had. She had done nothing wrong, therefore she should not be forced to stay and face someone else's danger. It was wrong for Imena to expect it of her. Andrea was the one who created the problem with the police. Andrea should be the one expected to resolve it. And if some innocent man's life really was in danger as a result of what Andrea had done to get that money for her father, then *Andrea* should be the one there trying to save him. Not her. None of this was her fault. She should not be forced to intercede in something she had nothing to do with.

Alisha closed her eyes to suppress the anger and the outrage that had been building inside her for two days now. It was not fair that she be forced to risk her first real chance at a vice-presidency because of something someone else had done, nor was it fair that she faced someone else's danger.

If only she could find some way to convince Imena of that.

Nine

Because the doctor did not believe Alisha when she told him her head and her shoulder no longer hurt, he ordered her to take a few sips of water he laced with laudanum.

Thinking she would hold most of it in her mouth and spit it out after they had left, she obliged rather than argued and was dismayed when the doctor then demanded to see an empty mouth.

Reluctantly, she swallowed the foul liquid and as a result spent the next seven hours sleeping soundly. When she managed to force herself awake again, it was already dark outside. Too dark for her to find her way in a city she did not recognize. A city filled with policemen who wanted to haul her back to that rat-infested jail.

Aware it would be much safer to wait until morning, she put on the nightgown Thomas had left out for her, then drifted off to sleep again, this time to be awakened by the smell of food and the rattling of a supper tray nearby.

Opening her eyes, she expected to see Thomas's face hovering above the tray and was baffled when instead she saw the face of the very man she had just been flirting with shamelessly in her dreams. In her dream, however, that handsome face had been smiling with adoration, not scowling like it was now.

"Thomas told me to bring you this," Rand said, gesturing to the large metal tray in his hands with a curt nod. Despite his grim expression, he looked remarkably handsome in the dark trousers and pale blue shirt he wore.

Remembering what he had worn before, Alisha decided blue must be his favorite color. Or perhaps he wore so much of it because he knew it brought out the amazing color of his eyes. Whatever the reason, he did look good in it. *Too good.*

"He said you hadn't eaten since this morning and should be hungry by now."

Alisha breathed in deeply the spicy aroma of the food, then nodded. "I am hungry."

Curious to see what smelled so delicious, she sat up and stretched her neck as far as her injuries would let her. "Very hungry."

"Good," Rand responded, then thrust the tray at her brusquely. He did not offer to help arrange her pillows like Thomas might. "Eat."

Alisha stared at him while she accepted the tray, surprised by his rudeness. Both in the dream that still lingered in her mind and during that initial meeting in his yard, he had been very much the gentleman. Not only did he offer her the safety of his home, he had seen to it that she had appropriate clothing to wear.

But that was before he thought she was Andrea Knight, cheat and liar. That was also before

Alisha tried to explain to him that she was not Andrea and therefore not to blame for what the woman did. Since then, he had become increasingly more provoked with her, as if all that had happened during those past few days was *her* fault.

"And what, pray tell, is eating at you now?" she asked, frowning with annoyance while she tried to balance the cumbersome tray on her lap to eat the rice-and-shrimp concoction piled on her plate. It looked a little like the food she had eaten at Rand's house days earlier, but the sauce was not quite as dark.

Rand blinked in puzzlement, then responded. "I guess what is *eating* at me, as you so strangely put it, is the fact that I deplore being around people who have intentionally lied to me. I prefer people who are honest."

Alisha's frown deepened into an angry scowl as she moved her water glass from the tray to the side table. "Then why are you here?"

"That's a good question," Rand replied, his blue eyes glittering. "Why *am* I here?" He crossed his arms while he shifted his weight to one well-muscled leg. "I keep asking myself that very same thing."

Alisha tried not to notice the way the shift in his weight caused his black broadcloth trousers to hug his sinewy body. She also tried to ignore the way the color of his shirt brought out the crystal clarity of his eyes. Eyes so blue and so pale they made her want to forget all her troubles and simply become lost in their depths—

and *that* made her angrier still. Angry with herself for being so easily affected by him.

"And did you come up with an answer?" she asked.

The lean muscles that shaped Rand's strong cheeks hardened upon hearing her impertinent tone of voice, and she found perverse satisfaction in knowing she could annoy him almost as much as he annoyed her.

"That is *not* the way to speak to the person who saved your virtue if not your very life by hauling you out of that jail."

Although Alisha knew he was right, she did not like being reprimanded as if she were a small child. "And just why did you save me from such a terrible fate? You never have quite explained that. What did you hope to gain by smuggling me out of there in the dead of night like that? Were you hoping I'd feel so grateful to you that I would hand over the three thousand dollars you think I stole?"

Rand lifted his chin in arrogance. "Dear one, I spent over that much getting you out of that jail. Three thousand dollars is not a grand sum to someone like me."

"Then why *did* you do it?" she asked, truly perplexed. "It certainly couldn't be because you like me." She knew he could barely tolerate her.

Then she remembered how beautiful and enticing Andrea's body was and knew the answer. Her anger increased. "I certainly hope it wasn't because you thought I'd be so grateful to have had my virtue saved that I'd willingly hand it over to you instead. You may be one gorgeous hunk of manhood, but you can just forget me hopping into your bed."

Rand's eyebrows arched, then dropped. He clearly had trouble following her figures of speech. "I never asked you to *hop* into my bed as you so crudely put it."

"That may be true, but as I recall you did say something about having figured out a way for Thomas to get out from under the six-thousand-dollar debt he owes you. And you were staring at my body when you said it."

"Oh?" he asked with an arched eyebrow, as if he had just caught her at something. "So you now admit that is your body and not one belonging to someone else?"

Alisha took a deep breath. He was trying to confuse her. "In a way this could be considered my body, at least for as long as I'm inside of it; but you are right. It is really Andrea's body, not mine. I should try to remember that. But you were definitely staring at *this* body when you said what you did. If you weren't planning to coerce me into your bed, then what?"

Rand's face perked up as if having taken a sudden interest in the direction of their conversation. His eyes glittered from some private thought. "Do you really think you'd be worth six thousand dollars in bed?"

Alisha paused a moment, aware that was exactly how that last comment had sounded, then looked back down at her plate. "Well, no."

"Too bad," he responded. A glimmer of a

smile wavered about his lips. "I was really very curious to find out what would make bedding you worth six thousand dollars."

Feeling suddenly uncomfortable, Alisha hurried to change the course of their conversation. "Then what did you mean by claiming to have figured out a way for Thomas to repay his debt to you."

Rand studied her a moment. "Why don't you ask him? He should be in here in a few minutes."

Alisha did not want to wait even those few minutes. She wanted to know now. "Because I'm asking you. What did you mean by that?"

"I'd rather he be the one to tell you. I think you'll prove more receptive to the idea if he's the one who explains it to you."

Frowning, Alisha dug her spoon into the rice-and-shrimp concoction. Its deliciousness made her feel a little less antagonistic.

"Okay, I'll wait for Thomas to tell me," she said, then shoveled a second spoonful into her mouth. Although the sauce was a little spicier than she had expected, the food was good and she was hungry.

Rand watched thoughtfully, then asked, "Why do you insist on calling your father by his first name? Don't you know how disrespectful that sounds? Why don't you call him Father or Papa like most daughters do?"

Alisha pressed her lips together long enough to swallow the food before responding, "I think you already know the answer to that. I've certainly told it to you enough times."

"Ah, yes, the amnesia," he responded sarcastically. His blue eyes glinted with renewed anger. "The reason you don't call him Father is because you don't remember that he is your father."

"Not true," she countered, just as angry.

Rand's eyes widened. He looked suddenly hopeful. "Then you are finally ready to admit the truth to me?"

Alisha bounced her foot impatiently beneath the covers. "I already have. The truth is that I don't call him Father not because I don't remember him being my father, but rather because he is *not* and never *was* my father. My memory is not the problem here. The problem is that I never laid eyes on that man before Saturday. What do I have to do to get you to hold on to that one simple fact? Why can't you just accept that not all things are what they seem?"

Rand's grim expression returned as he jerked the chair facing her bed around so he could straddle it. "Have it your way for now. But I think you should know I will one day hear the truth from your lips. Mark my words."

"These aren't my lips," Alisha returned, knowing the comment would enrage him more. Serves him right for not even trying to accept the truth, she thought as she resumed eating.

"Then you won't mind when I eventually claim them as mine," he said, then smiled when her head snapped up. He propped his arms across the back of the chair while he awaited her reply.

Alisha's heart tapped out a rapid rhythm. "I

thought I made myself clear: I have no intention of going to bed with you." The last thing she needed was to allow herself to be used like that again. It was bad enough she'd allowed Brad to take advantage of her all those years.

"You won't have to be in my bed when I first kiss you, though I admit, I do like the thought of that."

Alisha blinked, trying not to envision them in bed together. It was far too arousing. "I really think you should direct your energies elsewhere. You are headed for a major disappointment if you think I'm ever going to let you kiss me."

He stared at her for a long moment. His eyes sparkled with some untold amusement. "And I think it is time someone brought you down a notch or two—and as it turns out I happen to be just the man to do that."

"Oh, you are?" she asked as intrigued as she was outraged by his challenge.

"Yes, despite your strong, rebellious nature, I find that I am extremely attracted to you. More than I've been to anyone in a long, long time. Therefore I've decided to have you." He spoke of it as if it were nothing more problematic than deciding what to have for lunch.

Alisha fell silent a moment, not knowing how to respond to such arrogance. "You certainly have a lot of audacity to think you can maneuver me so easily."

Rand's smile turned seductive. "I never said seducing you would be easy."

Alisha could not believe how confident he

sounded. "You also never said it would be impossible, which is exactly what it would be— *impossible.*"

"Nothing is impossible," he responded calmly, then rested his chin on his arms as if he hadn't a care in the world.

Alisha studied him a moment. With the way his blue eyes sparkled and his dark hair caught the soft glow of the wall lamps someone had come in and lit while she was asleep, she could well imagine herself eventually giving in to such a man. It was a good thing she did not plan to be there long enough for that to happen.

Or was it?

Although a part of her was clearly put off by such obvious arrogance, another part of her was elated by the thought of having such a strongly attractive man in open pursuit of her— even if it wasn't really her he was after.

"And what makes you so confident you have what it takes to win me over?" she asked, unaware that much of the anger had left her voice. She was far too intrigued to continue being angry.

"I don't know that I have. But I do know that there is something different about you that makes me want to try."

Alisha wanted to laugh aloud at that last comment. There was something different about her all right. Like the fact she had been brought there against her will from the twentieth century.

"Try all you want. I don't plan to be here long enough for you to accomplish that goal," she stated, then felt an unaccountable sadness knowing that someone else would end up being his prey—the real Andrea, as soon as she returned.

"I wouldn't try running away again if I were you," he warned her, this time with no rancor in his voice. "The police are still out there trying their level best to find you again, and if or when they do locate you, this time they will be a lot more watchful. Your chances of escaping again on your own will be practically nonexistent. Even bribery won't save you from your fate a second time."

Alisha's stomach tightened at the thought of what fate that might be. She remembered the lewd comments she had overheard shortly after her capture. "I'm clever enough to stay out of their way."

"Yes, you've proved that twice already, haven't you?" he said, then flattened his mouth with annoyance. "I don't think you realize just how many of those hired thugs Miller has working on the local police force now."

"Nor does she know that Miller has offered a two-hundred-dollar bonus to the man or the group of men who finally brings her in," Thomas added, having entered the room in time to catch the end of their conversation. "Beau just came up to tell me he was downstairs putting together his order for the week like he always does on Sundays when a pair of officers stopped by to question him again. It was them who told him about the new reward."

"A reward that will make those men all the more eager to find you," Rand said.

"And it's why I'm so grateful to Mr. Kincaid for his generous offer," Thomas continued as he moved quickly toward the bed.

"And just what offer is that?" Alisha asked, suspicious of any offer Rand may have made.

Thomas's eyebrows dipped low, casting an added shadow over his bruised eye when he looked over at Rand. "Didn't you tell her about it?"

"No. I thought it would be better for you to be the one to explain."

"Explain what?" Alisha interrupted impatiently.

Thomas smiled. "Mr. Kincaid has offered to let you stay with him."

"He *what?*" she responded, knowing all too well what lay behind that generous offer. She glowered at Rand.

"Now, now, Pumpkin." Thomas held out his hands to stop her from saying something she might later regret. "I know what you are thinking, and this is not a case of charity. He has offered you a job."

"Oh, he has?" she asked with an accusing lift of her brow. "And just what sort of job has he offered me?"

Thomas's dark eyes sparkled while he explained further. "Mr. Kincaid is willing to forgive my gambling debt to him and pay off all my other gambling debts in exchange for two simple agreements from us. One is that you move in over there and go to work for him as a housekeeper for one year, which is ideal because you needed a safe place to stay for a while anyway."

"I thought his place was just as suspect as yours," she argued, deciding the two had formed a conspiracy against her.

"Oh, but they've already torn his place apart looking for you once, and after the complaint he filed with the mayor in which he has demanded restitution from the city for the damage done to his property as well as for having had his privacy invaded, they won't be doing that sort of thing again. At least not to him, especially after he personally assured the mayor that you were not in his house or on his property."

"And at the time you weren't," Rand said in ready defense of what he had done. "You were still here. He never thought to ask whether or not I had plans to bring you there in the future."

"How clever of you," came her caustic response— and he had the gall to accuse *her* of skirting the truth.

"He's even promised to start you off slow," Thomas continued. "Because of what the doctor said about your injuries, he will let you take on the work a little at a time."

"How truly kindhearted he is," she said with a tight smile. Her dark eyes bored into Rand's. "And did he say exactly what this *regular work* would include? Making his bed perhaps?"

"Among other things," Rand put in quickly. His blue eyes glittered with amusement. "But that's because your father has explained to me that you really are not much of a cook. Otherwise I'd assign you to the kitchen instead."

Another thing Andrea and I have in common, Alisha thought, for she never had cared much for spending a lot of time in the kitchen either. There were just too many other things she could do with her time.

"What do you say?" Thomas asked, clearly hopeful. "One year of working as a housekeeper in exchange for clearing me of all my debts. Just think. No more worrying about what Frank Potter or Gil Platt might do to me. We could start afresh."

"Didn't you say something about *two* conditions in this contract?" she asked warily while her gaze involuntarily strayed to the lines of Rand's sleek body, fascinated by the man's easy movements while he slowly swung his leg over to sit sideways. "What's the other agreement?"

"That I stay completely sober during that same year," Thomas explained. "He knows I'm not tempted to gamble as bad when I'm sober." He lifted his chin proudly. "And I've already gone two days without as much as opening a bottle."

"What it really amounts to is being paid over eleven thousand dollars for only one year of hard, *honest* work from you and one year of complete sobriety from him," Rand thought it necessary to point out.

The emphasis he had placed on the word *honest* did not go unnoticed by Alisha, a word choice she considered ironic since she did not believe he was being all that honest himself. He would want more than a year's worth of housework for his eleven thousand dollars— especially in a time when most wage earners made only a few dollars a week.

"And why do I have to live in your house while I do this work for you?" she asked in an attempt to catch him in his lie. "Why can't I continue to live here instead?"

Rand let out an annoyed breath, then ran a hand through his long hair. "You can't very well chance being caught while going back and forth, now can you?"

Although peeved by his tone of voice, Alisha knew he had a point there. Going back and forth would be a foolish risk, and it did sound as if she might be a little safer over there than she was here. "Exactly where in your house would you expect me to live?"

"Wherever you wanted," he replied with a lift of his hands, as if he hadn't understood the hidden meaning behind that question. "Given the situation, I would allow you your choice of guest bedrooms on the second floor or a room in the servants quarters either on the top floor or at the back of the ground floor. The choice would be yours." He reached into his pocket and pulled out a folded piece of paper.

"Just think of it," Thomas put in, wanting to convince her yet. "You'd have a bedroom a lot nicer and a whole lot quieter than this one to sleep in each night, and you would probably be saving my life by clearing me of those debts."

Saving his life? Suddenly Alisha leaned forward. Maybe by agreeing to do this, she *would* be saving his life. She would certainly be saving him from Frank Potter because Thomas would no longer owe him anything. If he ended up owing anyone, it would be Rand and Rand did not seem like the type to physically harm anyone. She could then go back to Imena with the assurance that she had done exactly what she had been told to do— saved this old man's life. Imena would *have* to send her back then. With that danger suddenly gone, there'd be no reason to keep her in 1882.

But the thought of giving in to Rand so easily irked her, especially after all he had said earlier.

"Does he plan to pay the money right away?" she asked, remembering that one of the men he owed had given him only a few weeks to come up with the amount owed.

"Yes." Thomas nodded eagerly, then nodded to the paper in Rand's hand. "He's put that in writing. It also says I won't have to pay him back a cent unless for some reason one of us doesn't live up to our agreement."

"That's true. If you both promise to do what I ask, I'll pay the money tomorrow," Rand told her, looking very smug as he opened the paper and held it out so she could see it. Clearly, he expected her complete cooperation in the matter.

Thomas nodded again. "I've already agreed to stay sober a year. Now all you have to do is promise to be his housekeeper for that same year. Will you do that?"

Alisha looked at the page and noticed the

bold signature of *Thomas Henry Knight* at the bottom just above a blank line that obviously was for her signature. She turned her head so she would not have to look into Thomas's pleading brown eyes when she answered.

"No. I won't." She refused to give Rand the satisfaction of hearing her say otherwise.

"But why?" Thomas wanted to know, unable to believe she had turned down the offer. "It's only for a year."

Alisha continued to look away. She felt guilty knowing she could help this nice old man out by simply agreeing to give Rand the next year of her life, but something inside her would not allow Rand to use her like that. "Because there is more to this offer than I think you realize— much more. There has to be another way for you to get together the money you owe."

Thomas looked as if she had struck him and was about to plead with her further when Rand interrupted. "Don't be so quick to refuse, Andrea," he said, then slowly stood. "Think about your answer very carefully. All I am asking is that you be a housekeeper and work just as hard as the other housekeepers without complaint for one year in exchange for payment of your father's gambling debts. I realize that means having to give up working downstairs for Beau, but that's something you would have to give up anyway, at least until the problem with Jeremy Miller is suitably resolved. Other than that, I am asking *no other requirement* of you." He looked at her a long moment, then stepped away from the chair. "I'll be back in the morning for your answer— after you've had a little more time to think about it."

Thomas waited until Rand's footsteps were heard on the wooden stairs outside her window before he, too, stepped toward the door. "He's right. You need time to think about what Mr. Kincaid has offered. I'll leave you alone."

After Thomas left, Alisha did think about the offer. In fact she could think of little else.

It was not until she had gotten over her initial feelings of animosity toward Rand that she finally realized that in all likelihood *she* would not be the one to have see that year out, Andrea would. Andrea, who had herself caused a great deal of their trouble by having cheated at cards and therefore deserved to work like a slave for a year.

By agreeing to give Rand the year he wanted, not only would she be helping out Thomas, the one man who had treated her with consistent kindness since she had been forced into 1882, she would also be accomplishing what Imena wanted all along. She would be stopping Thomas from being brutally murdered by the men he owed.

As unbelievable as it sounded, she had within her power to save a person's life. All she had to do was agree to Rand's conditions. But then again it shouldn't be up to her to have to save Thomas's life. He had gotten himself into that fix, therefore he should be the one to get himself out. The real Andrea could decide to help him if she wanted by agreeing to Rand's ques-

tionable offer after she was returned to her
body— but that should be her choice.

So why did Alisha continue to feel so guilty?
Why did she feel like she was somehow responsible for the life of a man she hardly knew— a
man she met only days ago?

By the time Rand appeared at her bedroom
door the following morning, Alisha had just
about made up her mind to agree to his ques-
tionable demands, thinking it would be Andrea,
not her, who would have to suffer the consequences. But when she saw how confident he
looked when he strode into the room, as if he
knew she had changed her mind, all willingness
to cooperate left her. Suddenly, she wasn't so
sure Thomas's life was in all that much danger
anyway. Just because someone had given him a
black eye did not mean they wanted to kill him.
Besides, their killing him did not make a lot of
sense. They could never get their money out of
a dead man.

"So have you finally come to your senses?" he
asked, staring intently at her. His cocky stance
reminded her of Brad, which made her all the
more determined to deny him what he wanted.

"Yes, just now." She met his determined gaze
with her own. "That's why the answer is still no.
I refuse to become your personal slave."

"You don't hold a winning hand," he said in
an unnaturally calm voice. "In time you *will*
change your mind." He then turned and strode
out of the room as confidently as he had stridden
in.

Ten

While darkness descended outside the bedroom windows yet a third time, Alisha sat on the edge of her bed listening to the loud music, scraping chairs, and the grating laughter from below, too frustrated to sleep, which explained why she was still fully dressed except for her shoes. She had too much on her mind.

Not only had her second attempt to go in search of Imena's small shop failed as miserably as the first, she felt burdened with guilt, knowing she had selfishly refused to help Thomas out of his current troubles all because of the anger she felt toward Rand. Or maybe it was because of the anger she still felt toward Brad, for, in small ways, Rand reminded her of her ex-husband. They were both strong, handsome, controlling men who were very arrogant and very used to getting whatever they wanted out of life and people. It didn't matter who might be hurt by what they did as long as in the end they had whatever it was they wanted. Their only concerns were themselves.

Oh, how she hated people like that.

If only she could have made it to Imena's

without having come across the police first, then perhaps she could have found some way to convince the contentious woman to return her to the future where she belonged.

Alisha wondered then if her having suddenly been transported back in time like that had anything to do with Andrea having gone to the voodoo woman and asking to be sent off somewhere out of harm's way. It could be that Andrea paid her a lot of money to help her or it could be Andrea was a close friend of hers, someone Imena would want to protect.

She chewed on her lower lip while she thought more about that. She remembered Imena having said something about Andrea having come to her frightened, but she really could not recall exactly what was said. She had been too bewildered at the time to listen.

But if it were true, if the switch had taken place at Andrea's request, that meant Andrea was probably content to be right where she was and would not want to come back and face all the trouble she had caused. *Well, that was just too bad. She* did not want to have to face that trouble either, and it was not fair for her to have to. Just because Andrea had proved too cowardly to handle her own problems did not mean she should have to. Surely Imena could be made to see that.

If she could ever find a way to talk with the woman. Alisha pressed her lips together with disappointment. Today she had not gone two blocks before spotting three men dressed in the dark clothing and stiff hat she had come to recognize as a policeman's uniform. Not wanting to risk recapture, she had headed off in an entirely different direction and within three blocks had run into two more policemen. At that point, she'd had little choice but to turn back.

She sighed softly, realizing that Rand may be mistaken about a lot of things, including herself, but he had certainly proved right about one thing: the New Orleans police were everywhere. Not only had she run into those five during her attempt to flee the area, she had since seen several pass along the street in front of the apartment. Some rode on horseback, a few in buggies or in wagons, but mainly they were on foot and usually walked in pairs or in groups of three, and although some were rather portly, many looked to be in fine shape and would probably outlast her should she try to make a run for it. Especially while in Andrea's body, which had proved not nearly as fit as her own body.

There was no getting by them the way things were, not when there were so many of them and only one of her. What she needed was a disguise of some sort. But what? She didn't have any clothes that would make her look like somebody else— not even her own. All she had was what was hanging in that cabinet, most of which was designed to attract attention, not divert it.

It was while she sat there thinking that she heard the stairs creak outside her window. Yet she had heard no footsteps. Even over the barroom noise below, she should have heard footsteps if someone was really out there. Unless of course whoever was out there did not want to be heard.

Knowing now that the top portion of her bedroom could be seen through the small window directly above those steps, she quickly ducked to the floor. With her heart hammering at twice the normal rate, she waited to see what would happen next.

Thomas sat staring at the half-empty bottle. He figured he could take one small swig from it and no one would ever know. Andrea wouldn't because she had already gone on to bed. Rand had told him he would not be back until early that following morning.

And, too, he had already gone down to sweep out Beau's back room and haul his rubbish out to the street bin about mid-afternoon. That meant no one from downstairs should be up to find out why he had not done his work yet. There should be no further interruptions until that following morning— and it had been three days now since he had sipped anything stronger than water. Three long, torturous days.

He smacked his lips while he considered how good that one swallow of whiskey would taste as it rolled gently down his throat. He wouldn't have to have any more than that. All he needed was just enough to remind him of the taste.

"Besides my year shouldn't have to start until Andrea's does," he argued aloud, but not so loud that she might hear him above the noise slowly building below. "I should still be allowed a swallow or two until after she climbs down off her high horse and finally agrees to go to work for that man. 'Sides, I don't understand why she's so dead set against working for him anyway. If she doesn't feel any need to cooperate with him, then neither should I. Why should I be the only one to suffer?"

Having convinced himself, he tugged the cork out with his teeth and was just about to put the bottle to his lips when he heard a loud, splintering crack out in the hall. Aware someone had just banged his door open, he hurriedly jammed the cork back into place and hid the bottle back in the bottom drawer of the sideboard where he kept it for emergencies.

"Who's out there?" he shouted angrily and headed immediately toward the narrow L-shaped hall that connected all the rooms to the only door that led directly to the outside. Having had some of the drunks from below come upstairs and cause him trouble before, he was prepared to be firm but not offending while ordering whoever it was back downstairs.

He came to a sudden halt when instead of some drunk looking for a handout, he found himself face to face with the police chief himself. And right behind him stood three of his men, all facing him with angry scowls.

Thomas's heart drummed a frantic rhythm when he realized why they were there and how important it must be to have dragged the police chief himself out into the streets that late at night. He swallowed hard, then took a defensive stance. "What do you think you are doing busting in here like that?"

"We're here looking for your daughter," came the chief's expected response as he stepped forward.

"But you've already had this place searched," he pointed out, hoping somehow to talk them out of coming in any farther. His whole body ached with the chilling knowledge that Andrea was in the next room, probably asleep by now and unaware of the danger. Because they were both accustomed to sleeping with a lot of noise around them, there was a good chance she did not notice the sound of the door banging back against the wall. "Two men were here just yesterday. They tore this place up looking for her. Took me most of the day to put everything back in order."

"That was yesterday," Chief Miller replied. He and his men headed immediately toward the room Thomas had just exited. "And that was before one of your neighbors spotted her running up those stairs earlier this afternoon."

Thomas's gut wrenched. What was Andrea doing outside during the bright of day? Didn't she know any better? "But that wasn't Andrea," he said in an overly loud voice, hoping to alert Andrea to the danger. "That was a friend of mine who came to visit me. She just *looks* a lot like Andrea." He moved over to block the men's way. He knew that as soon as they had thoroughly investigated the parlor, they would head on to the bedrooms. "There's no reason for you three to tear this place apart again."

"Get out of our way, old man," the chief growled between clenched teeth. He reached out a meaty arm and slammed Thomas's frail body against the wall. "We're taking that daughter of yours to jail and that's all there is to it."

"But you are wasting your time. She's not even here," he lied. He tried to ignore the sharp pain that shot through his back when he pushed himself away from the wall and stumbled forward to try again to stop them.

He proved just as ineffective the second time. Again the chief struck him hard and sent him reeling backward.

"Well, we'll just find out whether or not that's true, won't we?" he said after Thomas had fallen to the floor. "George, you step back outside and make sure she doesn't try slipping out a window or out another door," he told the smallest of the three men, then nodded for the other two to start their search. Together he and the larger two entered the room where Thomas had been.

In an attempt to uncover any possible hiding places, they shoved over the larger pieces of furniture, lamps and all, pulled the lid back on a steamer trunk, and yanked all the curtains off the wall.

Still hurting from the fall, Thomas followed them inside and cringed while he watched the sideboard crash forward.

"Please, don't do this again," he pleaded, knowing they had broken two of his bottles the first time they searched the place. "I swear to you she's not here."

"Then where is she?" the chief asked. He stopped helping the other two long enough to confront him.

"I don't know. I ran her off after I found out what she did to that man downstairs." He continued to lie, desperate to make them go away. "I couldn't stand to look at her after hearing about that."

The other two stopped their search to see what the chief would have to say about that.

"That's a crock," the chief replied, then reared his arm back and struck Thomas across the side of his head with the back of his hand. "You know where she is. I can tell by looking at you."

Thomas staggered back, briefly stunned by the powerful blow, but he did not fall.

"N-no, no, I don't." He reached out to steady himself against an overturned table.

"And I think you do."

Thomas raised his arms to protect his head when he realized Chief Miller planned to strike him again, but they did little to obstruct the blow. This time the force dropped him to his knees and caused him to fall forward into pieces of broken porcelain. When he sat back up, his hands and arms were bleeding.

"Please, go away," he sobbed, aware now he would not be able to stop them from taking his daughter from her bed. If only she had gone with Rand that afternoon like she had been asked. Then he wouldn't have to worry about what would happen when these men came to her room. "Please just go away and leave me alone. I've done nothing to any of you."

"Not until you tell me where your daughter is," the chief replied, then kicked him in the ribs with his booted foot, causing Thomas to double forward with renewed pain. "My brother wants his money back. Every last cent of it. He also wants to have a long talk with her about what she's done."

Thomas was not fooled. He knew Jeremy Miller wanted a lot more than a conversation with Andrea. "I don't know where she is. I told you. I haven't seen her in awhile."

When the chief realized the other two had stopped their search to watch, he snapped, "Don't just stand there gaping, go search the other rooms. Just because this man says she's not here doesn't mean it's true. Also, keep a close eye out for the money. No telling where she hid it."

While fighting a strong wave of dizziness, Thomas attempted to stand, but before he could find the strength to get to his feet, the chief kicked him in the side again. This time the pain was so sharp and so all-consuming, he crumpled to the floor and was unable to move.

The next kick struck him in the stomach with such incredible force it skidded him out into the hall. Aware it was just a matter of time before they came upon Andrea's bedroom, he tried to call out a warning to her in hopes she might hear him over the noise below, but each attempt to draw air into his lungs hurt too much to allow him to even speak. When the fourth and final kick came, he was almost grateful. In the darkness that followed there was no wrenching pain.

Alisha ran through the streets, terrified. She had gone to the bedroom door as soon as she had heard all the shouting in the hall and had watched helplessly through a small crack while one of the four men who had stormed into the apartment brutally kicked and beat Thomas until he was unconscious.

The memory of the blood splattered across the side of Thomas's head and down his clothing haunted her while she fled along the rain-dampened sidewalk in her stockingfeet. Because she did not recognize any of the streets around her, she had no way of knowing where she was or in which direction she was headed. All she knew was that she had to get far away from where she had been before what she'd just seen happen to Thomas happened to her.

Her lungs burned while the blood pounded in her ears at a hard and rapid rate, drowning the patter of her own footsteps while she ran as hard as Andrea's body would let her.

It had been like watching some old gangster movie. Those men were even more ruthless than she had imagined. Rand was right, they posed far more of a threat than she had ever realized. They behaved more like criminals than police, willing to beat an innocent old man senseless in their effort to get at her.

Tears stung her eyes while she clutched her purse against her chest with one arm and held her pink skirts high above the ground with the other as she continued running.

The short late-afternoon shower had left behind cooler temperatures but Rand hardly noticed while he sat in the garden staring off into the darkness with only one torch burning. He was too angry with Andrea for refusing yet again to come live there as his housekeeper. Why couldn't she understand that he only wanted to help her—though why he bothered was a mystery to him.

All Andrea had done since that first night she came tumbling over his garden wall so unexpectedly was lie to him about who she was and treat him like he was some sort of leper. Despite all he had done for her, she continued to distrust him. Continued to refuse to let him help her.

Rand raked his fingers through his long hair, a result of all the frustration building inside him. He was not accustomed to having a beautiful woman spurn him like that, especially one he had tried so hard to help.

Truth was, most women, beautiful or not, had always seemed quite pleased by whatever attention he gave them. So why did Andrea become so upset every time he came close to her? Why couldn't she understand that his offer of a job wasn't so he could work her like some slave or so he could trick her into his bed? It was so she would not feel awkward about coming to live in his house.

By giving her good, honest work to do, she would not only have something to help keep her occupied during these next few months, she would have an appropriate excuse for being there. An excuse the others in the house would accept without question.

If she did not come there in the guise of a housekeeper, the rest of his staff would undoubtedly wonder why she was there. Some of them, like Jolie, who loved to believe things were not quite what they seemed, would immediately decide she was there because she had offered him *other* services. Therefore, it really was to Andrea's advantage that she agree to come there as part of his staff.

It would also give the others a logical response should the police ask them if there was anyone new living in the house. "Only the new housekeeper," would be the answer. Hardly a response that would raise suspicion.

He shook his head grimly. All Andrea could see was the hard work she might be asked to do while she was there. She did not understand that by doing such hard work and behaving like any other housekeeper, she would be helping to protect herself from eventually being captured by Chief Miller and his men. But then again, because she had managed to escape them twice now— once on her own and once with his help— she probably did not see the real danger of being caught a third time. If only he could make her see the truth. Those men meant to have her.

Too frustrated to think about Andrea's obstinate behavior any longer, he pushed her beautiful image from his head and concentrated instead on the fact he had not eaten anything since breakfast. Remembering that Caroline had called out earlier something about his supper being ready, he pushed himself up out of the chair and headed toward the house.

He was still within range of the torch light when he heard a rustle of leaves behind him. He turned in time to see the gate that separated the garden from the carriage lane swing open and someone hurry through.

To his surprise it was Andrea. His heart leapt with an odd combination of hope and fear.

"Rand. You have to help me," she cried between short, rapid gasps for breath, her cheeks a darker shade of pink than the dress she wore.

Rand hurried toward her, prepared to fend off whoever was chasing her. When no one appeared in the gateway behind her, he turned to her, puzzled. "What happened?"

"Four men," she said while she continued to take in quick, hard breaths. "Three wore uniforms. They broke into the apartment. They beat Thomas until he was unconscious, then came looking for me. I managed to slip by the one standing at the top of the stairs and got away."

"Do you think he saw you?"

"I don't know. I never took the time to look

back. When my feet finally touched the ground, I started running as fast as I could," she explained, her dark eyes round with fright. "I was lost at first, but I kept running anyway. Somehow, I found my way to this street. When I realized where I was, I ducked inside your gate."

"And you don't know if you were followed?" Again he glanced at the gate, his heart racing with the fear of what could happen yet.

She shook her head. "I don't think I was, but I can't be sure. I didn't *hear* anyone behind me."

"Good," he said, thinking that boots on a wet sidewalk should have made a sound loud enough for her to hear, even in her panicked state. Aware she must be exhausted from such a long run, he hurried forward to close and lock the gate, then gestured to a set of chairs cloaked in shadows. "Now tell me again what happened. Start at the beginning."

Alisha accepted the offer to sit and, after finally catching her breath, told him everything that she knew. By the time she finished, Rand had a pretty good idea who the man was with the three uniformed policemen.

"That was probably the police chief himself. Miller must really be desperate to find you if he was willing to go there himself— especially at night." His face pulled into a deep, pensive frown. "I wonder why? Having his brother cheated out of a few thousand dollars shouldn't bother him that much." He studied her a moment, though he could see little of her expression in the darkness. "Is there something about all this you aren't telling me?"

"I've told you all I know," she said truthfully.

Rand's frown deepened, for she seemed sincere enough. But then Clay Miller was basically a lazy person who usually sent his hired thugs to take care of his business for him. It would take something more than the fact she had cheated his brother out of a few thousand dollars to make him that determined to find her. "Maybe he *thinks* you know or saw something you shouldn't."

"Like what?"

"I don't know," he said, trying to think. "Maybe something having to do with one of his shady operations. Something that could turn our new mayor against him. I'm sure he doesn't like the thought of Mayor Shakespeare turning one of those vigilante committees against him. I imagine he's been on edge ever since that new administration took office last year. I'm sure he worries that as soon as they get through shutting down the more corrupt gambling and bawdy houses, they'll turn their attention to the police department."

Alisha looked at him, perplexed. "All I know is what he told Thomas while he was beating him."

"Which was?"

"That his brother was determined to have his money back. Every cent of it." She paused for a moment while she mentally relived the incident. Pleadingly she said, "I never realized how much danger Thomas was in because of me. I thought his only danger was from those hoodlums he owes money to." She shook her head sadly. "I never should have agreed to stay there with him but then those men turned out to be a lot more violent than I ever thought. You have to help him."

"I'll have someone go over and check on him right away," Rand promised, knowing it would not look right for him to be the one to suddenly show up at their door, not when he had told the mayor he barely knew the girl. "If he's hurt as badly as you say he is, I'll have the doctor sent over there, too."

"No, I don't mean just for tonight. Those men are ruthless. They will be back again and again until they get what they want."

"I know. I tried telling you that myself."

She looked away for a moment, then lifted her chin proudly and returned his gaze. "I'm ready to agree to be your house servant."

"You are?"

"Yes, I don't dare go back there and I have nowhere else to go," she admitted. "But I agree to do this only under certain conditions."

He lifted an eyebrow. "Which are?"

"That in addition to paying off all of Thomas's gambling debts like you promised that you also pay back the three thousand dollars that was stolen from the chief's brother. And that you won't ask for the money back for at least a year even should Thomas start drinking again."

"That's adds up to over fourteen thousand dollars," he pointed out, though not in outrage.

"I realize that." She lifted her chin higher.

He studied her proud features a moment, amused by her unbelievable gall. There was certainly nothing humble about this woman.

"And will your services be worth that much?" he asked, his eyes sparkling at the thought.

Alisha bristled but knew now was not the time to worry about what might happen between them should she move in there. "If by the word *services* you mean a year's worth of housework, then I can promise that I will do my best." She could not very well promise what the real Andrea would do once she had been returned and found out what had happened in her absence.

"And you really think your best will be worth fourteen thousand dollars? Why, this entire house is barely worth over that."

"You were the one who made the offer to pay off Thomas's debts," she pointed out. "I just added the other three thousand to make sure he goes completely unharmed. I have to see to it that his life is no longer in danger, which it definitely is now." It was to be her bargaining point when she finally talked with Imena.

"But why would you care about that if you are not really his daughter?"

Because Imena told me I would not be allowed to return to my own time until all danger of his dying was gone, she thought but did not state so aloud because she knew Rand would never agree to pay off all those debts if he knew her plans were to ditch out on him the first chance she got. And if memory served her right, that voodoo shop was not all that far from Rand's house, perhaps six or seven blocks.

As soon as was safely possible, she would find the place and demand that the woman send her immediately back— or forward— or in whatever direction the twentieth century lay. It would be up to Andrea then to decide whether or not to go through with the promised year of labor, not her.

"I care about him not because he's my father but because he has been extremely nice to me and has taken very good care of me during these past few days."

Rand studied her a moment longer, his blue eyes reflecting more than a natural concern. "And what if I put a few conditions of my own on this new agreement?"

Alisha's insides tightened. She did not like that determined gleam in his eyes. "I already told you. I will *not* go to bed with you. I am not ready to start a new relationship with any man right now— no matter how handsome he is," she said.

Rand sighed heavily. "That's wasn't going to be one of my conditions. Why do you keep coming back to that?"

"Because fourteen thousand dollars is a lot to spend for only a year's worth of housekeeping."

"Very true, but that still was not going to be one of my conditions."

"Then what are your conditions?"

"One is that you quit pretending to be someone else when around me. If I happen to call you Andrea, you are to answer, although for protective reasons I think I will concede enough to introduce you to the others as Alisha Sampson."

Alisha took an annoyed breath but did not argue such a trivial request. At least she would still be Alisha Sampson to the others. She would again hear the sound of her own name. "And what are the other conditions?"

"Just one other," Rand said and looked relieved that she had not protested the first condition. "And that is that you speak civilly to me whenever you are around the other staff. No more snapping at me for no real reason. No more arguing with practically everything I say. I don't want the others thinking I will abide such foul treatment from those who work for me."

"Fair enough. I will agree to both if you will go tomorrow and pay off all those debts."

"Tomorrow it is," he said, as if it were not a problem to come up with that much money in so short a time. "But for tonight, I think you'd better sleep out in the summer kitchen. It would look a little odd for me to be bringing my new housekeeper in through the back door this late at night, especially when some of them are going to remember you from the other night. We want them to believe you are here as a housekeeper and not just some beautiful woman I want to have around. I'll bring you some food and something to sleep on later, after everyone has gone to their quarters for the evening."

"I don't need anything to eat. I had supper hours ago. But I could certainly use something to drink." Remembering how foul the water tasted by itself but that it had yet to make her ill, probably because Andrea's stomach was used to it, she tried to figure out something that might hide the taste. "You don't happen to have any iced tea, do you?"

"Tea with ice?" Rand asked as if repulsed by the thought. "You *want* your tea cold?"

"Yes. It tastes a lot better than it obviously sounds," she said and chuckled at the puckered look on his handsome face. Laughing eased a lot of the tension that had been building inside her. "Just bring me some tea with ice in it and a blanket, and I'll be fine."

She went willingly into the summer kitchen where she opened several windows just wide enough to allow a breeze, then waited for Rand's return.

Eleven

Several hours passed and Rand did not return with the promised tea and blanket. Exhausted, and knowing she needed sleep if she wanted to be able to face whatever the following day might bring, Alisha decided to make do with what she had.

After looking around for towels or even curtains in the summer kitchen and finding nothing made of cloth, she eventually took off the two ruffled petticoats she wore under her dress, having put them on for no other reason than to keep her skirt hems from wrapping around her ankles when she walked. She wadded one of them into a tight ball, then used her waist sash to tie it to her purse, and placed the resulting bundle under her head. She then used the other petticoat to cover her arms and head so that the mosquitoes the unprotected windows let in would not eat her alive.

Because there was no rug, or anything else with which to make a pallet, she brushed a spot clean, then lay directly on the hard wooden floor where she tried her best to go to sleep. But sleep would not come. She was too worried about Thomas. The brutal scene she had witnessed through the tiny crack in the bedroom door kept replaying in her mind. If only there was something she could have done to stop them, but it would have been one woman against four men. Thomas was already too far gone. Instead of helping, she would have made matters worse by giving them two people to vent their rage against instead of just one.

The thought of what might have happened to her should she have let her presence be known caused a sickening chill to wash over her. As angry as those men were, they very well may have killed her. Her stomach wrenched. What if Thomas were dead as a result of what happened? If only there were some way to know that he was all right, then perhaps she could finally find enough peace in her heart to sleep.

Frustrated and frightened, and so thirsty her tongue felt sticky and swollen, she lay peering over the rim of her petticoat, staring off into the darkness, wondering how she was ever going to get out of all the trouble she had so suddenly found herself in. How was she ever going to get safely past all the policemen patrolling this city and find Imena?

Alisha's tears were just moments away when she heard someone approach outside. Knowing it had to be Rand, she threw back the petticoat she used for cover and hurried to the door to greet him.

"You brought it," she said with relief just seconds after he entered. There was just enough moonlight streaming through the door and windows for her to see an enameled blue pitcher in his left hand.

"After finding out that pump over there beside the sink does not work, I thought I would die of thirst in here." She glanced at his other hand and saw only a blanket. "Where's a glass?"

"There should be one that just needs rinsing in one of those cabinets," he said and gestured to the cupboards behind her. "You want me to find one?"

"No. Never mind," she said, already grabbing the pitcher from his hand. "I'm so thirsty I'll drink straight from this."

Rand watched for a moment while she gulped down the cold tea he had brought her before he turned and closed the door. "Sorry you had no water but that pump hasn't been used since late last summer. It'll have to be primed."

Alisha paused long enough to glance back at the sink, but not long enough to ask him anything about the priming of a pump. She was still too thirsty.

"I'm also sorry that it took so long for me to get back here, but I had a few unwanted visitors."

"The police?" She stopped drinking. She tried to see his expression but it was so dark, she could barely make out his tall, lean shape.

He nodded, then placed the blanket he carried on a nearby counter. "They asked enough questions to make those who may have overheard them a little suspicious, so I thought I'd better wait until I was certain everyone was in bed before returning. Normally, they would all be in bed by nine o'clock, but William had a little trouble finding Dr. Owen. He wasn't home the first time William went by his house, and he wasn't where his wife thought he'd be."

"Then you've sent a doctor over to see Thomas. How is he?" she asked, almost afraid to hear the answer. "Or did William stay long enough to find out?"

"William didn't go over there at all. I was afraid the police would be watching your place to see who came and went, and might recognize William as being my butler and occasionally my driver. They would undoubtedly want to know why he was there, so I had him come on back here after alerting Dr. Owen to the trouble."

"So you don't know if Thomas is okay or not?"

"Oh, yes. The doctor came by here just a few minutes ago to give me a report. Your father has a couple of injured ribs and one eye is swollen completely shut, but he's going to be fine. The doctor says that with some good, stiff bandaging and a little pain medicine, your father should be able to get up and move around within a day or two; but he isn't to do anything that might strain those ribs for several months."

Alisha did not bother to argue the point that Thomas was not her father. At the moment that did not seem too important to her. "Was this the same doctor who came to see me?"

Rand nodded. "I've known Dr. Owen a long

time. I have always been able to trust him to keep certain matters to himself. He'll see to it that your father gets the care he needs without bringing up my name to anyone. No one need ever know that I'm connected to you two in any way. That keeps your presence here safe."

"Thank you," she said with all sincerity. "I appreciate what you've done." Having finally drunk her fill, she set the pitcher aside then moved closer to a window, hoping Rand would follow her into the moonlight. She wanted to be able to see his strong face while they talked. "I realize all these doctor bills were not a part of our agreement."

"And speaking of our agreement," Rand said as he did indeed follow her to the window, "I'll want to introduce you to the others early tomorrow morning, but I'll want it to look like you approached the house from the main street. That means you should go around, then approach the house from the front. I'll signal you when it's safe to do that without being noticed from inside."

She studied his face in the soft glow of moonlight. "How?"

He thought a minute. "By coming outside to read my newspaper. When I do that, you sneak out of here and go around to the front door. It'll mean that I've checked and everyone is away from the windows, which will probably be while Jolie is in the dining room cleaning away my breakfast dishes and the others are getting ready to do their own work. That should be about an hour after the sun comes up."

"And what about the money Thomas owes? When do you plan to pay that?"

"Shortly after you've gotten settled in, I'll go out and take care of Frank Potter and Gil Platt myself. But because I don't want the police to know for certain that I have had any association with you, I'll have to let Dr. Owen give the remaining three thousand dollars to your father. Your father can take it to Jeremy Miller himself." He paused for a moment as if trying to read her thoughts, then added, "And just to make sure your father doesn't get into a situation he can't handle, I'll have a few of my men from the docks follow him when he goes. I'm also planning to add an extra five hundred dollars as a bonus for what Miller has gone through so maybe he won't feel such a continued need for revenge. I'm hoping he'll consider the extra money his retribution."

Alisha studied Rand a long moment, aware he looked especially handsome in the shimmering glow of the moonlight. His blue eyes shone. "Why are you doing all this? What do you hope to gain from it?"

"Satisfaction," he said, then smiled when she cocked a doubtful eyebrow. "And *not* the sort of satisfaction you obviously think." He bent forward until his eyes were level with hers and his mouth but a few inches away while he studied her reaction to that.

"And how do you know what I'm thinking?"

She felt a perplexing leap of her pulse to have him suddenly so close. Despite a strong desire to look away so he would not know how deeply he affected her, her gaze roamed at will over his devastatingly irresistible features. He was such a incredibly handsome man.

"I can just tell," he said, then, while still standing only inches away, he lifted his hand and touched her playfully on the nose. His eyes glittered when he did. "You're worried that I plan to do more than what I threatened to do the other night."

Distracted by his touch, Alisha frowned. She did not remember any mention of a threat other than the hint that she might need saving from him. Her eyes rounded with sudden wariness. "What is it you threatened to do?"

"Just this," he said, then bent forward to press his lips gently against hers. "Don't you remember?"

The kiss was so short and so unexpected, Alisha did not have time to pull away.

She blinked while she tried to figure out whether to be alarmed that he had actually kissed her or disappointed that it had happened so quickly. It was the real first kiss she had experienced since her divorce. "Yes, I remember. It's just that I didn't think you really meant it. I thought you were just trying to annoy me."

"My kiss annoys you?" he asked, looking more amused than hurt.

"Well, no, but— "

"Good," he commented. "Then I'll kiss you again."

Giving her little time to protest, he pulled her immediately into his arms and this time kissed her soundly.

Alisha was left breathless. It was the most powerful kiss she had ever experienced. In all her years of marriage and in the many years of dating that had preceded her marriage, she had never once felt such a strong reaction to a mere kiss.

The strange, simmering warmth that suddenly filled her was like nothing she'd known. It flooded her body with a lingering heat, making her feel lightheaded. So lightheaded she could hardly think of anything but how exhilarating it felt to be held like that again. She did her best not to give in to the splendid sensations completely, knowing only too well what might happen if she did.

It was while she still fought the strong arousal he had created inside her that he suddenly broke away. His breath came just as raggedly as hers when he said, "I warned you that I fully intended to claim those lips."

"Yes, you did," she replied, trying to sound unaffected by the maelstrom of emotions still raging inside her but knowing that her rapid gulps for air had to be giving her away. "And now that you have, may we get on with other matters?"

"As long as you realize that I now plan to claim more than just your lips," he responded.

Two dimples appeared in his cheeks while he studied her startled expression. "I think you should be forewarned that I now intend to capture your heart as well."

Alisha's brown eyes widened. She was not used to such a direct approach. Obviously Rand Kincaid was not a man who liked to play a lot of games. "Then I think I should warn you that my heart will not be easily captured. It has become not only cautious but reclusive in these past few months."

"Why? Because of having lost your husband?" he asked with an instant scowl. Suddenly he looked wary. "I gather you loved this husband of yours very much."

"Yes. I did. But unfortunately he did not love me with quite the same intensity. He left me for another woman, which is why I now despise rather than love him."

"You are divorced?" Clearly Rand was surprised but not appalled, although he did look angry for some reason. "What sort of fool was this man?"

"The sort who likes to sample all the goodies around him. Sort of like you do," she responded. She did not intend her words to possess the accusing edge that they did.

"Me? How have your husband's actions turned you against *me?*"

"Because you apparently have a reputation for enjoying your women, too."

"And that makes you jealous?" He looked as

if he had a hard time making sense of everything she said.

"No, of course not. But it does let me know that you are just like him." And it made her realize she should not put more emphasis on that last kiss than it warranted. He was a man used to having his way with women. A man who had somehow sensed her need to be held and decided to take advantage of that fact. A need she herself had not realized until he'd touched her. Tears beckoned when she realized the void Brad had left in her life.

"No, it doesn't. He was married. I am not. Besides, I happen to know that he never even existed. Because I wanted to learn more about you, I asked your father about your previous marriage, and he told me you'd never even had a steady caller, although many tried to capture your attention. Why do you find it necessary to lie to me like that?"

Alisha's expression darkened as her honesty was questioned yet again. She met his defiant gaze with one of her own. "Andrea may never have had a steady caller, although I can't imagine why unless she just never had the time for such, but I have had several through the years. My problem is that I was foolish enough to have fallen in love enough to want to marry one of them. Had I known then what I know now, *that* never would have happened, which is why you nor anyone else will have that sort of control over me again. My heart is no longer open to such restrictive emotions."

"Aren't you forgetting your promise?" he asked, clearly as angry as she was.

"What promise?"

"The promise you made to stop pretending you are not Andrea Knight around me. It was one of the conditions to our agreement, remember?"

"No. All I promised to do was answer to the name Andrea when you called it. I never agreed to give up my identity."

Rand stared at her a long, angry moment, then spun sharply on his heel, headed toward the door. "Better try to get yourself some sleep," he said curtly. His words trailed over his shoulder while he reached forward to find the knob in the darkness. "Tomorrow will undoubtedly be a long day for you, Andrea. You will be asked to perform a lot of hard work, something you obviously know very little about. You will need all the rest you can get."

He stormed out of the kitchen and into the garden, slamming the door behind him.

Because of all that had happened in such a short span of time, Alisha still found it impossible to get any sleep that night. She lay on the blanket watching the sky slowly turn from black to a dark crimson rose to deep, rich, dusty blue. Knowing it was an hour yet before she should watch for Rand to appear in the garden, she continued to lie there staring sadly at a nearby window.

Even after she heard the sounds of birds chattering and dogs barking, she did not rise from the floor to start her day. Instead she remained lost in thought, remembering how well she and Rand had gotten along the previous night, if only for the few minutes that led to his kiss. Her heart fluttered at the memory of that kiss. No wonder he had so many women willing to do his bidding, even without the promise of marriage. He was a master of seduction.

Wouldn't it be wonderful to find someone like him in her own time? But then again, that would be asking the impossible. Even if there was such an enticing man, he would already be taken. Men like Rand rarely roamed free, especially those in her age group. By the time the really appealing men reached their late twenties they were already the permanent property of someone else.

Her forehead knotted when she wondered why Rand was not married. Why had some clever woman not reeled him in long ago? He was certainly handsome enough. So handsome it almost hurt to look at him. He was also wealthy and intelligent. Why hadn't some smart young thing snapped him up years ago?

Then she remembered Nicky's eagerness to oblige him and realized that Rand was not married because he did not want or need to be. There were enough willing women in his life to make him consider never settling down with just one. And why should he?

He was what the women of that time would

call a rake and what the women of her time
would regard as a playboy. He was exactly the
sort of man she did not care to become involved
with ever again. She had suffered enough heartache and humiliation in her short life.

So why couldn't she get that kiss out of her
mind? And why did it hurt to know that he was
the type of man who could never love just one
woman? What did that matter to her?

While still wondering if Rand would ever find
a reason to settle down, she heard voices outside.
Women's voices. Loud enough to catch her attention.

Curious to find out who they might be, she
pushed herself off the floor. Because she was
sore from all the running she had done the
night before and from the injuries she had suffered in the accident four days earlier, she hobbled to the nearest window. From there she
could see most of the garden area and crossing
the yard, headed in her direction, were two
women.

One was the large black woman who had
served her and Rand dinner the night she had
"dropped in." The other was a frail-looking
white girl who wore a shorter black dress with
gray stockings, no apron, and looked to be in
her late teens. They both wore white caps and
carried large buckets.

Aware they were headed in her direction, Alisha quickly searched for someplace to hide. The
only spot she saw that looked large enough was
on the far side of the largest iron stove, but she

knew that would shield her from view only if they did not come inside the room.

Her heart froze when she looked again toward the window and realized they were now close enough that she could tell what they said.

One spoke with a strong Cajun accent. "It do not matter to me dat dis day is cooler dan some of dose in de past weeks. Warmer days are coming and it time for us to get dis other kitchen ready for de coming season."

"But I still have washing to do," the other voice responded, clearly the younger of the two. "And Mr. Kincaid told me to get a room made ready for that new housekeeper he hired. Said she should be arriving here sometime today."

"Let her get her own room made ready," the older voice muttered. "It nearly de second week in April. It time to get dis other kitchen ready. Besides where dat other housekeeper going to sleep anyway? All de quarters are filled."

"He told me to ready a room on the second floor for her. Said she could stay there for now."

Aware the two women were just a few yards away, Alisha snatched up her purse, her petticoats, and the blanket on which she had just lain, then scanned the room a second time, hoping to discover a hiding place she had overlooked. It would ruin everything if those two found her there.

"Jolie!" Rand's voice carried across the yard, causing Alisha to turn and face the window again. "Where are you two going?"

Alisha held her breath while she waited to see if Rand could turn them around.

"Out to de summer kitchen," the older woman answered in a deep but loud voice. "It time we open it for de season."

"That may be but it will have to wait until Faye has gotten that room ready and you have gone to the wharf for fresh fish, lemons, and more ice."

Alisha edged closer to the window so she could see the women who now faced the house while Rand stood just outside one of the back doors facing them. A pair of dark pants clung to his slender legs and a white shirt lay fitted against his muscular frame by a pair of dark-colored suspenders. The white brought out the dark tone of his sun-bronzed skin.

"But dat can wait until de afternoon, can't it? I don't have to start cooking your fish till then."

"The fish could probably wait, but I'll be wanting the lemonade with my noon meal."

"You won't be going down to de wharves today?" she asked. There was a hint of annoyance rimming her voice. "Aren't you supposed to inspect dat new ship Mr. Lee sold you last week?"

"No. Not today," he responded, then explained, "I told Caroline earlier that I planned to be gone for a little while this morning, but I'd be back by noon. She was supposed to tell you that I plan to have my lunch here."

"Den I guess I'd better go and fetch dose lemons and dat ice right away," she muttered and headed immediately toward the house with the younger woman only a few steps behind her.

Alisha stayed near the window and watched until both had disappeared inside the house. As soon as they had stepped out of her sight, Rand turned and glanced toward the summer kitchen, causing Alisha's heart to jump for no apparent reason. He then strode casually back into the house.

Still watching through the window, Alisha felt an unexplainable sadness when he disappeared from her sight. Without appraising the emotion, she wondered how long it would be before he finally came outside to read his newspaper. She had been imprisoned in that small building long enough.

Jolie was still muttering to herself about having to go to the wharves on a Tuesday when William entered the kitchen only a few minutes later.

"And what's the matter with my fat and sassy woman this bright and beautiful day?" he asked. As was his custom at that time of the morning, he walked over and poured himself a cup of coffee from the stove. "You still angry because I got back so late last night?" he asked with only a hint of a Cajun accent.

Unlike Jolie, whose father was a true mixture of French and Indian, William had drawn his accent from others, therefore it was not quite as strong. "I told you I had no choice. I had to find that doctor for Mr. Rand and send him over to some man's house. I can't help it that you were already asleep when I arrived back."

Temporarily setting aside her other reason for being angry, Jolie eyed her husband suspiciously. "You sure you didn't go stopping off at de Sweet Apple for a little libation to calm your nerves?"

William raised his hand as if prepared to give an oath. "I didn't even go near that place. I didn't have time. I was too busy trying to find out where the doctor had gone. Had to see to it that he went over to Beauregard's to see about some friend of Mr. Rand's who was hurt there."

"That gambling place he sometimes has you to drive him to? You went there?" Again, her voice was edged with suspicion.

William shook his head, then pushed his red bandanna higher up onto his forehead so he could glower at her better. "Woman, I didn't say I went there. I said I sent the doctor there. Somehow Mr. Rand got word that one of his friends had been hurt and he wanted to make sure a doctor went over to see about him. He told me to come right on back as soon as I had talked to the doctor, and I did."

Jolie studied him a moment, then shrugged as if to say she finally believed him. "Well, you missed de policemen coming by here last night demanding to speak with Mr. Rand. Such an angry lot dey were."

William's scowl melted into a look of concern. "Again? They were here just a few days ago. What did they want with him this time?"

"I don't know. I answered de door since you were away, but Mr. Rand made me leave de room soon after they started talking. But I heard enough to know der was a grim fight over some woman. And it wasn't Miss Collingsworth who was named, nor was it one of his dames from the district. Looks like Mr. Rand has gone and found himself a new friend to interest him, one who means to cause him trouble."

"Was her name Andrea Knight?" William wanted to know. He remembered the name from the last time the policemen came. "Did they say something about this woman running from the police?"

Jolie's eyes widened. "I heard nothing about none of that. But den I barely heard de name. I was halfway out de room by de time dey spoke it, but I think dey might have said Andrea Knight. But I heard nothing about her having to run from de police. I was not allowed to stay long. All I heard was dat der had been a fight over a woman Mr. Rand had been protecting and dat some old man was bad hurt as a result. Happened over on Basin Street."

"Basin Street?" William stroked his chin thoughtfully. "Beauregard's is over on Basin Street. And that's where he had me send that doctor. Maybe the friend that was hurt is the same man the police came here to tell him about. But if that's so, how'd Mr. Rand already know about it? He was here alone all evening."

He continued to look puzzled for a moment, then quickly shook his head. "But then, it's none of my business how he found out. My business is trying to make you smile again. Now where are those comely white teeth of yours. I think I remember you having some." He bent low so he could get a better look at her mouth.

Jolie's lips quivered a moment, then broke into a wide grin. "Oh, you rascal! How can I possibly stay angry at anyone with you around to pester me. Come on, since Mr. Rand is not leaving here for a while, you can give me a ride to de wharves. Seems he has decided he wants fish for his supper tonight. Treat me nice enough and I'll see dat you get fish for your supper, too."

"And what can I have for dessert?" he asked, then looked down at her ample bosom with a playful leer.

He ducked just in time to avoid being popped across the forehead with the flat of her palm.

Knowing it could be a while before Rand came outside to read his newspaper, Alisha lifted herself onto a nearby counter so she would not have to stand the entire time she waited. She had barely made herself comfortable when she heard a door clatter shut. Glancing up, she noticed Rand headed across the yard to a small set of three chairs near the garden wall, newspaper in hand.

Aware the time had come to leave there, she hopped back down and quickly straightened her skirts and petticoats as best she could, considering how wrinkled and dirty they had become.

Having had plenty of time to consider her situation more thoroughly, she had made up her mind to do all she could to convince Rand's servants that she was one of them so they would not question her having been hired.

At the same time, she would show Rand that he was completely wrong about her. She was capable of doing whatever work she was told to do. Despite the nagging pain in her injured shoulder and the dull ache that still throbbed near the back of her head, she could handle whatever hardships came her way.

Even though this whole situation was grossly unfair and she had no reason to want to please any of them, she would stick with the plan as it was— at least until she was certain all Thomas's debts had been paid and Andrea's apology to Jeremy Miller had finally been accepted. But the very moment she knew Thomas's name was in the clear and it was safe for her to be on the streets again, she was out of there.

Twelve

Alisha glowered the whole time she rubbed the gleaming mahogany handrail. It had been three days since Dr. Owen had given that three and a half thousand dollars to Thomas. Three days since she had penned that letter asking Jeremy Miller to forgive her foolishness. Plenty of time for Thomas to have taken both on over to Jeremy Miller. But here it was already Friday afternoon and she had yet to receive word that the money had been paid and the apology accepted.

The last she had heard was that Thomas was still having trouble getting out of bed and that it might be Tuesday before he had the strength he needed to make the trip over to Felicity Street where Jeremy Miller lived. If not by Tuesday, then surely he would make it by Wednesday.

Alisha rubbed the wood harder.

Although she hated the thought of the man being in that much pain, she also hated having to wait any longer before trying her latest plan to make it past the police so she could finally locate that blasted voodoo shop. She had already been in 1882 a full week. That meant she had only two more weeks before her opportunity to return would be completely gone, or so Imena had indicated. Three weeks was all "the spirits" had allowed her.

Frustrated to know she had already suffered seven days longer than she should, Alisha clenched her teeth hard while she continued her angry assault on the wooden rail with her once-white polishing cloth. If only Rand would come home and tell her everything had finally been taken care of— that Thomas had finally delivered the money along with Rand's generous bonus and that all was forgiven. Then she could leave there with a clear conscience, knowing both she and Thomas were finally safe.

Until then, she would have to wait to see Imena. And she would continue to avoid being alone with Rand— other than those brief moments she went to him for a report of what had happened that day. That could not be helped.

Ever since those moments they had shared in the summer kitchen when she came to realize just how very attracted she was to him, she had tried to avoid any situation that left them alone for more than a few minutes at a time. She refused to risk being lured into a blind moment of passion with a man she hardly knew no matter how attractive he was or how starved she was to be held— especially when she would have to leave that man behind when the time finally came for her to return to the twentieth century.

She desperately feared falling in love with him. And it was something she knew could happen very easily. Rand was the sort of man any woman could easily love, and she simply could not afford another heartache in her life. At least not yet.

It was going to be hard enough to leave him behind as it was.

"You planning on rubbing a hole clean through that banister?"

Not aware that Faye had come up behind her, Alisha gasped then looked around. "You startled me."

"That's obvious," Faye commented, staring up at her from the floor below. She placed her hands on her slender hips and tilted her head to one side quizzically. "Is something bothering you?"

"No. Of course not," she replied, but when she saw the look of doubt on her new friend's face, she smiled. Faye had known her only a few days and already could tell when she was lying. "Well, maybe. I have to admit, I am getting a little tired of all this hard work. That's all we do from sunup to sundown. Work. Work. Work. And even though you and Millicent have shown me how to get my cleaning done more efficiently, I still am not finishing my chores as quickly as I'd like."

"Probably because you sit there and rub until the wood falls apart," Faye chuckled, then pointed to the spot Alisha continued to rub. "I really think you are finished there and can move on to those two tables near the door."

"You see? There's always more work for me to do," Alisha responded with a playful sigh.

Of all the people who could pull her out of a foul mood, Faye had proved one of the best. Perhaps it was because she always had such a ready smile.

"Well, at least we all have tomorrow afternoon and Sunday morning free to do as we please. That's what I wanted to talk to you about. Would you like to walk with Caroline and me to the dance tomorrow night? Everyone is going."

"Who is everyone?" she asked, even though she knew she dared not say yes and risk being seen by a policeman. Besides, if by chance Thomas did manage to give Jeremy Miller the money before then, she would want to use the opportunity of everyone being out of the house to dress in the men's clothes she'd stolen from the laundry and see if she could find Imena's small shop. Even though the danger the police posed should be minimal by then because they all should have been informed about the money's return, she would take no chance of there being even one officer who had failed to get the message. She did not enjoy being treated like a common criminal. Her scalp had not completely healed from the last time.

"Why, *everyone* is everyone," Faye answered, then counted them off on her slender fingers. "You, me, Caroline, William, Jolie, and even Millicent. It's a street dance and everyone who works around here is invited. Lots of unmarried men will be there."

Alisha wanted to smile at how excited Faye was

from the prospect of meeting someone special. It was the first time she had ever seen any real color in Faye's normally pallid cheeks. "Sorry, but I don't think I had better go to this one. I am really not feeling up to a dance right now. I would rather just stay home and read something out of Mr. Rand's library."

"But that means you'll be here all alone," Faye protested, then looked puzzled. "You mean you'd rather read a book than go to a dance and meet men? Don't you ever want to get married?"

"At the moment marriage does not interest me in the least and, yes, I really would prefer to be alone with a good book than be off in a crowd of people I don't know. The rest of you can go along without me."

"But nobody stays home on a Saturday night unless they're married or sick. Are you sick?"

"Not really, just tired. And although you might find it hard to believe, I really would rather stay here and enjoy the quiet than go with the rest of you to that dance."

"Please yourself, but I think you are making a mistake," Faye said, then shrugged her thin shoulders. "But if you change your mind between now and tomorrow night, be sure to let me know because you really will be all alone here. Even Mr. Rand will be gone. Tomorrow is his night to take Miss Collingsworth to the opera."

Alisha blinked at the unfamiliar name. "Miss Collingsworth. Who is Miss Collingsworth?"

"The fancy young lady who has her cap set

for Mr. Rand. Her family owns several restaurants over in the fourth district. Because every third Saturday night of the month is usually an opening night, that's when Mr. Rand takes her to the opera. It's expected of him."

"But I thought there were no special women in his life," Alisha said, surprised by the sudden jealousy she felt. "I thought he had the reputation of being a ladies' man." Or at least that was what he and Jolie had led her to believe.

"Oh, he does like to have his beautiful women around him, and he is known to see more than one, but Miss Collingsworth seems to be his favorite. He calls on her a little more often than he calls on the rest. Fact is most folks around here figure that one day he'll finally up and marry her, though I doubt it will be any day real soon. Mr. Rand is also a man who likes the freedom to come and go as he pleases. Still, I think it'll happen eventually. Mr. Rand likes children too much not to want some of his own." She smiled at the thought. "You should see how he dotes on that young nephew of his."

Alisha had a hard time visualizing Rand with children, although she had no trouble visualizing him surrounded by a whole harem of beautiful women wanting to bear him those children. She tried not to think of what it would be like to have someone like Rand make love to her. "What does his nephew look like?"

"A little like he does. Although the boy has blond hair like his mother, he has big pale blue eyes like his Uncle Rand." Her smile widened.

"Oh, he's going to be a heartbreaker, that one. Five years old and already has every one of us wrapped around his little finger. We all look forward to his visits."

"Oh, and how often does he visit here?"

"Usually about four times a year. Mr. Rand's sister likes to come to the city at least that often to do her seasonal shopping and go to the opera a time or two or maybe to some fancy ball." Faye continued to smile fondly with thoughts of Rand's sister and nephew, then looked at Alisha with a cocked eyebrow. "You see, even the Widow Williamson likes to go out and enjoy herself on Saturday nights. You are the only one I know who does not."

"Not again," Alisha moaned and pressed her lips together as if annoyed when what she really did was repress the urge to grin. Faye had a way of working any conversation to her advantage. "You never give up, do you?"

"Just thought I'd give it one more try. You are going to miss out on a lot of fun."

"Still, I'd rather stay home."

"Well, don't forget that if you do change your mind, you're welcome to go along with us. We won't be leaving here until six."

"I'll keep that in mind," she promised and watched the frail young woman head toward the back of the house. Faye was such a gaunt young thing. What with her light blond hair, her pale green eyes, and her fair skin, she looked like a ghost, especially when contrasted against the black dress she wore.

If it were not for her constant laughter and the sparkle ever present in her eyes, Alisha would think the girl was downright unhealthy. But except for the fact she was a little slower and a little weaker than the rest of them, nothing pointed to her being especially ill. Still, Alisha had to wonder what a good diet and a few hours out in the sun each day would do for her.

Deciding Faye was right, she had worked enough on the stairs, she tossed the polishing cloth into her cleaning box, then fought all the new aches and pains her body had developed over these past few days, as she headed for the tables near the front door. For some reason the cleaning of all three entrances had fallen on her alone, and even after she finished this one, she still had the side door to do.

Just as she set her box back down and reached inside for the furniture oil, she heard the front door open and smiled when she saw William come strutting in with a single, long-stemmed red rose held beneath his nose.

"Have you seen my woman?" he asked, lowering the rose.

"I think she's still out in the summer kitchen," Alisha told him and gestured toward the back of the house.

William smiled, revealing a set of startling white teeth, then held the rose out as if it were some sort of trophy. "Think she will like the flower I bring her?"

"Yes, I think she will."

"Enough to let me back into my own bed?"

His smile fell to a boyish pout. "Imagine her getting so angry with me over such a foolish thing. How was I to know that faro game would last into the night like that? I was not told."

Rather than risk sounding as if she had taken sides in one of the many arguments between the two, Alisha simply shrugged then pointed out, "I'm not the one you need to convince of that. Jolie is."

She then glanced at the still-open door behind him. "Where is Mr. Rand?"

She had learned early on that if she did not put the word *mister* in front of Rand's name that eyebrows tended to jump, especially William's.

"He's coming. Just stopped to say hello to one of the neighbors." He bent toward the large mirror that hung just above the table and checked to make sure his collar was straight before turning and heading toward the back of the house with his usual swagger.

Alisha chuckled when she heard him practicing aloud what he planned to say to Jolie. Those two. When they were not arguing, they were busy forgiving each other and making up. Rare was the moment when they were not doing either. Because of that, there was seldom a dull moment between them, which meant there was rarely a dull moment in that house.

Knowing she still had quite a bit of work to do and very little time in which to do it, Alisha quickly removed everything from the nearest table. When she did, she caught sight of her reflection in the same mirror William had just used and paused for a moment. It had been a week now but she still had a hard time adjusting to the odd fact that she was really someone else— at least for now.

While watching the reflection, she poured a thin trail of the yellow oil across the top of the narrow table, then reached for her polishing rag. She was busily rubbing the liquid into the wood's gleaming surface when Rand appeared in the doorway.

"My, my, I must say you are taking your new duties far more seriously than I ever thought you would. You may still be a little slower than some of the others, but I do have to admit that I haven't had any real trouble out of you yet. Not at all what I had expected."

Alisha's heart did its usual little leap upon hearing Rand's voice, but she kept working. She did not want Rand to know how easily he affected her or how pleased she was to hear that he appreciated her efforts. He might misinterpret her reasons. "Is that a compliment?"

"Yes, considering I thought you would try to botch your work more often than you have. And you've had only one temper tantrum. I am not only pleased, I am impressed."

Alisha grimaced at the memory of what she had done the morning she had been ordered to rehang the curtains in the dining room by herself, but then she really should not continue to feel so bad. She had already paid him back for the broken window by having worked several extra hours. "I couldn't get the curtains to look right no matter what I did. I was frustrated at the time."

"I'll say," he agreed with a disarming smile.

There was such amusement in his voice, Alisha glanced up to see his expression and became momentarily distracted by the deep dimples in his cheeks. Although she continued moving her polishing cloth in slow, easy circles, her gaze remained on Rand's handsome face as he continued.

"Jolie's still talking about the word that came out of your mouth just seconds before you hurled that curtain rod through the window. You really should watch that before someone realizes just where it was you picked up that sort of language. You don't want any of your fellow workers figuring out that before you came here you worked in a gambling house, do you?"

"No, of course not," Alisha said, then pushed an errant curl away from her face and looked back down at her work. "It really is not like me. It won't happen again." At least not for as long as *she* was in Andrea's body. She had no idea what sort of language Andrea herself might decide to use when she was returned to her original time period and discovered herself having been contracted as a servant for a year.

"Good," he said and stepped closer. "I don't want anyone becoming at all suspicious about you. So the less you act like someone who might have at one time worked in a gambling house the better."

Her heart gave another little leap when she

realized he now stood only a few feet from her. Remembering what had happened the last time he had stood that close, she decided to put distance between them and took a quick, precautionary step toward the far end of the table. "You're right. It's just that I am unaccustomed to this sort of work." And obviously so was Andrea, judging by how sore her body felt as a result of those past few days of labor.

"That's why I'm so proud of you."

Though he did not continue to pursue her, his smile deepened, reminding her yet again of how dangerously attractive he was. She watched him as he set the lightweight coat he carried onto that portion of the table she had already polished and loosened the black ribbon he wore for a tie.

"Proud?" Alisha had not expected the compliment and felt instantly warm all over. It had been ages since anyone had said they were proud of her, probably since before her parents' deaths. "I'm just doing what I promised to do. After all, you have more than fulfilled your part of the bargain; now it is up to me to fulfill mine." Or it was until the real Andrea finally returned and took over.

"That reminds me." His smile immediately faded. He glanced around to make certain no one was nearby, then spoke in a low, serious tone. "Your father went over to Miller's house today to give him the money and that letter you wrote."

Alisha's eyes rounded with hope. *At last!* "And did Miller accept them?"

"No. He refused both."

Alisha's heart sank with despair. It felt like a tiny part of her had been torn away. "Why?"

"Because he says *you* have to be the one to return that money to him. His reasoning is that you were the one who cheated him out of it, therefore you should be the one to gather your courage and return it."

Alisha's stomach clenched at the thought of having to face a man like him. She placed her polishing rag aside and wiped her hands on her apron while she studied Rand's grave expression. "And what did Thomas say to that?"

"That either Miller take the money or not, but that you were not going to come anywhere near him."

"But if I don't, doesn't Thomas run the risk of being severely beaten again? Don't you think Miller might again try to get to me through him?"

"Probably. But such action will do them no good. Your father will never tell them where you are. We all know that Miller will do far worse than administer a beating should he ever get his hands on you. You've made a fool out of him, Andrea. Miller and his brother are not the type of men who can live with that."

"So the police are still out trying to find me."

Rand nodded grimly. "Harder than ever. Word is that the reward for your capture is now at a thousand dollars, and as you know that's more than most men make in an entire year, especially those working on the police force—crooked or not."

"Then I don't dare show my face on the street just now," she muttered, aware her plan to escape just became a lot more dangerous.

"No, not if you value your life."

A chill skittered across Alisha's shoulders, then darted down her spine, raising goose bumps. "You don't think that they'd actually kill me, do you?"

Just having asked the question aloud caused a sudden rush of panic. Although she abhorred the thought of being molested by the likes of those men, even if the body was not hers, she certainly did not want to die in 1882, especially for something that was not her fault.

"After seeing what they did to your father, I don't know what they might have planned for you. And what's more, I don't care to find out."

"You saw Thomas?" She looked at him questioningly. "I thought you were going to stay away from him for fear the police would see you two together."

"I saw him from a distance, and he looks pitiful. He can't stand erect because of his ribs, and his face is a mass of bruises and cuts. Andrea, these are not kind people. They have no qualms about killing anyone who causes them trouble."

Alisha felt another cold rush of fear. "But I thought you said all they wanted was my virtue. That's frightening enough, but you didn't mention anything about them wanting to *kill* me. I thought all they wanted was to rough me up a little, then put me in jail for a few days."

"That was before you managed to stay hidden for so long. Your father has since told Dr. Owen that Miller and his men are *very* angry about that and that they have threatened to hurt him again if you don't come forward and take your punishment within the next few days."

"And you think they will kill me if I do," she repeated grimly. She pressed her hand over her mouth while she thought more about it. The situation was far more serious than she had realized.

"Yes. I think it has now become a matter of principle to them. They will want you to pay dearly for having caused them so much trouble and for having humiliated them the way you have. Keep in mind, not only did you cheat the chief's brother out of all that money, you've managed to escape some of the police force's best men twice already. They are all taking a lot of hounding for that. But then as long as you stay here where they can't find you, none of that will be a problem."

"Maybe not for you, but then you aren't the one being threatened by it all, are you?" she asked, her tone both amazed and bitter. How could he take the possibility of her death so lightly? "You aren't the one who's been made a prisoner here as a result."

Rand held up his hands. "Don't get upset with me. I'm not the one who created this problem. I am not the one who was foolish enough to cheat a man like Jeremy Miller out of all that money."

"Neither am I!" she said, frustrated that he still thought differently. It was upsetting enough to be trapped in 1882 and inside someone else's body, but to be constantly doubted made her want to scream.

Rand's expression darkened. "Don't start that I'm-not-really-Andrea-Knight speech of yours again. I'm in no mood to hear it."

He jerked his coat off the table and started to walk away but then stopped. "You know, I would think you'd be grateful enough for everything I've done for you thus far to stop lying to me. But you are not. You continue to lie to me at every turn. And for the life of me, I don't understand why."

"Is *that* why you're helping me?" she asked angrily. "So I'll feel grateful to you? Is that what prompted you to help?"

"Partly," he admitted. "And part of what prompted me is the fact that I've seen what those men can do when they are angry. Even to a woman. Or maybe I should say *especially* to a woman. Because of my shipping company, I am out on the docks almost every day. I've seen the bloody, mutilated bodies that are found there—both men and women. Bodies that are rumored to have been dumped there by the police themselves. And although I have no idea why, I would rather not see anything like that happen to you."

"Oh? So now you hope to convince me that you care?" She didn't know why she sounded so spiteful. His generosity far outweighed any underlying motive he might have. "How very noble."

Rand's blue eyes glinted. "I'm not trying to convince you of anything. You asked a question and I answered it. That's all. And if it makes you feel any better about me, one of the many reasons I have decided to help you in any way I can is because I don't appreciate men like Miller. I don't like what they get away with in this city. It's time someone showed them they are not as invincible as they think."

So, it was personal vengeance, she realized, glad finally to know the real motivation behind his actions. It was not just to get her into his bed, it was his way of striking back against some of the social injustices of his time.

Suddenly she saw Rand in a different light. Although Rand and Brad were alike in many ways, they were also different in many others. Brad manipulated people's lives for the sheer fun of it. At least Rand had a reason for what he did. While Brad was out to make no one but himself happy, Rand was out to hinder the crime that ran rampant in his city. While Brad was a selfish lord true only to himself, Rand was more the champion of causes.

"So you admit it's not for *my* good that you are doing all this," she said, still amazed by the revelation. "It is for *yours.*"

"It's a little of both I guess" he admitted. "But even if I do stand to gain a bit of personal satisfaction out of what I've done, I'd think you would still be grateful enough for the help you've received thus far to stop with all these lies. I don't like knowing that even after everything I've done to help out, you still don't trust me enough to be completely honest with me."

Frustrated, he reached up and jerked his tie off, then flung it over his arm alongside his coat. "I just don't understand why you continue to lie like that. It's not as though you have me fooled. I know who you are and what you've done, and in spite of knowing all that, I remain willing to do what is best for you."

Alisha eyed him skeptically. He was sounding a bit too noble again. "If you are so determined to do what is best for me, then why do I have to continue with all this hard work?" She gestured to the table that was now little more than half polished, then at her black dress and white apron, both spotted with patches of dust and grime. "Why is it I wake up every morning so sore I can hardly climb out of bed?"

"Because I happen to think that this *is* what is best for you," he answered in ready defense of himself. "You're not the type to take charity no matter how badly you need it. Your father told me that was why you went to work where you did and at such a young age. I don't happen to think it is a good idea for any woman as beautiful as you are to work inside a gambling house. So now you don't have to. You have a far more respectable job right here."

When he saw how unimpressed she was by everything he had just told her, he countered her scowl with a playful smile. "And you certainly can't complain about the wages. Not many women I know have the ability to earn well over fourteen thousand dollars in only one year's time. Truth is, not many of them earn that much in an entire lifetime. Not even those women who sell their personal pleasures in the better houses on Felicity Street. I know it is hard for you to see the advantage right now, but in the end you will be much better off because of what I have done." He paused. "At least you will still be alive."

Alisha could not very well argue against those points and felt ashamed for having complained to him at all. It was not as if she would have to work for him for the rest of her life. She should be able to find her way out of there within a few days. And even Andrea would not have to work there for more than a year. Hardly an injustice, considering what she gained in return. "I know I don't have the right, but could I ask you to do me one more favor?"

"What's that?" He looked at her warily, clearly not trusting how quickly her temper had subsided.

"Would you please try to see to it that Thomas is safe from Miller's men? I'm afraid for him. Imena has already told me that he will be killed if I don't do something to stop it."

"Imena?" Rand's dark eyebrows drew into a question while he contemplated the name. "Who is Imena? The name sounds familiar for some reason."

Alisha hesitated, knowing that if she told him the whole truth he would become angry with her all over again for continuing the bizarre story of a voodoo priestess having brought her there from the future. Instead, she offered only part of the truth. "She's one of those people who can see into the future. And what she has seen is Thomas's early death."

"I don't know if I believe in soothsayers, but as it turns out I've already taken care of that request. I have already hired two men to alternate keeping an eye on him just like I've hired a pair to watch my house. That should keep you and your father safe enough for now."

Alisha's forehead wrinkled. She was again perplexed. If Rand's real goal was merely to aggravate a few of the men he felt had ruined his city, why would he bother putting out more good money to hire protection for her and Thomas? How could protecting them from harm possibly help him in his quest to pester Miller and his men, especially if he was being so careful to keep his involvement a secret.

"By the way, Dr. Owen told me to tell you that your father sends his love to you and wants you to know that a friend named Ruby is taking good care of him and that he wishes he could come see you. But then he understands only too well how dangerous that could be for both of you. He'd rather wait until something has been done to calm Miller's desire to harm you or until he's finally turned his anger toward someone else."

Alisha felt a small pang of guilt because although she cared for the old man deeply, she could not honestly send her love back in return. Or could she? Perhaps that was part of the reason she worried so about him. Perhaps she did indeed love the man and in much the same way a daughter should love her father.

"Ask Dr. Owen to tell Thomas that I understand the danger and I don't expect him to try to come see me." Tears stung her eyes when she realized just how painful all this must be for the dear man. He had no way of knowing that Andrea was not really there, that his beloved daughter was not the one in danger right now. The poor man must be beside himself with worry.

Rand frowned, then pushed his soft brown hair away from his face with a quick flick of his fingers, evidence of his annoyance. "I wish you'd stop referring to him by his given name like that. Why can't you just call him what he is— your father? Why can't you give in at least that much? It would mean a lot to both of us."

Alisha thought about the request for a moment, then realized it could do her no harm. They deserved that much from her. "Okay, then ask Dr. Owen to tell *my father* that I understand why he has to stay away right now. And tell him that I'm glad he has someone like Ruby to take care of him."

For some reason having called Thomas her father felt genuinely good to her, and she smiled. "Have him also tell Father that I don't want him doing anything that might cause himself any more harm. Especially not in the next few weeks. He has to have time to heal." And she had to have time to get to Imena's before anything happened to him.

Rand smiled, too, satisfied to have gotten that far with her. "I'll tell him."

He turned and headed toward the stairs. He felt deeply pleased by what he had accomplished that day. Not only had he finally gotten Andrea to admit aloud that Thomas Knight was her father, he had hired four of the best marksmen from the Johnson Detective Agency to protect both her and her father from further harm.

He could rest a little easier that night.

Thirteen

Having Rand admit he was both pleased and proud of how hard she had worked during her time there made Alisha want to work all the harder. She liked seeing him smile and liked being the reason he did so. It made her feel good about herself and made being stuck in the insufferable year 1882 a little more bearable. And working hard allowed her to get Andrea's body into better shape so she would have more fortitude should she suddenly have to make another run for her life.

But mostly she worked hard and long because she really did like pleasing Rand and because she had fallen so far behind that day, largely due to brooding. Because she had promised Jolie to finish all the ground-floor entrances that day, she worked beyond what was normally quitting time for Rand's servants and was nearly two hours late entering the main kitchen for her supper.

It was well after eight o'clock. Only Jolie remained in the kitchen at that late hour. She stood before a cupboard putting away what was left of the clean dishes. Everyone else had gone to bed.

"Thought maybe you not plan to eat tonight," Jolie said, glancing over her shoulder at Alisha.

When she did, Alisha glimpsed the dark red rose displayed proudly in Jolie's dark hair and smiled. Obviously darling William had been forgiven— again.

"I wanted to finish my work before I ate," she said, then pushed several stray locks of hair off her damp forehead with her wrist. With very little breeze coming off the water that night, she had worked up quite a sweat during the last few hours. She had discarded her white mopcap long ago because the perspiration it collected burned one of the small cuts she still bore from the accident. Her underclothes, which she could not discard, now clung to her like a second skin.

Jolie gestured toward the mesh door which led to the shell-covered path to the summer kitchen where Alisha would find a plate sitting on a still-warm stove and a heavy cloth draped over it. "Dat what Faye told me. But when it turned so late and still you not come back to eat, I wondered if you planned to eat at all and if I should continue to keep your plate warm. I wondered if I should take it on outside and feed dat food to de cats in the alley like I do the table scraps. Because it so late, I did not know what to do. Why you not wait until tomorrow to finish your work? No one will think bad of you for dat."

"Because I'll have other chores to do tomorrow."

"Well, you surely do look tired. It a good thing you do not have to walk up but one flight of stairs tonight. I don't think you would make it up to de top floor where most of us sleep.

Alisha found just enough energy to smile. Jolie was the only one who did not seem to find it strange that she was allowed to sleep in one of Rand's nicer guest rooms. Or if she did think it odd, she never mentioned it. "The way I feel right now, I might just crawl over into the corner there and sleep right on the floor like some poor injured pup."

Jolie chuckled, then closed the cupboard door. "Since you know where de food is and can wash your own plate, I think I'll go on to bed now," she said, then touched the red rose in her hair with the tip of her finger. "William is in a very loving mood tonight."

"I don't doubt it," Alisha said, knowing he was still on the defensive for what he had done the night before. "You go on up. I'll make do on my own. Besides, I think I'd like to have a quick bath before going up to my room."

"You certainly know where de tub, de screen, and de kettles are. You one of de bathingest people I ever known."

"It helps keep me cool," Alisha said in ready defense of herself, knowing that the others bathed only twice a week— *if* then. How they tolerated being that sticky and grimy for that long was beyond her.

"You and Mr. Rand." Jolie shook her dark head. "Always wanting a bath even when you don't need one."

Alisha shrugged as if to say she could not help

it. She liked bathing even though what she would really like was a nice, long shower. It had been over a week since she had felt the delicate rush of water cascading over her tired skin.

"I see you in de morning. Don't forget to turn out de lamp in the other kitchen when you go to get your food and bring it back here to eat. Don't worry about dese." She gestured to the lamps around them. "Mr. Rand will get de ones down here when he comes in from wherever it is he went."

"Ran— " Alisha started to ask, then caught herself. *"Mr.* Rand is not here?" She had assumed he was either in his study reading or had already gone to bed. "But it was only a couple of hours ago that I saw him." Only a couple of hours since he had come very close to luring her into the garden. Her heart fluttered at the memory.

"Dat about the time he left. He said he had something important he wanted to take care of tonight and left out all by himself right after he finished his meal. Said he would probably be very late acoming back and I was not to bolt de door. Don't you bolt it either."

Alisha felt a sudden heaviness when she realized that the important something he wanted to take care of was probably himself. He had undoubtedly gone to see one of his many lovers— maybe even the beautiful, voluptuous Nicky, whom she remembered having met the night she first entered this time period.

Alisha had been told by the rest of the servants that it had been well over a week since Rand had been with anyone *special* and, according to them, a week was an incredibly long time for him to go without having entertained at least one beautiful young woman either in his home or in his coach. House gossip had it that Mr. Rand was not one to go long without his pleasure.

Her heart ached just knowing that was probably why he had left the house that night, although she had no idea why it should. Her dark scowl deepened when she tried to find a reason behind such a troubled reaction. If she had not known better, she might think she was jealous. But that was ridiculous. She did not know Rand Kincaid well enough to be jealous.

Pushing such perplexing thoughts aside, not wanting to have to come to terms with the ache still building inside her, she waited until Jolie had left, then walked out to the summer kitchen to get her food.

Since she was wanting a cold bath anyway, she did not stop to put any water on the stove to heat. Instead, she went ahead and turned out the lamp Jolie had left burning, then carried her food back across the yard to the main kitchen. There she ate her fill, then tossed the scraps outside with the rest.

After she washed her plate and glass, she began filling the tub with cool water. Although Jolie usually put only a few inches of water into the metal tub whenever she prepared a bath, Alisha wanted to submerge as much of her aching body in cool comfort as possible. She continued to haul water until the tub was half full, knowing her body weight would push that water the rest of the way to the rim.

It was not until she had set the pail aside, positioned the screen so that the bathing area was hidden from general view, and began unbuttoning her dress that she realized she had nothing to put on after she finished.

Too tired to go upstairs for the robe or one of the nightgowns Rand had provided her during her first day there, and finding that someone had already carried the clean laundry upstairs to the appropriate rooms, she decided she would have to make do with a couple of towels. But because the ones they provided were not as large or as fluffy as those she normally used, she knew she would need at least two to cover her more private areas and even that would leave plenty for view.

Still, she did not see that as much of a problem. It was after nine o'clock, and with Rand away and the others already in bed either on the top floor or in the rooms off the back of the house, she should be able to make it all the way upstairs without being seen.

Eagerly, she placed the towels on a small stool only a few feet from the tub. She then plopped a small piece of soap and a body brush directly into the tub and checked again to make sure the curtains of the only window with a view of her bathing area were pulled together.

Thinking everything finally ready she returned to the task of unbuttoning her clothes. Once unfastened, she gently peeled out of the heavy, sweat-soaked garments, then dropped them on the floor with a flop.

Enjoying the night air against her bare skin, something she did not feel often because of the many clothes she was expected to wear, she stepped into the tub, then scowled when she sank into its small confines. The round tub, though certainly functional, was so small she had to sit with her knees practically tucked under her chin. The water came only as high as her breasts, and the only way to sink her shoulders was to place her legs out of the tub entirely.

She certainly missed the huge pink and gold bathtub at her apartment that doubled as a whirlpool, and it galled her to know that Rand had a nice private bathing room at the back of the house with a large, footed porcelain tub, a heater for the winter, and both hot and cold water; yet she and the others were expected to take their baths in a small metal tub, in the kitchen, behind a small folded screen.

Scowling, she reached into the water for the small chunk of white soap she had tossed there and briskly lathered her skin.

Although it did not happen often and he had not intended for it to happen that night, Rand was stumbling drunk and he knew it. He had just spent the last two and a half hours sitting alone at a small table in one of New Orleans's most exclusive men's clubs sipping his whiskey straight— all because he could not work up the desire to take one of the many hostesses upstairs for a few hours of entertainment.

Something was obviously wrong with him. For the past week, whenever he saw what he normally would consider an enticing woman, his mind immediately compared her to Andrea Knight, and no matter how attractive or how vivacious she was, the lady always paled in comparison.

But then nothing could compare to Andrea's dark, expressive brown eyes or her shy, dimpled smile—unless maybe it was her own quick wit and that unfailing determination to live her life on her own terms. Even when being manipulated into working for him, she had agreed to it only after she had established her own rules. She had not simply accepted what everyone thought was best for her.

She definitely had a mind of her own.

In that respect Andrea was different from any woman he had ever known, so different and so fiercely independent that he longed to know her better. But she had made it perfectly clear to him that she did not want him getting to know her at all. She did not even want friendship from him. But then again, friendship was not what he wanted from her. His desire for her went well beyond that. Which was why he could think of no one else, not even when surrounded by beautiful women trained to accommodate a man's every need.

Andrea was in his every thought whether he wanted her there or not. It was as if he were obsessed by her. When he was not lying awake at night trying to figure out a way to capture her interest, he was asleep, dreaming about having already done so. Even when trying to work, she pulled at his thoughts. No matter how hard he tried, he could not completely rid himself of her image even for a moment.

But that was not the most frustrating part of the present situation. The most frustrating part was that Andrea Knight now refused to have anything to do with him.

Ever since that night he gave in to his growing desire and kissed her, she avoided him. No matter what he did to try to gain a few moments alone with her, she had managed to stay clear of him. The woman always had an excuse to be somewhere else. Always had something else more important to do.

It was almost as if she were afraid to be alone with him. Afraid that if given the opportunity, he might try to kiss her again.

Obviously Andrea had not enjoyed the kiss as much as he had originally thought— and certainly nowhere near to the degree he had enjoyed it. And that hurt his pride as much as it injured his heart. Never before had a woman shunned his advances with such adamance— never to the point of having invented a cheating husband just so she could scorn him for his own philandering. And not once had a woman claimed to be divorced as a way to cool his ardor.

But what was even more perplexing than her continued aloofness was the fact she seemed so eager to please him in every other way. At first she had botched nearly every chore given her, whether because of incompetence or by design he was not entirely sure; but that soon changed. Since then she had worked hard and long, improving her skills with each day's passing.

She had proved determined to do a good job, despite the circumstances that had brought her to him. So much so that shortly after supper that evening, he had gone in search of her with hopes of convincing her to go out into the garden with him to enjoy a cool glass of lemonade, but she was still working.

He had planned to invite Faye, too, so Andrea would feel more comfortable about going and so the others might not think he was singling her out, but instead of her being in the kitchen finishing supper with the others like he had expected, he had eventually found her still on her hands and knees, polishing the floor near the side entrance.

Despite his effort to convince her to stop, she continued with her work. She claimed it would not be fair to the others for her to quit before the job was done.

Rand wondered if maybe she was taking her responsibilities a bit too seriously. He pulled his carriage to a halt outside his house, then sighed. Perhaps her refusal was for the best. Had he managed to convince her to stop working long enough to sit and talk about herself, it would have been a conversation peppered with lies.

Despite all he had done for Andrea and her father during that past week, she still did not

trust him enough to tell him the truth. He may
have finally gotten her to concede that Thomas
really was her father, but she had yet to admit
anything else of consequence to him. No matter
what he did to try to earn her confidence, she
remained very distant toward him.

What does it take to win such a woman? he
wondered, knowing he wanted her to do much
more than clean his house. He wanted her to
be a *part* of his house. A part of his home. For
the first time since Christina Williamson, he was
actually considering marriage.

Frowning at the memory of what it felt like
to be jilted by a girl he so deeply loved and at
the tender age of eighteen, he staggered out of
the carriage and headed for the gate. Tina had
promised to marry him just as soon as she had
returned from that women's college in New York
she was so determined to attend, only the promise had proved empty because she never came
back. Instead, she stayed and married one of
her own professors, leaving her brother to be
the one to tell him the painful news. Was it any
wonder it had taken him this long to allow himself to be that deeply in love again?

His frown faltered when he realized that that
was exactly what was happening to him. After
all these years, he had finally allowed himself to
fall in love again. Only this time with a woman
who refused to even talk to him. *What logic.*

While considering his own stupidity, Rand
struggled a moment with the contrary gate latch
and wished he had thought to tell William to

leave it open for him. It was a minor oversight on his part, but a direct result of the frustration he had felt when he left.

After finally liberating the latch, he pushed the divided gate apart, then headed back to the carriage. Noticing a man standing in the shadows across the street, he knew it was one of the four detectives he had hired from Johnson's. He glanced in both directions to make sure no one else was on the street, then nodded discreetly to the man who in turned touched the brim of his hat, then patted the side of his coat where he kept his pistol.

Rand smiled briefly from the strong sense of security he felt knowing that someone was out there protecting his house and those inside it from any peculiar activities.

Although he thought it unlikely that the police would do anything to either him or his property again— not after the trouble he had caused them that last time— he liked knowing someone was out there ready to prevent trouble should he be wrong. Besides there was always the possibility that Miller might send hired thugs to do evil work.

Glad he had hired the men, Rand drove the carriage onto the drive, then closed the gate and barred it before continuing on inside the carriage house. There he unhitched the horse and led him into his stall, wishing now he had asked William to stay up and take care of the animal for him. He'd had far too much to drink that night and wanted only to go on inside and up to bed.

Muttering about having to do everything himself, he made sure the animal had water and oats, then quickly curried his coat, knowing if he didn't, the animal's hair would dry matted. Finally, he finished stabling the horse and was able to turn out the lamp and head toward the kitchen door.

Because he neglected to light a hand lantern and carry it with him, mainly because his mind was still too focused on Andrea, he stumbled on a small tree limb that had fallen across the path. Angry at his own drunkenness, he clomped up the steps, jerked the door open, and stumbled inside the lighted room.

While still holding on to the now-closed door, more for the support it offered than anything else, he heard a sharp gasp followed by the sound of water splashing.

He blinked with confusion. "Who's there?"

When no one answered, he noticed that the bath screen was up and that there was a lamp burning on the other side. "I said who's there?"

"Me. And I'm taking a bath. Go away."

Rand recognized Andrea's voice and blinked again. Why would she be taking a bath so late at night? He frowned at the oddity, but then slowly smiled when it dawned on him that if he could get to her clothes before she did, he finally had her.

With the agility of a much more sober man, he ducked around the screen and made a grab for the two towels he spotted on a nearby stool at the same time he snatched the clothes off the floor.

He saw Andrea begin to get out of the tub to make her own grab for the towels, but she dropped back down the moment she realized he was headed there, too. She sat with part of her body submerged in the frothy water and her knees drawn up to her chin. Her long hair had been tugged forward to cover the rest. But despite the effort, she could not hide all her bare beauty from him. He stared for a moment at the soft ivory shoulders peeping through the dark tresses and at the way the ends of her hair floated provocatively at her sides.

"Well, now," he said with a cocky wag of his head while he tossed the clothes haphazardly over the five-foot screen. He purposely held on to the two towels. "Looks like I finally have the advantage."

"What advantage?" she asked with a splendidly defiant lift of her chin, retaining as much dignity as a woman in her situation could.

"What advantage?" he repeated with arched eyebrows. "I'm not entirely sure, but I do believe that I am the one who holds the winning hand here and that these are my aces." He dangled the towels just out of her reach, wishing she would lift up and make a futile grab for one of them. How he would love to glimpse her treasures. "Do you happen to have anything that beats my pair of aces?"

"Stop playing games," she demanded angrily. She held out her hand but not her arm, revealing no more of her body to him than he had already seen. "Give me those."

She hugged her knees closer when instead of handing the towels to her, he tossed them on the floor well away from the tub.

"Pick those up and return them to me now," she tried again. Her eyes glinted like dark jewels in the lamplight.

Rand shook his head defiantly. "Nope."

"Rand, you have two choices. Either give me those two towels or give me back my clothes." She was so angry now her whole body shook, something that brought his attention back to the sudsy water, where he noticed tiny patches of clear water breaking through the quivering layer of bubbles that floated on top.

"Madam, I do believe that you are in no position to be giving me orders at the moment," he stated determinedly, then moved a few feet in hopes of getting a better view through the clear water. He frowned when he could make out nothing of consequence. "Get them yourself if you want them."

"I will not."

"Suit yourself, but as your bubbles there continue to disappear, I believe you will find the need for your towels continue to grow until finally you will choose to go and get them." He smiled as images of that played in his mind. Originally all he had planned to do was force her to sit and explain why she had been avoiding him during those past few days. But having seen her sitting there in the soft glow of that nearby lamp with absolutely nothing to hide her nakedness but her long, dark hair had caused him to alter those plans a bit. "Until then, perhaps we can pass the time by talking for a while. Let's see." He stroked his chin thoughtfully, the whole time swaying slightly from side to side.

He frowned at his inability to steady himself and wished now he had not drank quite so much whiskey while brooding at the Customhouse. He'd certainly like to be able to remember when morning came whatever it was he was about to see. "What shall we talk about? Oh, I know. Maybe we could discuss the fact that you have been avoiding me these past few days. We could discuss why you haven't let me have even one little moment alone with you since you started to work here when all I want to do is get to know you better. Is that really so much for the man who saved your virtue if not your very life to ask?"

"Rand, you are drunk!" she replied.

"And you, woman, are naked," he quipped. He grinned when he realized just *how* naked. There wasn't one stitch of clothing on that entire beautiful body.

Alisha's expression darkened with intent. "That happens to be the very reason why I want those towels returned to me."

"And that also happens to be the very reason why I want them to stay right where they are." His grin widened. "At least until you decide it worth your while to dash over there and get them. Until then, I guess you could say I hold you captive. You are not getting away from me this time, my beauty."

Alisha took and released a long, deep breath before speaking slowly and quite distinctly. "If you do not hand me those towels or my clothes right now, I am going to throw my head back and scream at the very top of my voice until I wake up every person in this house." Her eyes narrowed and her nostrils flared in preparation to fulfill that very threat.

Rand scowled. He had not considered that possibility.

"Damn," he cursed aloud, then bent over, picked up the two towels, and hurled them at her. Because his aim was off, largely due to his drunkenness, both towels fell into the water and became instantly soaked, but that did not prevent her from wrapping them both around her.

Irritated to know she had *again* gotten the better of him, he glowered at her a moment, then stalked angrily out of the kitchen.

"That damned, contrary woman," he muttered while he stormed up the stairs, taking them two at a time. "She is still too big for her own britches."

Despite his anger, a devilish grin replaced his dark scowl. *What britches?*

The woman wore only towels.

Alisha was careful to take the back stairs down to breakfast the following morning. She was afraid Rand might still be angry with her and she was not ready for another confrontation. But as it turned out, he had already come downstairs, eaten his breakfast, and left the house, making her precautions unnecessary.

She wondered if his early departure on a Saturday was due more to embarrassment than the business engagement he had claimed to have. Perhaps after having sobered, he realized what a jerk he had been and did not want to be reminded of such behavior. Or it could be that she was reading much more into the situation.

But Alisha did not have time to dwell on such matters for long. Faye would not let her. She was too busy trying to convince her to go with them to the street dance that night. But Alisha was determined to stay there.

After a long, mostly sleepless night, she had decided that there was no reason to put it off any longer. That coming night would be the night.

Not only had Jeremy Miller flatly refused the money Thomas tried to give him that would have more than repaid his loss, he had refused to as much as touch her carefully written letter of apology. That meant the danger of being captured would always be there. Waiting would change nothing.

That was why, as soon as everyone left, Alisha planned to slip into the men's clothing she had taken, hide her bulky hair beneath one of Rand's large bowler hats, then as soon as it turned dark enough to shadow her face, she would slip out into the street and try to find

Imena's shop. With any luck, everyone would accept her disguise and think she was a man. But just to be cautious, she would do everything she could to avoid any of the policemen she encountered along the way.

With her stomach squirming and knotted, knowing that by morning she would be either safely back in the twentieth century or dead, Alisha had a hard time concentrating on her chores that morning. By midafternoon, when it came time to quit work so those going to the dance could get ready, she was consumed with worry, knowing all that could go wrong with such a risky plan. But she refused to let her fears get the better of her. Danger or no danger, she would see the plan through.

The last hours of that day passed at a snail's pace until finally it was time for everyone to leave. Jolie and William left first, wanting to stop and collect Jolie's cousin along the way. Millicent followed only a few minutes later. Then finally it was Faye and Caroline's turn to leave.

"Alisha, are you absolutely certain you don't want to come with us?" Faye tried one last time to convince her to go.

"Yes, I'm quite certain," Alisha said, glad now that Rand had decided to introduce her to these people by what he thought was her invented name. Even though he had done so for purely protective reasons and not because he believed her in any way, she was glad that Faye would be telling her goodbye while using her real name.

In the short time Alisha had been there, she had become very fond of the quiet, fragile young woman, and even though she was so much the opposite of Roni, whom she was so used to being with, she would miss her.

A sharp pang of longing shot through Alisha when she thought of Roni. Although she truly liked the people around her, she missed her best friend dearly. She missed being able to kid with her and missed trying to outquip her whenever they were in one of their more playful moods. Alisha had learned early on that people in the 1800s took whatever she said seriously, even when said in jest. It was not that they did not have a sense of humor, because they did, it was just different in many ways and that had taken some adjustment on her part.

It became immediately obvious that these people had not been exposed to the frivolous sort of banter that occurred in modern sitcoms or during most late-night talk shows. At times that was refreshing, but at other times she missed being able to taunt and tease, and be teased.

Despite the many problems she knew she would face upon her return, her heart fluttered happily at the thought of finally being back home. It had been over a week since her abduction. Over a week since she'd seen her friends or had sat at her desk.

"You two just run along and enjoy yourselves. I'll be fine."

Faye frowned then looked at Caroline as if hoping the older girl would offer a viable reason for Alisha to change her mind. When that did

not happen, she finally shrugged then did a little curtsy to show off her burgundy-colored
dress.

"You look beautiful," Alisha lied, for although
it was a lovely dress, the dark shade made Faye's
skin look just that much more pale. The girl had
no color. "The men there are going to be quite
impressed."

Faye came as near to blushing as Alisha had
seen her. "Just as long as one of them asks me
to dance." Sighing, she gave Alisha one last im-
ploring look, then shrugged when it was apparent Alisha would not change her mind. "I'll stop
by your room when I return and tell you all
about it."

"Only if I'm awake," she cautioned, not wanting anyone to realize she was gone until morning. She did not want to take the chance that
they might try to track her down before she was
able to find Imena. "If I don't answer when you
first tap at the door, wait until morning."

Faye nodded. When Caroline headed toward
the front door, she waved and quickly followed.
"Goodbye, Alisha," she called as she hurried
across the veranda, then down the steps.

"Goodbye, Faye, I'll miss you," she responded
quietly, knowing the two were too far away to
hear her anyway. For a moment she felt very
sad. She knew, if all went right, that would be
the last glimpse she ever had of her new friends.

She stood near a window and watched while
they hurried off to join another group of
women, also colorfully dressed. She sighed wist-

fully while she watched, knowing how much she would miss them.

She waited until they were no longer in her sight then went upstairs. She was still feeling a little melancholy when she passed the door to Rand's room, knowing she would miss him most of all.

Hoping to indulge herself in one last memory and knowing she needed a belt to keep the clothing she planned to wear from falling off of her small frame, she stepped inside to have a look around what turned out to be a decidedly masculine room.

The walls were stark white with mahogany trim that matched the floor. A dark blue carpet the same shade as the heavy drapes lay centered beneath a massive fourposter. Other furniture included two large chests of drawers— one with a swivel mirror on top— an elaborately designed wardrobe, a commode, a night table, and a small grouping of comfortable chairs, upholstered in dark blue.

While looking for the belt she needed, she noticed several articles scattered across the top of one chest. With a heavy heart, she picked up the porcelain-backed hairbrush and touched it to her own hair, then held it tenderly against her breast while her thoughts strayed to that night in the summer kitchen when he kissed her so unexpectantly.

How gently but masterfully he had kissed her, so unlike the quick, hard kisses Brad had bestowed upon her whenever he felt the need. If only she had known what she was missing then perhaps she could have shown Brad a better way, but then what good would that have done? He would just take what he had learned and offer it to other women.

Tears filled Alisha's eyes when she realized she might never have a man in her life whose kiss or even whose smile would affect her as powerfully as Rand's did. How desperately she would miss him after her return.

In a way, she wished she could have seen him one last time before leaving. Even though it would make little sense for her to tell him goodbye, since eventually this same body would return to him with the real Andrea inside, she longed to hear his sultry voice and see those pale blue eyes sparkling above that dimpled smile one last time.

Filled with sorrow, knowing now that she had come to care for Rand far more than she should, she set the brush back down, then did what she could to shake the gloom cloaking her. With a narrow leather belt in hand and a heavy ache filling her heart, she headed off toward her own bedroom.

There she changed into the blue shirt and black trousers she had taken from the laundry days ago and strapped them to her with the belt. She then twisted her hair into a tight ball and anchored it into place with the plain black hair-combs Faye had loaned her earlier in the week. When she glanced into the mirror to view the effect of her disguise thus far, she was perplexed to see how shapely she looked even in the baggy clothes.

With nothing to bind herself and time running out, for it was already turning dark outside, she decided to just make do the way she was. She would stay to the night shadows, and if she came across a policeman on the street, she would walk with her head turned away and shoulders hunched forward.

Counting on the fact that there were always a half-dozen or more hats on the wall rack just inside the front door, she gave her bedroom one last glance, pleased with how neat she left it. She then took her purse out of the drawer where she had kept it hidden beneath the underclothes Rand had bought her, and headed downstairs.

She stopped beside the door that led into Rand's study and considered leaving him a note. She wanted to thank him for all he had done for her but realized that would only confuse matters once the real Andrea returned. As would a note left for Faye or any of the others.

She closed her eyes against the sharp, sudden pain those last thoughts had caused and recognized it for what it was. Jealously. She was jealous of Andrea—jealous that she would be the one returning to a man like Rand, a man obviously interested in her and who had the power to make the earth move with just one kiss. It was then Alisha realized just how deeply she did care for him. She pressed her eyes shut to keep her grief from overwhelming her.

The awful truth was that she had fallen in

love with a man she would never see again. The
pain she felt now would be a long time in healing, but there was nothing she could do about
that now. What she felt for Rand was already a
part of her.

With her hour of reckoning clearly at hand
and knowing that if she didn't collect her wits
about her before leaving that house she could
end up killed long before reaching Imena's
shop, she again pushed her gloom aside and focused on the matter at hand. She hurried on to
the front door. Her breath came in short, rapid
bursts while she quickly selected a hat. Within
a very few minutes, she would be on her way.

Filled with a conflicting combination of fear,
sadness, and excitement, she moved toward the
mirror where she quickly tucked every last curl
out of sight. While checking to make sure the
hat was secure, she gazed at the reflection curiously, knowing that would probably be the last
time she would have to stare at Andrea's face
instead of her own, then picked up her purse
again and headed immediately for the back
door.

Because she remembered Rand mentioning
there was a detective hiding somewhere out
front, she decided to go out the back way. She
was just reaching for the latch when suddenly
the door swung open and Rand stepped inside.

His face registered immediate anger.

Fourteen

"Where in the hell do you think you are going?" Rand thundered. His blue eyes glinted with rage. He slammed the door behind him with a loud, shattering crack.

Alisha swallowed hard. She had never seen him look so angry. She had never seen *anyone* look so angry. It took all the nerve she had just to answer him.

"Out."

"Out? Out where?" With an expression filled with fury, he took a menacing step toward her, his arms stiff at his sides.

Alisha's heart drummed a frantic rhythm as she quickly backed away, all the while trying to come up with a calming answer. Anything besides the truth, which she knew would only enrage him more. "To the dance. I was curious to see the festivities and thought if I went in a clever disguise no one would realize who I was."

Knowing the purse might get in her way should she suddenly find a need to take flight, she set it on a nearby counter while continuing to back away from Rand.

"And you think *that* is a clever disguise?" he

asked. He continued to move steadily toward her while gesturing to her breasts, which pushed out the lines of an otherwise flat shirt. "You think that people will look at those clothes and not notice the shape beneath them?"

Aware she was about to back herself against a wall, Alisha stopped and lifted her chin in defiance. "Not if I pull my shoulders in and stay off in the shadows."

"There are no shadows at the dance. The place is very well lit, as are the streets along the way." Still angry, he took one last step forward, then grasped her sharply by the shoulders. His fingers dug deep into Alisha's tender flesh. "I can't believe you'd try something so dangerous. You can't be trusted at all, can you?"

Alisha winced from the pain. "You are hurting me."

Rand did not ease his grip. He was still too angry. "When I think what might have happened if I hadn't decided to come back here and apologize to you for the way I behaved last night," he said, forcing his words past tightly clenched teeth. "It makes me want to throttle you."

"I'm sorry. If it means that much to you, I won't go." Again she winced, for his grip tightened more.

"You're damn right you won't go," he vowed in a whisper so fierce it sounded like a growl. "Because I'm not going to let you step one foot out that door."

Alisha continued to grimace from the pain his

grip caused, then looked at him beseechingly. It was that pitiful gaze that made Rand finally realize the death hold he had on her. Finally he let go but did not step away.

When he spoke again, it was in a much calmer voice. "I'm sorry, it's just that you scared me half to death with what you tried to do. I didn't mean to hurt you like that." He shook his head at the irony of what had happened. "Truth is I came home because I wanted to help protect you. I knew that everyone else would be going off to that dance and that would leave you here alone."

"I thought you had a man outside protecting the house," she said, wondering now if that were true.

"I do, but I'm not sure that's enough. At least not tonight. Not when everyone knows that my regular staff is away at that dance. If the police even suspect that you might be here, tonight would be the perfect night for them to try to steal you away."

"So you came home because you were worried about me?" she asked, finding that thought oddly comforting. Suddenly the pain in her shoulders no longer mattered.

"Yes, and to apologize for what I did last night. I was a little drunk."

"A *little*?" Her eyes rounded at the understatement.

"Okay," he admitted and the first glimmer of a grin tugged at his ample mouth. "I was very drunk. The truth is, I haven't come home quite that drunk since my youth." The smile that broke his face was flanked with boyish dimples.

"And what happened last night that made you come home that drunk again?" she asked, pleased the harsh lines of anger that had spoiled his handsome face had disappeared. Knowing now that she would not be leaving that house anytime soon, she pulled off the hat and set it aside. Carefully she removed the combs from her hair and let the heavy mass fall loosely across her shoulders. Suddenly, it felt very awkward to be standing there in front of him dressed so much like a man. "Or do I dare ask?"

Rand's smile quickly faded and a look of seriousness returned. "I was angry with you for refusing to stop working long enough to talk with me last night. You've been here since Monday, and except for those few minutes out in the summer kitchen that first night, you have repeatedly refused to be alone with me. Why is that?"

Alisha was surprised by the anguish she saw in his dark expression.

"Because I'm afraid to be alone with you." There was just something about having Rand that close to her that made Alisha want to be honest with him.

"But why?" he asked, clearly baffled. "What have I done to make you afraid of me?"

"No, not of you. I'm more afraid of me and of what I might do should I ever catch myself alone with you again. Rand, you are a very attractive man and I am a very vulnerable woman right now. That could prove to be an extremely dangerous combination if we ever found ourselves alone together."

"Dangerous how?"

Alisha looked away. "Dangerous in that I could end up falling deeply and forever in love with you."

"And that's bad?" He scratched his head.

She reluctantly returned her gaze to his and quivered when she noticed how intently he studied her. He wanted the truth. "It could be for me. That's why I don't dare be alone with you.

Rand returned his hands to her shoulders, this time to hold her gently in front of him. "But we are alone together now," he said in a deep, beckoning voice. His eyes became heavily lidded.

Alisha swallowed, unable to pull her gaze away from his handsome features. "I know."

"And are you afraid?" He bent slightly so he could better see into the depths of her dark eyes.

She felt a vibrant, invisible current pass between them.

"Yes."

"Too afraid to let me kiss you?"

Alisha's heart leaped wildly at the thought. She remembered only too well the power hiding within his kiss. "Rand, if I were to let you kiss me now, there's a strong chance we'd end up in bed."

"And that's supposed to discourage me?" he asked, already dipping toward her mouth. "As you might recall, I've wanted you from the start. You are already a very real part of me."

Even before Rand's lips touched hers, Alisha knew she was lost. Her pulse raced and her body felt weak, as if her bones had suddenly turned to liquid.

Although certain she would live to regret her actions, she could no longer deny what she felt for Rand. Nor could she deny how, at that moment, more than anything else, she wanted him to make love to her. She wanted to feel his sturdy arms around her again. Wanted to know what it was like to be held and loved by a man so powerfully strong, yet so amazingly tender.

With a hunger that must have been growing since that very first night she met him, she leaned forward and met the kiss halfway.

Rand groaned in response to such unexpected willingness. He wrapped his arms around her and pressed her soft body hard against his.

Alisha felt exhilarated beyond belief. The emotions that washed through her were more powerful than any she had ever known. They consumed her completely. It was hard to believe that she had opened her heart again so easily after what Brad had done to her. She had thought she would never love again, yet here she was more deeply in love than she'd ever been.

Closing her eyes to better enjoy the many sensations sweeping her body, she slid her hands up behind his neck. Although he already held her firmly in place, she pressed herself against him harder still, all the while wishing there was some way she could pull herself right on inside him.

With equal ardor, Rand's arms closed tighter around her while he dipped inside her mouth with his tongue.

Alisha shuddered in response to the sensual assault. She had never felt such an immediate craving for any man. Even though she was well-aware that this was just one short fleeting moment and not something that could ever be a permanent part of her life, she did not consider pulling away.

Despite all this, she could tuck this interlude away in her mind and carry it with her forever. It would always remind her of the very real love she felt for this man. She longed to have at least a memory to cling to. So much so, she dug her fingers deep into his flesh and pressed him closer. Never had she felt such an immediate need.

Nor had Rand. Andrea Knight was different from any woman he had ever seduced. That much was clear to him from the onset. And knowing that made what was about to happen between them all the more exciting.

Aware Alisha was just as swept away by the passion that had engulfed them as he was, he felt no qualms about pursuing that which they both needed. Fervently, he moved one hand to cup the fullness of her breast and caressed it through the soft linen of his shirt. He could tell by the firmness and rigidity of her nipple that she wore nothing underneath. Obviously, she had dressed like a man in earnest. That both pleased and amused him.

As she had showed no resistance to the intimacy he had displayed thus far, he reached for the buttons of her shirt. Starting with the one at her slender throat, he slowly worked downward. When he had the shirt half-undone and realized just how wondrous the treasures were that awaited him beneath, he could tarry no longer. With both hands, he ripped the shirt open. The remaining white buttons scattered in all directions.

Alisha's eyes flew open at such a fine display of passion and felt as proud as she was excited to know he was that eager to see and touch her. Not wanting to hinder his progress, she arched her shoulders back to make it easier for him to tug the shirt off and out of their way.

When her shoulders thrust back, her breasts lifted up, causing him to moan with expectation while he hurried to unfasten the belt that held the trousers she wore in place.

Because Rand had never taken trousers off a woman before, he found it not only odd but strangely provocative. His whole body ached with anticipation when he knelt to tug off her boots, for his actions put his face only inches from her taut stomach.

As soon as her boots and stockings were removed, he quickly tugged the baggy trousers down over her slender hips. It took just a moment more to untie the cotton bloomers she wore and discard them as well.

By the time he had the last of her clothing removed, he was so frantic with need that he virtually tore his own off; then, despite their strongly aroused passion, he returned to the simple task of kissing her. He reveled in the feel of her naked breasts pressing firmly against his bare chest. So much so, it nearly drove him to madness.

Meanwhile Alisha's body absorbed the pleasures hidden in Rand's ardent embrace and the wonderful feel of his mouth as it effectively commanded hers. The deep ache of longing he had aroused inside of her flamed into a furious fit of desire. She pressed herself harder against him, eager to experience all there was to experience from this one encounter. She knew it would be a long time before she again felt such true passion— if ever.

Hungrily, she pressed her fingertips deep into the strong muscles of his back, marveling at how that drove him into a further frenzy. Aching for release, she broke away from the kiss and looked pleadingly into his pale blue eyes. Silently she encouraged him to find a place for them to lie down— before her knees collapsed on her right there and they ended up making love on the hard, cold kitchen floor.

Rand understood the unspoken message, and she gasped softly when instead of leading her by the hand like she had expected, Rand swept her into his arms and carried her away.

Not wanting their passion to lessen, he held her high in his arms, continuing the wondrous act of kissing her.

Thinking he was probably headed to the par-

lor just down the hall where they would have
their choice of several comfortable sofas, she was
further surprised when he turned and carted
her up the stairs instead.

Within minutes they were inside the warm,
velvety shadows of his bedroom. There, he gently laid her in the center of his massive bed. He
paused just long enough to part the drapes closest to the bed, allowing a stream of moonlight
to splash over her before he lay down beside
her. Fighting the desire to take her immediately,
he pulled her into his embrace again and kissed
her gently.

Lightly, he dipped the tip of his tongue past
her parted lips and again savored the sweet taste
of her, and was warmly rewarded when she did
the same.

Enjoying this simple exploration of each
other, knowing that in time their passions would
soar yet again, he rolled so that he lay partly on
top of her. While he allowed his lips to remain
on her sweetly demanding mouth, he eased his
free hand down over the smooth curves that
formed her body, aware of how much more la-
bored her breath became with each gentle
touch. He felt a beautiful sense of accomplishment just knowing he was capable of giving her
such true and basic pleasure. Because of that,
he held back his own growing response and continued to carry her from one height of arousal
to another. He wanted this to be an experience
she would cherish forever.

Alisha was again lost in the twisting torrent

of emotions that Rand had so masterfully stirred to life inside her when once again he cupped her breast with a strong hand and gently played with the tip until it grew rigid. Liquid fire coursed through her while her needs spiraled ever higher. Every part of her yearned for release.

Closing her eyes, she trembled with expectation while his skilled touch sent wave after delicious wave of pure ecstasy teeming through her body. Writhing from the gentle torture, she arched her back and thrust her breasts ever higher, knowing his hand would follow. When he finally broke his kiss to gaze down at her writhing form, she moaned aloud her protest and reached out to bring his splendid mouth back to hers.

Rand obliged her with another long, plundering kiss, but then brought his lips away again, this time to trail feathery kisses downward until he finally arrived at one of her swelling breasts. Deftly, his tongue teased the tip with short, tantalizing strokes while his long hair teased the sensitive skin surrounding the breast. He nipped and suckled the hardened tip until she cried aloud from the sheer pleasure that brought her. Then, just when she thought she could bear no more, he moved to the other breast where again he suckled, nipped, and tugged. Alisha bit the sensitive pulp of her lip while her body trembled. Never had a man gone to such lengths to ignite her passion.

Not certain how much longer she could endure his tender torment, she grasped his shoulders to encourage him to stop this delicate torture and bring her the release she so desperately sought. But despite her urgings, his mouth continued its sweet assault, and she shuddered from the delectable sensations that continued to build inside her until she felt certain she would burst with ecstasy.

The delicious ache that had centered itself low in her abdomen grew steadily stronger, and her whole body craved release from the sensual agony that burned inside her.

"Rand," she murmured, only vaguely aware she had spoken the name aloud. "Now."

Her head tossed from side to side while Rand suckled first one breast, then the other one last time before finally moving to fulfill her blistering needs. Once inside, with smooth, lithe movements, he brought their wildest longings, their deepest needs to the ultimate height they both so desperately sought. When release came for Alisha, it was so wondrous and so deeply shattering that she gasped aloud with pleasure. Only a moment later, the same shuddering release came for Rand.

With their passions finally spent and satisfaction cloaking them with its warmth, he rolled over onto the bed beside her and cradled her gently in his arms. For nearly an hour they lay perfectly still, listening to the steady rhythm of each other's heartbeat, bound together in each other's embrace, too amazed to speak.

Alisha lay in quiet awe, for what had happened between them was like nothing she had experienced in all her years of lovemaking with Brad. She felt pleased knowing that when she finally returned to her own century she would have that most wonderful memory to carry back with her. The memory of what it was like to be made love to by a man who knew exactly what was needed to satisfy a woman both sexually and emotionally.

She closed her eyes and, for a moment, wished that sort of passion could be hers forever but at the same time knew it could not. Although their evening of lovemaking had temporarily cushioned the disappointment she felt from having her earlier plans so easily thwarted, she knew that time was running out for her. With less than two weeks left, she would have to try leaving again very soon.

Rand waited until after eleven o'clock before slipping his arm from around Alisha's warm body and rolling off the bed. Thinking her asleep, he walked quietly toward his dresser where he lit a single lamp, then opened one of his drawers.

Having felt him leave, Alisha opened her eyes and quietly watched the lithe movements of his magnificent body for a moment. As he pulled a pair of folded trousers out of the drawer, she asked, "Where are you going?"

She rolled over onto her side and propped herself with a steady elbow.

"I thought I'd better make a quick trip downstairs to gather up our clothes before the others return," he said, then smiled at her playfully while he stepped into the trousers then slid them up over his lean hips. "Or should I say to gather up *my* clothes since that's who they all belong to. The others might think it strange to find so many of my clothes strewn about the kitchen like that." Without bothering to put on a shirt, he stopped beside the bed, then bent over to kiss her first on the forehead then at the corner of her mouth. "I'll be right back. Don't you dare go away."

"But I'll have to return to my own bed before they all come back," she protested, though in truth she did not want to go. Not yet. She was too happy being in his bed, pretending that she belonged.

Rand looked at her, puzzled. "Why leave? No one else sleeps on this floor."

"I know. But Faye plans to come by my room and tell me all about her evening as soon as they return. When she peers inside and sees that I'm gone at such a late hour, she'll wonder where I am."

"I'll shut your door so she will think you are inside asleep," he said and bent to kiss her again, this time on the other corner of her mouth. "She'll never have to know where you stayed the night."

A breeze wafted through the nearest window and caught the front locks of his tousled hair, reminding her how soft his hair had felt when grazing her bare skin.

"But I can't sleep here."

Rand's blue eyes sparkled with mischief. "Who said anything about *sleep*?" He bent yet again, this time to kiss her fully but quickly on the lips. "Certainly not me."

"But if I don't get any sleep I won't be able to stay awake tomorrow morning."

"Why is that a problem? Tomorrow is Sunday. Everyone but Caroline will sleep late, and the only reason she will be up early is because she goes to church." He kissed her again. This time he caught her lower lip with his teeth and tugged gently. His blue eyes darkened with more than mere devilment when he then bent lower and kissed the tops of her breasts individually. "I told you. I'm not through with you yet."

Alisha's body tingled at the thought of yet a second round of such passionate lovemaking but held fast to the notion she should leave. "Rand, I was wrong to let that happen. Especially when you consider my situation."

"Are you trying to tell me that you didn't enjoy what just happened between us?" he asked doubtfully while he bent again to kiss one of her nipples. He offered another of his slow, heart-stopping smiles when instead of pulling away, she moaned softly, then rolled onto her back and held her arms out to him.

"Of course, I enjoyed it. You are a master at lovemaking," she admitted, though sadly. "I know I will never have another man in my life like you."

"As well you should not," he responded and bent to kiss the other nipple, this time tugging at it lightly with his teeth. His eyes twinkled when her eyelids drifted close in response. "I'll not have my wife taking an outside lover."

Alisha's eyes flew open instantly. "You'll *what*?"

"I'll not have my wife taking an outside lover." He paused, then peered at her quizzically. "Didn't I mention that I love you and that I want to marry you?"

"No you did not," she answered, knowing that if he had, she would never have allowed him to make love to her. It was bad enough that *she* would suffer a traumatic loss when the time came for her to leave, but she did not want him to suffer one as well. It had never occurred to her that she might mean more to him than his other lovers.

"Then let me mention that now," he said, grinning at the perplexed expression on her face. "I've spent all day thinking about it. I want you to marry me. I want such pleasure to be mine forever."

"But I can't marry you." She sat up and hugged a pillow to her.

Rand's grin faded immediately. "Why not?"

"Well, for one thing we are far too different," she said, stating the obvious first. "We come from two entirely different worlds."

"True, but those are differences we can overcome. All that matters is that we love each other and that we long to make each other happy," he said, then narrowed his gaze while he stared at her pointedly. "You do love me, don't you?"

Pressing the pillow harder against her aching

heart, Alisha looked at him for a long moment, then nodded. She could not lie to him about how she felt, not after what had passed between them.

"Then marry me."

"It's not as simple as that," she said, wondering how angry he would become if she tried again to explain that she was from another time period or that she would soon be going back.

Not feeling up to having another argument, especially after they had started to get along so well, she finally just shook her head and remained firm. "I love you but I can't marry you." Tears filled her eyes, knowing that if the situation were any different she would be sorely tempted to say yes and marry him. He would make a wonderful husband. But as it was she could not even consider that. Could not even fantasize about it, for the resulting disappointment would be too great.

Upon seeing her tears, Rand sat down on the bed beside her and pulled both her and the pillow into his arms. "If you are turning me down because you've had another lover, then don't. I have already realized that fact and I don't care. I love you no matter what you might have done."

Alisha squeezed her eyes shut, knowing he had to be the most generous, most forgiving man she had ever met. If only she *could* stay and marry him— but that was such a ridiculous notion. She belonged in the twentieth century. "Marriage just wouldn't work for us."

"I'm sorry, but I cannot accept that answer.

At least not yet. I love you too much to let you go that easily." He lifted a corner of the linen pillow cover and gently dabbed at the moisture that glimmered in the corners of her eyes. "Will you at least think about it?"

Knowing she would be able to think of little else, even long after she had returned to her own time, she opened her eyes again and nodded, but refused to look at him. It hurt too much to see such a hopeful expression. "Okay, I'll think about it. But I can't promise that I'll change my mind."

Rand continued to hold her close. "Just as long as you leave the door to marriage open for me, that's all I ask for now."

Alisha could hold back a heavy flow of tears no longer. Breaking free, she wrapped herself in his comforter and sobbed uncontrollably while she fled his bedroom. He followed only as far as his door.

Fifteen

Alisha got little sleep that night. There were too many rampant thoughts plaguing her. Too many emotions struggling for her attention. She had to deal with being disappointed, afraid, and in love all at the same time, because not only was she still stuck in 1882 where she did not belong and where her life remained in danger, she had a whole new problem facing her. Foolishly, she had allowed herself to fall in love with Rand, knowing she would soon have to leave him behind.

Because of how very much she had come to love him, she was deeply saddened by his beautiful proposal of marriage and at the same time a little leery of it. She could not help but be skeptical at how easily those sweet words of endearment had rolled off his tongue. How well she remembered Brad's lavish declarations of love, delivered even after he had slept with that precious little secretary. It was hard not to equate Rand's eloquent avowals of love with those of her unfaithful husband.

But even if it turned out Rand's declarations were sincere, it was not *her* he loved. He loved the woman he thought she was. He loved the woman he wanted her to be. And even though it was not really her he loved, she *did* love him and knew how much she would miss him after she had finally convinced Imena to send her back into her own time.

If only it were possible to meet someone like Rand Kincaid in her own time. It would make getting over him that much easier. But she knew the chance of ever finding another man like Rand was almost nonexistent, and that seemed very unfair.

Filled with frustration and anger, and an ever-growing sadness, Alisha finally gave up on falling asleep and walked over to the window to watch the morning sky turn first purple, then crimson, then a deep, dusty blue. It was not until the savory aroma of fresh bread drifted up through the open window and prodded her empty stomach that she realized she had not eaten since lunch the day before. Because everyone else had planned to eat at the dance, she had been left to fend for herself and had been far too focused on making her getaway.

Suddenly very hungry, she slipped into the only dress she had that was not black and went downstairs to see if perhaps the enticing aroma had come from their own summer kitchen. Because she was not expected to work that day, wearing the light pink garment did not seem inappropriate.

To her disappointment, when she entered the kitchen where Rand had taken his first kiss, she found it empty. Rather than stay where the memories of that unexpected kiss were far too vivid, she walked out into the garden. There she found the still morning air and the sound of the birds chattering in the trees so delightfully compelling, she lay down in one of the chaise lounges and enjoyed the serenity.

The cheerful sounds soothing her troubled heart, she closed her eyes and was just starting to doze from lack of sleep when she heard shouts coming from inside the house. Because there was panic in the shrill voice, she hurried inside to see what was wrong.

Finding no one on the ground or second floor, she ran all the way up to the third floor. There she found everyone gathered in Faye's room. Most of them wore their bedclothes. Only Rand and William were dressed, though Rand wore only a pair of trousers.

Alisha stood in the doorway listening, trying to determine what had their attention. They all stood facing the bed.

Her heart skipped when she heard Rand tell William to ride over to the hospital and get a doctor— any doctor.

"What's wrong?" she asked, stepping to the side as William rushed past her.

When Rand turned to her, she saw concern pulling at his face.

"It's Faye. She won't wake up."

Alisha gasped with horror, then rushed forward. Her heart twisted with brutal force when Caroline stepped aside and she saw the frail girl lying on the tall bed, motionless, a portion of her pale blond hair spilling across her face. Fearing her dead, she pushed the hair back as she reached for a slender wrist, then sobbed with relief when she felt a weak but steady pulse.

"What happened?" she asked, looking every bit as worried as Rand when she laid the limp arm back down on the rumpled sheet.

"We don't know," he answered, then bent forward to rub Faye's cheeks vigorously with his palms. His skin looked dark brown in comparison to hers. "Last night she told Caroline to wake her early so she could come down and tell you about some man she'd danced with, but when Caroline came in here to do just that, Faye would not awaken."

"And there was nothing wrong with her last night?"

Caroline shook her head, then circled to the other side of the bed. Her eyes filled with tears while she watched Rand continue his attempt to bring Faye around. "When we got home, she complained of being a little tired, but then we all were. It was very late by then."

"I remember she also complained about being a little dizzy the other morning," Millicent put in, then looked at Rand apologetically. Her wrinkled hands curled into tight knots. "She became so lightheaded she nearly fell off a stool while washing windows."

"Why didn't you say something?" Rand asked, frowning.

"Because she told me not to. Said it was nothing to worry about. Said it was just something that happens to her now and again and that the feeling never lasted long."

"She told me the same thing," Jolie put in, her fearful brown eyes gazing at Rand. "She told me after I saw her stumble while climbing de stairs. Said it was not to be worried about. Said it was because she had not eaten."

Rand now looked even more worried as he bent over Faye's prone body again. This time he cupped his hands against her pale cheeks as if to warm them. "I just hope William hurries."

The next twenty minutes crawled at a snail's pace. No one left Faye's side while they all took turns calling her name and rubbing her skin, trying to bring her awake. Finally, Rand heard a carriage come to a halt and rushed to the window, where he could see a portion of the street below.

"Good. It's Dr. Owen," he said, then headed immediately toward the door. Maybe he can figure out what's wrong with her."

In minutes Rand returned with the doctor at his side. "There she is."

Dr. Owen set the black satchel he carried in a nearby chair then quickly waved everyone out of the room. "All except you, Jolie. I want you to stay with me. You will be my nurse."

Alisha opened her mouth to protest, not wanting to leave for any reason, but she realized by the doctor's grim expression that he would brook no argument.

She followed the others out into the hall

where they waited as a group for nearly an hour before receiving any news.

When the doctor finally opened the door and came out of the room, he looked deeply troubled. Alisha's pulse throbbed with quiet force while she waited to hear the news.

"Rand, I think I'd better have a word with you alone," he said. Because Jolie had remained in the room with Faye, he indicated they should take a walk together down the hall.

Rand pushed himself away from the wall where he had leaned for the past twenty minutes, but when he noticed the concern on everyone's faces, he did not try to follow. "These are her friends. They want to know what's wrong with her, too."

Dr. Owen looked at them for a moment, then nodded. "Very well. But I think maybe the women should sit down first."

He gestured toward the chairs Rand had brought out into the hall earlier. Chairs that until just a few minutes ago had been quietly occupied by the women.

Caroline and Millicent did as they were told and sank back into their chairs, but Alisha was too distressed to sit.

"What's wrong with her?" she asked, forcing the words past the constriction in her throat.

Dr. Owen hesitated a moment, then stated simply, "Faye has a fatal illness. I'm afraid the young woman in there is dying."

Dying? Alisha pressed her hand over her mouth to keep from crying aloud and was barely aware when a pair of strong arms eased her gently into the chair she had but minutes ago refused.

"Yes. It appears she has leukemia."

"And what's that exactly?" Rand wanted to know. He stood beside Alisha's chair, a comforting hand on her shoulder. He knew how much Alisha liked Faye. The two were always laughing and teasing each other whenever they worked together.

"It's a disease of the blood. There is such a large number or destructive white cells being produced in her blood that it has already affected her kidneys and her liver. The girl has been living with the resulting pain off and on for quite some time."

"And how do you know all this? Wouldn't you have to do tests to determine something like that?"

"The tests have already been done. Dr. Lee diagnosed it months ago. She told me so herself."

"You mean she knows?" Caroline's eyes widened at the thought.

"That she has leukemia, yes. But that she has at the most a few months to live, no. Evidently Dr. Lee led her to believe she has much more time than that. But then, too, the disease might not have been quite so progressed when he last saw her."

Millicent cut her troubled gaze to the closed door. "She's awake?"

"Awake and tired, and in grave need of rest, but you three can go in and talk with her for a few minutes if you'd like. Just don't stay long and don't mention what I've told you. Don't tell her how little time I think she has left. That should be up to her own doctor to tell her."

Millicent and Caroline exchanged glances, then headed solemnly toward the door. Alisha remained seated, trying to better comprehend all that she had just learned while listening carefully to the rest of what the doctor had to say.

"Rand, Faye will become progressively worse over the next few months while this disease continues to inflame her internal organs one at a time. I can give her medicine to make her more comfortable, but nothing will stop her death. You need to contact her family right away so they can care for her. Do you know where they are?"

Rand stared at him a long moment, his blue eyes rimmed with sadness, then answered quietly, "she has no family. She's been on her own since she was fifteen."

Alisha had not known this. She pressed her eyes closed. *Dying and alone.* Faye did not deserve that.

"Then you have nowhere to send her?" The doctor rubbed his tired jaw a moment while he thought more about it.

Rand shook his head. His gaze was lost to whatever dark thoughts had entered his mind. "She can spend her last few months here. I don't mind."

"But it's not your responsibility to take care of a dying servant," Dr. Owen told him. "I can send her to a county home. There are nurses there who can help take care of her."

"No." Rand lifted his gaze to the doctor's and again shook his head. "That won't be necessary. I can hire a nurse to take care of her here. These women are her friends. She'll want to have them around her when the time comes. Besides, I have not heard very good things about those county homes. I don't want Faye living out her final months in such a place."

"Are you sure?"

Rand nodded, then gestured toward the stairs.

Alisha watched with hot tears scalding her cheeks while he accompanied Dr. Owen downstairs to make arrangements for getting a day nurse. Although she had no idea why, she had not expected such kindness. What a truly exceptional, caring man Rand was. How could she ever have ever compared him to someone like Brad?

Trembling, she waited until she was all alone in the hall, then surrendered to the painful emotions that boiled inside her. She pressed her hands over her face and wept bitterly.

"Smells good," Alisha commented while she waited patiently for Jolie to slice the still-warm bread and put a piece of it on the tray beside the small bowl. It was her turn to take Faye her lunch and then sit with her long enough to allow the nurse a chance to come downstairs to eat and take care of her personal matters.

"You tell Faye if she eat all dis, I have a giant piece of blackberry pie waiting for her," Jolie said as she laid the bread beside the soup bowl. She smacked her lips together. "Tell her I make it fresh dis morning."

"I will," she promised, eager to go up to the third floor and see how Faye was.

It had been only two days since Caroline had found her lying in her bed unconscious, but in those two days Faye had grown remarkably better. So much so, she declared herself ready to get out of bed and back to work, but both Rand and the doctor had said no. She was to do nothing to tire herself.

As expected, when Alisha entered Faye's bedroom, Faye was sitting up in bed looking through one of the many books Rand had brought her from downstairs. Although Faye could not read beyond what an eight-year-old might, she loved looking at the pictures and trying to make out the captions. It kept her entertained for hours.

"Time to eat," Alisha told her, hurrying across the room and setting the footed tray on the small table beside her bed. When she noticed the nurse sitting on a stool beside Faye's dresser carefully pulling everything out and placing it into wooden boxes, her first thought was that the doctor had somehow convinced Rand to send Faye to a county hospital after all. Her heart wrenched at the thought of Faye dying there among strangers. "What's going on here?"

Faye smiled as she set the book aside. "Mr.

Rand is moving me down a floor," she answered, her words slow but distinct. Because of the laudanum, she was not as quick-witted as usual. "He says it's too hard on everyone to have to climb two flights of stairs to come see me. He's putting me in one of those guests rooms near yours. Says I will be able to see out into the garden from there. It will be nicer than having a window that looks down on a carriage lane."

"Yes, you will like that," Alisha agreed and wondered if Rand's kindness would ever end. She then turned to the nurse and suggested she go on downstairs to eat. "Before William comes in and devours all that fried chicken Jolie just made."

"Fried chicken?" Faye asked. She frowned at her usual bowl of beef soup while the nurse, who was an older woman, stretched from having sat too long, then hobbled out of the room. "When do I get to eat fried chicken again?"

"When the doctor says you can. Until then, you eat the beef soup he's had Jolie make just for you."

Faye scowled but accepted the tray. Then, with a little vigor, more because she still had no strength than because she was tired of the soup, she reached for her spoon and started to eat.

Alisha pulled the tall padded armchair where the nurse usually sat closer to the bed so they could talk.

"So how do you feel today?"

"I'm still a little tired, but other than that I'm

fine," she answered with another slow smile. "The medicine the nurse gives me has stopped the hurt I had in my side completely."

"You mean you were in pain but didn't tell anyone?" Alisha frowned.

"I didn't want anyone worrying about me," Faye replied sincerely. "But I'm much better now, and it won't be long until I'm up and helping the rest of you again."

Alisha felt bittersweet comfort in Faye's sweet smile. Although she did not care to think such morbid thoughts, she could not help but wonder how many more such smiles the pretty young woman had left in her fleeting life. With that thought pulling at her heart, she blinked several times and looked away.

"What's wrong?" Faye asked after dipping her spoon into the hot soup and bringing it halfway to her mouth. "You look like maybe you are about to cry. It's not because of me, is it?"

"No, of course not," Alisha lied, not wanting to upset her. "Why would I cry because of you? Because maybe you think I can't handle the extra work?"

"No, because you know that I'm dying," she said so matter-of-factly that it caught Alisha completely off guard.

When Alisha offered no immediate response to that, Faye set down her spoon. "I don't mind talking about it. I really don't. Truth is, I would like to talk about it, but everyone keeps changing the subject. Even the nurse."

"That's because it is too painful a topic to

discuss," Alisha admitted, finding it odd that Faye did not sound more distraught. But then Faye still thought she had years yet to live. "No one wants to talk about death."

Faye sat perfectly still for a long moment. "I do."

Alisha's heart wrenched at the quiet sincerity in Faye's voice.

"Alisha, you have been so nice to me. In the short time I've known you, you have become one of my closest friends ever and I have something very important to ask you."

Alisha swallowed hard, her emotions so close to shattering that her voice trembled when she replied. "What?"

Faye paused a moment to think about what she had to say, then said very softly, "Please be here to say a prayer over me as my soul slips from this world into the next. When it looks like my time is near, please come and stay by my side until I'm gone. I don't want to be alone when it happens."

Alisha closed her eyes against the pain that pierced her soul. It was such a simple request, but one she could not fulfill. Despite a growing desire to be with Rand and despite the deep compassion she felt toward Faye, her plans to leave had not changed. According to the doctor's latest estimation, with good care Faye should live for a couple more months. Alisha planned to be gone long before then. Had to be. Imena had given her only the three-week time span, and eleven of those twenty-one days were already gone.

"Please?" Faye tried again for a response. She reached out and touched Alisha's arm with an icy hand. "I want someone with me when my time comes to die. Someone who will hold my hand and pray for the deliverance of my soul. Promise me."

Faye gazed at her pleadingly, so pleadingly that Alisha could not tell her no.

"Okay, I promise," Alisha finally agreed, although reluctantly. "When the time comes, you won't be alone." She sucked in a deep breath in a useless effort to ease some of the constriction near her heart. She hoped one of the others would step in and make up for her absence so that promise would not turn out to be a complete lie. "Now, can we please talk about something else?"

"And what do you want to talk about?" Faye asked, looking satisfied to have Alisha's promise.

Alisha thought a second. "Tell me again about the young man who asked you to dance," she said, knowing that subject would keep Faye talking for the rest of her time there.

Jolie and William stood at the foot of the front stairs talking when Alisha came back from taking Faye's empty tray out to the summer kitchen. She hurried to them. She had waited all day to catch the two alone and did not dare forgo this opportunity.

"Jolie, William, can I talk to you about something important?" she asked. She tried not to think about the betrayal Faye might feel when she woke up that following morning and was told that she was already gone.

"And what is that?" William asked. He turned to look at her questioningly.

"I have something important I want to ask of you." She spoke now in a much quieter voice, in case someone else was nearby. "Something I think just might help Faye get better instead of gradually worse."

"And what is dat?" This time it was Jolie who asked.

Alisha took a deep breath, then placed her latest scheme into motion. "First let me ask if either of you happens to know of a voodoo woman named Imena. I don't know her last name, but I think she has a little shop somewhere in this part of the city."

Jolie's eyebrows arched. The question had clearly caught her by surprise. "Why you want to know?"

"Because I'd like to have William take me to her tonight after everyone else has gone to bed. I know this might sound a little far-fetched, and it is certainly something we would not want to discuss with the others, but I would like for William to drive me over there so I can ask if there is anything she can do to help Faye."

"You think a voodoo queen might make her well again?"

"I don't know, but the doctors have already

admitted that they don't know of anything else that can be done medically to help her. I thought maybe a voodoo woman might know of something. They are supposed to have great powers," Alisha explained, knowing only too well just *how* great those powers could be. She was living proof that they had the ability to pull people from one century and place them in another. There was bound to be something Imena could do to help someone like Faye. "Even if she can't make Faye well again, perhaps she could give us a charm or something that would make her feel better."

And if William would agree to take her there inside a closed carriage, she could try to kill two evil birds with one stone, so to speak. Not only could she speak to Imena on Faye's behalf, she would also have a chance to speak to her on her own behalf. She could finally ask to be sent back. After all, it had been eleven days since her arrival there, and Thomas was not only still alive but, thanks to her agreement with Rand, he was living that life debt free.

"I have given this matter a lot of thought and think it would be well worth our effort to try to convince the woman to use her magic to help Faye."

"Not me," William said holding up his hands. He shook his head. "You are not about to catch me anywhere near that voodoo witch."

A tight knot pulled at Alisha's chest. "Not even to help Faye?"

"Not even to help nobody. It's too risky. I

heard tell that some people walk into that place and never come out." He took a quick step back. "I'm not going anywhere near there."

Alisha's heart ached with disappointment. she had not expected him to be so adamant against helping her. "But all I'm asking is that you drive me over there. You won't have to go inside." She preferred he didn't. That way he would not be there to overhear her ask Imena to send her back. He would not have to know that a change had taken place and would probably attribute the confusion the real Andrea would have upon her return to something evil the voodoo woman did. "You can wait outside in the carriage."

"Not me." Again, William shook his head. "You never know what will anger that sort of woman and make her want to put one of her evil spells on you. Find someone else to take you if you have such a mind to go— or walk, but I'm not going. And that's all there is to it." Rather than chance being talked into something he did not want to do, he turned and strode toward the back of the house.

Alisha watched with such an expression of sadness and defeat that Jolie took pity on her.

"I see what I can do," she said, resting a brown hand on Alisha's shoulder. "Maybe his mind will change."

"Oh, please, do try," Alisha said, pleadingly, aware it was the safest plan devised thus far. She knew that unless William cooperated she would have no choice but to try venturing off again on foot. And so far she had not managed it as far as three blocks without running into a policeman.

Jolie squeezed her shoulder reassuringly. "I do what I can, but it may take a little time. He be a most stubborn man."

Alisha bit her lower lip at the mere mention of it taking more time. She had only ten days left, that is if Imena proved adamant about her three-week limit. If only she knew why. What happened after that time that made it impossible to send her back? "Just remember that Faye has only a few months left and that she will only get worse with each day's passing. The sooner we get her some help, the better."

"I do what I can," she repeated with an understanding nod, then glanced up the stairs and looked suddenly surprised. "Hello, Mr. Rand. I did not know you came home."

Alisha gasped and spun around to find Rand slowly descending the stairs. Her heart hammered with the fear that he might have overheard some of their discussion.

"I returned to see how Faye was," he answered, looking at Alisha curiously. "And to get something I left in my room." He patted his coat pocket. "What is wrong with you two? Alisha looks as if I just scared three years off her life."

Afraid Jolie might tell him about her latest plan, she quickly answered, "There's nothing wrong with me. It's just that I didn't hear you coming. You startled me is all."

"Have you eaten?" Jolie asked, frowning. "I

have nothing left of our own meal, but I can find you something."

"I ate hours ago," he admitted, then stopped to stand beside them. He continued to look at Alisha curiously. "What were you two talking about? You both looked so serious."

"Nothing," Alisha answered again before Jolie could speak. "We are just worried about Faye." She shifted nervously beneath Rand's probing blue gaze and prayed he would accept that reply.

"Jolie, would you go tell William that it looks like there's a big rainstorm coming in from the north." Though he spoke to Jolie, he continued to stare at Alisha. "He'll want to secure the stable. And tell Millicent and Caroline to close the windows along the north side of the house."

He waited until Jolie was well away before narrowing his gaze accusingly. He bent down so that his eyes were level with hers. "Now what were you *really* discussing?"

"I told you." She swallowed hard but continued to meet his gaze. "We were discussing Faye."

"Then why is it I don't believe you?"

"Because you never believe me." Her expression flattened at the thought.

"And could that be because you so rarely tell me the truth?"

Thinking that comment unfair, Alisha glowered at him, but just when she opened her mouth to give an appropriate retort, someone knocked on the front door, distracting them both.

Her first thought was that it might be the police coming to search his house again.

"Should I hide?" she asked, already looking around for the best place.

"Just step over to the side. If it was someone who looked like he could cause any real harm, the detective would have stopped him. It's probably just a peddler," Rand told her, but as a precaution he went first to a window, where he lifted back the curtain and peered outside to see who had knocked.

He glanced back at Alisha questioningly when he did not recognize the woman.

A second knock sounded just as he reached for the knob— this one more persistent than the last.

"Can I help you?" he asked of the short, dark-haired woman who stood trembling on his doorstep. His eyes widened with immediate alarm when he noticed blood splattered across her pale green dress.

"Are you Randall Kincaid?" she asked in a frightened voice, then stepped inside although yet uninvited. When she did, she caught her first glimpse of Alisha standing off to the side.

"Andrea!" she cried, then burst into sobs as she clutched her skirts and hurried toward her. "Its your father. He's been beaten and he's nearly dead."

Sixteen

Alisha stared at the terrified woman who for some reason looked vaguely familiar to her, even though she had no idea why she should. "Why? What happened?" Instinctively her arms went around her.

"Some men came," she answered between rasping sobs. Her whole body shuddered from the onslaught of her emotions. "They weren't in policemen's uniforms like before, but they had pistols and clubs, and they forced their way through the door. They wanted to know where you were. And when Thomas wouldn't tell them, they started beating him with their clubs as hard as they could. I could not stop them. I tried, but they just threw me aside. I'd have shot them all but I didn't know where your papa had put his gun."

"Papa has a gun?" Alisha asked, not realizing what she had just called him, just concerned that the poor man had felt frightened enough to arm himself. In all the years he had lived above a rough-and-tumble gambling house and saloon, he had never felt the need to own a firearm. He had admitted being afraid of such weapons.

The trembling woman nodded, then wiped away her tears with the back of her hand. Although she still shook violently in Alisha's arms, she had calmed a little. "Beau gave it to him. Not too long after that last time he was so badly beaten. But he put it away somewhere in his bedroom so it wouldn't be stolen."

"And they didn't give him much of a chance to go and get it," Rand surmised. His blue eyes glittered with anger. "How many of them were there?"

"Five. Or six. I'm not sure. They came in so suddenly."

"And what about the detective I hired? Where was he during all this?"

"Dead," she answered solemnly. "Beau found him out in the alley with his throat cut. They probably caught him from behind."

Alisha gasped at the brutality but remained steady. This was no time to get hysterical.

"Ruby, where is Papa now?" she asked, although she was not sure how she knew the woman's name. Then it dawned on her that Rand had mentioned something about a friend named Ruby helping to take care of her father. The same Ruby who had helped take care of her during those first few hours after the carriage accident. She supposed that could also be the reason Ruby looked vaguely familiar. While still somewhat delirious from the accident, she must have come awake just enough to see Ruby's face.

"In his bedroom, where he managed to crawl before collapsing," Ruby answered, then started sobbing again. "He's still alive, but he's in terrible pain."

"And did you send for the doctor?" Rand asked. His frown deepened.

"Yes. Beau went for one. They should be back there by now."

"Then I don't understand. Why are you here?"

"To tell Andrea what those men told me to tell her. That they will be back to kill Thomas if she doesn't come out of hiding by sometime on Thursday. I thought she should be told."

Rand's explosive reaction was immediate. "And you couldn't have sent someone else with that message? Don't you know that by coming here yourself you've now put both their lives in danger? Don't you realize that those men or the police who hired them could have been waiting outside to follow you, knowing you'd come tell Andrea?"

He threw up his hands and glowered at her. "And if they did follow you here, not only do they now know that Thomas did indeed know where his daughter was, they also will conclude that either she is right here hiding in my house or that I must be a direct link to her whereabouts."

He went to the window to see if there was anything suspicious happening outside. A gust of wind from the approaching storm caught his hair and blew it off his forehead.

Ruby's face paled. "I didn't think about that." Her body stiffened when she looked at Alisha, who stood with her arm still around her shoulders. "I'm sorry. I just wanted you to know." She then looked again at Rand, who still surveyed the street. "And I wanted to know what I should do next. Those men meant what they said. They will come back to kill Thomas if Andrea doesn't come forward by Thursday morning."

"Then we'll have to send him away," Rand said, having reined in his anger long enough to consider the matter further. After a few more seconds he stepped away from the window. "Maybe we can send him to that cousin's house in Texas. The one where he planned to send Andrea at first."

Ruby shook her head. "We can't. He's already learned that his cousin no longer lives in Daingerfield. The local telegraph operator sent word back that Jeff has since moved farther west but wasn't sure where. Besides, Thomas could never make the trip. Not now. He's hurt real bad." She pressed her lips together to fight a fresh onslaught of tears while she absently traced the outline of the darkening bloodstains on her dress with her fingertip. "He was barely conscious when I left."

"Then I'll have to find somewhere else to send him. Somewhere closer." He looked at Alisha. "Your father will be safe. I'll see to it."

Alisha smiled, knowing he meant that.

"But as for you," he continued, looking again at Ruby. "There's still the chance that no one followed you. I'll have to get you out of here unseen. Come with me. We need to find William." He led her off toward the back of the house. Just before they reached the end of the hall, he turned to look back at Alisha, who had not moved, and smiled reassuringly. "I'll take care of this. I'll find some way to keep you both safe."

Alisha was amazed at how far Rand was willing to go to help the man he believed to be her father.

Later that same night, he saw to it that Thomas was secreted off to his sugar plantation where he could be given further medical care, continue to stay sober, and eventually be put to work. Rand hired two men to help Thomas walk right out the front of the saloon, using their shoulders for support.

All three had pretended to be happily but stumbling drunk, covering the fact that Thomas could barely walk. Because it was not an unusual sight to see three men come out of Beauregard's supporting each other's weight like that, they had had no trouble getting him into a buggy and driving straight out of town.

That meant Thomas was safe once again, something Alisha was certain Imena would be pleased to hear. If she ever got the opportunity to tell her.

By the following weekend, with time rapidly running short, Alisha became very antsy. She felt like a prisoner in Rand's home because no matter how or what she tried, she was unable to unearth a way out of there. At least not one that would go completely undetected or that was at

all safe. After having learned what those men
had done to Thomas and to the detective Rand
had hired to protect him, she wanted to keep
herself as safe as possible. She did not want to
end up lying in an alley somewhere with her
throat slit like that poor detective.

And after what happened Tuesday, Rand, too,
became far more cautious. He went out that same
day and hired more detectives to protect his
home. Now, at least three men were posted front
and back, and at all hours. That left little chance
of her leaving that house on foot unobserved.

There was now only one feasible way for her
to slip out of there unseen and that was inside
a closed carriage with William driving. But William still refused to do that for her, although it
was clear by some of the questions he had asked
recently that his position was slowly weakening.

He had wanted to know just how close to
Imena's shop he would have to park and how
long he would have to wait there—but he had
yet to agree to take her there.

Everything now fell on Jolie's shoulders. It
was up to her to persuade her husband to go
against his cautious nature and take her to see
Imena. For Faye's sake.

Meanwhile Alisha made the best of a continuing bad situation by spending much of her free
time with Faye and by trying to get along better
with Rand. Having decided that nothing could
be gained by doing otherwise, she had stopped
trying to convince him that she was anyone but
Andrea Knight, and that had put him in a much

better mood than he had been in the days prior. That and the fact that no one had yet attempted to break into his house to see if she was hiding there.

Even so, she did what she could to avoid being alone with him, knowing only too well what would happen if she did not continue to steer clear of him. It was going to hurt her enough when she left. She did not need to add to the heartache by becoming any more attached to him, which was part of the reason she spent so much of her evenings in Faye's room entertaining her. She knew Rand would not approach her with more declarations of love or inquiries about marriage with Faye sitting right there listening to every word.

Still, a part of her yearned to be with him at least once more before she left.

"What do you mean he's not there?" Chief Clay Miller asked, then leaned heavily against the side of the creaking buggy so he could glare directly into Heath Butler's ugly, bearded face. How could one man be so inept? "Where the hell is he?"

"No one seems to know," Heath answered, then glanced back at Beauregard's. "They say he just up and left in the middle of the night one night, never to be seen again. Didn't even take all his clothes. I checked on that."

Chief Miller's scowl deepened and the carriage creaked again when he leaned closer still.

"What about the woman? Didn't you say there was a woman with him the other night?"

"Yes, sir, there was. But she's disappeared, too. Her name is Ruby Brooks, and she also works here, usually serving tables." He gestured towards Beauregard's with a jerk of his thumb. "But yesterday, she just up and didn't show up to work. No one knows what's happened to her either. I know you told us to do something with her to make sure she can't identify any of us for what we did to Thomas, but we can't kill her if we can't find her."

"Damn!" Clay sat back in the padded seat so forcefully, it caused the whole buggy to bounce. He turned to his brother with a look of dark rage. "Now what do we do?"

"I don't know, but we have to do something," Jeremy answered, his expression just as grim. "Especially now that we know Andrea was seen nosing around the warehouse later the same night she cheated me out of all that money. It's pretty clear she knows about the guns and opium we have stored there."

"Yes, and if you told her that much you probably also told her how we came to have them and what we plan to do with them. And if that's true and she ever surfaces long enough to tell anyone with any real authority, we could all end up in jail for a good part of our lives."

He slammed his fist hard against the tufted leather seat. "Damnation, Jeremy, why do you have to get so gabby when you drink?" He did not wait for a response. Instead he leaned forward toward Heath again. "And we all know what happens to policemen or corrupt city officials when they are thrown in jail with some of the very men they helped put there."

Heath swallowed hard then nodded as he reached up to rub the scar near his left eye with the stub of his finger.

"That means we have to find out where this Ruby Brooks has gone. Find her and I think you'll not only find Thomas Knight but maybe even Andrea."

"I'll keep asking around," Heath vowed.

Chief Miller sighed with annoyance, knowing that if Heath's horse hadn't stumbled and broken its leg so shortly after the woman took off, they probably could have found Andrea Knight that same day. Damn their rotten luck!

"And when you finally find them, you don't take *any* chances this time." Chief Miller looked back at his brother scathingly, a brother he no longer believed deserved the opportunity to bed the wench before killing her. "Don't bother trying to arrest any of them. Not even Andrea. I know my original orders were to see to it that she was brought to me alive, but I've changed my mind about that. Just go ahead and kill all of them on the spot. All I want to see are bodies."

"I'll pass the word," Heath promised, then turned to go back inside the saloon where two of his fellow policemen waited.

Chief Miller stared after him a moment before he turned again to his brother. "I think we'd better consider raising the reward another five hundred. We need that woman dead."

Early Sunday morning, Faye awoke with a sharp pain in her right side followed by an extremely high fever and the inability to sit up in bed for long stretches of time. Rand sent for her doctor immediately and was told that the leukemia had caused one of her kidneys to become so large it had quit functioning. With the other kidney already so swollen it was tender to even the slightest pressure, the doctor predicted that she had only a couple of weeks left, if that.

Because of the severity of her pain and because of the fever, the doctor instructed the nurse to double the dosage of opium they had been giving her and to start keeping cold rags wrapped around Faye's head and draped over her body. And because Faye had become very restless, even while heavily drugged, Rand asked the nurse to start staying with the girl round the clock. A bed was brought into Faye's room for that purpose.

He also made sure that during the nurse's one day off that someone stayed to watch Faye. Which was why Rand was in her room Sunday night when Alisha went upstairs to check on Faye after supper.

When Alisha stepped inside the dimly lit bedroom, she found Rand standing beside Faye's bed, gently stroking her cheek with the back of his fingers. He was so absorbed in thought he did not notice her enter.

To Alisha's surprise, Faye was awake, but barely, and staring up at him.

"Don't worry," Rand said. His eyes glittered in the soft light of the only lamp burning in the bedroom while he gazed down at her. "You will not die alone. Alisha and I will *both* be with you when the time comes."

At hearing such sincerity in his voice, Alisha's heart flowed with tender feelings toward him. She felt relieved knowing that someone would indeed be with Faye when the time came. Rand did not make idle promises.

Faye smiled weakly then closed her eyes. A few seconds later the contented expression faded, and she slept.

"How is she?" Alisha asked softly as she came to stand beside Rand.

Rand looked at her, then glanced back down at Faye's pallid face before motioning toward the hall. "Let's talk out there."

He waited until they were in the hall but where he could still see Faye's sleeping form before answering. "Her condition is not good. The fever is down some but not entirely gone. She still has sharp pains in her side whenever she moves and has a dull pain when she doesn't. Dr. Lee and Dr. Owen have both told me that she will never get any better than she is now. Because her organs are so badly affected and because her body is already so very weak, she'll live these last few weeks in pain more than not. That poor girl."

Because the light was much better in the hall, Alisha saw Rand's face more clearly and stared at him with amazement. There were big shimmering tears in those blue eyes.

"But at least she has you and all of us to help take her mind off her pain," she said.

Sadly, she lifted her hand to caress Rand's cheek, an action that not only comforted him but comforted herself as well, for she was hurting, too. In the two weeks she had been there, she had become very fond of the sweet-natured blonde.

Rand responded by tilting his head against her palm. "It's just that I feel so helpless. At least with Miller and his men, I have something or someone tangible I can fight, and because of that, I have a very good chance of winning."

His gaze wandered to where Faye lay perfectly still, her skin as pale as the sheet beneath her. "But with this leukemia disease, there is no way to fight back. There's nothing anyone can do to save her. There is no cure."

"Which is something I think you should remember," she said, sharing his pain, for she, too, felt helpless whenever she was with Faye. "There is nothing you or I or anyone else can do." She knew that even during her own time some people died from leukemia.

Still caressing Rand's warm, rugged cheek, Alisha gazed into his tormented blue eyes for a long moment before hearing footsteps coming up the stairs. She quickly pulled away.

The nurse, coming back on duty, nodded to Rand when she walked past them, but said nothing before disappearing into Faye's bedroom.

Rand watched sadly until the older woman

had settled into the chair beside the bed. Without a word he turned and walked away. Alisha followed. Although she knew exactly what was at risk, she wanted to continue comforting and being comforted by him. She followed him down the hall and into his bedroom, knowing where their emotions would lead and how that would result in her falling even more deeply in love with the man. But for some reason, such consequences mattered little to her at that moment. As did any of the other consequences.

It had occurred to her shortly after the first time they made love that she had taken absolutely no protection against pregnancy, but at that same time she also realized it was not *her* body that risked such a thing. It was Andrea's. And after everything Andrea's absence had put her through thus far, she did not feel all that guilty about exposing the cowardly woman's body to the prospect of motherhood. It would serve her right for having ducked out on her responsibilities the way she had.

But then again, Alisha did suffer a twinge of jealousy just knowing that should their lovemaking result in the creation of a child, Andrea would be the one to carry the baby inside her and Andrea would be the one to nurture it and love it once it was born.

Sadly, Alisha pressed her hand against the flat of her stomach and wondered what it would be like to be pregnant with Rand's child, to feel the baby move about inside her. She remembered how badly she had yearned to have a child

while married to Brad; but children had never
been a part of Brad's plans. He did not have a
the time nor the desire to be a parent and had
tried to convince her she did not either.

Alisha also remembered how badly her own
mother had wanted children. Problem was,
though, that because of medical problems her
mother could not have any children of her own
so she and Alisha's father had chosen to adopt.
Having heard about the newborn left on the
front steps of a New Orleans's church in a blan-
ket-lined box shortly after Easter in 1969, they
put a request in to adopt that child and asked
to be able to raise and care for it as if it were
their own.

They'd wanted the baby even after the doctors
had warned them to expect the child to have
serious health problems because the tiny infant
had legally died twice while being taken to a
local hospital. Each time it was several minutes
before they were able to resuscitate her.

But despite a very real possibility of brain
damage, which fortunately had not occurred,
Carole and Reginald Sampson still wanted that
child. And Alisha was forever grateful that they
did, for she could not have asked for kinder,
more loving parents. She smiled again at the
thought of what it would be like to have a child
of her own to cherish in that same manner. She
would be a loving mother. She was sure of it.

Rand waited until they were both inside the
shadowed bedroom and he had closed the door
before bending to light a small porcelain lamp

nearby. He adjusted the wick until the globe offered a soft yellow glow, then turned to gaze at her in the muted light.

"So you have had a chance to think about my proposal?" he asked, already taking her into his arms. "Have you thought about marrying me?"

Alisha felt warm and giddy all over just knowing what would surely follow.

"Yes, but I have not yet come to a decision," she answered, rather than try to explain again that marriage for them was out of the question.

"No? Then maybe you need a little more persuading," he suggested. His blue eyes glittered at the thought.

Eagerly, she stared at his strong, sun-browned features, knowing now that it was the strenuous work he did on the docks and on his ships that kept him so fit. He was not a man who shied away from hard work.

Her heart fluttered when he dipped forward to take her mouth in a sweetly demanding kiss.

Aware that within a very few days, whether William agreed to help her or not, she would have to leave there, Alisha slipped her arms around Rand's strong shoulders and held him close. She longed to have him make love to her at least once more before being forced to leave his side forever. She closed her eyes against the sudden ache that flooded her heart and refused to allow the painful thought to reenter her mind. All she wanted was to enjoy the moment and pretend they would be together forever.

Holding on to that fantasy, she pressed herself

harder against him so he would understand that she wanted him every bit as much as he obviously wanted her. Although she refused to talk marriage with him, for it was not up to her to make such lasting promises, she would share the love in his heart and the warmth of his bed one last time.

While the kiss continued, Alisha slowly lifted her arms and freed her long dark hair from the combs she had used to keep the bulk of it off her neck. She wanted to feel its softness cascading across her shoulders while Rand slipped his strong fingers through the thickness.

Her heart pounded excitedly when his hands moved first to stroke the soft tresses, then to unfasten the many buttons that ran down the back of her dress.

Wanting to hurry the pleasure she knew awaited her, she slid her hands between them and unfastened his buttons as well. Soon they were both gloriously naked and unable to resist the bed that beckoned them. Falling onto its softness together, they remained entwined as one, each eagerly sampling and searching the body of the other.

While Rand's mouth trailed a fiery path down the slender column of her throat toward her aching breasts, she threaded one hand through his long hair, then with the other grazed his chest hair, marveling again at how different their bodies were.

With their passions fully ignited and their innermost yearnings spiraling skyward, Alisha lay on top of him as their bodies finally joined in the age-old union of love. Together they soared, their emotions climbing ever higher until at last they attained the cherished goal and shared the most complete, earth-shattering fulfillment that was possible.

Contently, they fell back onto the bed, cloaked now in the warmth that came from having known such true satisfaction. But unlike that first time, Alisha did not rush to leave Rand's bed. Knowing how very little time she had left to be with the man she so desperately loved, she remained in his bed and slept happily in the crook of his arm. It was not until the following morning when she awoke just before dawn that the happiness dissolved and left her with a deep, hollow feeling.

She lay there staring at him in the growing light, memorizing every detail of what he looked like while he slept.

Oh, how dreadfully she would miss Rand after she left. She wondered how she would ever survive the pain.

Seventeen

Late Monday afternoon William finally spoke the words Alisha had been waiting days to hear. "Okay, I'll do it. I'll take you to see that voodoo witch you want to see. We'll go Wednesday night while Mr. Rand is away at his meeting. That way he won't have to know what fools we are." He shook his head as if unable to believe it himself. "I just hope the trip there does some good for Faye. I hate seeing her in so much pain. She's such a sweet child."

"I'm sure it will do some good," Alisha said, elated. "And thank you."

"Just you keep your promise to be inside only a few minutes," he warned with a deep scowl. His nostrils flared. "I don't want to be sitting outside that woman's place any longer than I have to."

"You won't," she vowed again. "When should I be ready to leave?"

"A little after seven. That'll give me plenty of time to saddle two horses, deliver you over there, and— "

She interrupted him in mid-sentence. "No, not saddles. I'm afraid of horses. You'll have to take me in one of Rand's carriages. Preferably the coach so no one will see who I am."

William's frown deepened for a moment, but then he shrugged. "That should still give me enough time to hitch up the coach, drive you over there so you can talk to her, and get us both back before Mr. Rand returns. I sure don't want him finding out what we've done. I'd sure hate to lose my job over this."

"You won't. And I'll be ready," she promised, then smiled reassuringly. "Don't look so worried. This will turn out for the best."

"I just hope we don't end up having to haul Faye over there for that woman to work some of her magic," he muttered. "I don't think we could hide something like that."

"We won't have to. If it turns out that Imena has to be in the room with Faye to help her, then she'll just have to come here to do it." It was the least the woman could do considering all she had put her through during the past seventeen days. "How far away is Imena's place?"

"It's a little over five squares east of here. Shouldn't take us long to drive there."

With the problem of getting safely to Imena's finally solved and believing she could yet salvage that promotion she was due by claiming to have suffered some rare form of amnesia, Alisha went happily upstairs to sit with Faye awhile.

While regaling her with some of the incidents of the day, she noticed the pain ever present in Faye's expression and wondered if there really might be something Imena could do to help

Faye fight the leukemia. The woman certainly possessed some very powerful magic, more than *she* would ever have thought possible.

"No one answers and the door's locked," Heath said, stating the obvious. He looked to Chief Miller for further instructions.

"Are you sure this is her house?" The chief bent forward and cupped his face with his hand in an effort to see through the glass and the lace curtains drawn across a nearby window.

"That's what I was told," Heath responded. "The yellow clapboard with dark green shutters."

The chief looked at the house, then at Heath, then at George and shrugged. "Then break the door down."

Heath took a step back and gave the door a swift, hard kick. He smiled smugly when it shattered open on the first attempt.

George entered the small house first. He lit a nearby lamp to make sure no one was hiding inside those darkened rooms with a weapon of some sort. After deciding the house was safe, he signaled for the other two to follow.

"What do we do now?" he asked after he settled the glass globe back onto the small lamp, then moved to light another.

"Start looking for something that might indicate where she's gone," the chief replied. "I still think that if we can find Ruby Brooks, we'll also find the other two. Her disappearing so soon after the old man did is too coincidental."

George turned to a nearby sideboard and started pulling drawers out and scattering the contents across the wooden floor while Heath entered the next room and performed a similar search. The chief poked at some of the more curious items with his boot but did not participate in the actual work.

Within minutes, Heath returned to the front room with a pair of strange-looking white shoes. "Chief, it looks like you might be right about that Ruby Brooks knowing where Andrea Knight is. These are the same shoes Andrea had on her feet that last time we arrested her. I remember them because they look so odd. Like nothing I ever saw."

Chief Miller took the shoes and looked at them curiously, then searched inside them with his hands. When he found nothing hidden there, he set them aside. "No clues there. Keep on searching. We have to find out where they've gone."

After rummaging around for another twenty minutes and finding nothing else that indicated a connection between Ruby and Andrea or even Ruby and Thomas, Chief Miller walked over to one of the lamps George had lit and picked it up. "That's enough. There's nothing else here. Get on outside."

He waited until Heath and George had stepped back out onto the front steps before shattering the lamp hard against a nearby wall. He watched the bright flame leap across the wall, instantly following the trail of splashed oil.

The fire rushed to the floor, where it quickly spread to the many items strewn there.

"That's for helping to harbor a criminal," he muttered just before he turned and walked slowly out of the house.

Despite the eventual pain Alisha knew she was headed for, she could not resist accepting Rand's invitation to join him in his bedroom again the following night. She had experienced such bitter-sweet happiness there the night before.

She still refused to discuss marriage, but she did not hold back telling Rand how very much she loved him, nor did she hold back showing that love.

She wanted him to know that he had affected her every bit as strongly as she had affected him. Which was why she again stayed the entire night in his room, despite knowing that some of the others in the house knew where she now slept and talked about it in low whispers. But then it was not *her* reputation being tarnished. It was Andrea's. And she felt it would serve Andrea right to come back and find herself the center of such speculative gossip.

Again that Tuesday night, knowing it was to be her last night there, Alisha went to Rand's bed for what she knew would be the last time. Because of the sadness that engulfed her, she had a hard time holding back the tears after they made love. Just like she had a hard time holding back the tears when it came time to tell Faye goodbye the following afternoon.

Just knowing how soon she would be gone from there made everything Alisha did Wednesday that much more important to her. And when Rand came up to her bedroom looking for her just after six o'clock to tell her that he was leaving for a few hours, she pulled him into her arms and kissed him long and hard.

Baffled but pleased, he vowed to return to her as quickly as he possibly could.

"The meeting itself shouldn't last but a couple of hours. I should be back here before nine o'clock." His gaze roamed her beautiful face, then her hair, which she wore in a twist high on her head. "If it weren't such an important meeting, I'd stay right here with you instead. But the mayor is working on plans to pass a few new laws that will allow him to form a special police force to crack down on the crooked gambling houses and the bawdy houses known to drug their patrons and rob them. There are also plans to discuss what might be done to stop the corruption that has become evident in our own police department. And I certainly don't want to miss that. It's time the good citizens of this city banded together and did something to stop those criminals once and for all."

He then smiled mischievously while he let his gaze roam seductively over the form-fitting bodice of her work dress, accentuated by the triangular shape of her apron bib. "Don't go to bed without me."

He bent to kiss her again, this time lightly on the cheek, and Alisha's heart felt as if would break into a hundred little pieces when she watched him turn and walk jauntily away, secure in the thought that she would be there waiting for him when he returned.

But Alisha knew that was not likely because if Imena proved at all cooperative, which she had every reason to be since Thomas Knight was still alive and safe, that would be the last time she ever saw him.

With tears brimming and her heart yearning to call him back for one last embrace, she hurried down the hall and into his bedroom so she could watch him saunter across the yard, swing up onto the horse William had just saddled for him, then ride away. She waited until she could no longer see his strong body atop the tall dark horse before slowly turning away.

Having promised William to be ready and knowing he had already returned to the carriage house to get the coach ready, she went first to Faye's room to offer her sleeping friend a silent goodbye, then on to her bedroom to remove her apron and retrieve her purse from the drawer where she kept it. When she returned downstairs, she had only one person left to tell goodbye and that was Jolie. Caroline and Millicent had left earlier that evening, having asked Rand for permission to go visit a friend on her birthday. Alisha had told them goodbye then.

While fighting an overwhelming sadness, Alisha visited with Jolie in the kitchen while she prepared Faye a supper tray to take to her room. Alisha's heart raced with apprehension while she waited for William to finish outside.

When he finally entered through the back door to tell her it was time, she stepped over and gave Jolie a brief hug.

"Goodbye."

Jolie looked at her, puzzled by such a fond embrace. "Are you afraid of not coming back?"

"No, of course not," she lied, knowing that if William thought her afraid, he might back out. She could tell by his sullen expression that he was still very troubled about their plans. "I just felt like hugging you is all."

William gestured toward the door, but before Alisha could respond, they heard a loud knock at the front door.

"I'll go see who that is," he said, frowning with annoyance. "Then we have to go."

Alisha nodded, but curious to know who had come calling at that late hour, she and Jolie followed him halfway to the door. They stood in the adjoining hallway, just out of sight, listening. Instead of a cordial greeting, they heard William sternly ask, "What do you men want now?"

"We want to see Mr. Kincaid," came an angry retort. "And we want to see him *now.*"

"He's not here. He's gone to a meeting and won't be back for at least another hour. You policemen will just have to wait and come back then unless you'd like to leave a message with me."

"We'd like to leave a message all right, but

not with you. We want to talk to the servant named Alisha."

Alisha's heart drummed a frantic rhythm when Jolie suddenly shoved her toward the back of the house then hurried around the corner to help William manage the men at the door. Alisha slowly retreated.

"Alisha isn't here right now either," she heard William say while she continued to back silently away. "She and two other servants went over to a friend's for a birthday party."

"And would those other servants be named Millicent Raynor and Carolyn Wiggs?"

There was a long pause before William finally responded. "Yes, why?"

"Because we just had a long talk with both of them, and they were the ones who told us Mr. Rand had a new housekeeper named Alisha Sampson working here."

"And why would dat matter to you men?" Jolie wanted to know.

"Because judging by the description they gave of her, the new housekeeper's real name is Andrea Knight, and Andrea Knight is wanted for committing a crime. We've been looking for her for nearly three weeks."

Alisha did not hear the rest of what was said because as soon as she had stepped back inside the kitchen, she hurried out the back door and sprinted across the darkened yard. But this time she did not turn and go out the front gate where there could be yet more policemen waiting with the horses, nor did she go out the back way where she knew one of Rand's detectives stood guard and might try to stop her. Instead she tossed her purse into the bushes so she could use both hands and quickly scaled the section of garden wall that lay closest to the summer kitchen. She knew from having looked out Faye's window that another courtyard lay on the other side.

Certain no one had seen her climb that wall or drop to the other side, she hurried across to yet another wall and scaled it, too. This time she found herself in a narrow, dark alley.

Remembering the name of the street where William said Imena lived and remembering that he had mentioned her place being about five blocks to the east, Alisha took off running in the same direction that she knew the sun rose. With the New Orleans police hot on her trail and nowhere else safe to hide, she had little choice. It was now or never.

Staying in dark alleys as much as possible and glad now to be wearing a black dress, though it was long and cumbersome, she hurried toward the area where she had last talked to Imena. To her relief, she had to sidestep only one policeman during her hasty flight, and she did that by hiding inside a large empty crate until the man eventually strolled past her.

A little more than an hour after having left Rand's house, Alisha found Imena's small abode. By the time she arrived at the front door, her hair was a streaming mass and she was badly out of breath but otherwise unharmed.

Knowing it was not safe for her outside, she knocked only once then tried the latch. She found the door unlocked, so she quickly stepped inside. The front room was cast in dark shadows, but she could tell from the light that spilled from the back area that someone was on the premises. She found Imena in the hallway, dressed again in black silk.

"You have to help me," Alisha said, forcing the panicked words through short, hard gasps for air. She was so terrified by all that had happened, she could hardly think. "You have to send me back to my own time. There are policemen linked to the underworld who want to kill me. And the man you wanted me to save is no longer destined to die. He is in a safe place several miles north of here. There is no reason to keep me here any longer. You have to send me back into my own body and bring Andrea back here to hers. *Now.*"

Imena looked at her curiously. "But you *are* Andrea. No one is inside that other body waiting to return here."

"But there has to be someone there," she argued, caught off guard by such an unexpected declaration. She had lived seventeen days believing that she and Andrea Knight had traded places; it was too confusing now to be told otherwise.

"You are wrong. When I first sent you forward, you entered the unoccupied body of an infant who had just died. And that same body, though now older, was left unoccupied again when you were brought back here. That is why

I gave you only three weeks to save that life
you'd endangered and return here. That other
body you occupied can remain vacant only so
long before those keeping it alive will decide
such attempts are useless. If you or *someone else*
does not return to take over that body within
two more days, then just as the sun goes down,
the body you once occupied will be deemed
without a soul and allowed to cease its functioning."

Not really understanding what Imena was trying to tell her but in too much of a hurry to
discuss such details, Alisha said quickly, "Well,
you won't have to worry about sending anyone
else. I have already saved the life you wanted
me to save. Thomas Knight is still very much
alive and safely hidden from further danger.
You can send me back now without any misgiv-
ings."

Imena continued to look at her curiously. "Who
is Thomas Knight?"

"The man you told me was destined to die if
I did not do something to save him," Alisha said,
frustrated by the games Imena seemed bent on
playing. Her breathing was now normal, but her
heart continued to hammer at a rapid rate. It
sounded to her as if Imena planned to back out
on her promise. "Remember? You told me I had
twenty-one days to reverse his death and return
here. And I did it in nineteen. You have to send
me back into the future now. You promised."

"But it is not a man by the name of Thomas
Knight who dies," Imena told her, still frown-

ing. "It is a man by the name of Randall Kincaid. I saw this just hours ago. You have not succeeded."

Alisha stared at her, horrified. *"Rand?* It is Rand who dies?" Her heart froze for an instant, then resumed beating even more strongly.

Imena lifted her hands and pressed them gently over her eyes. After a few seconds, she nodded. "Yes. I am right. Randall Kincaid is the one you needed to save. But you have failed. He has this very night been taken from his home by four men in dark clothes armed with pistols and clubs. He is now in a small warehouse near the waterfront and is being beaten unconscious."

"No! That can't be true," Alisha wailed, shaking her head violently. Not Rand. Not her beloved Rand. Why, he wasn't even home, so how could he have possibly been taken from there?

Imena continued to hold her delicate hands in place and stood perfectly erect. "But it is true. The men are angry with him. They want him to tell them something about you. But because he loves you more than life itself, he refuses to tell them what they want to hear. He will eventually be beaten until he is dead. He will breathe his last breath before the sun rises again." She lowered her hands and looked toward Alisha with wide eyes filled with despair. "Your smile will be his last thought."

Alisha had never felt such anguish. "You have to be wrong. Rand is too clever to let them get the better of him like that."

"Being clever could not save him. They were

waiting for him and he was taken unaware as he entered his house. Do you really want this man's death on your conscience?" she asked, then sighed and shook her head. "It is too late anyway. There is no way for you to save him now. Even if you offered your life for his, they would still kill him, for he has seen that which he shouldn't. Perhaps he was destined to die, for even with you still here it will happen."

Imena let out another heavy breath, then motioned toward the back room with a wave of her slender hand. "There is certainly no wisdom in having two lives lost. Come. I will explain to the spirits and ask them to let me return you to my great-granddaughter. At least this time you will journey forward with their sanction as you should have then. I will no longer bear the responsibility alone."

Alisha continued to stare at Imena, torn by all that she had just been told. She had a choice. She could go back right now, be safe again, and try to forget all about these people and the seventeen days she had just spent there. Try to forget that her beloved Rand was off in a warehouse somewhere being beaten to death during the very moments of her leaving, or that her friend Faye would also soon die but without either her or Rand there to comfort her.

Or she could stay long enough to find Rand and try to save his life before returning. It wasn't as if she *had* to go back at that very moment. She still had two days.

"Do you happen to know exactly where it is

they've taken Rand?'' she asked, having made her decision. She would gladly risk her life to save Rand's.

Imena closed her eyes a second time. After a moment, she nodded. "To a small empty warehouse that faces the water and has a large brown bird painted on one side. It looks like the eagle with its proud wings spread wide. The building, it is old and it is not safe. Part of the floor has fallen in.''

Knowing the general direction of the wharves and aware she still had to avoid running into policemen along the way, Alisha took off into the night yet again, this time to find Rand.

Oddly, after only a few blocks, the area around her felt familiar somehow, although there was no reason for that. And because the streets and buildings did seem so suddenly familiar, she had little trouble locating the small dilapidated warehouse that stood down and away from most of the other buildings in that district. It also stood well away from what few ships were docked in that area and was a good distance from the nearest paved street.

Though the closest street lamp glowed hundreds of yards away, she still managed to make out the dark shape of an eagle emblazoned across the side of the small building. She also noticed that there were three horses tied to a small, wind-torn tree only a few dozen yards away. A carriage was parked in the shadows of a much larger tree that shaded the nearest street. Someone was indeed down there.

Clambering down a slight embankment, she approached the secluded building from the darkest side so she would not be seen and noticed a dim light glowing through two of the side windows. Both windows were too high for her to see inside, however.

Quietly, she moved a large wooden barrel that stank of dead fish to stand directly beneath one of the two small windows. Lifting her dark skirts up out of her way, she hoisted herself on top of the creaking barrel and peered inside. She prayed that Imena would prove wrong. That Rand had somehow outsmarted his captors and was at that very minute on his way to the mayor's house to get help.

She gasped, her heart slamming hard against her chest, when instead she saw Rand inside lying on the rotting floor of a small room. His once strong, agile body was crumpled and bent. Blood covered both his face and his clothing.

Through the dingy window she could also see two armed policemen sitting in chairs nearby. One fiddled with a torn pocket while the other nursed a large bruise on the side of his face. Obviously, Rand had not gone down easily.

Not far away from them, two portly men in gray suits stood arguing near a closed door, their backs to her.

Knowing that she stood a few yards from the only door to the outside other than the one that opened out onto the dock area facing the water, she decided the door where they stood probably

led into another room or into a hallway of some
kind.

She felt in no danger of being discovered and
leaned forward to get a better look. When she
did, the barrel shifted beneath her, causing her
to fall forward against the wall with a thud.

Aware she had made enough noise to be heard
from within, she sucked in a deep breath and
peered inside again. Her heart hammered loudly
in her ears while she waited for one of the men
to react, but they evidently had not heard the
noise above the arguing because no one looked
in her direction.

Pressing a hand over her thudding chest, she
again looked at the two men in gray suits and
realized that one of them was Chief Clay Miller.
She recognized him from that night he had broken into her father's place.

Alisha felt a cold, terrified rage take hold of
her when she realized that Imena had told her
the truth. These men had beaten Rand until he
was unconscious, and unless she did something
drastic to save him, he would die before dawn.

While she desperately tried to decide what to
do next, the two men dressed in suits left the
room. They were still arguing when they came
outside just moments later.

Having heard the door open, Alisha dropped
lithely to the ground, then ducked down behind
the barrel she had just used. She pressed her
back against the wall and closed her eyes, praying they would not come in that direction. If

they did, they would see her and she would lose her chance to save Rand.

Alisha's heart hammered with a brutal force while she listened carefully. For the moment it appeared the men planned to stand right outside the door.

"Well, Clay, if you'd just let me handle that, we'd have already gotten him to tell us what we want to know. *I* would have been a little more careful."

"My men did all right considering the fight he put up. After all, he's not dead. Just unconscious. He'll talk yet."

"And what if he doesn't? What are we going to do then?"

"We kill him, then dump his body into the water like we do anyone else. Would you quit worrying so much? We'll find that woman yet, and when we do, we'll murder her, too, and finally be done with it. But what's so frustrating is that Kincaid *knows* where she is. I can feel that in my bones. He knows exactly where she went."

"I get that same feeling. But what if he never tells us what he knows? What do we do then?"

"Then we send someone back over to his house and try again to get one of the servants to tell us where she's gone. Shouldn't be too hard to pry that information out of them if they have it. They have no reason to protect her."

"But what if they do try to protect her? What if they don't tell us a thing?"

"They will eventually— if they know. And even if they don't know where's she's gone, they can probably be persuaded to do what they can to find out. No matter what, we will find out where that woman has gone. And we will find out tonight. Also, before we do kill her, we will need to find out what became of her father. Chances are that if she told anyone about the guns and opium, it was him. We can't chance letting him live."

"Well, it's clear she didn't tell Kincaid. If she had, he would have gone right to the mayor with the information. You're right. I think we should forget him for now and try instead to get one of those servants to tell us where she's gone. And if it turns out they don't know and have no way to find out, then we'll have to come back here and try again to get Kincaid to tell us. One way or another, we have to find out where she is and we have to find out before she has a chance to come out of hiding long enough to give our secret away."

Alisha's eyes rounded. Until now she had not realized that guns and drugs were involved. She had thought they wanted her solely because she had cheated Jeremy Miller out of all that money. Even so, the fact that guns and opium were involved did not surprise her. Not after seeing what they were willing to do to Rand to protect themselves.

"We have to protect our operation any way we can," Chief Miller continued. "Jeremy, you ride on over to the police station and see if Heath and George have arrived back yet. Tell them not to leave. Tell them I plan to meet them there in a few minutes. We still have more work to do."

With her breath now coming in short, restrained bursts, Alisha listened to the scuffling sound of one set of footsteps along a graveled path that led to the paved street. Because the building was perched on a narrow embankment, she could not see the carriage from where she sat, but within minutes it clattered away.

She remained perfectly still even after Chief Miller had stepped back inside. She could tell by his voice that he had not walked far into the building, but far enough that she could not quite make out what he said. She prayed that he was ordering the other two men to leave with him. That would make getting Rand out of there just that much easier.

But to her despair, when he stepped back outside, his words were, "And keep this door closed and bolted. Don't open it for anyone but me."

Alisha's heart sank.

"Eric, you will know that it's okay to open it when I knock twice then pause and knock twice again. Otherwise, the door stays shut. You got that? And I'll send someone back with the food you wanted in about an hour. Surely you two can last until then. Oh, and whoever brings the food will know about the special knock."

"Don't forget to send something to drink with it," came the response from inside.

"Just don't you and Craig forget to keep that door closed. And if Kincaid does come to before I get back, which I doubt, be sure to lock him up in that closet like I told you. I don't want him getting away."

"We'll take care of him," came the promised response. Alisha heard the door clatter shut again.

She listened carefully for the sound of the chief's footsteps but heard nothing to indicate he had actually left until she heard the whinny of a horse then the clopping of its hooves as it left.

Alisha waited until he'd had time to ride several blocks before slipping out from behind the barrel. Cautiously, she searched the shadows to make sure the man that the chief had just spoken with was not still outside. Confident she was again alone, she searched the debris scattered along the side of the tattered building until she found a large heavy, loose board lying amid the clutter.

Picking it up like a club and knowing she had to do something to save Rand before anyone else came, she sucked in a deep breath, then stepped over and knocked loudly on the weather-beaten door.

Twice. Pause. Then twice more.

Eighteen

"Yeah, what did you forget?" the man who answered her knock asked as the door slowly creaked open. When he found no one there, he took his pistol out of his holster and stepped around the door, which opened to the outside. He turned out to be a tall man, but not a muscular one. "Chief? What's wrong?"

Closing her eyes and using all the strength inside her, Alisha smashed the board across the side of his head, causing blood to splatter across her face and arms. The tall man crumpled to his knees, wobbled a moment, then fell face forward onto the hard earth.

Too panicked to be sickened by the sticky feel of blood, Alisha dropped the board and snatched the pistol out of his hand. Now armed, she spun to face the door just moments before the second man rushed outside to find out what had happened. She cocked back the hammer just in case the gun needed it.

He spotted his companion lying on the ground just before he noticed her. He had already drawn his gun but had not yet aimed it.

Now he was afraid to. She had caught him off guard.

"Drop it," she said in a deep, determined voice. A tight knot formed inside her chest while she waited to see if he had enough sense to comply.

The man stared at her for a long moment, then slowly opened his hand. The pistol fell to the ground with a soft thud.

"Don't shoot," he said, then lifted his hands high over his head to show that he meant her no harm. There was just enough light spilling in through the doorway behind him for her to see that his whole body shook.

"Don't *make* me shoot," she countered, so relieved to know she would not have to, that her legs suddenly felt weak. It was bad enough that she may have already killed the first man. She did not want to be responsible for two deaths. "Just do what I tell you and you can come out of this still very much alive."

"W-what do you want me to do?"

"First step back inside." She was amazed at how calm she sounded when she gestured toward the door with a quick wave of the gun barrel. "But do it slowly."

The man obliged her by backing into a small hallway that led to the room where Rand still lay unconscious. He stumbled once on a small hole in the floor where several boards had rotted out, but did not fall. Still the sudden movement was just enough to make Alisha that much more aware.

Once inside the corridor, where a lighted lantern hung on a nearby peg, she could better see her opponent's terrified expression. She was glad to note that not only was he smaller than the other man, he was older. And so frightened that his skin looked stark white against the dark material of his tattered uniform.

"Go on in that room there," she continued, never pulling her gaze away from his. "Then I want you to get into the closet where Chief Miller told you two to put Rand should he wake up."

The man immediately complied, and again Alisha followed with the heavy pistol held steady in both hands. She fought the urge to look at Rand when she first entered the room, knowing that until she had the other man locked safely away, she dared not take her sight off him.

"Okay, I'm inside," he told her, still holding his hands high above his head. "Now what?"

"Now close the door."

He looked almost relieved when he reached forward, then pulled the door close with a loud crack. "Okay it's closed."

With the pistol still pointed toward the door, Alisha eased closer, then quickly shoved the large metal bolt into place. With no time to consider what might have happened had the man refused to cooperate, she tested the door to make sure it was secure, then spun away. When she caught sight of Rand still lying there in a pool of his own blood, his body unmoving, her heart plunged to the pit of her stomach with a sickening thud.

"Oh, Rand, what have they done to you?" she cried, then sank to her knees beside him. She reached forward to cradle his face between her hands and felt another sharp pain pierce her heart. It hurt to see how truly battered he was. His face was not just bloody and bruised, one side of it was swollen and distorted. If it were not for his long hair, his curling lashes, and his strong, muscular build, she might not have known him.

"Rand, wake up," she tried again. "We have to get out of here." She rubbed his cheeks vigorously with her hands, the same way Rand had done the morning he tried to wake Faye from her coma. "Please, Rand, wake up."

Aware of the time that had passed and knowing that someone was due to arrive there with food in a very short while, she tried again, this time bending forward and shouting close to his ear. "Rand, wake up!"

Next, she shook him, though gently, for she wasn't sure how bad his injures were. "Please, Rand. Wake up!"

Panicked, she stood and tried to lift him up by the shoulders, but he was so heavy she could barely budge him. When she realized she would never be able to drag him all the way to safety, she tried again to wake him. A hard, throbbing ache filled her when he still did not respond. She had to rouse him somehow. If only she had smelling salts or a bottle filled with ammonia.

It was then she remembered the barrel she had used earlier to boost herself to the window. The one that smelled like dead fish. Quickly she hurried back outside, grabbed a stick, and stabbed it into the contents of the smelly barrel. Fighting her own urge to gag, she hurried back inside, then placed the tip of the reeking staff beneath Rand's nose.

"Please, Rand, wake up," she called again, and her heart soared with renewed hope when he suddenly jerked his head to the side, then sputtered awake. One eye opened and his lips moved, but no sound came forth.

"Come on," she said after she was certain he understood her. "I've taken care of the two men who were here with you, but we have to get out of here before anyone else shows up."

Rand blinked the one eye that wasn't swollen shut and nodded that he understood. With her help, he managed to roll over. With a contorted expression he forced himself up onto his hands and knees. From there he slowly drew himself to his feet, then grunted as if to announce he had done his part.

Even with Rand stumbling and disoriented, Alisha managed to get him outside and up into the saddle of one of the two horses still outside. After making certain he had enough of a hold on the saddle that he would not fall off, she returned to the man she had knocked unconscious and checked to see if he was still alive. When she discovered that he was, she rolled him inside, then closed the door and blocked it shut with the barrel and a lot of other items she found lying about outside. Soon she had debris stacked several feet high.

Before returning to Rand, she bent to pick up the pistol the second man had dropped and shoved it as far as she could into her skirt pocket. She placed the other pistol inside a leather satchel attached to the saddle, then untied the horse from the tree.

Putting her fear of horses aside, she climbed up behind Rand and reached around his slumped form for the reins. But before she could ask Rand what to do to make the horse go, she heard a carriage coming in their direction at a rapid clip.

To her horror, it was the same fancy carriage that she had seen parked on the street earlier. Obviously the chief's brother had returned for some reason. With his pistol drawn, he bounded out of the carriage before she had time to free her own pistol from the pocket inside her skirt.

"So there you are," he ranted, glowering at them both while he kept the pistol aimed at Alisha's head.

Angrily he reached up with his free hand and dragged Alisha off the horse, bringing Rand down with her. Rand landed on his side with a pained grunt, rolled over onto his back, then did not move.

Aware Rand had been knocked unconscious again, Alisha tore into Jeremy Miller with all the rage of a madwoman.

After knocking him onto the ground, they wrestled back and forth with the pistol between them until Miller, being stronger and larger, finally earned the advantage and pinned her back to the ground.

"Looks like I finally have you," he said as he sat astraddle her waist, his body bent so he could continue to hold her by the upper arms. His thinning brown hair stuck out in all directions and his expensive suit was ragged from the struggle. "I've been waiting for this night for nearly three weeks." His eyes glinted in the darkness when he released one of her arms, lifted his hand high, then slapped her hard across the face with the back of his fist.

"Let go of me," she said through clenched teeth, too angry to sense the immediate slash of pain. She tried to wriggle out from under him but found him too heavy for that. When she did manage to free her arm again, she made another grab for her pocket, hoping to retrieve the gun quickly enough to shoot him but discovered she must have lost the weapon during the struggle. She turned her head from side to side but could not spot it lying in the darkness.

"Let go of you? Not for all the gold in California," he replied, then grabbed her hand and pinned it beneath his knee before slapping her a second time with his free hand.

This time she felt a sharp, shattering pain as jagged flashes of white light darted across her vision. For a moment she nearly lost consciousness, but she managed to stay alert. She had to. For Rand's sake.

"You are going to pay dearly for what you've

done and for what you know," he spouted, then reached for the stiff collar of her bodice. Sneering, he tore the front of her dress open with his one hand and peered down at the white chemise he exposed beneath. "You will curse the day you ever crossed me."

Knowing it would do no good to try to convince him that he had the wrong person, she started squirming again but found she still could not free herself. An icy chill washed over her when he then reached for the top hem of her chemise and gave it a sharp tug. Although the material did not tear, the shoulder ties came loose and exposed her breasts to his greedy sight. She managed to free the hand he had trapped beneath his knee and made a wild grab for her clothing, but he caught her by the wrist before she could actually cover herself and pinned the arm above her head. She tried kicking him, but he was too high up for her to make contact. There was nothing she could do to stop him.

Terrified, she closed her eyes. She did not want to witness whatever he planned to do next.

"I finally have a chance to teach you a lesson," he said and bent forward to rub his stubbled face against her soft flesh while he continued to hold both her arms pressed firmly to the ground.

Alisha cringed and tried once more to struggle free but could not make him release her.

"Get off me, you fat, filthy pig!" she cried in anger.

"After I am through," he told her, then let

go of one wrist just long enough to slap her again, forcing her to reopen her eyes. "And after you are dead."

Laughing at the terror evident in her huge brown eyes, he raised up to unfasten his belt but stopped suddenly when he heard a loud shot ring out in the darkness.

He jerked his head around to see where the noise had originated, then turned to face Alisha again with a look of utter disbelief. Gently, he slipped his hand into his coat and pressed it over his heart. When he brought the hand out again, it was coated with blood.

"He shot me," he said with amazement while he stared at the liquid glistening on his fingers. "The damn fool went and shot me in the back."

Alisha watched with a mixture of horror and relief as he slowly toppled sideways, one leg still draped over her. Wiggling free, she saw Rand wavering unsteadily beside the horse, a pistol in his hand. Yet before she could rush forward to prevent him from falling, his legs gave way and he again sank into oblivion.

Rousing him, she managed to get him back onto the horse, draped across the saddle, where he fell unconscious again. She put the pistol he had used back into the saddlebag, then quickly she retied her chemise and tucked the loose part of her torn bodice into the top. Knowing that would have to do, she again pushed her fear of horses aside and climbed up behind him.

Not knowing where else to go, and also knowing that the man with the promised food could arrive at any moment, she slapped the reins like she had seen other people do and was relieved when the horse headed off in the general direction she wanted to go. It did not take her long to figure out how to maneuver the huge animal, and she headed immediately for Rand's house.

Even though she knew that the chief or some of his men might be there trying to find out more about her, or could come at any time, she rode into a nearby alley. She left Rand still draped across the horse, then quickly climbed over the garden wall.

Blood-splattered, bone weary, and running now on pure adrenalin, Alisha slipped inside the back door and headed toward the back stairs in search of William. She found him sitting on a stair about halfway up, dabbing at a large, gaping wound on the side of his face with a wet cloth. He told her that Jolie was upstairs in their bedroom tending to a similar injury.

The policemen had already been there again looking for Andrea, and like last time, William had been the one to open the door. They wanted to know where Andrea had gone, and he had told them the truth. He did not know. She had run off earlier— only minutes after she'd realized there were policemen at the door.

Despite his claim not to know, the policemen proceeded to beat both him and Jolie in an attempt to make them remember something they could have forgotten. The police might have done the same to Millicent and Caroline had they come back yet. Fortunately they did not return until afterward.

Though badly injured himself, William came to Alisha's aid immediately and asked no questions as he climbed over the garden wall behind her. It was after he had hoisted Rand's battered body up over one strong shoulder and had headed for the back gate that Alisha realized no one had come out of the shadows to investigate their activities. What had happened to the detectives?

Fearfully, she scanned the shadows and gasped with horror, when she spotted several men lying beneath a pile of rubbish, not moving. Obviously the police had found out about the detectives and had taken care of the ones on duty that night before even approaching the house.

Her whole body shook at that realization.

"Hurry," she whispered to William, even though he was already halfway toward the gate that led to the main garden close to the carriage house. She paused long enough to retrieve the pistol, then followed with it cocked and ready to shoot. "We have to get him to safety."

"You don't have to tell me that," he whispered back, then waited just long enough for her to lift the latch before continuing on.

As soon as they were all inside, Alisha bolted the gate shut, then again turned to follow William, who was already several yards ahead of her. There was just enough moonlight for her to see that Rand's weight was causing William to stagger.

"Where are you taking him? To his room?" she asked, wondering if the strength in William's shoulder would last long enough for him to do that.

"No. Not there. With those three detectives now dead, it's too easy for the police to get to him up there. I'm putting him in the summer kitchen, where there will be only one door for us to guard."

Thinking that probably best, Alisha hurried ahead of them to open the door. "Lay him over there on the worktable. It's plenty big."

She lit a lamp but turned it down dim so the glow would not be noticed from the outside before hurrying to see to Rand's injuries.

"I don't really know what's going on here, but it's clear to me that you and Mr. Rand's lives are at stake," William said with a grim shake of his head. "The police have been by twice tonight trying to find out whatever happened to you. I knew something was mighty wrong the first time when they forced Mr. Rand to go with them, but when they came back again without him, I knew some serious trouble was going on. But I didn't know what to do. Couldn't go to the police because they were the ones who took him, and I don't know how to get in touch with the other three detectives Mr. Rand hired. The ones who work in the daytime." His eyes clouded and his voice was strained when he repeated, "I knew there was some serious trouble going on but didn't have no idea about what to do."

"What did you tell the police?" Alisha asked,

wringing the water out of a dishtowel she had found in one of the drawers. Now that the summer kitchen was in use, there were plenty of towels and washcloths on hand.

"I told them that you had taken off like a frightened rabbit and that I didn't know where to." He stood there watching Alisha gently cleanse the blood from Rand's many cuts and bruises for a long moment, then added in a less strained voice, "I'll send Jolie out here with blankets, a pillow, and clean bandages. Then I'll go get the doctor." He stepped toward the door but paused. "Now, if for some reason I don't get back before those police come here again looking for the two of you, you be sure and use that gun. Don't you think twice about it."

Alisha glanced at the weapon she had laid on table beside Rand and nodded. She would have no problem shooting the men who had done this to Rand. "Just be careful, William. Those men don't care who they hurt."

"Don't I know," he responded, then lightly touched the still-oozing cut on the side of his face just before he disappeared from sight.

It was almost an hour before William returned with Dr. Owen, but in that time Alisha had managed to stop most of Rand's bleeding and, with Jolie's help, held towels filled with ice against the areas of his body that appeared the most swollen. It was all she knew to do.

"How is he feeling?" William asked as he closed the door and bolted it shut.

"I don't know," Alisha admitted with a worried frown. Her heart twisted with renewed anguish when she glanced down at the badly wounded portion of Rand's face. The whole left side was swollen and discolored. Just as discolored were some of the areas around his ribs and across his back. Plus there were several places where the force of their blows had split his skin open. How could anyone do such a horrible thing to such a wonderful man? she wondered. Her anger still boiled inside her. "He hasn't come awake since you left."

"Mr. Rand, he not said a real word in all dis time, but been moaning something terrible," Jolie added, looking every bit as concerned as Alisha.

Alisha stepped back to let Dr. Owen have a better look. "Did William explain to you what happened?"

"Not fully, but I think I pretty well know," the doctor told her. "Rand explained much of what was going on the second time your father was so badly beaten. But then it doesn't really matter to me how it happened or why. All that matters is that he needs my help. I'll do what I can for him." He began by rolling out the wick of the lantern Alisha had placed on the table so he could have better light. "Jolie, are you ready to be my nurse?"

Because there was now enough light inside for

people to see from the outside, William set about pulling the curtains closed.

"I hope you are not going to ask me to leave," Alisha said firmly, remembering how that same doctor had ordered everyone but Jolie out of Faye's bedroom that first day she slipped into unconsciousness.

"No, but I would like for you and William both to keep a watch for more trouble," the doctor replied while he hurriedly tugged out of his coat.

"All right," Alisha agreed. "There's no way to know what those people might do next. Could be anything."

She decided to wait to explain the additional gravity of their situation: that Rand had just shot and killed Jeremy Miller, the chief's brother and one of the city's most corrupt councilmen. As soon as his body was discovered and the men she had imprisoned inside that warehouse had a chance to talk, there would be hell to pay.

"Then you take this pistol," Dr. Owen replied, indicating the weapon still lying on the table. "And William, you take mine. I want both of you guarding that door while I try to patch Rand. I don't want any violent interruptions."

Not needing to be told twice, William accepted the pistol Dr. Owen handed him, then went to sit on the bottom step outside the door while Alisha pulled a chair over and sat inside staring through parted curtains. Occasionally she glanced away but only long enough to gauge the progress the doctor made.

It was nearly midnight before Dr. Owen finished working on Rand's many injuries. He had just turned his attention to Jolie's injuries when suddenly they heard Millicent's shrill voice calling out from a second-floor window. "William! William, come quick!"

William headed toward the house immediately. Not knowing what he faced, he held his gun ready. Minutes later, he returned to the summer kitchen, his eyes large with renewed concern.

"Doctor, it's Faye. She's coughing up blood."

"Faye?" Alisha replied. *What next?* She clenched her hands into fists to keep from crying aloud.

Nineteen

Without a word passing between them, Dr. Owen grabbed his satchel while Jolie snatched up some of the items he had left lying on the table beside Rand.

"You and William stay here. Continue protecting that door while I go see about Faye," he ordered as he rushed passed Alisha. "Don't let anyone get to him."

Shaken, Alisha turned down low the four lamps the doctor had used. Because they did not want anyone who might be watching the house aware that anything out of the ordinary was going on inside the summer kitchen, Dr. Owen and Jolie made their way through the garden without a lantern. The only light spilling across the courtyard other than a dim, silvery blush from the partial moon came from inside the house itself.

Alisha waited until she saw one of the back doors open and the dark forms of Jolie and Dr. Owen slip into the house before she spoke again. "William, you go on back outside and keep watching those shadows for signs of trouble while I cover Rand with a light blanket and make sure he's comfortable."

It was not really cold that night, but Rand was lying on the hard wooden table wearing only a torn remnant of his underdrawers. The doctor had cut away most of his clothing before going to work on his injuries.

William did as told, and while Alisha stood vigil over Rand, Dr. Owen, Jolie, Millicent, and Caroline did what they could for Faye. After another hour, Dr. Owen appeared in the door of the summer kitchen looking haggard and worn. He asked William to help him move Faye to the summer kitchen while Millicent and Caroline prepared a couple of sturdy cots for his two patients. He felt Faye would be safer there, and it would be easier to watch over both of them if they were in the same room.

By the time both patients had been heavily sedated and made as comfortable as possible on the canvas cots, everyone in the house had been informed of the terrible events of that night. But only Alisha knew that Rand had killed Jeremy Miller.

It was because of the increased danger to them all that she decided to tell them everything. Everything except the one little fact that she had come there from another time. That one detail, albeit true, would make them think she was lying to them. Even if it did not anger them, hearing such a strange tale might cause them to doubt everything else she told them. She had to keep their trust.

"Well, if you are really Andrea Knight like you say, did you cheat that man out of all that money?" Millicent asked, frowning over all she had learned thus far.

Alisha pondered how to answer that. Now that Imena had told her that she really *was* Andrea Knight, though she still was not sure how that could be, it had become much harder to answer that particular question with a resounding no. Apparently she was both Andrea and Alisha, but how could she possibly explain that?

Fortunately Jolie saved her from having to answer at all.

"What difference dat make?" Jolie snapped. "What matters is dat she and Mr. Rand are in danger and we have to help."

Millicent narrowed her gray eyes indignantly but did not respond.

"Also keep in mind that all of you could be in danger, too," Alisha cautioned. "Chief Miller is the type who will try to retaliate for the death of his brother. Some of you may want to leave until the danger is over."

"De danger, it matter to me none," Jolie responded with a defiant lift of her bandaged chin.

By then the doctor had tended to everyone's injuries, big and small, including a large scrape on the side of Alisha's face where Jeremy Miller had struck her.

"I take whatever dose men do to me." Jolie looked down at Rand, then at Faye. "I stay right here and care for dem both. Alone if I have to."

After hearing the deep emotion tearing at Jolie's voice, everyone chose to stay— especially after having been told that Faye was so much worse. After Dr. Owen gave her a thorough examination, he had sadly announced that she had only a week to live, if that.

That gave them very little time to show Faye how much they loved her and how much they would miss her after she was gone.

Because of the seriousness of their conditions, Dr. Owen stayed with his patients until nearly dawn, then left with a promise to return late that afternoon. But in case either patient should take a turn for the worse while he was gone, he told William where he would be. Otherwise, they were to try to keep them both quiet and sedated. He gave Rand and Faye both one last look, then grimly shook his head as he walked out the door.

Rand did not come to again until after four o'clock that afternoon. Faye, though, slipped in and out of consciousness several times, each time pleading desperately with whomever was in the room to take some of the pain away. Jolie responded each time by giving hr a little more of the medicine Dr. Owen had left. Because Faye was destined to die anyway, he had told her not to be too concerned with the possibility of giving her too much medicine. Keeping her comfortable was far more important. As long as she could keep the medicine down, she should be given all she wanted.

Although Millicent, Caroline, and William were in and out of the summer kitchen during most of the day—running errands, bringing food prepared in the main kitchen, or merely checking to see if there had been any change for the better— Jolie and Alisha rarely left the room. Alisha had decided early on to stay put until either she was certain Rand would be all right or until her time there was finally gone. She still had until late the following afternoon to have William hitch up that coach and take her back to Imena's. As long as she arrived there before sunset, she should still be allowed to return to her own century with no trouble.

Because she still had one day left, Alisha returned to the house long enough to bathe with a damp cloth and change out of her torn and bloodied clothes. She then sat vigilantly by Rand's side while Jolie remained close to Faye. But no longer did they stay there out of a need to guard them.

Early that morning more than two dozen detectives had appeared at Rand's door, armed and ready to defend him and his house from further attack. The men who worked for the Johnson Detective Agency had taken the deaths of their four colleagues personally and immediately took up strategic positions both inside the main house and outside.

Because the doctor's orders had been to keep the two quiet, sedated if necessary, they had decided not to move the patients back into the house even though the danger was now greatly diminished. They thought it would be better to wait until they had a doctor's permission before transferring them to the house.

Meanwhile both Jolie and Alisha sat in wooden chairs near the two cots, watching and waiting. That was where they were when Rand suddenly came awake and in a panicked state cried out Andrea's name.

"I'm here," she assured him, then stepped forward so he could see her. She took his hand and held it gently in her own. Joy filled her heart to overflowing when he turned, focused on her face, then smiled with relief. Rand was not only alert but able to see. His vision was not damaged by the blows he had taken in the head. "I'm right here."

Rand's hands trembled and his uninjured eye teared, forcing him to blink several times while he studied her smiling face. "I dreamed you were dead. I dreamed that I sent you to the plantation to hide with your father, and chief Miller found out and came after you. I dreamed that he shot you both." His hand tensed inside hers. "Right through the heart."

"Well, as you can see, I'm still very much alive. And so is Papa. No one else knows where you've sent him," she assured him, then wondered just when it was that she started thinking of Thomas as really being her father. "Papa is just fine. He has your sister taking very good care of him."

Rand stared at her a long moment, clearly relieved, then glanced curiously at his surroundings. "Why am I out here?"

Alisha explained, then told him that even though they were now well protected, enough so they had the door and all the windows open to allow a breeze, they continued to keep him there because the doctor had not been back to tell them it was okay to move him.

She lowered one hand to his face and gently caressed his battered cheek. Even bruised and with a swollen left eye, he was endearingly handsome. Not caring that Jolie might be watching or what she might think, she bent to kiss him lightly on the forehead.

"I'm sorry this had to happen to you. You don't know how guilty I feel or how angry this makes me."

"I'll mend," he said and attempted a smile, but grimaced at the pain that caused him.

Although not entirely comfortable in the wobbly cot, Rand agreed to stay put until the doctor returned and gave permission to move him. Even so, he refused to take but half the medicine Jolie tried to force on him.

"Now that Jeremy Miller is dead, killed by my own hand, the danger is far worse than ever before. I have to be alert should his brother decide to do something rash. Besides, I don't hurt all that much anyway."

Alisha studied him skeptically. She knew by the way he winced after each slight movement that the last statement was a lie. But she did not try to convince him to take more of the medicine.

For the next few hours, Rand remained awake, listening to William's intermittent reports of what was happening outside his house. For most of the afternoon, the police had passed back and forth along the opposite side of the street in groups of four and five but had yet to approach the house.

It was not until the doctor returned and *demanded* he rest that he and Faye were taken back inside the house and William stopped bringing him any information.

Finally Rand slept and left the protection of his house in the hands of the many detectives. He knew someone would wake him should anything significant happen.

It was not until darkness had settled that anyone advanced on the house. Three men dressed in police uniforms knocked on the front door and demanded to speak with Rand.

"We know he's in there," the largest of the three said with a dark, determined scowl.

"I'm sorry but Mr. Rand is resting," William stated calmly but scornfully.

"But we have something important to discuss with him," the policeman replied. His expression became even more grim when he glanced beyond William and saw three well-armed men standing nearby.

William returned that stern expression with one of his own. "Then maybe you'd better tell me what that message is so I can pass it on to him."

There was a long hesitation then, "I don't know. We were told to talk to him direct. The chief might not want us telling this to nobody else." He looked at the other two as if soliciting a response. They did so by leaning toward him and whispering gruffly near his ear. After a brief discussion, they decided to go ask if it would be all right to send their message through William. Several minutes later they returned to do just that.

William listened carefully to what they had to say, then went directly upstairs to tell Rand.

Alisha left Rand's room to go check on Faye, who lay in the bedroom just down the hall. She had heard Faye's painful moaning and knew that Jolie had gone downstairs to get more ice chips to help cool her latest bout of fever. Since the nurse had been sent home until things calmed down, that meant Faye was temporarily alone.

"Faye?" she called out softly to her friend as she came to stand beside the bed. Aware of her pain by the contorted expression on her face, Alisha bent to pick up the damp cloth Jolie had been using to keep her face cool. "Faye, what's wrong?"

Faye's eyes fluttered open, but it took her several seconds to focus on Alisha's face. When she did, tears instantly filled her pale green eyes and her words came in short gasps. "I'm in so much pain. I hurt all over."

"I know," she responded and sat down to stroke Faye's cheeks with the cool cloth. "And I'm sorry. I wish there was something I could do."

"There is," she responded, then looked pleadingly at her as she grabbed Alisha's clothing with amazing strength. "You can take one of the pillows out from under my head and hold it over my face. Please. It wouldn't take long to smother me. I promise I will not fight."

Alisha stared at her, horrified by the thought. "But I can't do that."

Faye pressed her eyes closed for a moment. When she looked at Alisha again, the tears spilled past her temples and into her pale blond hair. "Yes, you can. You must. I can*not* bear this pain anymore. You don't know what it is like."

"But I can't do that to you," Alisha repeated, pleading with her to understand. "I don't have it in me."

"Does that mean I have to continue to suffer?" Faye asked with pained annoyance. "Just because you don't have it in you to bring me the peace I need?"

Aware Faye was serious, tears filled Alisha's eyes, then spilled down her cheeks. There was no way she could have a hand in bringing Faye's life to an end, no matter how much her friend hurt. "Faye, you don't want to die. Not yet. Please, let me go find Jolie so she can give you more medicine. The medicine will help take some of the pain away."

She tried to stand, but Faye had such a grip on her dress that she could not easily pull away. Fortunately, Jolie appeared at that moment and hurried to administer more of the laudanum Faye needed. Several minutes later, Faye slipped off into a another fitful sleep and Alisha stayed just long enough to tell Jolie about her tearful request.

Jolie shook her head, dismayed. "I hope she not ask me. I never could do such as dat. But I no want to tell her."

Satisfied Jolie meant that and desperately wishing she could be in two places at once, Alisha returned to Rand's bedroom to take care of her own patient.

When she entered, she noticed that William now stood beside Rand's bed talking to him in deep, low tones. She could tell by the serious expression on William's dark face that whatever he said to Rand was important, so she did not interrupt. Instead she moved closer where she could hear.

"That's what they said," William continued grimly, his mouth drawn tight. "They said that you could prevent a lot of bloodshed and misery if you'd just agree."

Rand frowned, then glanced at Alisha. When he saw her questioning expression, he explained, "Seems our noble chief of police has realized the serious trouble he could be in for what he and his men did to me yesterday, and he wants to strike a deal. It appears that my having lived has caused him some unexpected problems."

Alisha found it hard to believe that the chief was so willing to offer a compromise. He did not seem like the type to give even an inch, no matter the consequences. "What sort of deal?"

"If I agree not to bring to light anything that

happened to me last night or why, and if I agree not to mention anything I may have seen or heard while they held me prisoner, then he will not press murder charges against me," Rand responded bitterly. "In other words, if I keep quiet, I will not have to worry about hanging for having murdered a man."

Alisha gasped. *"Murdered?* But you shot his brother because you had to. To protect me. True, that horrible man died by your hand, but that can't be considered a murder. Surely they can't hang you for having saved another person's life."

Rand nodded, and his expression became all the more determined. "You're right. It was not murder. That is why I'm not about to give into his demands. Not only do I plan to expose the chief's actions and those of his men, but I am quite willing to let a jury decide whether or not I should be punished for Jeremy Miller's death. I may have shot him in the back like he said, but I had good reason. And *I* happen to have a witness. The *only* witness. You. You are what will save me."

Alisha felt a sharp pang of guilt, for she knew she would not be there to help defend him. She would be gone by the following afternoon. "But what if they don't believe me?"

"Oh, but they will," he replied, then arched an eyebrow meaningfully. "That is as long as you don't start trying to convince the entire jury that you are not really Andrea Knight, that you are someone else. That would be one time when you'd have to stick to telling the truth for both our sakes."

"But what if they ask me if I cheated the man out of all that money?" she asked, hoping yet to find some reason, however small, for Rand not to count on her testimony. "I could go to jail for that."

"You shouldn't have much problem there. Not after the jury hears how hard you tried to make that situation right again. You need to remember that we have Thomas and Ruby both safely tucked away at the plantation. They both can verify that you tried to pay the man back his money and even offered him a five-hundred-dollar bonus to boot."

He paused a moment, then narrowed his gaze. "I'm not backing down. They took on the wrong man this time. I'm going to bring the chief and his crooked little operation down. With your help, I'll expose them all for just what they are."

Alisha looked away guiltily. He would be confronting those men without a witness.

"I think maybe you should reconsider," she said. "If you don't back down on this, lots of innocent people could be killed. He is the type to take his wrath out on anyone he thinks might be close to you."

"He won't be able to do much of anything if he's in jail. And even if he tried, he would never be able to get at anyone here. We practically have an armed fortress here. No, I've made up my mind. This city cannot remain under the domination of men like Miller. Our police force has needed to be purged for a long, long time, and now I have the power to do just that." Rand's blue eyes glinted. "Those men are coming down."

Alisha's heart twisted. "But what if you fail? What if you end up being sentenced to hang?"

"That is a chance I'm willing to take. I am not running from my responsibility."

"Besides," William put in, looking very proud of his boss, "no jury in their right minds would find him guilty. Not after I tell them how they came here and took him away at gunpoint. Then you could tell them how he shot that man in an effort to save your life."

Alisha bit back an angry retort. Why didn't William mind his own business? Without her there, Rand could very well end up sentenced to hang. "I think it would be a lot safer if he would just go along with the chief on this matter."

"No," Rand said with finality. "I'll take my chances and face Miller in court." He turned to William with such a look of cold determination that it caused Alisha's skin to prickle. "Go on back down and tell those men I said no. The chief will answer for all he's done. You also better warn the staff and detectives that there may be more trouble, because the chief is going to be furious after hearing that answer. Until that man is behind bars, no one in this house is safe. Also, I'm going to want to send a letter to the mayor right away. He needs to know what has transpired. Have someone bring me the lap desk and fresh ink."

* * *

Later that night when Alisha returned to her bedroom, instead of sleeping, she wrestled fiercely with her conscience. She knew if she left the following day as planned, Rand would have no witness in court. With her gone, it would be easy for the chief to claim that Rand had murdered his brother in cold blood. After all, the evidence showed that Rand had shot him in the back and at a distance, indicating there had been no threat to his own safety. And knowing the type of man the chief was, he would probably cajole his own men into lying and have them claim to be false witnesses to the shooting. Rand did not stand a chance without her. She had to stay.

For Rand's sake.

And her own.

Tears flooded her eyes when she realized the truth. The thought of returning to her own time no longer appealed to her. Although she would miss Roni dreadfully and would have trouble adjusting to such an entirely different way of life, she would much rather stay right where she was and be Andrea Knight, the future bride of Rand Kincaid, than return to the twentieth century and be Alisha Sampson, the broken-hearted. She needed nothing more than she had at that very moment to make her happy.

But if she stayed, what would become of Alisha Sampson?

Imena had mentioned two possibilities: either

send another spirit in her place or let the body she had once occupied simply die again and be gone. She wondered which would happen. Did Imena have another person in mind to send? If so, would that person go of her own accord or be forced into it much like she had? She also wondered if the person would be able to adjust smoothly to the new time period and if she would get along with Roni, who would not be aware of the change and would want to remain her friend. She knew that Roni could be pretty darned temperamental when she wanted.

Alisha felt her only real pang of regret.

Roni.

She knew she would never see her best friend again. Roni would never know how truly happy she was or that she had finally found a man worthy of her. A man of such strong moral character and sound principles. A man she loved more than life itself.

It made her sad knowing that Roni would never know any of these wonderful things, nor would her dear Aunt Lila, who had always believed she deserved better than Brad. They would never know of the extreme joy that now filled her heart— unless . . .

Her brown eyes widened at her next thought. There might be a way to let Roni know what had happened, after all.

Alisha thought about that for a long time, then realized exactly what she should do. But first she wanted to see Rand so she could tell him that she had finally made her decision. She would indeed marry him. Then she had to find William.

Filled with more joy than she had ever known possible, and even though it was well after midnight and Rand was finally resting, she slipped into her white nightrobe and hurried to tell him her decision. She did not want to have to wait until morning.

With her heart overflowing with happiness, she slipped quietly into his bedroom and lit the lamp beside his bed. When that did not wake him, she stared down at his sleeping form for a moment. Even battered and bruised, he was truly the most handsome man she'd ever met. She smiled as she sat down on the edge of his bed and called out to him softly.

Rand's eyes fluttered open upon hearing his name, and when he saw who sat beside him, he smiled contentedly. "I was just dreaming about you."

"Oh?" Alisha responded with an answering smile. Unable to keep from touching him, she rested her hand on his shoulder. "And was it a good dream or a bad dream?"

"Oh, it was a *very* good dream." He lifted a hand to push an errant curl off her cheek while his gaze roamed wistfully across her face. "I dreamed that you came to me dressed much like you are now, all in white with your dark hair loose and cascading down over your shoulders, just like it is now. You came to tell me that you had changed your mind. You had decided to marry me after all."

Alisha smiled and bent forward so that her long hair spilled over his chest and shoulders. Her mouth was only inches from his when she spoke again. "Then you must still be dreaming, because that is exactly why I am here. I really have changed my mind. I do want to be your wife. I want to have your children, lots of them, and I want to be able to make love to you for the rest of our lives." Her brown eyes glittered with love as she glanced down at his form. "As soon as you think your battered body is well enough to handle it."

"For the rest of our lives?" he asked. Returning her smile, he peeled back the covers and gently pulled her to him. "Then we might as well start right now, because that's just the sort of thing this body was made to handle, battered or not."

Then with tears shimmering, he drew her lips to his and kissed her passionately.

Alisha's heart soared to new heights when he reached for the sash of her robe. She knew she had found the sort of happiness that would last through all time, and nothing could ever take that away from her.

Epilogue

Roni glanced over at Alisha's aunt resting in a large green upholstered chair and realized how haggard and drawn the poor woman looked and knew that she looked much the same. It had been three weeks now, and Alisha had yet to come out of her coma, but at least she was still alive. Despite the fact that there had been no real sign of brain activity in all that time, the doctors had managed to keep Alisha living with the use of machines.

She glanced at the many monitors, computers, and apparatuses plugged into Alisha's limp body and knew the time was coming when Alisha's aunt would have to make the decision to let her niece go. Alisha would not want to be kept alive like that. It was so degrading. And senseless. Because without a brain, without the ability to think, there was no real life. But even so, Roni knew it would be a hard decision to make. She was just glad she was not the one who would have to make it.

"It's all my fault," Roni said softly while gazing down at her friend's lifeless form. With a fresh onslaught of tears, she lovingly brushed

Alisha's hair back with the tips of her fingers. It amazed her that after all she had already cried, she still had tears left to shed. "I'm the one who persuaded you to go into that voodoo shop in the first place." She paused to wipe part of her tears away with the back of her hand so she could see. "If it weren't for me, you never would have been attacked while trying to flee that awful place."

She shuddered at the thought of what else might have happened that day had she not gone back inside to find out why Alisha had not followed her outside. Because in the few minutes she had waited for her friend to emerge from behind her, someone had come out of the blue smoke and struck Alisha across the back of the head with something blunt, then had proceeded brutally to rob her of her purse and clothing. Roni was just glad she had been able to interrupt her assailants before any further physical harm had come to her. At least Alisha had not been raped.

With anger still roiling inside her, Roni glanced again at Lila, who had come awake to listen to her diatribe. "I still think that voodoo woman was an accomplice. I don't know why the police refused to arrest her."

"They say they have found no evidence that can prove she was involved," Lila reminded her with a morose shake of her head.

"That's because they don't *want* to find that sort of evidence," Roni said. She let her gaze wander to the quietly beeping monitors while she continued, "They want the woman to go free." She shook her head, then her eyes widened when she noticed that the lines on one of the monitors had suddenly become more jagged. They bounced at a more rapid rate up and down the screen. She then glanced at another monitor and noticed the same thing.

"Look," she said, her voice breathless while she pointed at the dancing blip. "Something's happening."

Lila turned and gasped.

At that moment Alisha's eyes fluttered open, and Roni's heart surged with hope. "Alisha!"

"Oh, my word," Lila responded, pressing her hand over her heart. "She's awake."

Alisha blinked, then squinted in an attempt to adjust to the flourescent light streaming down from the large fixture directly over her bed. After a few seconds, she turned her gaze to Roni, who stood gawking at her.

"Who are you?" she asked, then blinked again.

"Who am I?" Roni asked, so overwhelmed by what had happened that she was half laughing and half crying. "Why, I'm Roni Belomee. I'm your best friend."

"And I'm your aunt," Lila added, having come forward to have a closer look.

Alisha shook her head as if not understanding any of that, then glanced around at all the equipment that crowded her hospital room. She frowned, clearly perplexed by what she saw. "Where am I?"

"In a hospital. In New Orleans." Because the doctors had warned them that should Alisha wake up, she would probably be disoriented at first, Roni was not too worried that Alisha did not recognize them. Most patients having been in a coma that long awoke very confused.

"A hospital?" Alisha's frowned deepened.

"Yes, don't you remember being hurt?"

"No." She shook her head, looking more baffled by the second. "All I remember is the dream I was having just before I opened my eyes."

Excitedly, Lila hurried out of the room to find a nurse.

"What sort of dream?" Roni asked, then leaned over her friend so she could look at her more easily.

Alisha's face twisted with thought. "I dreamed that I was terribly ill. And when it was learned that there was no cure for my illness and no hope that I would ever get better, I was taken to a strange woman who was supposed to be able to take the pain away. I had taken a lot of medicine, but I do remember that I was in terrible pain at the time. I also remember a new friend I had made taking the strange woman aside to explain my ailment to her, and the woman nodding that she understood."

She wrinkled her face and looked again at Roni. "What did you say your name was?"

"Roni. Roni Belomee."

"That's strange. My friend told me she was sending me somewhere in her place. Somewhere

where I would feel better again. And she said when I got there, I was to tell someone named Roni how very much she appreciated her friendship and that she was happy now. Happier than she has ever been before. She also told me I was to trust you, that you would also be my friend." She paused, then shook her head. "But that's about all I remember. It is all so vague."

"That was some weird dream," Roni agreed, then grinned. "But then, like me, you have always had an active imagination." She reached forward to stroke Alisha's cheek lovingly. "Don't worry, your real memory will eventually return, but until it does, I'll act as your memory. And one of the first things I think I should remind you is that not only am I your dearest and most trusted friend, I am the *only* person you let drive your new BMW."

Alisha's forehead notched. "What's a BMW?"

"Oh, I *do* have a lot to explain, don't I?" Roni said happily, then sat down on the edge of Alisha's bed to make herself more comfortable. "Where should I begin?"

CURES
from
The
Counselor

Dedication

To the Creator of the lives of those who tell
their stories in this book,
Thank You for all that You've given to me—
so much, much more than mere human words
can communicate.

CURES
from
The
Counselor

Clint Conner

Whitaker House

CURES FROM THE COUSELOR

Clint Conner
570 Morningside Drive
Lancaster, OH 43130

ISBN: 0-88368-349-0
Printed in the United States of America
Copyright © 1995 by Whitaker House
Images © 1995 PhotoDisc, Inc.

Whitaker House
580 Pittsburgh Street
Springdale, PA 15144

1 2 3 4 5 6 7 8 9 10 / 04 03 02 01 00 99 98 97 96 95

Contents

Acknowledgments

I want to thank Dick and Donna Masheter, without whose help in obtaining and learning to use the computer on which these pages were originally recorded, they would all still be unwritten except in my mind.

Anyone who has read a first draft of anything I've written knows that more than thanks are due my wife, Bonnie, for her patient, painstaking labor of love as she transformed my original "masterpiece" into something readable. She and our daughter, Corrie, also put up with my frustration (and sometimes, irritation) in trying to write between clients, family times, raking leaves, mowing grass, and shoveling snow. Part-time writers who labor at home probably shouldn't! But as one who has had to, I've found myself surrounded by grace from two most wonderful people who cared, prayed, and put up with both me and the project. I bless them forever.

I also extend my gratitude to Whitaker House and editor Sharon Hemingway for their diligent efforts as they have served as midwives in the birthing of this book into print.

Clint Conner
Lancaster, OH

Foreword:
A Counselor Confesses

When Whitaker House published my first book, *Not without Cure*, one of its chapters told the story of a counselor who discovered he needed counsel and help the same as his clients did. This man from a dysfunctional family had become a Christian, had supposedly solved his personal problems, received training as a counselor, and was living happily ever after in beautiful Ohio.

Just like his counselees, he soon found that most personal problems are solved over a span of time by a process, not instantaneously, despite our cultural conditioning for "quick fixes." Soon after the book came out, that counselor found himself dealing with rationalizations and denials he thought were gone. He had to confront hurt and self-protection previously unopened to others or given to God as completely as needed—new depths of insecurity and anger that surprised him by their very existence. He had supposed past prayer had completely healed him.

Crushed to the point of depression, realizing that in the phrase popular then, that he still did not "have it all together," he did the only thing one who wants to walk with God must do: he humbled himself before God. The counselor's prayer went something like this:

"Father, I have told others that healing is not instantaneous but rather a process—part of our ongoing walk with You. I have paraphrased Psalm 32:5, *'I'll continually unfold my past to You, God, until everything in it is revealed to Your satisfaction.'* I told them that David did not have to do that for You because You already knew everything about him. David needed to confess and pray that way for himself, until he understood and was healed. He must have stopped somewhere in the process before he should have. It seems he denied what he was really like and what his real problems were. Otherwise, he would never have murdered and committed adultery or lied about it.

"I have done the same. I stopped short in praying all I needed to pray. I must follow the counsel I give others. I must pray over old attitudes and relationships, as I did before, but with the aid of the new perspectives You are revealing. I need to pray over new things, too, things I've never seen before...."

God interrupted him and communicated through the Holy Spirit these real words: *"Son, anyone who thinks he is different is still conceited. Healing is no different for you than for any of your clients. It is conceit to assume that you will ever completely know yourself.*

You'll never have it 'all together' before you reach heaven. My methods vary, but I do not deal differently with My children. Repent of your conceit. Receive healing for the insecurity beneath that conceit. You'll have more insecurity to pray about before I am finished. Many more nooks and crannies in your soul and spirit need to be made whole. But do not strive to discover these. It is a work of My Spirit."

I am that counselor. Sufficient conceit remains in me that I wish this were not so. I travel on the same journey as you, dear reader. Many are the days I am happy and enjoying the trip, but like everyone else, there are days when I long for the "quick fix," to be the total package marked, "the totally sanctified man of God—always holy, always godly, always righteous, completely healed."

I wait impatiently for God's appearing. Other times I do what we all should do: cooperate with the Lord in preparing myself and others for His appearing. I should be grateful that I'm no different from anyone else, grateful that His promise to complete the good work He has begun until the day of Jesus Christ (see Philippians 1:6) is for me as well as for you.

The Cure Remains the Same

Cures from The Counselor tells more stories about people who successfully solved

9

problems and the process they went through to do so.

In the years since *Not without Cure* was published, the clinical names of some conditions have changed while others have been added. Amid all these changes, one constant has remained: the cure. It is still the same as it was twenty years ago, two thousand before that, and back to the first people who felt or thought to themselves, or said to another, "It seems I have a problem here." This book isn't just about new people with spellbinding, psychologically "in vogue" stories to tell, including their treatment process; it is about the cure and The Counselor that process brings them to.

That first writing experience two decades ago left me saying, "I'll never do that again!" But during these years, two sons became men, and the deaths of two of the three additional children we conceived led to change in me. Those changes caused us to name our daughter who lived, Corrie Bethany, meaning "cherished girl," "from God's grace." These same changes led me to see every client as cherished and the grace that's in the cure for each one.

I don't know you, but I do know this: something in one of these stories is there just to bring the cure with blessing and grace to you, too. *Domine vobisium et cum spiritutia.* "May God be with you and with your spirit," and may you find your way to The Counselor as you read *Cures from The Counselor.*

Chapter 1

Adjusting to Aging

"Some of us die before 'our time' is up because we've taken 'our times' out of God's hands and placed them in our own hands. 'Our times' are indeed, intended to be left 'in His hands' (Psalm 31:15)." —The Author

A s I write these words, I am healthy, happy and seventy-six years old. My story, however, takes place ten years ago when I was a retired widower living in Florida, on a modest, fixed income. I retired at sixty-two and with my wife moved to the Sunshine State. Three years later she died of cancer. Two months later my son went through a nasty divorce which affected my relationship with my two grandchildren, who were my pride and joy. Suddenly they were distant both geographically and emotionally. They began to treat me and their father as enemies rather than family.

My relationship with my son changed, too. When I returned North in the summer to fish, we were estranged. He was preoccupied with his own pain, as one might expect. He blew up at me one rainy evening, yelling at me at the top of his lungs, and after that, no matter how hard we tried, we could never go back to the easy, if superficial, camaraderie we'd enjoyed before.

I began to pity myself, counting my losses: my wife, two grandchildren, and now my son who was slipping away from me. Illogically, I didn't count my daughter and her family as much as I should have. My son meant too much to me. I felt I had lost everybody and had only "things" left: fishing, my little boat, shuffleboard and golf with my friends—but these things changed from joys to duties to ordeals.

Soon, I wasn't eating or sleeping regularly. I spent days in my mobile home, some without dressing and a few when I never left my bed except for a cup of coffee and a sandwich.

One day I made two lists: in one column, those things I had left worth living for, and in the other, my future options. Six-and-a-half hours later, I had nothing under the first column and one item under options—suicide.

I bought two boat anchors and put them in my car trunk with two other anchors, two blocks of cement, and some rope. The next morning I penned an apology to my son and daughter, trying to reassure them that my death wasn't their fault.

I bought some bait and headed for a liquor store where I bought a six-pack and some wine.

I wanted to catch one last fish, get as drunk as possible without losing consciousness, tie the anchors to my belt, rope the blocks to my ankles, and take the last plunge.

Although I was unreligious, I believed God would understand my reasons and that whatever good I'd done in my life would outweigh the bad.

It was an infuriating day: not a single nibble for three hours. Drinking beer before four p.m. was more than I could bear. Boats occupied the secluded spots I'd marked as good places to die.

So, I dropped the idea of catching one last fish and was ready to get blitzed and jump when a boat appeared with two men in it. They fished all day next to me like someone had ordered them to. I could find no other place secluded, private, and deep enough to do the deed, even though I toured the lake again and again looking for other places.

Finally, I decided to do it after dark. About dusk I caught my only fish, then let it go. I kept drinking the warm wine and hot beer, but it was hard going. I snuggled close to the bottom of my boat so I wouldn't cast a silhouette. Anchored near shore in a deep water cove, I wanted any observers to think the boat was empty. I could hear voices floating across the water as I began to prepare myself mentally for what I was about to do. That was the last thing I remembered before passing out!

My next sensation was a strong hand shaking me and a loud voice saying, "Wake up, Harry." Another voice mentioned the anchors and blocks attached to my waist and feet. I'd thrown up and urinated on myself. My neighbor and life-long fishing buddy, Smokey, had stopped by my place that evening. When he found my car and boat still gone so late at night, he went into my mobile home and found the suicide note. He called 911. Within fifteen minutes the rangers were spotlighting every boat on the lake, asking night fishermen to keep an eye out for me.

The rangers took me to the park office where Smokey and a deputy sheriff were waiting for me. I had to promise to call the suicide prevention service and my son and daughter. Her reaction I could predict. She was a Christian. I had no idea what my son would say.

Smokey and I left, after he promised to keep an eye on me and see that I followed through with my three calls.

Smokey wouldn't leave me alone. I'd told him I'd call my daughter, to set her at ease, but refused to call my son or the suicide prevention office. He threatened to call them for me, or call the sheriff's office and have me confined to the psych ward, if I didn't. Then he went to sleep in my old easy chair which he had pulled in front of my door. He meant it when he said he'd keep an eye on me.

I made the calls. The woman I spoke with on the suicide hotline told me she'd tried suicide. Embarrassed in front of Smokey, I tried to explain to her why I'd tried.

I don't know if it was hearing a female voice again, or knowing someone else had felt just like I had, or the anonymity of her not knowing me, but I found myself not hanging up until an unburdening of my soul and forty-five minutes had come and gone, as had Smokey when he realized I needed the privacy to really talk.

To my surprise, our conversation ended with me hearing myself say I'd consider professional help, attend at least one meeting of a suicide-prevention support group, and call her back to let her know how it had gone and what I was going to do next.

At the time I intended to do every one of those things as much as I ever meant to do anything. But without knowing why, a few days later I found myself sneaking off in a cab for the airport. I took the first flight I could get for Columbus, Ohio, where I could escape to my daughter's. I was running from the increasingly embarrassing mess I had made for myself as news of what I'd done quickly spread from acquaintances to strangers.

My shame and embarrassment compounded as I thought about Smokey. Only the night before, he had agreed to stop spending nights at my place. I knew he would still be watching my lights and car, like the loving "hawk" he had become when it came to my life. "I'll go home if you promise not to...you know..." which I interrupted with, "Yes, I know, and I promise I won't."

But I hadn't promised not to sneak out my back yard between two trailers to a waiting cab on the street behind. I vowed to call Smokey from the airport seconds before I boarded my flight to tell him what I'd done.

Other thoughts cut off my guilty reverie. What needed to be said when my other airport call was made to my daughter's home? "Can you stand your old man spur of the moment for a few days?" Of course I'd hear, "Sure, Dad. When do we pick you up?" What I had tried days earlier had poised her toward me in the best of the many sensitive and compassionate ways she had about her.

I just hoped she'd be sensitive enough to keep from talking to me about her religion. Although she had gotten better about it over the years, whether she ever said anything or not, the religion issue was always there between us. We both knew it. The last time it had only been a simple statement as I was leaving: "Good-bye, Dad, I love you and we'll be praying for you. You know I don't want to spend eternity with just Mother and not you, Daddy."

A lump came to my throat whenever I remembered those words. I thought it was because of her soft voice and the tear in the corner of her eye. Those words seemed to pop into my mind a hundred times a day for what seemed like weeks until fishing, shuffleboard, golf, and card games crowded them out.

On more than one occasion, I had kiddingly told her that her efforts were useless to get old-time religion into an old man who would just have to take his chances when it came time for him to "head upstairs to meet the other Old Man." I knew how to cut her off, to let her know that although we were both smiling, we were at the stopping point in our conversation on that subject.

As the cab turned off for the airport exit, I found myself thinking of new stoppers for what I was sure would be a new level of, "Dad, what's just happened proves how much you need the Lord" comments from her and her husband. And what about my grandchildren, those wonderful little creatures who could still put a smile on my face? Would they have been told, and if so, what would I say to them? What would be my reply to their, "Grandpa, how could you try that when you know we love you and pray for you so much?"

My call to Smokey got me cussed out royally, but with love underneath that I could feel and hear. I could hear the same love in my daughter's voice when I phoned her and she said, of course, to come.

A few hours later as we conversed on the drive from the airport to her home, love was still evident. But I also heard a firmness, too, when she said, "Smokey phoned before you arrived, Dad. You know he's not really angry, just terribly concerned because you didn't follow through with your promises to get real help before you left. We all know you came here until things blow over at home and you can head back, sneak into your old routine, and not do any more about getting help than you did before you came. You probably won't be here long enough for the kind of counseling and help from a group you refused at home.

"Well, I made up my mind before you came to listen to the Holy Spirit and speak what I believe He has given me to say to you rather than give you only my words. Here's what I believe God has said: *'Let him stay as long as he wants. Don't preach while he's here; don't nag him to do certain things when he leaves. Ask him one thing only: to give you his word as a man—not under the pressure of his word as your father—to keep one counseling appointment while he's here, choosing from a list of several counselors you give him.'*"

As we rode along, I jokingly said I'd do the same thing she did with everything life confronted her with—pray about it. Immediately, however, I sensed by her silence that my attempt at humor had hurt her rather than lighten a heavy subject. Reaching across the seat and patting her hand, I promised I'd "sleep on it" and meant it.

That night when I bent to give her the goodnight kiss she'd received every night of her life when we still lived together, she pressed into my hand that list of names and phone numbers. Imagine my amazement ("miraculous" had never been a word in my vocabulary) when upon awakening the next morning to be immediately drawn to that list.

God uses whatever little shreds He can get a hold of in our heads and hearts when He's trying to apprehend us one last time. In mine it was a thought: "Conner—an Irish counselor—guess he can't be all that bad. I'll go out this afternoon for some pipe tobacco, call him, and when I get back say I talked to him. Everyone will assume I saw him and this whole thing will be over. I'll have a few good days here, then figure out what to do about life (or death) after I leave." I really didn't know if I would attempt suicide again or attempt to make a life back home. I just wanted to be left alone about getting help and be treated like nothing had ever happened.

Most of us survey life—especially our own—from a perspective that says big events are life-altering: starting school, graduating, marrying, having children, moving, changing jobs, getting religion, etc. A closer look shows us that lots of little things are just as life-changing.

That phone call proved to be one of those life-changing, life-altering "little things" for me. I "just happened" to phone Conner at a time when a scheduled client unexpectedly canceled, freeing his time to talk to me. My phone conversation brought questions I had never thought of previously, feelings and emotions I didn't know I was capable of, and hope that there was not just a future for me but a different one than the past I'd known. I know now all this occurred not because Conner was a great counselor with just the right penetrating questions and skillful techniques, but because Jesus is alive and gives each of us a chance to decide before we meet Him whether or not He'll be our Judge alone or our Savior.

"John," Conner said, calling me by the fictitious name I'd given him with an otherwise honest account of my suicide attempt and the events leading up to it, "from what you are telling me, you think you're running from a life that can only get worse and more empty to a god you believe to be a 'Man Upstairs' who won't send you to hell because you've done your best. You need to ask yourself a couple of things before you make the final decision again to end your life. Is the God who is the only God—Jehovah God—different from what you believe Him to be? If He is, He may have a different scale for 'measuring' us when it's all over, different than the 'I've-done-my-best' scale you think He uses—so different, John, that it could be a scale on which you get a failing grade!

"But let's not start with how God rates us. Let's first consider what He's like compared to what you think He's like, and how (or where) we discover this."

When I admitted that I thought creation revealed God, adding the standard non-Christian line, "I can worship God as well while I fish and watch the sun come up as any guy sitting in a church pew," Conner asked me if I saw people as an even higher form of God's creation than nature or fish.

Before I answered, the Spirit of God gave me the first spiritual revelation I'd ever had, other than a generic belief in Him. I saw that everything wonderful, happy, fulfilling, peace-giving, as well as everything positive I'd ever known, felt, believed, or done had been God's way of trying to get me to hear these words: *"Harry, the worth you felt when you graduated wasn't just personal satisfaction with achievement, it was mainly Me saying you have unique worth as the pinnacle of My creation—a human—the only one like you who will ever be. How you felt when your wife accepted your marriage proposal wasn't just her love that warmed your heart, it was Mine, too. I love you, and want to have a spiritual marriage with you through My Son if you'll receive it. Even the emptiness you felt after she died was to get you to see eternal emptiness before you die and enter it forever. The wonder of your children's births, and now your grandchildren—their natures, giftings, love for you—are all Me, too, Harry, trying to get you to look up. Your daughter's words, your wife's prayers now and just before she died, those of others you don't even know who have been praying for you, My intercession for you, and now the voice of this man you are talking to and this revelation by My spirit—all are attempts to reach you and turn you around before it is too late."*

All these thoughts seemed to come as in an instant while at the same time I was thinking, "Could this really be God?" One second it seemed plausible, the next, doubtful.

The thoughts and feelings I was having as I hung up the phone weren't coming like any others I'd ever had. Underneath I knew it meant that if they were from God, He was, indeed, nothing like what I had imagined. And if He were different than what I had always believed, His people-measuring scale must be a lot different, too.

What had been an almost finalized decision to kill myself before I made that revealing phone call was unceremoniously being replaced by two others: Was that God "speaking" to me? If so, would I respond to Him or not?

Within minutes of that call, I began to recall what Conner had been saying to me at the same time I was hearing what I know now to be God's voice. "As you ponder the eternal implications of another suicide attempt, please remember this: if you succeed, God will have allowed you a permanent solution to a temporary problem—age-related depression—a problem that has been resolved by thousands of other depressed, aging people who found the courage to keep on living, some with God, others without. Before you try again, probably successfully this time, think through the implications for yourself, your daughter, your son, your grandchildren, your friend in Florida, and others. Because while you are caught in the effects of your suicide in the next life, they will be caught in its effects in this world. Your buddy may do the same thing sometime just because it seemed to solve your problems. You'll have that to answer for, in addition to the effects on your kids and grandchildren who may never stop blaming themselves, wondering if they had just done something differently—prayed more, loved more, whatever— maybe they could have kept you from doing it. Even if they get past those regrets, they'll never get whatever God has for them through their only remaining parent/grandparent because you're no longer around.

"Since you refuse to come in or see any other counselor here, at least promise me you'll let me drop you a note when you get home with names of counselors like me where you live. And I'd like for you to call back once more before you leave."

I said I might call back before I left. I didn't. I did do one honest thing, however, for which I'll be eternally grateful: I gave Conner my true Florida mailing address, and to my surprise, had a letter waiting for me when I arrived with the name and number of the organization that could refer me to local counselors who were spiritually qualified to help me.

Before I even left my daughter's to return home I had pushed the "revelation on the phone" experience off my mental screen, not really thinking any more about it until a second one came as I opened Clint Conner's letter. All I can say is I'm glad I didn't do myself in between the airport and home because the Holy Spirit overshadowed my thoughts and feelings once again.

I called Clint early the next morning, spending another hour with him on the phone. The presence of God was once again very real and somehow I knew, although I seemed to be turning ever so slowly away from death and toward life, God didn't have many more divinely supernatural experiences like that for me—maybe no more at all.

After hanging up and reflecting on our conversation, the silence was broken with a loud knock at the door. It was Smokey, practically knocking the door down. I sat him down and told him right then and there I was deciding there was a God I didn't know from third base, and if He'd made the world and people He had to be a whole lot bigger and better than my tiny mind had ever imagined. I told him that three times now, He had overwhelmed me with thoughts about Himself and how He has been working in my life. I went on to promise Smokey I would make an appointment this time with a counselor like the one I'd been on the phone with when I "felt God." And I assured him I wasn't ever going to kill myself—he could bet on it!

I found myself saying, "Why take a chance of going to hell by dying without God, or even worse, sending myself there because I wasn't qualified for heaven?" I had no idea how to go about that, but I was going to find out.

Poor Smokey just about dropped his false teeth! He hadn't been sure he would ever hear his old buddy say he'd quit the suicide business, and now he was hearing religious words, too, from someone who hadn't been any more open to God than most old men until that very moment. I could tell that although he was glad I wasn't going to be dying, he wasn't any more excited than I used to be with the thought of having somebody close to him involved in "religion" in a serious way.

I kept the promise to see a counselor right away. When I did, I found out no one can receive God without receiving Jesus. *"No one comes to the Father except through Me,"* Jesus said (John 14:6).

I did that—received Jesus. I did so very early one morning when I loaded my boat (this time leaving all my fishing gear at home), and headed for my favorite spot on the lake, and prayed. I received God the Son into my life just as a different sun was gracing the sky in one of those unique Florida sunrises.

When I docked a couple of hours later, I realized I had spent most of that time praying. These weren't the "now we thank You for our food" or "now I lay me down to sleep" kind I'd heard my kids say, but real prayers about giving my life over to Him to live, not die, and to live that life however He wanted me to for Him.

There were some pretty strange looks when I docked and everybody saw me with no poles, bait, or fish. I began to chuckle, then roar hilariously when I realized those looks meant those friends at the marina thought I had chickened out on another suicide attempt. Trying to control my laughter, I decided right then to give my first witness about Jesus, making an effort to convince some pretty skeptical old characters that I wasn't drunk or suddenly "mental" but had really become a Christian.

They all know now I really became what I said I had that day nearly ten years ago. I still fish and dock there and "work on" the ones who are left just like my daughter used to "work on" me.

For several months I saw the counselor whose witness picked up where Clint's had left off. This, along with some pills prescribed for depression which I took for awhile, and my conversion all helped me get where I could stay mentally focused and benefit from the counseling and prayers for my healing.

It wasn't long before the Holy Spirit helped me find a church where I not only discovered a spiritual family right away, but the most wonderful woman who became my wife a couple of years later.

I've aged a lot in some ways the last ten years, but feel like I've gotten younger in others. In each and every area of my personal and married life with a new person, all my aging problems, all hers, and all of ours have been prayed about to The One who understands all about aging because He's older than time itself. He is far more than just the "Man Upstairs," as I used to believe. Even more than that, He has as much, if not more, for us older folks who know how to appreciate Him and the life He gives us, than younger people who often don't think of or take time to get to know Him like He is.

When you come as close as I did to ending life, it seems somehow sweeter. Growing old with another beside me and Another within, along with life itself, are three of the greatest gifts I know of!

Afterwords[1]

Harry is right. This story could just as easily been about a widower or depression or suicide. I gave it the title of *Aging* because it graphically describes several of the problems older people have: losses, loneliness, and the depression that results, to mention only three. Other elderly folks live with illness, disease, pain, or major problems with living standards related to reduced income; others must face increasing dependence and loss of the familiar such as their home, driving privileges, old friends, as they live out their remaining days with relatives or in nursing homes.

These and other problems lead some seniors into depressions they are not even aware of, and in others, increases what has been a life-long feeling of melancholy or sadness. Still others have had what I call a life-long existential depression because, like Harry, they've waited until the end of life to figure out what it is, who they and God are, what they've really been created for, and where they're going when they die.

I've started with this story for three reasons. First, when someone tells you life isn't worth it, take them seriously. You don't have to know that older widowers are five times more likely to successfully end their lives than those in any other age group to take seriously the "Harrys" you meet. Second, although it is important to learn all we can on a subject like aging, depression, or suicide, nothing you know will ever be a substitute for spending time with a person. Two telephone calls and some postage were certainly worth my time in Harry's case. Third, whether you know nothing, little, or lots about a subject, if you'll bathe whatever you do in prayer, the Holy Spirit will pour all God's grace and mercy into and through it to accomplish whatever the free will of the person involved will allow. The presence of God came to Harry because Jesus loved him, because his daughter and first wife had prayed for years, and because I prayed as I talked to and wrote him—not because I was a counselor or because of what I knew. He'll do the same for those you talk to and pray for if you ask Him to.

---

[1] We've purposely changed the spelling of "afterwards" to "afterwords" to indicate words after those used by the person telling the story. They are my words—the author—to highlight certain things in the story just told which may be applicable to your life or to someone you know.

Chapter 2

Alcoholic Offspring

"All of us are born helpless. When we realize it, loneliness grabs us. We attempt to diminish or submerge this loneliness looking for love and nurture from others and from things. Shame and guilt follow from these selfish, manipulative acts. Unless Christ redeems us, what remains is our lot in life." —The Author

I joined a support group to recover from my background and the life it had led to. I listened to the lecturer list some of the characteristics of people reared by addictive, dysfunctional parents like mine: isolated, poor self-image, approval-seeking, easily intimidated yet controlled, guilty, victimized, seeking relationships with other victims, unable to achieve intimacy. I thought, I've got so many of these characteristics, I'll never get better.

Up to that point, nothing had helped me: not counseling, advice, books, a different attitude toward my parents, avoiding them, trying to manipulate them to treat me differently—

nothing. Nothing could change how I felt inside or how I treated others.

The group helped all of us to see what was wrong with us. It proposed very few solutions. It could not give me or anyone else the power to carry out those solutions or to make the radical changes we needed to make.

For example, one evening the group dissected the roles we played in our families. Some were black sheep, while others had been the scapegoat, clown, or heroine. There were other roles: missing child, caretaker, junior (substitute) parent, etc.

I was overwhelmed. As an only child, I'd played all of those roles at one time or another, from dutiful daughter to bad rebel. I took notes furiously at that meeting, wanting desperately to change.

What little I was able to modify left me feeling no better. So, after a few months, I quit the group and fell into the worst depression of my life which is where I was when Amy, an old girlfriend, moved back to town, called and told me about a new kind of counseling and counselor who'd helped her with lifelong problems. Her enthusiasm was so contagious that I called her counselor for an appointment.

When I asked the counselor what was so different about her counseling, she replied that she was a Christian. Amy was sheepish about this when I confronted her about it later, admitting that she hadn't said anything about the counseling being "Christian" for fear of scaring me off. She explained how she'd become a Christian and was referred to this counselor by the people who'd helped her find spiritual answers.

I liked the counselor but was wary when I returned to see her for our second appointment. I had no religious inclinations and Christianity struck me as the worst of available religions. I viewed Christians as bigots, because they insisted that their religion was the only way. If I ever became religious, I told myself, I'd pick a tolerant one, a religion that believed that all roads lead to God.

I explained this to the counselor and she said that was an issue between God and me, not between me and her. What lay between us, she explained, was what I wanted from counseling and how we could get that started.

Defining that was easy enough: I wanted to escape the dysfunction of my family and past. To that the counselor wisely suggested I drop all my dysfunctional labels and focus instead on what I wanted to be rather than labeling what I was. "When we meet next," she said, "tell me what you want to be and what would be required for you to achieve that."

Making the wish list was easy. I wanted to fall in love and marry a wonderful man and live happily ever after as a wife and mother. I wanted to jettison my depression, anxiety, and low self-esteem. I wanted peace and happiness.

Figuring how to get from here to there was the hard part. I had no idea how to do it, so I copied a list of how-to steps from a book I'd read about overcoming a dysfunctional past. A good list, but it left me precisely where I'd started with the support group: trying to incorporate qualities from a list.

How could I change feeling the way I'd felt all my life? It seemed hopeless, so I called Bonnie, the counselor, and told her I wouldn't keep our next appointment or be scheduling more. I explained my dilemma and my conclusion that I wasn't getting any further with her counseling than I had with the support group or any other remedy I'd tried.

She suggested I keep one more appointment anyway. If it didn't help, she said, I wouldn't have to pay for it. That sounded fair enough, so I agreed.

After listening sympathetically during that appointment, Bonnie asked me a question. "How much would you have to be involved with God to overcome the ways you feel and act?" I was suspicious, but she hadn't tried to proselytize me, so I relayed, honestly, that if adopting religious beliefs or values would change the way I felt, permanently, then I'd accept them.

I began to see where this was leading. If I could live life, if I could change my life without God, I'd never ask for His help, would I? Most people never accept what they don't need—or don't think they need. Few get help with what they can take care of on their own.

After that session, questions troubled me: Was there a God—the Christian God? Had He allowed my efforts at self-esteem to be frustrated to drive me to Him before my life ended?

If He did exist, I loved and hated Him. I loved Him for trying to get my attention and hated Him for frustrating my self-help efforts. If He didn't exist, then death was truly the end and none of my struggles and pain would matter five seconds after I was gone.

Many Christians call this process of questioning and wondering about one's relationship to God "conviction." I never cared for that word. I prefer now, in retrospect, to think of it as "attraction." God was simply trying to attract my attention.

The Holy Spirit gave me a sense of God's presence and placed those questions burning in my mind: questions about God's nature, how to know Him, and how to have a personal, not abstract or merely intellectual, relationship with Him. Then came the overwhelming desire to have that relationship. In my counseling appointments during that attraction time, the Holy Spirit used Bonnie to answer my questions and to lead me to exactly the right book, article or Bible verse for my needs.

After several months, Bonnie looked across the table and said, "You must decide whether you are going to continue hearing about God, letting Him warm your heart—which is all He can do as long as you keep Him on the outside—or if you're going to let Him in your life so He can start changing you." There it was. A decision. I had to decide one way or another. Not to decide, ironically, was actually deciding against God.

I began to see that my experiences in my dysfunctional family made me feel inferior and inadequate. Now, for the first time I saw the mistrust my background had bred in me. I wanted to believe in God. But I didn't want Him, or anyone else for that matter, coming into my life. Much in my life was rotten, but at least it was predictable and controlled. I couldn't count on it remaining that way if Someone else was living within me, especially God. He might do or want something I didn't!

I took three months to weigh my decision —my dilemma, actually. One quiet summer night I lay in my bed. A silent voice said, "Faith isn't waiting and waiting to see if I'm trustworthy before you let Me come in. Faith is letting Me in. It's a decision, not a feeling."

The relationship had to come first. My mistrust of people had kept me from establishing a relationship with God. I knelt by my bed, asked for God's Spirit in my life, received Jesus' forgiveness for my sins, and told Him I trusted Him to run my life as He pleased.

I felt different. I acted differently, too. No more isolation, no more poor self-image, no more insecurity. I was at peace with myself. I felt like someone who'd come at long last to the end of a long journey home.

That was over two-and-a-half years ago. A couple of weeks ago, I was cleaning my apartment and came across one of my self-help books. Looking over its lists of dysfunctional characteristics, I found only a couple out of the fifteen or so that had originally applied to me

Better yet, many of the good characteristics I had wanted have come into my life, thanks to Christ, whose character is being formed in me. And, thanks to His presence (not self-help), they've stayed with me.

Afterwords

I would add this note: As Leanne Payne reminds us in her book, *Healing Presence*, practicing His presence isn't worshipping or relating to the God now within, but the Transcendent One who also exists outside us. He who is separate from us must be worshipped.

Chapter 3

Angry Adoptee

"If God is sovereign, then we ought to examine where we've been in life, where we are, and where we're going in reference to Him—the First Cause—not the secondary causes, the causes of who's done what to us and why, what's happened, etc." —The Author

My story begins twenty-three years and nine months ago when a seventeen-year-old boy and a sixteen-year-old girl conceived me out-of-wedlock. Seventy-two hours after I was born, my biological parents gave me up to my adoptive parents whose physical characteristics and nationality matched those of my parents better than other applicants at the time.

My adoptive parents were determined to be good parents. They read all the books and pamphlets they could find on the care and upbringing of adopted children. They meant well, but nothing they did worked.

I loved them—but only to a certain point. They were comfortable with me—up to a point.

Beyond those points, however, lay a chasm none of us could bridge. We never really bonded. As the years passed, we saw that it was more serious than "hadn't": we were unable to bond. We headed in opposite directions.

My parents were moral. I wanted to be immoral. They never lied. I never told the truth. Whatever they wanted, I wanted the opposite. Whatever they desired, I wanted nothing to do with it.

By thirteen, my rebellion against them involved an insatiable desire, an obsession, to find my mother. I needed to talk to her, to find out why she had abandoned me.

Six years and a lot of effort later, I found her. I can still see the horror on her face when I revealed who I was. She turned white, grabbed the door for support, and explained that she'd married but had never told her husband about me. If I ever came back, she threatened to kill me if her husband ever found out. She not only hated my father and herself for the pregnancy, but also me!

When I tried to ask the questions that had been burning in my heart for a lifetime, she shoved the words back into my mouth. She had no answers for me and nothing to explain except that she would have me arrested as a trespasser if I didn't leave immediately.

I broke down and pleaded with her not so much for answers to my questions, but for acceptance and love. She slapped me and screamed hatred. The scream and the sound of her neighbors' doors opening snapped me out of my trance. I realized suddenly that if I didn't get out of there, I would be arrested. So. I beat it, driving eighteen hours back home without stopping to · eat or rest. I knew I'd never go back. I knew that I'd never get the answers I had sought. I knew I'd never hear a kind word or feel a soothing touch from my biological mother. My attorney had been right to try to dissuade me from finding her.

As soon as I got home, I asked my boyfriend to marry me. I thought marrying might ease the hurt of rejection. It didn't. Neither did having a baby, but becoming a mother did set me on the road to solving my problems.

As my child grew from toddler to a little girl, I could sense that she had many of my problems. She'd inherited them in her spirit long before the way I handled and treated her could have communicated these pains to her. Although my problems remained unresolved, the "mother love" in my heart wouldn't let my daughter go through life carrying the hurt, rebellion, and rejection I had.

I heard no voices but a knowing came into my heart that said, "Jillian won't really be healed unless you are." I believed that, but I tried to heal her myself by going to parenting classes, reading books, watching videos, and listening to radio and TV programs. I talked to relatives and friends, attended lectures, all to no avail. My relationship with my daughter worsened.

Seeking help and advice from a high school girlfriend, I was mildly surprised when she suggested that attending church with her would lead me to a solution for my daughter and me. I'd not been religious. My adoptive parents hadn't reared me in any particular faith. I agreed to go, though, thinking it wouldn't help but so desperate without any other alternative.

I thought that if God existed, He must be mean to allow the pain my daughter and I suffered, but there I was in my best dress, standing to sing a hymn, as a choir walked down the center aisle of a new suburban, neighborhood church. Sun drenched the stained glass windows as I hoped against hope that "religion" might help where nothing else had.

Religion didn't save me. Christ did. As soon as I understood that He paid the price for my sins, I gave my life to Him. At first, I felt that all my problems were solved. For the first time in my life, I felt clean. I didn't feel guilty for my many mistakes as a parent and, for almost a month, seemed to quit making them.

Then, one morning, they started again. Jillian accidentally spilled her juice, and I flew into a rage, my mouth exploding at her in such a fierce way that I knew that more than the spilled juice was eating away at me. Worse, when I tried to fix the damage I'd done, we wound up in the same painful place we'd always been before I became a Christian. She was hurt and rejected me when I asked for forgiveness and tried to make up for my rage.

Devastated, I wondered if any change had actually taken place in my life. Within weeks, I was convinced that if such people as Christians really existed, I wasn't one of them. The "same old things" were happening. It was then I considered suicide for the first time, wondering if I had the courage to take my life, how I'd do it, and what would happen to my daughter and loving husband if I did. Would he find a good woman to raise our daughter and love him?

I'd quit the church where I'd become a Christian by this time, but my girlfriend didn't give up on me. I told her to leave me alone, but she said, "Okay, Jill, I won't call anymore, but you can't stop me from praying for you and Jillian. I hope you get counseling from some people I know. If you ever do want to call me, don't let your anger or embarrassment at 'cussing me out' today stop you. Nothing has changed with me."

I hung up. Dropping Jillian off with a neighbor to baby-sit for me, I went off to sob uncontrollably by myself. Hours went by. My husband finally came home after work, but I cried through dinner, and when I still hadn't stopped crying three hours later, he said in his soft-spoken way, "I've said all I know to say. I've done things I didn't know how to do to help you. I can't get into this Jesus and church thing you've been into, but I have prayed to-night and you aren't better. You're worse. Promise me you'll just cry and not kill yourself or wake Jillian to apologize to her one more time. I'll go downstairs to sleep. I can't jeopardize my job by missing work because I've not slept all night. If you can't promise, then I don't know what to do except take you to the psycho ward."

I promised. A couple of hours later, I fell asleep crying as softly as I could. I awoke feeling like I'd been beaten. My eyes were swollen shut. Exhausted, I heard the words *Conners* and *Lancaster* resounding in my head like a needle stuck on a record. This was the name and location of the counselors my girlfriend had suggested I see.

I had no idea who or what "the Gipper" was, but the expression, "give it one more for the Gipper" hit me. I decided to call the Conners in Lancaster and try the one remedy I hadn't tried: counseling. I didn't do it for God or myself, but for my daughter.

A few days later, I began my first counseling appointment by saying, "Help me stop hurting my daughter. I've given up on myself, but give me something that will stop me from hurting her." I didn't mention suicide, but the Holy Spirit informed them. I admitted that I was thinking of killing myself if counseling didn't help.

As I left my third appointment, Clint explained from Scripture the idea of fasting. He asked me to forego some food I really enjoyed and to use that time to pray. I did so between then and my next appointment two weeks later.

I drank only water one day, going without solid food for three meals and no coffee for another three days. I devoted mealtime to prayer for my daughter, my biological and adoptive parents, and for me. I prayed for my healing because in those appointments, the Holy Spirit had taught me that Jillian needed a healed, whole mother as much as she needed healing for herself. My healing was, in effect, a factor in her becoming healed.

I returned for my fourth appointment knowing we'd planned to spent most of it in prayer. Still, I wondered how much difference prayer could make in life in general and my life in particular.

How do I explain what happened to me through those healing prayers then and in later appointments? First, I asked for and experienced something that had only been intellectual for me up to that time: being a new creature in Christ—being *"greater"* even than John the Baptist, as the Bible says. As those words were prayed over me, God restored me— not to innocence or perfection—but to wholeness by the power of the Holy Spirit. He restored me to what He gave Adam and Eve when He forgave them for their sin of disobedience in the fall.

Next, the Holy Spirit Himself engrafted (or, if you will, impregnated) within me the desire to continue—to continue to live, to continue to grow spiritually toward the Lord as servant, parent, mate, friend.

Then we prayed that the part of my soul that had never been born might come to birth and grow from infancy to maturity, and that I would experience the effects of bonding like I never had. As we prayed, I was given a flashback to when I visited my biological mother. I saw the venom of that day wash over me from the second my mother knew she was pregnant up to the present. I hadn't forgiven her rejection of me which only perpetuated the venom, passing it to the next generation, my daughter. As I had reaped, so also did I sow.

Next, we prayed for spiritual balance and health. I prayed that God would give me a healthy, appropriate attitude toward my own and the opposite sex. Another flashback showed me how, unconsciously, I'd accepted and agreed with my biological mother's hatred of me. I had, in a sense, appropriated it and hated myself just like she did.

God lifted this dark, heavy burden from me and an inaudible, yet real voice said, *"Jill, while you were still a sinner, I died for you because I love you. If you are to be Christlike toward others, then you must be Christlike toward yourself. I love you unconditionally, but I can't love and accept you for you. Only you can do this. Accept yourself in the same manner you've accepted Me—completely. Choose to love, accept, and forgive yourself as unconditionally as I love you and forgive you."*

My belief that I was different—and not as good as others—melted away, transforming into a feeling of acceptance. Christ healed the wound.

Isaiah asks, *"Can a mother forget her child?"* (Isaiah 49:15) and promises that our Heavenly Parent will never forget or forsake us. Even if He wanted to forget us, He couldn't. My mother was trying to rid herself of something she couldn't expunge—the God-given "natural" bond in her soul for her child. She hadn't rejected me. She rejected motherhood because she felt inadequate to mother me and overwhelmed with guilt for the circumstances in which she'd conceived me. Love wasn't absent. She was struggling to blot out the love that was there, a love God gives all mothers. She really hated herself for what she'd done, not me. Likewise, I never hated Jillian. Like my mother, I hated myself which led, inevitably, to hurting my daughter in the same way I'd been hurt by my mother.

Those healing prayers didn't cause instant maturity. They were, however, a beginning. I had been unable to make it as a Christian and non-Christian before those sessions. Freed from the effects of original sin, of my sins, of others' sins against me, I was able to start growing spiritually and emotionally for the first time in my life.

The real test of spiritual healing is the fruit it produces. I am tension-free, able to talk to and love my husband. I can talk normally to my daughter, and I'm able to nurture her and not abuse her. I am able to pray for my biological parents that they will receive salvation and healing, too. I pray this not just for my sake or their sake but for Christ's sake because anyone's salvation makes Him happy.

I pray for my adoptive parents, too, and for my husband and daughter. They're not Christians yet, but are moving in that direction, each touched by the Holy Spirit through the example of the changes they can see in my life. Those changes witness more effectively than words can.

I also prayed for and witnessed to my attorney, the one I had consulted when seeking to find my biological mother. I told her she'd been right and apologized for not having listened to her advice. I told her that I called because I had become a Christian and that Jesus had prompted me to contact her.

Finally, I've prayed over what I have written here that it would witness to and encourage you, whether you are adopted or not. If you need healing as I did, it's there! Let Jesus into your life and ask for all that salvation brings—

life eternal and a healed life internally now. He promises to give it.

Afterwords

What the Holy Spirit revealed to Jill appears to me to be confirmed by modern psychological research. Some observers explain second pregnancies by unwed mothers as caused by "problems in their backgrounds." I suspect these girls seek a mother/child bond that cannot be cut by legal adoption following a first pregnancy, but can only be ministered to and healed by the God who created it. This God-created bond may also explain the tenacity which biological parents and their children display trying to find one another. Deliberately bringing biological parents and adopted children together was unheard of when we entered the counseling profession.

Jill's experience with her biological mother underscores the necessity and importance of praying for and determining God's will before initiating such contact. We live in an age of "God, give me what I want" even by Christians, but all of us must keep in mind God created us, knows us, and desires our best; therefore, our desires must be predicated on His if they are to have any chance of success.

Chapter 4

Anorexia and Bulimia

"Years ago when people in this country were emerging from the privations of the Great Depression and World War into a time of plenty and prosperity, this saying became popular: 'Some people eat to live, others live to eat.' I wonder if it isn't the guilt of existing, among others, that's described in this chapter which cause some people to stop eating to live (or vice versa) and begin (not) eating to die?" —The Author

The words "death" and "hell" could be used interchangeably in place of "anorexia" and "bulimia" for this story without being either melodramatic or inaccurate. I was a bulimic. My sister is anorexic.

Others call what we did an eating disorder. I'd call it first-degree murder. The premeditation in what we were doing may have been unconscious, but that didn't make it any less an intentional killing of ourselves—suicide.

The understanding of this horror story of how I got started with a food-thing that I later led my sister into I'm telling you from a hindsight perspective. When I was going through those painful, destructive years I didn't have a clue about why I was doing what I did nor what to do about it.

We grew up with a father who loved his job as a professional engineer, his favorite sports teams, and his wife and children—in that order. I don't think he ever loved himself. I guess that was why he was such a workaholic, always trying to make up for whatever it was he didn't like in himself. Unlike our vocal mother who always had something to say, usually negative, Dad said very little to any of us. When he wasn't at work, he was absorbed in TV or what it took to keep the house and lawn looking the best in the neighborhood. I didn't come away from what little contact I had with Dad feeling like I'd been with a mean, rejecting man, but rather with an empty and unaccepting one.

I think most of the reason Mom was negative and critical so much of the time was because she'd lived all of her life dominated by her mother. Grandma lived with us, ruling not only Mom, but all of us and everything around the house most of the time. She was even louder and more negative than Mom.

You could almost feel the death wishes Mom had—first for Grandma, then for her marriage. And somehow in our spirits, both of us girls knew we were the only reasons Mom hadn't left. Most kids feel their parents had them and maintain a home for them because they love them. What we felt was two people enduring us until we grew up and they could leave each other. It came out a different kind of death wish than the literal one Mom had for Grandma and Dad, but it was a death wish nonetheless.

Although I didn't know it at the time, those kinds of relationships and that kind of atmosphere not only created a hunger in me for real love, they also created the feeling that I was an impotent little kid in a dangerous environment that I desperately wished something or someone would come along and give me power over. Because I was a child, I had all kinds of dependency needs, but no one I could trust to meet them. My life was further complicated by all kinds of self-hatred because I subconsciously thought that if I were like other kids whose parents love them, mine would love me, too. Since they didn't, and neither parents nor kids are perfect, I concluded the reason my parents didn't love me must be my fault.

If you are wondering why someone could think food would solve the problems in a mess like our family, the scenario went like this for me. When you can't trust or depend on anybody you know for giving you love, you settle for a substitute you can depend on. Food is always dependable to give you the same feeling. Even though sweet tastes and a warm, full feeling aren't love, when they are as close as you can come to the real thing, you take what you can get and substitute them for what you really lack. Bingeing made me feel like I was sweet and warmly loved even though I was only full of sweets and warm food.

"Okay," you say, "I can see how that makes sense in a twisted kind of way, but I don't understand the purging that follows the bingeing of bulimia." I can explain that, too. When you have as rotten a self-image as I did because you think nobody loves you, pleasure becomes a cardinal sin. Believing you have no virtue leads to believing you never deserve pleasure. Bingeing is a pleasure, so you feel you shouldn't have it, or at least keep it once you've gotten it. Something must undo it, remove it, take it away. Purging does exactly that! Vomiting removes the pleasure of bingeing. When you flush the contents of your stomach down a toilet, you're not only getting rid of what brought pleasure, you're no longer the impotent little child. You feel like you've got power. You're in control. No more unmet dependency needs. You can depend on predictable food *and* yourself. You're in charge, and when you eat, you feel loved.

I got to the place where I experienced a high when I binged, much like people describe getting from drugs when they say it is like an emotional orgasm for them. Then when I purged I punished myself—and my parents, too, after they found out. At the same time I used food to punish them, it was as though I were trying to please them at the same time, saying by my behavior: "I'm dying. This is killing me. I'm getting rid of me, which is what you want—me to be gone so you can leave each other. Does that make you happy? Have I finally pleased you? I hope you'll tell me 'yes' so I can quit before I really do die!"

I never heard those words, "stop!," "we're pleased," "we love you," "we don't want you to die!" So, my rituals went on, moving me inexorably toward both emotional and physical death. I wonder if most of the people who commit suicide quickly instead of slowly like I was wouldn't have their lives saved if they could have heard those same words I was looking for—"I love you"—spoken not just once, but repeatedly by someone who meant them and whose love was unconditional. I learned later in counseling that people have used rituals since the beginning of human history for a variety of reasons, two of which are to control what they can't cope with and to control what they don't understand. Bingeing and purging were my rituals.

I didn't see it at the time, not even when I began to steal food from groceries and convenience stores, that bingeing stole or took "love" and gave it to me. But a person with no self-worth taking love feels guilty; that's where purging comes in. Vomiting was unpleasant for me at first but it soon became my high, my joy, almost a sense of happiness I looked forward to. Why? Because it cleansed me by giving me an exhilarating feeling of being clean. It was the only way I had for cleansing myself from anger and guilt.

Although it felt like it removed guilt and anger, of course, it really didn't. They were still there, and so the ritual had to be repeated over and over again. I heard later in counseling that failure to really remove something leads any of us to repetitive behavior which attempts to appease. But at the time it was going on, I knew only that while I ate I felt good, then bad—terribly, terribly bad—until I purged. Afterwards I felt great, a feeling which I could tolerate only briefly before I needed to feel good and bad again. The whole cycle would start over.

Life cannot go on forever like that for anyone. It didn't for me. I, the controller, the one seeking control of impulses and life itself had become the one who was controlled!

My parents took my sister and me to a counseling center that specialized in eating disorders. They hospitalized my sister and started me in individual counseling, a support group with other bulimic girls, and in family counseling appointments with my parents and eventually, my sister.

Although all of that counseling never got me to stop bingeing and purging completely at the time, I now believe it saved my life until a time came when I did quit. What we learned about anorexia and bulimia never phased my sister. But what I found out I was doing to my body scared me enough that I began to cut down on my frequency of bingeing and purging, and even stopped it altogether for periods that sometimes lasted weeks.

If my story were a book instead of a single chapter, I'd tell you how life—if you can call what I was living a life—went on. Suffice it to say, high school graduation came and went, followed by a series of marginal, minimum wage jobs and few relationships with anyone other than the people I met through the counseling agency where my contacts, even though sporadic, nevertheless continued.

One rainy, Sunday morning, not long after I had turned twenty, found me flipping the TV dial in my bedroom looking for a good movie. A television minister was concluding his program on a channel I soon changed, but what he said so intrigued me I made a mental note to watch his entire program the following Sunday.

I did, and that led to nearly six months of Sunday mornings spent hearing the Gospel of Jesus for the first time in my life. One of those Sundays I bowed my head, closed my eyes, and repeated aloud the same words the minister asked viewers to pray. Those became not mere words but a prayer of commitment to Jesus Christ, and I became a real Christian.

Not much happened for the next few months. I didn't meet any other Christians or go to church anywhere. I did try to read the Bible some and started praying about a lot of things. I kept watching the TV minister on Sundays, too, and I began to realize I never binged or purged on Sunday after becoming a Christian, not even once.

I know many people (Christians included) criticize TV preachers, and I can understand why. They have good reason to in some cases. But for lots of people, a television church is the only one they are ever going to try when they are like I was.

When I told my parents what I had done, they thought anything was okay if it helped stop the bulimia. My counselor cautioned me about religion and church, and my sister was so totally against God and anything in relation to Him that she became angry and rejecting of me whenever I brought the subject up.

With that kind of discouragement and very little encouragement, it is a wonder I didn't totally give up. However, the Holy Spirit has a way of finishing what He starts (see Philippians 1:6). My twenty-first birthday was on a Sunday. As I watched that minister who by then had come to feel like a friend, I heard him say that anyone watching who wasn't getting over their problems ought to think and pray about seeing a Christian counselor.

When I heard those words, I felt like they were Jesus' birthday present to me. On my break at work the next morning, I phoned the Christian television station that aired the program and was given the names of some Christian counselors in the area.

The next day I called the Conners. I guess I was intrigued by what a husband/wife couple who counseled together would be like. I spent the next six months seeing them and also a volunteer they introduced me to, somebody to get together with between counseling appointments who would talk to and pray with me when I felt like bingeing. She was someone who had successfully solved the very same problems I had with food.

It took me awhile to get to the place of saying, "I'm going to quit bingeing and purging forever," and I slipped a couple of times even after I did say it. But I could see that unless and until "I quit forever" is what someone does say, they can't really start to get well even if they do slip like I did. Quitting for good was the point I finally got to, now over two years ago. I've had over seven hundred days without reverting to what I'd done for over two thousand days before that.

God healed me through prayer during that period of extensive counseling. He responded to the prayers I prayed as well as those of the Conners and my friend, the volunteer, for me. These prayers released the grief my bingeing and purging behavior expressed. Prayer healed my feelings about and reactions to my parents and theirs of me. I even prayed about my sister's birth and the jealousy I had over who I felt she was that I wasn't.

Accompanied by the unconditional love and genuine concern I received, prayer accomplished in me what the relationships with my family never had. Things too numerous to detail here, except for two I want to share.

When I became a Christian, I didn't know that Somebody all-powerful not only forgave my sins but came to live in me, too. The awareness that Jesus Christ actually lived within me was a life-changing revelation which helped me stop trying to manipulate everyone—God included—by my behavior.

Clint related a story to me about how God had told one of his sons that if he let Jesus throw a ball through his hand that his inability to throw it would be overcome. I gave my problem to Someone within who could overcome it and all my other problems through me!

Secondly, I saw that although people have different symptoms (behaviors), they are really trying to solve the same problems, whether they take drugs, are alcohol addicted, into sex, or bingeing and purging like I was. What all those behaviors really do is cut off a piece of you and throw it away each time you indulge in whatever you're doing until you die because there is nothing left of you. The Conners told me about people they'd seen who literally cut pieces of their flesh off as an expression of their self-contempt. I saw for the first time I was doing that very thing with my soul and body every time I binged and purged. In short, six months of counseling prayers led me from the healing of my addiction to the healing of the despair that my behavior expressed.

What I started out fooling around with in high school so I could be thin and popular like other girls became more than something to try. It became something that possessed and almost killed me. If you are a teenager with thoughts of trying what I did, never start. It will lead you into hell on earth.

Now that I am out of the hell I was in, and even doing some volunteer work myself with teen-age girls who need a friend, I tell them the same thing I am telling you. You need power beyond your own never to start, or if you have, to quit. Only One greater than you are can destroy the stronghold for such an addiction.

Afterwords

If you re-read this chapter, you'll not only see the dynamics of bulimia and the way this young woman got over it, you'll see something else that is extremely important for all of us, whether we have this problem or are just reading about it. Bulimia and anorexia are two of the most dangerous addictions because the people who have them do not realize they are killing themselves a little bit at a time, and short of that, physiological damage to the body is often irreversible.

For the person in bondage to the addictive and ritualistic behaviors inherent in bulimia and anorexia, a greater, more powerful ritual is needed—the "ritual" of unconditional love, demonstrated repeatedly and consistently until the bondage has been replaced with love bonds that cannot be broken.

Chapter 5

Attention Deficit Disorder

"I have calmed and quieted myself like a child quieted at his mother's breast. Like a quieted child is my soul."
—Psalm 131:2 (Author's paraphrase)

"**D**ave, if you don't stop wiggling and sit completely still, you'll lose your mind." I cringed when I heard my son's playmates saying things like that to him. I cringed not only for him but because it took me back to childhood memories when I heard things like: "What's the matter with you, Dave? Got ants in your pants?" or, "You act like a bag of augers, Dave. For cryin' out loud, will you just sit still!"

I could solve my son's peer problems by telling his friends they either had to stop teasing or quit playing and go home. But I couldn't solve the problems Davey's hyperactivity created for him at school.

By the time Davey finished second grade, we had been told that the regular classroom teachers had done all they could. In addition, unless a local doctor who specialized in treating learning-disabled children was able to help him significantly over the summer, he would be assigned to special classes the following fall.

I couldn't stand the thought of that for my only son. I had gone through school in classes like that for the emotionally and mentally handicapped because I couldn't sit still long enough to learn. Compassionate teachers helped me get into an auto-mechanics training program after I dropped out. I blossomed in that program because I didn't have to sit still for hours on end and I was studying something I liked.

Even though I left school without a diploma and with a mind that was still like a pinball machine, I had a trade and no problems. No problems, that is, until a few years later when I was faced with a son who was looking at ten more years of school with a mind like his father's—seemingly incapable of keeping one random thought after another from flitting in and bouncing around, which were followed by a hundred others.

Those thought patterns were not really the only problems. School reports described Davey as "impulsive," "easily distracted," "hyperactive," "motor-driven," and "attention-seeking." In reading those words, all I could see was that my son was facing ten more years of pain like I had experienced.

Although I remembered kind teachers from my classes, I could not remember even one compassionate classmate. Bigger boys pounded on me, and smaller ones had been just as abusive with their mouths. The girls were not a whole lot better. Some teased or made cruel remarks; most had nothing to do with me. In either event I felt rejected. I came out of those years of classes little more able to learn than when I began, but with a host of behavior problems I had not had when I started. I did not schedule an appointment with the doctor because I wanted to—I did it to save my son from the same thing that almost destroyed me.

In that first appointment, the doctor, bless his heart, gave us what we had been looking for and what we needed: both an accurate diagnosis of what was wrong and what to do about it. I can say "bless his heart" now, however, that is not what I felt at the time. After some tests on Davey, he sat the three of us down and proceeded to say things that were difficult to hear, producing a variety of emotional reactions inside me, not the least of which was anger. He began by saying, "Davey isn't retarded or dyslexic. And he isn't mentally handicapped in a neurological sense. But he can become more or less learning disabled depending on what you and he do from now on, every day."

He went on to explain Davey was suffering from an attention deficit hyperactive disorder

(ADHD, or ADD, for short), and although he would be prescribing some medication to help with the remission of Davey's behavioral problems in the short term, he was referring us to a couple who did counseling for the real treatment that was needed for the attention deficiency rather than the learning/hyperactivity problems which were its symptoms. He cautioned us that Davey's learning disability could increase or decrease significantly depending on what we did.

The appointment concluded with our doctor handing us the couple's business card, saying they had helped others like us in the past but they weren't the only ones out there should we prefer to go to someone else. What mattered was that we saw someone, especially if we wanted him to continue prescribing, testing, and otherwise monitoring Davey. In other words, counseling was not an option!

A few minutes later as we sat in the car reading the words "special interest in Christian counseling" on that business card, my wife felt intrigued, but I felt trapped, along with the anger and fear that go with such a feeling. I might have been considered a lot of things by a lot of different people, but being a Christian wasn't one of them! I was about as far from that as one could get and wasn't interested in getting any closer. And I surely didn't want to see anyone that specialized in Christian counseling just in case they tried to take me in that direction. No, I definitely did not want to go there.

Our efforts to find help quickly elsewhere were unsuccessful, and because we had enough success with the medication slowing Davey down that we wanted the doctor to keep his case, we agreed to contact this couple. I was determined to let their counsel help my son and equally determined not to let it make a Christian out of me. And it didn't.

What it did do was give us a real understanding of Davey's attention deficiency by exposing what it was in us as mates and parents that both helped precipitate it and keep it going.

The counselors said their understanding of the neurological side of ADD was that the brain centers related to concentration and the ability to pay attention didn't function as effectively in AD people. An inordinate effort was required of them to control thoughts, get rid of those they needed to, and concentrate on that which did need their focus. They said the intensity level required to maintain normal thoughts and emotions caused most people to give up and live their lives as prisoners of their impulses, be they thoughts, feelings, fantasies, or all three.

Without asking what went on in our family, they added that they believed those under-developed attention centers in the brain of someone suffering ADD could become just as developed as those in others if certain things happened.

First, the communication which took place in the relationships the child had with other family members had to become firm yet kind in a consistently soft-spoken way. Soft-spoken was one thing I was not, but I could see the point. I just had not seen it during those first seven all-important developmentally critical years of my son's life. As children block out the pain, fear, and anger produced with loud discipline and parental arguments, which they all do as the sensitive little people God has made them to be at the outset of their lives, something else happens in that blocking. Not only is the attention to the "bad and unhappy" blocked, but the critical development of "attention-paying" areas is blocked, too.

The Conners, our counselors, went on to say a peaceful verbal and relational environment would keep added damage and deficiency from occurring. However, it would not necessarily heal what had already occurred. When my wife asked if it were possible to undo what had occurred in the past—that is, heal the hurts which had affected Davey and the resulting AD—we were confronted with the "Christian answer" I had been dreading.

The way the Conners put it was this: True healing from what had occurred could only come from God, and then only if what had caused the problem stopped (in our case, the loud, insensitive handling of a sensitive boy), mutual forgiveness, and replacement with the kinds of attitudes and words that would cause someone to want to hear, think, feel, and pay attention. To do all this, they added, was usually too difficult for people to do consistently without the power of the Holy Spirit in their lives.

I did not go back to hear any more. Fortunately, my wife did. I went off to find support for something other than a Christian answer to our problems. The nurse at work introduced me to a social worker who was angrier at Christians and their "answers" than I was. Even though neither of us came up with anything that really worked with Davey, we continued to project our inadequacy with so-called solutions into what my wife and the Conners were doing with Davey. I criticized her continued involvement with them, but I didn't forbid it. That was the only smart thing I can say I did during those all-important months.

While I griped, sulked, and unsuccessfully tried to quit yelling, I saw the Christian counseling I hated help my wife and son. They became Christians, joined a church, and began through healing prayer to recover from the effects of years spent in what we had thought was an okay, perhaps even better than average, typical American home.

My wife's success with changing her tone of voice to what the counselors said Davey needed, and what at the time I thought to be stubborn insistence that we enroll Davey in a Christian school for third grade, not only brought the "can't-learn" wall down around Davey, it began to make some cracks in the anti-Christian one around me.

I did not understand what my wife meant about the spirit of this world being over the public school and a different Spirit being over Davey's new school. However, I could feel what she was talking about when I went to a parents' meeting and met teachers, tutors, and other staff who treated him like I wished I could but did not seem able to.

By then Davey was no longer on the prescribed medication and continuing to improve according to the IQ, personality and psychological tests the school district required the Christian school to administer for all special students. The only explanation was that God was healing him and those around him, except for his father who steadfastly resisted giving in to what he needed even more than his son did.

I resisted, that is, until the night of the Christian school's Christmas program. Seeing my son able to sit quietly, repeating without a flaw all the lines he'd memorized for his role in a play, behaving himself, and displaying the same joy and happiness that I saw on his mother's face not only that night but at home, all combined to break something hard and cold in me. I had tears in my eyes all the way home and for the next two days.

I'd have never asked to go along to the next appointments with the Conners if it hadn't been for those tears, and even at the time I couldn't quite believe what I heard myself saying: "I want to go with you." I did go. And when I did, I heard an explanation for my tears that brought even more.

"Dave," the counselors said, "there aren't many parts of life that aren't a mirror-like picture of what God is trying to say to us about ourselves. Tears have a message for us; dreams are his disguised messages to us; what children play tells us what God is trying to let us know that they are going through; what's happening in our relationships is His picture of what we are reaping from what we've sown in prior relationships. Even the numbers and letters associated with our learning problems carry much that is symbolic for us, and are often God's messengers of what's wrong and what's needed in our lives."

"Dave, you need to see your son's problems and yours before his altogether differently than you now do. They aren't curses from a petulant God. They are something you've needed and when they've served their purpose(s), they can pass out of your lives through God's healing if you give them to Him for that purpose. And when you do, you'll find He not only removes and heals, He replaces.

Einstein was dyslexic; whether He ever gave God the credit for it or not, God replaced his dyslexia with the tremendous gift of intellect we're all aware of as evidenced by all his great achievements. Fanny Crosby, a Christian poet-songwriter saw God transform the problems her blindness created for her by giving her nearly two thousand hymns and songs to write, including 'America the Beautiful,' even though she never *saw* any purple mountains or amber grain.

"There are lots of ways to diagnose people and just as many ways to define their problems. You can look at your son and yourself through one of those grids and say he's an ADHD and I'm an ADHD, RT, even though you've learned to control your hyperactivity and gotten yourself a job where the AD doesn't affect your performance a whole lot. But all you have with that diagnosis is a description of symptoms. At a far more basic level than that, you are two creatures of God's that He very much wants to do His will in because He loves you both. He has already started that with your son and your wife because they have given their lives to Him through their faith in Jesus. He'll do that with you, too, if you do what they did—by faith, receive Jesus and commit your life to Him."

The tears that had been glistening in the corners of my eyes for days became like a flood as I heard those words. I felt an overwhelming sense of Jesus' presence in that room and saw in my mind's eye a little boy—me—with words spoken by angry parents coming at him like darts, each shattering a piece of me as they struck different parts of my head and body. Those shattered pieces broke off and turned into big, black tears.

As I gave myself in that moment to that presence—Jesus—He touched those pieces of me lying all around me in shattered puddles of liquid blackness. As He did, as fast as lightning bolts, they returned to the place on me where they had been before the angry words broke them off.

When the vision was over, I was left a shimmering, bright, whole person. The counselors said that was a picture of my completed healing. And it was. Several appointments later, I was no longer the little boy on the inside, one of those one in every seven or eight with a learning disability who walks sideways through life instead of straight ahead when it comes to the things of behavior, learning, and the mind.

What God did during those appointments healed me from things my ancestors did before I was conceived that I had inherited spiritually, as well as what had happened to my spirit in my mother's womb before I was born and ever heard those stabbing words I was healed from during the vision. I'm glad for what the world was able to do for me and my son with tests, medication, and special classes, but all that pales into insignificance beside the healing Jesus gave us.

My mind may not be ready for me to take some kind of job that would require an intellectual for it to be done successfully. However, I've apparently changed enough to be transferred within my same company to a department working on computers. Something I'd never been able to finagle successfully despite years of trying, God gave me within months of my tearful, total commitment to Him.

As God's healing continued in me, replacing what had become broken and confused with what's been restored and blessed by Him, I found an embryonic musical talent to go along with my developing computer skills. I now sing with the church choir and am taking guitar lessons from one of the men in our church orchestra.

Most important of all to me and my family, besides being a Christian, I now can control my voice when I talk to my wife and son. God told me if I gave Him my voice, He would speak through it, not in the way He did with Jesus or people in the Bible, but in the way I needed Him to when I would otherwise just be popping off and yelling on my own without Him.

It's wonderful to be able to read and concentrate on computer manuals or music when you have tried unsuccessfully hundreds of times before on your own, without God. Yet the best part of my healing is what my "new" voice is like with God, or otherwise put, what His Voice is like speaking through me.

The Bible says God is no respecter of persons. That means He has a healing for **every** AD person. If you have this condition I hope and pray you'll be one of the people who also experiences God's healing like Davey and I did. That's the main reason I share our story: for others, for you!

Afterwords

When the physical alone is healed it is wonderful, as it is when the emotional is touched by God's Hand. But when both are touched together, along with the relationships in the healed one's life, it seems even more wonderful still.

May all of us find God healing our voices and speaking through them and us just as He did Dave.

Chapter 6

Battered Batterer

"Anger felt is destructive. Expressed on things it's more destructive still. But when vented on another, it destroys the human soul and spirit as little else can or does." —The Author

The judge glared at me. "A suspended prison sentence, probation until I tell you you're off, court-ordered counseling at the county treatment program for wife and child abusers, and no return to the residence of your wife and children until I receive a report from that agency saying you are ready to go back. You may think how a man treats his family is his business but when he physically beats them in this county, it gives me the right to step in on their behalf and stop him. And if what I am giving you today doesn't stop you, I'll see to it that the prison sentence I'm suspending gets imposed. That would stop you for a good long time, and put you in a place where the people you'll be with don't take kindly to people who treat their families like you've treated yours. There you'll find out firsthand what abuse is like. Do you understand me?"

I managed a "Yes, your Honor," from between clamped lips that barely concealed my seething rage. Where I'd come from, no man told another man what to do or interfered in his family life.

I hadn't grown up with any more respect for the law than I had for my wife whom I had abused even before we married, nor my two children who'd felt the sting of my slaps and beatings from their infancy on, just like my father had treated me and all but one of my seven siblings. He never laid a hand on our oldest sister for reasons none of us understood.

I guess you'd say I was a real tough case. Neither going to a group meeting where other abusers and I had to tell what we'd done to our families nor individual counseling which tried to give me coping mechanisms (which turned out to be little more than "count to ten" and "contract to keep your temper") were helping me get over being a tough case.

Even tough cases think about themselves and try to figure out why they do what they do. At least I did. But I couldn't figure it out. My wife wasn't some provoking shrew. My kids weren't terrible problems. It certainly wasn't that I didn't love my family. I couldn't blame alcohol—I didn't drink other than an occasional beer—and I didn't use drugs either. I liked my construction job, wasn't angry at my boss or anyone else I could think of, and didn't have any major money or health problems. No, I didn't have the first clue why I acted like I did, yet here I was doing the very thing I vowed as a kid I'd never do when I grew up: beat my wife and kids like my Dad had done!

After that judge's lecture, I behaved. Behaved with a capital B. Then my counselor got the judge to lift the restraining order that had kept me from going home and the probation that had me reporting to the court.

My first night back home, Ruth said she wanted to talk with me. Typical of most dysfunctional men, I responded, "It really isn't necessary to say anything, honey. I know I've been to blame for our problems even if I don't know why. It's been me 100%. But those days are gone. Our problems are over now! This is the new me, babe, so you can say whatever you want." Silently I hoped she'd make it quick with whatever she had to say so we could get to what I wanted: bed and having intercourse.

I was only half listening when what I heard Ruth saying suddenly got all of my attention. It began making me very, very angry, lots angrier in fact than I'd ever felt when I had abused her before. At the time I thought it was because the woman who had never raised her voice to me—not even when I was hitting her—was telling me that if I ever laid a hand on her or Jerry, Jr., or Pammy again she wouldn't pack their bags and leave until I cooled off like she'd done countless times before. No, she'd pack my bag, and I wouldn't be coming back when a judge said I could, I'd only be coming back if and when she said I could!

The second thing she wanted to tell me and did that night was what really infuriated me. I knew she'd been going to see a couple who advertised themselves as Christian counselors. Ruth had been interested in Christianity for a long time, but I'd strongly discouraged it because of the bad taste religious conversions I'd seen as a kid had left in my mouth. What I didn't know was that Ruth had already become one. The very second she told me, I went from red alert to the emotional equivalent of 10,000 degrees—smoking ears and nostrils and gnashing teeth.

Although a kindly Sunday School teacher, showing me the love I didn't get at home, led me to Christ when I was seven, a fanatical mother who portrayed God as a "Be-No" (there will be no cars, be no tobacco, be no high school dances, be no long hair, be no...her list was endless), left me in the same unhappy place I'd been in life before I became a Christian. By the time I was twelve, I'd not only forgotten all about that commitment, I was also in total rebellion against any of the godly behavior that should have emerged from me because of the physical and verbal abuse of one parent and the religious straight-jacket imposed by the other.

Despite the fact I was blowing gaskets all over the place on the inside, for once in my life I kept my cool on the outside. I heard myself saying, "If going to church and taking the kids with you is what you want, I won't stop you, but I'm not ready for religion again so don't expect me to go with you and don't bring any of it home to me."

Ruth agreed and our conversation ended with her telling me she'd respect my feelings about religion. She added that I was going to have to realize she was deadly serious about my respecting her when it came to her own faith and to keeping my hands (and mouth) off her and the children if I didn't want to find myself and all my things on the porch.

It didn't take long for a guy with my attitude and background to lose it, just like I had a hundred times before. I found myself begging Ruth to "forgive me just one more time," as she packed my bag after I'd beaten both kids and been real mouthy with them and her. As I alternated between pleas and threats, I heard her say, "Jerry, you either take your things and leave, or I call the law. But if I do, you'll be going a lot farther than to one of your friends to stay. You'll go to jail tonight, court on Monday, and to prison after that, because the judge was serious about you serving the rest of the sentence he 'shocked' you out of if you ever appeared before him again."

I left. I didn't see Ruth again until a few days later when I asked her to meet me for coffee after work. I fully expected a groveling apology and a "never again promise" would get me back in my house later the same night. But although I knew I was dealing with a "new Ruth," I didn't know how new until she said, "Jerry, the judge told you once you couldn't go home until he was satisfied you were okay. Our home isn't his; it's yours and mine, and that makes what happens in it our responsibility. I don't know how you propose to be responsible, but the way I'm handling what I'm responsible for—the children's welfare and mine—is to not expose any of us to living with you again until you've really changed. Your promises aren't good enough anymore. You never keep them. The social worker and probation officer were wrong when they said you were ready to come home. The only person who'll know when you are ready to return is God, and we're not living together again until He tells me you're ready. It is not good for us or you when you fail."

It was a good thing we were in a public place because I found the mention of God bringing my anger back to epic proportions once again. I knew Ruth was right, but I didn't like it and definitely wasn't ready to admit it.

There's nothing quite like living with a couple of buddies instead of his family for a few weeks to motivate a man to do what he's needed to do for a lifetime—change!

Something was happening to me. Instead of trying to lie my way back home like I'd done before, I found myself this time really wanting something to happen to me that would make me a different man, different enough to be able to live with three people I loved without hurting them over and over again like I'd been doing for a lifetime.

When I shared my feelings with Ruth on one of our weekly coffee "dates," she suggested I get some counseling that could really help me change. Naturally she suggested the couple she'd been seeing.

For the first time in my life, I didn't find myself balking at an idea that was going to put me on the path of something or somebody religious. I'd seen the changes that were taking place before my eyes in my wife and children, and I desperately wanted change for myself that would be as real. I just didn't want to live the Christian life as I had been taught it was supposed to be lived to get that change. Maybe I wouldn't have to, I thought. Maybe there was a way I could get the one and avoid the other. I made up my mind to at least see.

Part of me hated the backbone becoming a Christian had given my wife; another part of me respected her and the counseling that had led her to it. This was enough to venture seeing the same counselors for myself.

A few days later I found myself seated in the office of a man named Clint Conner, who was saying: "Jesus said when He came into a life He brought everything needed to restore that life to normal, but He never sent those things into a life in any lasting way without coming along with them." My worst fear was true. Ruth wouldn't give me the reconciliation I wanted with her, and now I was being told God wouldn't give me the temperament change I wanted unless I was reconciled to Him!

It looked like I'd run out of options. I'd tried so many times myself without Jesus. Even I was as tired as Ruth was of my failures and broken promises. Newly turned over leaves turned out not being any different than old ones had been, and techniques for stress reduction and so-called coping I'd been given in previous counseling had not worked any better than my efforts before them. I was literally a man with nowhere to turn but up—to God—yet as unwilling as I'd ever been to do so. Humiliated but not humbled, I was ready to sacrifice my family to keep from becoming a committed Christian.

Then the only thing that ever could have changed me happened. And change me it did. I found out my dad had cancer. He got very bad very fast in a few short weeks. Before he died, he asked Jesus into his life. Before he went back to the hospital for what turned out to be the last time, he asked my mom and the four of us kids who still lived in the area to come over on a rainy, dismal Sunday afternoon. As we all stood around his bed, he gave us each copies of the same letter, a letter he'd already mailed to his other children. In it was an emotional but sincere apology for the abuse and everything else he'd done to us along with a request for our forgiveness and a promise to pray daily as long as he lived that each of us would find the same salvation and peace with God he had.

Just seeing the real peace Dad had and his repentance for all the terrible things he'd done over all those horrible years would have been enough to convince anyone they needed to become a Christian, too. But there was more. I saw him for the first time in my life smile at my mother and touch her lovingly when he held her hand. He asked us if they could pray for each of us. When they finished, there wasn't a dry eye in that room. When I left, it was still just as dismal outside, yet it seemed like a thousand suns had lit up that day when I walked out of there, and the heat and light from them was warming something long cold and dead somewhere down in the depths of my heart.

I didn't know enough at the time to call it God's healing presence, but I knew when I walked out of that room I had experienced a little taste of what God would bring into my life if I let Him. And it wouldn't be the "Be-No" religion I'd seen long ago and more recently imagined.

I also learned that when you walk away from a commitment to Jesus, regardless of who you are or how old you are, you get evil back in your life in a worse way than before you became a Christian (see Matthew 12:43-45.) Clint had me command spirits who had come into my life during the years I was away from God to leave in Jesus' Name. That brought a great deal of freedom from my anger, a freedom that included anger at God and the anger that caused me to abuse. It's a freedom that has continued until this day.

I learned, too, the person I was most angry with was me. First, I hated me because I thought my parents hated me. I must have been a terrible person or they wouldn't have treated me like they did. Then I hated me more and more each time I broke a promise and abused my family again. When I saw Jesus could forgive me for His own sake, but only I could forgive me for me—meaning forgive myself—I prayed about that. I also repented for the anger I had never dealt with toward my parents and asked God to heal me and to break the cycle of abuse from one generation to the next in our family.

This didn't all happen a lifetime ago. Actually, at this time it's been only a little over a thousand days. But although three-and-a-half years may not seem like a long time to you to go without screaming and hitting, for someone like me who has done it all through life, it *is* a long time. It *is* a miracle.

I've become angry in those three years, plenty of times. But now I have something I didn't have when I tried to use the techniques secular counseling taught me. I have God's power and instructional "techniques"—His, from His Word. This combination works.

Now when I get angry I either start whistling one of the praise choruses I've learned at church, or pray for myself and sometimes ask Ruth or one of the kids to pray for me, too. You know something? It's just impossible to hit somebody when they are praying for you or speak abusively at the same time you are praising God!

I have no idea how many violent sexual rapes will be committed in this country this year, but I know there is another kind of rape of people's lives and souls just as violent—the kind I did. I know this, too: virtually all of those rapes will be committed by men and women who could quit just like I did if they would only do what I did. They need to find out Jesus isn't a "Be-No" and let Him take over their lives, healing the hurts of which those rapes are an expression, and empowering them with His Spirit to handle their emotions righteously.

If telling my story stops even one person like me—perhaps you or someone you know—it's been worth my sharing it.

Afterwords

Seeing God as a "Be-No" like Jerry did, or in some other unrealistic, wrong light (cruel, or accepting of all regardless of what they believe, etc.) has kept millions from commitment to the real Jesus. If the enemy of God and all those He has created, the Devil, has orchestrated this kind of deception in you, you can change that by making the same commitment Jerry did to The God who loves you and gave Himself for you.

Chapter 7

Chronically Fatigued

"Being unaware of our hatreds doesn't make them less wrong; only wrong in a different way than when we're aware of them." —The Author

Asking for a phone number from an organization that lists Christian counselors, I called the Conners only to discover that they lived beyond a reasonable commuting distance for me to consult with them. Because no other Christian counselors lived near me, they offered to consult with my by phone.

I was happily married, a Christian in my forties, and diagnosed as having CFS—Chronic Fatigue Syndrome. I was listless, energy-less, nearly bedridden, and unable to care for my husband and children or do what God had given me to do.

At the time I was diagnosed, not much was known about either the causes or treatment of CFS. I had consulted with four doctors before the diagnosis of CFS was even mentioned.

I asked the Conners if they believed CFS was caused by physical or, perhaps, emotional factors. They advised me to continue the treatment my doctor had prescribed, but they also encouraged me to set aside a specific time to look at my condition and pray about it this way:

> *God, I come to You through Jesus, asking you to reveal to me any spiritual, emotional or mental reason that is a factor in my having Chronic Fatigue Syndrome.*

"Few doctors and medical researchers know much about the spiritual, so they omit it or ignore it in their diagnoses and treatments. Sometimes what they see as a cause is really an effect," the Conners said. I decided as long as I didn't refuse to follow my doctor's orders, how could praying hurt?

The Conners wondered if some of the CFS they'd seen wasn't a variation of burn-out, a condition caused by overwork or when people continue to do what they dislike or have come to hate. Perhaps those who suffer from CFS haven't given their negative feelings about what they dislike to God in a complete way. Whether conscious of it or not, they end up literally sick and tired of people, jobs, and their lot in life in general.

Jesus was so worn by His work that storms didn't wake Him even as they were sinking the boat He was in. He worked as hard or harder than any of us do, yet He was never burned out, never suffered CFS because He was renewed by spending significant time with His Father. He was never worn out doing His Father's work (see Mark 1:35-39, John 5:19).

The Conners believed that one could avoid CFS by following our Lord's example: by spending quality time with The Father in prayer and doing only what The Father would have us do.

"Many get tired and worn down," they said. "Why not pray about how you feel about your life and what you have been doing? Find out whether you have been living life out of your strength or Jesus has been living His life through you. Have you been giving Him the wear and tear of your life? You're too tired to do anything but pray, so try this. If you don't find a counselor in your area, call us when you've done what you know to do in prayer. Let us know what happens."

Several weeks passed before I had the strength to even pray. When I did, I discovered lots to pray about.

I hadn't been wearier than anyone else until my husband changed jobs and we wound up moving to the boondocks. It wasn't where I'd hoped or imagined we'd live. I discovered my anger at having my husband thrust new responsibilities on me after our move, responsibilities he'd handled before it. I was angry at having to taxi children all over the place. They were old enough to go places, but not old enough to go on their own.

I found out that some of my anger was also directed at God. I was frustrated and angry that I had to watch what I ate—constantly—or put on unwanted pounds.

As I prayed, as I discovered the hidden sources of my discontent, my strength and energy returned, not all at once, but gradually. Now I have normal energy, but a completely different attitude about life. I am more grateful and humble now.

I'm not accusing anyone with CFS of a lack of gratitude or humility. Different causes may well provoke CFS in different people.

I've worked out a way of avoiding a recurrence of CFS. Once a week during the time I've set aside for prayer, I make a list of things I've done and endured that I wasn't a hundred percent enthusiastic about. I give that list to God, ask Him to remove the negative effects of it, and to forgive anything sinful in my attitude toward it.

Others may need more than prayer. Both medicine and prayer are healing agents—just different forms of it.

In my case I was fed up with life and hadn't realized it. I didn't drink or drug my feelings. I didn't have an affair or consider suicide. I burned out, dropped out, and found a way to stop doing what I hated and nobody could blame me for it. I had a physical, not emotional problem. I could even feel sorry for myself.

Prayer helped me. If you have CFS and know the Lord Jesus, you can pray, too. Prayer won't worsen your CFS; it makes you better.

Afterwords

A spiritual law might be stated this way: whatever you haven't expressed or given to God, you will internalize. Some internalize and get ulcers. Others develop forms of arthritis. Is it possible that some people internalize unwanted feelings that affect their energy levels —and that those levels can be restored to normal through healing prayer? It is worth considering.

Chapter 8

Codependent Cover-up

"For each one should carry his own load."
—Galatians 6:5

I went into my usual litany of instructions. "I'll call your father's foreman when I get to the office and tell him he's too sick to come to work....Tom, get the car off the lawn and in the garage....Sue, you clean the vomit up in the bedroom after your dad gets up and be sure and have a glass of cold tomato juice and some coffee made for him....Oh, and start the chicken before I get home."

The kids and I had all done these jobs so many times over the fifteen years my husband and their father had been alcoholic that I am sure they'd have done them perfectly without a word from me. But codependent people need to "spell out" the nature of the burden for themselves before they carry it out.

I'd taught the children well, too. They never heard me complain about any of the hundreds of duties and requests I'd allowed their father in his alcoholism to put on me. So neither of them had ever uttered a complaint either. Not ever, that is, until that morning.

Suddenly, Tom wheeled around and shouted, "No! ___ _____! I'm not backing that ____ car off the lawn ever again so the neighbors can watch me put it in the garage and say, 'Well, old Tom must have tied one on again because young Tom is getting the car in for him again.' I've had it with that drunken ___ __ _ _____. I used to help cover up for him thinking he'd appreciate it and straighten up. He's never done it. Never! And then I think, 'I'll do it for Mom's sake. She needs me to help her out and he'll have less to yell at her for.' But no matter how much Sue and I do for him, you keep thinking of other new things to do for him, and no matter what any of us do, he still yells at everybody about something. Helping, covering up, none of it does any good. I'm not **ever** doing anything again to help that _____ ____ man with anything!"

I was dumbfounded. I had never even heard Tom complain, let alone swear before. I didn't know what to say or do.

After an awkward silence, I began with a sputtering, "You can't refer to your dad like that! He's your father!"

Tom interrupted, "Not anymore to me he isn't. A father gives and loves. He hates and takes. He may be my father on a piece of paper but to me he is no different than any other no good drunk!"

Again, I didn't know what to say. I couldn't stand up to a son rebelling openly for the first time any more effectively than I could a husband who was expressing his rebellion in drunkenness for the thousandth time. Silently I picked up my lunch from the kitchen counter and went out to put the car in the garage before catching the bus for work.

Later that day in the break room, I found myself in tears as I told what had happened to a woman who ran the shoe department with me at the discount store where we had worked together four years. When I finished, she lovingly but firmly admonished me with these words: "If you want to give your life over to someone else to destroy, that's your prerogative, I guess. But when you start making other people's lives sacrifices too, especially your own children whom you are supposed to be protecting, that's pretty darn serious. I don't blame young Tom for reacting like he did! And if you have any sense, you'll see the handwriting on the wall. Sue is next. If you don't stop what you are doing, it will be too late for all of you, and none of it is going to make Tom, Sr. any better. It hasn't in all these years."

I knew she was right. Absolutely right. But I had no idea how to stop what I was doing or what to do instead if I ever could bring myself to change my ways.

I was stuck and I was scared. Stuck about what to do and how to do it, and desperately scared for the first time in my life. I had been shocked into awareness for the first time that what I had been doing was costing my children their lives. To hear my behavior was costing me would never have stopped me, but telling me I was the cause of my children's destruction was something else altogether, and probably the only thing that could ever have stopped me in the course I had set for myself.

After years of doing nothing except perpetuate Tom's behavior, suddenly I was like an animal in a feeding frenzy trying to find answers, anything that would stop what was happening to my children! I shared my plight with everyone who would listen, getting every kind of advice. It was the same friend at work who first heard my story who now helped me see what was happening and suggested I see a professional counselor who went to her church. But I guess I wasn't really ready to do *any-thing*. At least I wasn't ready for church or anyone connected with one at that point.

Almost a year went by. I'd read several secular books and articles about dysfunctional families and codependent people, picking up in the process a whole new vocabulary and way of looking at and discussing things.

My insurance at work had paid for me to attend an eight-week group for codependents, and I continued to get together with one of the group members for coffee and conversation about our families after the sessions ended.

After a year of information and enlightenment and some changes in what I did for Tom and what I requested the children to do for him, I found myself with a husband who still drank, a son who had moved out to live with my sister, a daughter who was taking out her frustrations about life with her father by becoming verbally abusive toward me, and as much inner turmoil as I had ever felt. Enough, in fact, that my doctor had prescribed nerve pills.

The tranquilizers helped my anxiety some, but couldn't help my thinking about my situation enough to keep me from continuing to talk to and seek suggestions from everyone I knew. My friend and co-worker finally pointed out to me that people were out of suggestions, and I was on the verge of making a nuisance of myself. Our conversation ended with her saying she had given me the courtesy of a year of listening and watching me go through everything I had tried that hadn't helped. She advised that I needed to try the counselor she had suggested once before or else stop bending her ear with my problems and requests for help.

I settled for a compromise: I would attend her church and let her introduce me to the counselor. If he seemed different than most religious people I'd met, I would ask him if he thought seeing him could help my family.

The next Sunday found me in a church service different than any I had ever been in, including one I attended with my grandmother as a young girl. Everyone from well-to-do, educated professionals to middle class and poor, singing and fellowshipping with an enthusiasm for God that I had only previously seen displayed for sports teams.

What they did and how they did it put me off somewhat, but both the people and what I felt internally in that meeting attracted me enough to go ahead and meet Clint, the counselor, describing my situation to him and asking if he thought he could help me.

After the service ended and we'd been introduced, I was fifteen minutes into my story before I realized how inappropriate I sounded. Red-faced, I apologized, saying I wasn't really trying to get something for nothing. Bursting into tears, I stammered, "I've tried all I know. I need some help that will work!"

Expecting to be quieted and sent on my way with a business card, I was amazed to find my tears understood instead of stopped, given time to finish my story while someone listened thoughtfully, and offered an appointment time for which I would be charged according to my income if insurance didn't cover it.

Clint listened just as thoughtfully a few days later during the appointment. At the end he said these words: "I think what will help you most is for me to introduce you to a woman who used to be more codependent than you but isn't any longer. I've given her training to become a lay counselor, and I supervise what she does, so I'll be in touch with what is going on with you. Because she is both a woman and a volunteer, she can help you in some ways, perhaps, where I couldn't. I would like you to give this a try. After a few times if you don't feel it is helpful, I'll either start seeing you again or refer you to someone else, whichever you prefer."

I thought I needed more than a lay volunteer to counsel me, but the idea of seeing someone who had been worse than I was so intrigued me that I agreed to Clint's plan.

He introduced me to Michelle a few days later. We hit it off right away. After she had listened as thoughtfully to me as Clint had, she handed me a cassette tape that contained her story about how she had been healed from codependency. I agreed to her suggestion that I listen to it before we met again.

Listen I did, more than once. I found myself drawn to an account of a woman telling how all of us have been created with a place within designed to have a relationship with The One who created us. However, people without such a relationship with God still had that internal, God-given need to posit themselves toward somebody or something. Michelle used the example of a weathervane that, because it is weak and powerless of itself, ends up being pointed by and toward the thing that acts most strongly upon it: the wind. The tape ended with a moving account of how Michelle had not only given her life to Jesus Christ but given Him the job of changing her then workaholic husband instead of trying to change him by her codependent behavior.

A second year of trying to solve my problems has gone by since Michelle and I first discussed that tape. Now I could make a tape of my own because of all that has happened.

It is one thing to see that you are so husband-controlled that you've allowed your husband to assume the place that Jesus wants to have in the control of your life—the One you live for and try to please. It is another thing altogether to tell Jesus you are removing your husband from that control and that He may have it instead.

I realized the main reason it was so hard to do that was because I could avoid facing myself and my problems when I had my husband for a focus. I knew from Michelle that if Jesus were there, He would ask me to become somebody, to grow up instead of trying to get my husband to do so. That was scary! It was something I had never done. Focusing on his problems had been a defense for avoiding mine.

All those years that I'd *seemed* so responsible, I had actually been avoiding it. Rather than letting God give me my identity, I'd let my husband define who I was and what I did. He was God for me. He was doing the things in my life that God wanted to do. Our whole family had become a Tom-controlled monarchy!

I saw that the first year of seeking help had only pointed me toward different people: my children instead of my husband, not toward my Creator. My life was still being given to creatures instead of to the One who asks all those He has created to give their lives entirely to Him.

I felt like I was a ghost who had been wearing clothes and a mask to cover the fact that I possessed no real face. If I were ever to become a real person, I would have to make the same commitment Michelle had.

I did, not openly in front of my family or others at first, but just quietly one still summer eve when Sue and Tom, Sr. were gone. I sat on our porch swing moving gently, looking up at a sky filled with stars, saying, "Jesus, I feel like the black emptiness between those stars. I want to be like one of them instead, something that gives off a glow that You and others can enjoy, just as I am being blessed right now by their white brightness. Come into my life. I give it—me—to You so You can make me into the woman You want me to be rather than the shallow caricature of one I have become because I've let others be my God."

That prayer made my second year of seeking help altogether different from the first one. In the first year, I found a name or label for myself: codependent. Although labels are not inherently wrong in and of themselves, if we don't have the power of God working in us in relation to our problems, we automatically give power to the label.

Before my first year of problem-solving efforts, I had a problem but didn't know what it was. Once I was given a name for it, I spent a year learning all about it and trying to solve it humanly. Then I met Jesus. I began to experience His presence and power and began to find a Christ-controlled rather than man-controlled cure that has resulted in the following.

When I stopped doing everything for Tom, Sr., he became physically abusive. When the violence didn't stop, at Clint's suggestion and with Michelle's support, I had a legal separation drawn up. Tom had to voluntarily sign it to make it legal. I told him that if he did, I would stand by him until he quit drinking and we got back together. If he didn't agree to the separation, I saw no alternative but to obtain a restraining order and begin divorce proceedings. His violence toward me and what he was doing to the children were major enough to fit the biblical definition of fornication (gross sin) that Jesus said justified divorce in some cases.

Tom signed, and at this writing the children are both living with me. Tom is at his brother's. He has done some drinking there but not as much as before. He has also attended Alcoholic Victorious meetings and is nearing a decision to see Clint for counseling.

We both have a long way to go. Tom and the children are not Christians, and I am a new, relatively immature one. But I know this much. I have stopped sacrificing myself and my kids. I've tried the therapies that seek to empower us to solve our problems without recognizing we are too fallen to do so. Now I am in a place where I am daily seeking God and His plan for my life and His power working through me to implement it.

I recommend the same to anyone reading this who has the same problems we do. I don't know how things are going to end up or what the future holds, but now I know the Lord holds that future.

Codependent no more, I am dependent on the Lord and His ways which are infinitely better than my own were for me, and, I might suggest, better than yours are for you.

Afterwords

Dependency is such an interesting phenomenon. After listening to secular psychology tell us to rid ourselves of it and become independent, we find we have been created with it inherent in us. The question becomes not, will we be dependent, but rather, upon whom or what will we depend—another, self, things, or the Lord!

Chapter 9

Depression, Loss, and Grief

"Some depressions begin for a variety of physiological reasons. But most occur when people hold on to someone or something that is gone, then internalize their anger about the loss."
—The Author

I told myself what I'd told hundreds of clients: "It's normal to feel bad about trying circumstances, but when you move from feeling bad about what's happened to feeling sorry for yourself because you have to endure what's happened, you're indulging in self-pity. Then healthy grief becomes unhealthy depression. Don't hang on. Don't disengage or withdraw. That leads to depression, too."

I told myself: "The only healthy thing to do is accept what's happened. Thank God. Release it to Him."

Even if you understand the situation intellectually, however, it doesn't make it easier to accept emotionally. I had trouble moving the solution from my head to my heart.

My wife and I were in our forties, my boys in their teens, nearly grown. Except for caring for foster children occasionally, we assumed our "parenting" roles were nearly finished.

Unexpectedly, the Holy Spirit began to change our plans. Prophetic words from others, some strangers, and prophetic words to us proclaimed we'd give birth to a beautiful little girl. God gave one woman a truly inspired poem about us and a daughter.

Scripture has always been our primary source of guidance. God confirmed to us through more than one verse that we would have a daughter, and then gave us a desire for a baby girl, a desire that stood the test of time and went far deeper than mere emotional whim. All that remained was the "when."

Our answer came on Valentine's Day when I awoke with these words in my spirit: *"In your prayers you have lamented that Valentine's Day has been stripped of the meaning of true love as I intended it. I shall redeem the meaning of this day and of love in your life by making it the day you and your wife conceive in holy Christian love a beautiful girl who will serve Me all the days of her life."*

A few months later, the doctor's calculations confirmed what we already knew: our daughter had been conceived on Valentine's Day. God had told us that Carrie Susan, the name He inspired us to choose for her, was created on that day.

Three Christian physicians, close friends of ours, stood around Bonnie in the delivery room. Two immediately offered to pray when the third said, "The baby is already dead, and she's starting to deliver now."

In shock, I couldn't believe it! I felt as if I had been torn in half. I knew my friend would not joke about a baby being dead. What he said had to be true, but I simply could not accept it.

In seconds it was over. The prayer was said, the baby delivered, and my wife taken to an operating room for the usual post-miscarriage surgery. When she woke, I told her everything would be okay, but I didn't believe it. Later at home, I found myself alone in a darkened room, staring at a ceiling I couldn't see. Life sounded all around me. Cars and trucks whizzed by on the busy highway in front of our house, but inside I felt only life-lessness and emptiness. I felt the presence of death at that moment more intensely than ever before, far stronger than when my father, grandparents, and close friends died.

Suddenly, unexpectedly, I was angry, furiously angrier than I'd ever felt before. I hated the doctors. I was furious with my wife. Most of all, I hated God with a vengeance. I had no reason to hate any of them, but I did.

I wanted revenge for what felt like a sadistic act by a vengeful God, but all I felt was the impotence all of us feel when God has permitted that which we are powerless to change. I spit these words at God: "You're all powerful! There is nothing I or anyone else can do in the face of what You've let happen here. But I hurt so bad from it and it's a hurt You allowed to happen, a hurt You could have prevented but didn't. I want to hurt you back. What could I do to hurt You? Only one thing. I'll be a Christian no longer. I'll say I'm no longer Yours and mean it! When I get over this I'll not feel this way, but I sure do right now. I don't know how to get over it where I am now. I don't know what to do and don't want to talk to anyone who does. That includes You, God!"

When the words stopped, my tears flowed. I sobbed and wailed into a pillow to muffle my grief from the neighbors. Part of me was surprised that I cared how anyone else felt. I cried myself to exhaustion, only able, at last, to fall asleep.

I awoke to these inaudible words of the Lord in my spirit: *"My son, I didn't lie to you when I promised your wife would bear a beautiful daughter who would serve Me all the days of her life. I didn't reveal this: she would serve Me here in My presence from the day of her birth. Had I told you months ago, you'd have spent that time in sorrow, knowing when death was coming. If I revealed the time of death to My children, none would live in joy in their earthly lives."*

That made sense, but I simply could not shrug off the emotional impact of my baby daughter's death. It felt as though it had been frozen into my soul. I was encased in it.

I awoke to a sunny spring day. I knew I had to call our friends to tell them that Carrie Susan was dead. My call to our pastor began with unintelligible sobs but eventually I was able to say, "If God tells me why this happened I may be able to make it out of where I'm at."

His reply wasn't what I wanted to hear. It was what I needed: "God may never tell you why. Whether He does or not, you must thank Him for this or only part of you will get over this and another part won't. That part will never go on with life or God. It will stay where it is right now."

His words angered me. How could we ever thank God for what seemed to be the worst thing that ever happened to us. But I knew my pastor was right. I'd given the same advice, in fact, to many. I needed the very words I'd given to others.

I couldn't pray when I hung up the phone. Today I know God would have enabled me to pray then had I asked Him for the words. But a few days passed before I said: "God, in my emotions I don't feel what I'm going to say. In my mind I don't believe it. In my spirit and with my will, however, I choose to thank and praise You. You are God. Desperately I want to know why this has happened, but if I never learn those answers, You will still be my God. I will never say anything but thanks when I think of her death."

I felt God speak these words in reply: *"I've taken your baby who belonged to Me anyway. All babies belong to Me. Now I have returned to claim you, not to dwell in My immediate presence as your daughter does now, but to live for me in your earthly life. I can be with you as you were before this happened. Saying thanks is a good beginning. But she is gone, and you are not letting go. Release her to Me and ask Me to release her from you. Don't just ask for that release. Tell Me you receive it. And continue giving thanks until it is real in your mind and feelings, not just the choice of your will."*

Ten years plus have passed. We have another child, age nine as I write this. We've endured the loss of another baby, too, a little boy.

Why didn't they all live? I don't know. Why did one die rather than another? I have no idea. Why did God want us to have children after my older sons were grown? No answers. (see Psalm 131:1-2). However, though we have no answers, we are blessed with peace and certainty—certainty that whatever His reasons, God allowed it to happen for good, not cruel purposes.

I've heard that a celebrated Christian leader declared that all problems begin as a wrong response to God. If he, indeed, said it, he's right. If you examine your trials—trials

that have not necessarily become problems—
honestly, I am convinced you'll see an opportunity to respond the wrong way to God. God
risks that we will refuse to continue our walk
with Him. We were called to make a judgment
just as we did when we were converted: Is He a
good God? Will we follow Him in spite of what
He has allowed?

For a week ten years ago I made the mistake of initially responding to God this way:
"You are a bad God, and I quit. I refuse to live
the Christian life further. I believe You're
there, but I hate You for what You let happen
to us. The only revenge open to me is to remove myself from You."

Some people hang on to what's gone, and
that leads to depression. Others go the opposite way, disengage, withdraw from life, and
wind up the same way—depressed. Some disengage by seeking a new home, job, marriage,
etc. Still others try to rationalize and thereby
minimize their hurt. Others work harder.
Some turn to explicitly sinful behavior seeking
revenge for their hurt.

Depression can be a message—a sign-
post—that we've depended on God, self, and/or
others wrongly. Bear in mind that depression
can lead to chemical imbalances, to alcoholism
and drug abuse, but it always begins with a
bad choice or response to that which God has
given or allowed.

You have only two choices with depression: to try to usurp God's place and substitute someone or something for that which God has taken. Or you can come to Him and say, "I accept this. I thank You in the midst of this. I give You this loss and myself in it completely to You."

Remember: God loves us enough to stick with us through our bouts of self-pity, despair, depression, in our tantrums. He loves us enough to shake out every shakable thing until, as the Bible says, only the unshakable remains (see Hebrews 12:27). He loves us too much to take choice from us. He is there to help us when we choose Him and His way.

Counselors are not above or immune from trials. This trial was ours. Through this trial God made real to us what many of our clients had suffered. Many suffer more deeply for a longer time than I did. Some depressions have other causes.

This chapter is not a clinical text on depression. It is a chapter for ordinary people who struggle with things that can depress anyone, and it offers as valid a cure for those situations as it brought to ours.

Chapter 10

Fractured Feminist

"Any creation, including woman (or man), can become all that was intended for it only when it fulfills the purposes of its Creator and functions in tandem with Him."   —The Author

My interest in feminism was planted in college, blossomed in graduate school, and bore fruit once I'd earned my degree in social work. I was committed to a cluster of feminist-related issues: abortion, sexual harassment in the workplace, wife abuse. Name the issue, and I had lobbied or marched for it or worked on it somewhere. I devoted myself to these causes part-time until I quit work to have a baby. That gave me the leisure to make the liberation movement my full-time job.

For years things went well for me. Some of my feminist causes linked up with homosexual rights and other advocacy groups. I devoted myself as energetically to them as I did to my original causes.

Then the energy drained out of me. At first I attributed it to overwork, but cutting back on work didn't help.

I took a sabbatical. That didn't work either. I had to hire help for the house and children while I laid around, listless, wondering how and why this had happened to me.

Neither my doctor nor a specialist could find a physical cause for my condition. Neither my husband nor my friends—most of whom were social workers and counselors—could help me.

That left seeking counseling. I saw two psychiatrists, one psychologist, spent a lot of money, and got nowhere. I was still listless. I had no solution, and my condition made my husband irritable and impatient. My two girls were beginning to relate more readily to the baby-sitter than they did to me. My friends wondered whether I was a malingerer or a mental case.

Then on a sleepy, rainy Monday morning, I awoke suddenly. Startled, I knew I *had* to call a former classmate's field-work supervisor. Somehow I knew this man had the solution to my problems. I don't know how I knew, but I was certain that Clint Conner held the answer.

My friend, who had introduced me to Conner, was a Christian. I remembered she told me that she appreciated having a field-work instructor who understood the spiritual dimension to people's problems.

I disliked Christians, who struck me as always trying to convert you. Their values were the antithesis of mine. Only my apparently hopeless state drove me to consult a Christian.

I called Clint, briefly described my problem to him, and he suggested that I see his wife who was also a counselor. He perceived, and rightly so, that part of what I would have to deal with was related to womanhood and women's issues. Perhaps, he said, I would have less reason to feel that my counselor was biased on these issues if I saw a woman. That made sense, and I agreed.

After listening to my description of my troubles, Bonnie Conner's first question was: "Do you believe in God? If so, who is He?"

I replied angrily that I didn't see what God and His nature had to do with my problems. I'd not thought much about God over the years and didn't want to start now at the beginning of my counseling.

She replied that that was fine, but I had to know that she believed that God is a Spirit. She said that He wanted me to know that my listlessness was neither illness nor disorder, but was a *loving* message from God. He wanted to warn me that I'd given myself over to a false conception of femininity. This had drained me of my true feminine identity. Bonnie said that if I'd give myself to God, He would heal my emptiness by filling me with His life and my lost womanhood.

Infuriated, I declined to schedule another appointment. Bonnie remained unperturbed. She said she'd pray for me. She also told me that God would confirm His existence to me and what He'd given her to tell me about the cause of my listlessness. Then, perhaps, I'd change my mind about the cause of my condition.

Bonnie was convinced that I had a spiritual problem that could be healed only by spiritual means. I didn't accept any of this—until I had a dream.

The next night following my session with Bonnie, I went to sleep before eleven o'clock, slept nearly four hours, and then awoke with near total recall of a dream given to me by a *real* God with a *real* solution to my problem.

The dream began with a beautifully furnished house. Suddenly the house was engulfed in a flood that washed it away from its foundation and carried it along in the current. One room after another was flooded. The furnishings were ruined, then the windows were washed out, and the doors were smashed by the flood waters.

After the roof was blown off, the shattered remnants of the house came to rest on the uppermost part of a mountain. I watched as a tornado approached the house from the North. Opposite this, the sun burst gloriously through the clouds in a clear, deep-blue sky. Then I woke up.

Like most people, I always wondered what, if anything, my dreams meant without paying them much attention and forgetting them rapidly. Not this one. I knew the house represented me. Like the contents of the house, what I was had been progressively taken away from me and destroyed. The dream's message was clear: God had placed me in a temporary refuge (the mountain peak) where I could choose between Him (represented by that blue sky and sun) or destruction (symbolized by the approaching tornado).

I knew this dream had come to me from the God Bonnie Conner believed in. So I called for a second appointment and shared my dream with her.

She agreed with my interpretation and added that in Scripture the direction North symbolized both physical and spiritual death and that South represented resurrection. She believed that the Holy Spirit was telling me that the house's contents were my emotional (soul) life. The house was my spirit. The choice was mine—one direction led to spiritual death, the other to spiritual rebirth.

I wasn't angry this time. I was hungry for answers to every question about spiritual matters. I didn't quite know what those questions were. I had hope now that everything would return to normal. But I had a lot more to learn.

In later sessions Bonnie explained the differences between the head (mind, emotions or soul) and the heart (the spirit). A Spirit-God could only be apprehended and known spiritually, not just intellectually by believing in Him. Even the devil believes intellectually that God exists and, in this sense, is a believer.

But God is Someone, not an idea or concept. He desires to be known personally. God can be known as a Person, through Jesus Christ. The same power that resurrected, regenerated, and healed Him is available to heal any sufferer with any problem, provided the person first receives Christ as Savior.

Kneeling beside my bed that night, I prayed to Jesus, telling Him that I wanted Him to take not only my emptiness, but also me, for His eternal possession. In bed for the next two hours, I experienced the incredible sensation of being filled. I can describe it only in these terms: it seemed like I was engulfed in a warm, gentle tide of oil that filled every nook and cranny of my being. It flowed from a Source that, until that night, I'd never known.

My "filling" didn't solve all of my problems. My family had provided me with some human love, but there was a spiritual void in it. I was empty for two reasons: first, for what the women's' movement had done to me—emptying me—and, second, what my family had not done for me. The Holy Spirit began to fill those needs with Himself.

Christ gives Himself in many ways to each of us: as Healer, Teacher, Wisdom, Comforter, and Protector, to name just a few. In each circumstance, He comes to us in whatever role we need Him.

I have known Him for two years now. Next to forgiving my sin, His strength is the gift I most appreciate. He gave me strength to resume the care of my home and family. He's given me strength to face a husband who neither understands nor supports my spiritual commitment. He's given me strength to endure the scorn of many of my friends in the women's movement.

The Lord has given me strength to work in the true women's movement, the Christian women's' movement. I counsel single mothers and help lead a women's Bible study. I've never felt stronger physically.

If you're involved in the counterfeit women's movement, I pray that you'll find the courage to do what I've done: come to the only One who truly understands woman. Jesus created woman. Only He can heal us from the hatred of her, the fear of true femininity that lies at the core of the women's movement as we know it in this country.

Real liberation for anyone lies in Christ. Real identity lies in knowing Him personally. Discarding what the women's movement calls tyranny and oppression brings only emptiness, not fulfillment—fractured identity, not freedom within.

Afterwords

Sooner or later in life, each of us is confronted with something beyond our best (strongest) human coping efforts. Often such an experience leads us into anger and bitterness. At times, however, it leads some to say their first serious prayers and into a relationship with the God to whom they are praying. My guess is that if all of us became so related, crises wouldn't need to be God's medium in our lives.

I recommend Leanne Payne's audio tapes on feminine ambivalence, entitled "Misogyny," for those wishing a detailed treatment of the problem. They're available from Pastoral Care Ministries, Box 1313, Wheaton, IL 60189.

Chapter 11

Homeless Prodigal

"A father to the fatherless, a defender of widows, is God in His holy dwelling. God sets the lonely in families." —Psalm 68:5-6

Growing up in a Christian home with parents who believed the biblical promise: *"I have never seen the righteous forsaken or their children begging bread"* (Psalm 37:25), I never dreamed I would one day be numbered among the homeless. After graduating from college, I sped to the big city to launch what I was sure would be the first step in a fabulous business career. I knew that, eventually, I'd be CEO, then chairman of the board, and so on. For four-and-a-half years my life rolled along on the fast track of my plan.

Then it happened—a leveraged buyout of my company by another one. I was history.

Left with severance pay and a secretary to type resumes, I was sure I'd have a better job with a better company within days. My former employers brought in a "career restructuring" consultant company to help me find a new job. Their real function was simply to ease me out in such a way as to minimize my hard feelings and protect the corporate public image. I expected almost immediate employment.

I didn't get it.

Christmas came and went. I pretended to be working where I always had. You see, I couldn't tell my family and church friends, all of whom equated work with righteousness and unemployment with failure and evidence of major sin in your life that I had lost my job. Their reactions months later when they found out validated that belief.

After four months of unemployment with no money left and no prospects of a job, I could no longer afford to tell no one. I contacted one of my former high school teachers who owned his own small business.

He didn't have to be a genius to figure out that my inquiries meant I was unemployed. Although he was polite, I could read the silences among his words. They said, Your old employer must've let you go for a good reason. Why hasn't someone else hired you by now? I must've overestimated your abilities when I gave you high marks in high school. Best of luck. I can't help. I sensed my predicament embarrassed him and he wouldn't help me when he concluded our time together with a polite variation of the old line, "Don't call me, I'll call you."

Through him, however, my secret was broadcast to everyone I knew. He promised me "every assurance of confidentiality." As my counselor said later, "Those who promise to keep your secrets think they really do. It's those they tell who don't."

In this teacher's case, his sole confidante was his wife who, in turn, told her most trusted friend who told her best friend who told someone else until the news reached not only my friends, church, and college but also my parents. I didn't know they knew at first.

Meanwhile, I ran out of friends as well as funds. Although I had deluded myself into thinking I'd done a good job hiding my increasingly desperate dilemma, people were suspicious about a guy who'd previously always wanted to golf, eat out, and buy another tee shirt, but who now appeared suddenly to hang out for a few days to sit around "shooting the breeze" instead of going out and spending money. My discreet inquiries about business opportunities in their areas provoked several of these friends to put two and two together and ask: "What happened? Were you fired? If you need money..."

I dreaded those two words: "fired" and "handout." Their sound, the merest suggestion that either word might be associated with me and my predicament kept me from telling the truth. Later, I would discover that it wasn't those two words denying the truth. It was me.

My pride kept me from accepting a couple of less prestigious, less well-paying jobs that with diligence and effort I might have worked into something similar or even better than my lost job. That pride kept me from minimum wage jobs that would have saved me from what I believed to be the last straw—repossession of my car by a "repo man" who was the most sarcastic human being I ever met.

How low I sank! No job. No friends. I'd used my friends as far as my dishonesty had allowed. No apartment. No car. I'd lost everything except what God was after—my pride.

There was only one place for me to go. I landed in a Christian shelter for the homeless. I had nothing except a plan that I thought would preserve my integrity and story until I landed that perfect job I was praying for.

I had it all figured out. I still had part of my wardrobe in storage. I'd take a daily job or two per week and hope no one saw me riding buses to the storage unit to change clothes and go to job interviews.

But I miscalculated again. I may have been competitive in my profession, but I was no match for my shelter mates in competition for the kinds of temporary work that came to us through the job manager. There were also the class prejudices that I, as a "professional," seemed to excite and exacerbate. Consequently, I was left with barely enough work to pay for my daily needs for toiletries.

So, I slunk for two months from one temporary job to another (when I could get one) during the daytime, hoping no one would see me, and trying to relax at night. Still, I couldn't settle down.

I had no resumes circulating. Having become unemployed just as a recession was starting, my rare job interviews through employment agencies didn't land me at the top of an employer's "hire now" list. Too many unemployed workers with my education and experience were looking for work, too.

Still, I must confess that Somebody was trying to tell me the recession was not my most serious problem. Rather, it began to dawn on me that my problem was me. I was extremely proud, so it was not an easy lesson to learn that to get out of the hole I was digging for myself I needed to jettison that self-pride and learn to depend on God.

To succeed a man needs a whole spirit and a broken will. I had it backwards. My spirit was broken, but my will was as intact as it had always been. But the Holy Spirit has His own ways and means committee.

One evening when I returned to the shelter, I found a note on my pillow that read: "See me when you get in tonight." As I talked to this weekend night staff person, I found myself opening up. Crying, I admitted feelings of nothingness. Having lost hope in my future, I felt my past slipping away, too. "Nobody cares," I said, "and maybe I'm becoming 'nobody' too."

My friend helped me see that I shared the common feelings and experience of the homeless. My problem and theirs is not primarily material. It was spiritual; as my counselor later put it, "born from wrong belief about God and myself and wrong responses to both."

My friend said, "To God and the staff here you are no more important than any other person in the shelter, you just happen to have a good education and work experience many residents don't. Within the will of God, we try to tailor a man's recovery program to both his gifts and needs. We'd like to refer you to a counselor. He adjusts his fee according to the income of his clients. If you'll put up five bucks from your last pay we'll pay twenty toward your appointments and he'll see you once. If you prefer not to see him after that, we'll talk about it."

That conversation brought me relief and hope. Those positive feelings gave me hope about seeing the counselor, too.

The counselor, Clint Conner, taught me to pray—not in the shallow way I'd prayed as a boy and later as a businessman, but prayer for forgiveness and healing from my insecurities. These, I learned, had been the source of my pride and subsequent downfall.

I'd grown up in a Christian home where nobody missed church but everybody missed an authentic relationship with Christ. Prayer healed my too-intellectual walk with God. It helped me confront my family and friends with the truth.

It is one thing to pray for the death of pride. It's another to participate in the funeral of that pride.

I discovered that my parents had already heard of my "fall." They hadn't said anything to me. They respected my freedom enough to let me handle it or share it with them as I wished.

My father took a long time recovering from what had happened to me. He's probably still embarrassed about that period in my life, especially when he's with his business associates. I'm one apple that didn't fall far from the tree where pride is concerned.

I moved back home where my mother, true to her basic nature, saw that I was well fed and cared for—which answered my desperate need to know that I was loved then by at least one human being no matter what I'd done or how I'd failed.

A few years have passed. I found a job with a newly formed company. I didn't earn what I had before, but it was a start back up the business ladder. I have married a Christian, a deeply spiritual woman, and further counseling has helped me to learn to deal with those basic insecurities out of which my pride had developed.

So the tragedy of my fall, my homelessness, turned out to be, instead, a wonderful blessing. I had thought life would be a bowl of pitless cherries because I had accepted Christ as my Savior as a boy. I discovered I needed a real Jesus for my adult life, and that spiritual homelessness is far more impoverishing than material homelessness.

Afterwords

Although this story is not typical of most of America's homeless, I've presented it here because I think it illustrates a spiritual problem which is often the basis for homelessness.

First, many are poor through no fault of their own. Many of us are biased in two ways toward the poor. We accuse them of laziness, or dismiss poverty as a "socio-economic problem" beyond our individual ability to correct.

Second, prayer is a vital part to the answer to the homeless problem, but not just prayer for the homeless themselves. We need to pray about *our* pride and selfish unconcern with those who have less.

This story illustrates just to what foolish lengths pride will drive most of us, and pride afflicts all people, regardless of their station in life. One of the seven deadly sins, pride is Satan's favorite tool, the one he most loves to see us lost in because it is the same one that brought his downfall. With pride, he can make fools of us all.

Note how this man lost identity, significance, hope and meaning of even his past existence when pride drove him to homelessness. The depression and dread he felt are experienced by all the homeless regardless of the particular circumstances that drive them into the streets.

Jesus can heal them and restore their losses. But He comes not only to heal and save them, He comes to put them in and on our hearts.

He wants very much to do both.

Chapter 12

Hypnotized Homemaker

"Our beliefs about anything don't change its fundamental nature, origins, ends, and/or what it produces." —The Author

The brochure read, "Do you need to lose weight, reduce stress, stop some besetting sin...then sign up for our workshop with a trained hypnotist." My aunt had taken it out of her church's bulletin and sent it to me.

Although she was a Christian as were lots of people in her church, it didn't change the fact that neither they nor the pastor had the discernment to ask the questions I asked my pastor about it: "Is there anything in the Bible about hypnotism? What should a Christian believe about it?"

I hoped desperately his answer would be, "It's okay, go for it," because I'd tried unsuccessfully to lose weight with every diet, diet program, and every other method I'd ever heard of except for hypnotism.

A couple of days later, he called to say he thought hypnotism was okay unless it was used in some occult way. He'd talked to my aunt's pastor who said the hypnotist was a Christian and had never used hypnotism in any way other than for helping people with their problems. He didn't see how it could hurt me, and that it might be the very thing that would help me, suggesting I at least try it, but not go back after the first session if anything seemed wrong.

Three weeks later, I found myself seated in a church multi-purpose room with fourteen other people. Their various addictions and woes had caused them to seek the same magic answer for their problems that I was looking for.

None of us seemed to know what to expect. I doubted it would be like the old movies where one concentrates on some metallic object suspended and swinging back and forth like a pendulum while the hypnotist chants in a monotonous whisper, "your addictions are cured."

An hour and a half later, I had my answer. I found I'd been led through a group "relaxing and emptying process," followed by what could best be described as a power-of-suggestion reconditioning (against my eating practices), and a mind-over-matter reconditioning to establish new eating habits.

Although some of you may be interested in the hypnotism techniques themselves, they are not really worth your time. What does merit attention is to look at the fact they worked and why.

They worked like magic—for awhile. I lost twenty-six pounds in three-and-a-half months before the wheels started to come off. The same thing that had happened to me every other time I lost twenty or thirty pounds started to happen all over again. That's right, I gained it all back. Only this time something happened to me that had never happened before. I went beyond my highest weight ever and put on pound after pound to a weight gain I'd never seen before in my life!

The hypnotist's solution when I phoned her was to see her in her private practice for a fee that I could only call exorbitant if I were trying to be kind, and highway robbery if I were being totally honest. If our insurance company hadn't said they wouldn't pay a hypnotist I might have gone anyhow because I had no idea where else to turn. My weight was scaring me so badly I knew I had to do something.

My pastor and friends offered prayers and well meaning "sound bites" of advice, none of which helped. The pounds just kept multiplying. I kept eating, gaining, and worrying until my husband came home from work one day with a woman's name and phone number on a piece of paper. He had asked his noon-hour Bible study friends to pray for my weight problem, and afterwards one of them gave him Bonnie Conner's name as a Christian counselor in the area who had helped other men and women with weight problems.

I'd never heard of her and was leery of any referral after the hypnotism experience. But I couldn't go on like this so I decided on at least scheduling a "check-her-out" appointment.

During that session I found myself listening to a logical and biblical explanation of what had happened to me that was at once so helpful and simple I found myself wondering why I hadn't thought of what I was hearing.

Bonnie began by having me look at verses in Leviticus 19, Psalm 58, Daniel 2, and 1 Timothy with her to see what Scripture said about enchantment and spells and those who use such devices. As we studied contemporary meanings of the biblical words used in those and other passages, I saw that in the meetings I had attended I'd given myself over to the influence of another person and their suggestions, and opened my spirit to mental powers rather than the power of God. In 1 Chronicles 10:14, God was as angry at Saul for not coming to Him as He was over Saul's going to another spirit for answers.

In our second appointment as Bonnie and I looked at additional Scripture, this time in the sexual area, I saw how the things that the god Baal—the male sexual idol—and goddess Ashtoreth—the female sexual idol—made to happen were actually caused by demons who influenced the sexual activities, alcohol abuse, and occult worship that those who came under their influence practiced.

It suddenly hit me! I had come under the influence of a spiritual principality when I gave myself to an irredeemable system and methodology that's been under the influence of that evil power since Satan's fall. That which is inherently evil can **never** become or produce good.

As Bonnie and I prayed for me to come out from under that Satanic influence and for the part of me that had been effected to be given back to God and under His influence again, I could actually feel a change of kingdoms taking place in my heart.

It became very clear that who (the source of power) brings results, not the results in and of themselves, is the ultimate measure of a thing. After initial success with hypnotism— that is, some weight loss—I actually got worse than I'd ever been and could not get better no matter what I tried.

After repenting for my involvement in so-called benign hypnotism, and forgiving the Christian hypnotist and the church pastor who had recommended the program, I committed my weight problem to God, acknowledging Him as my Source for the power needed to lose weight. I also sought additional counseling from Bonnie to resolve the issues underlying my weight problem, and followed godly principles of good nutrition and exercise. This combination led to the loss of the thirty pounds I had lost so many times before, and now twenty beyond that. Yes, I've lost the twenty more I always needed to lose but had never been able to do before, and have maintained this victory in the three years since the counseling and weight loss started.

Some of the women I've shared my experience with have said, "I was hypnotized for weight loss and didn't have your experience. It worked for me. I'm fine, weight-wise and spiritually."

If you are saying the same thing as you read this, I 'd say to you what I said to them: "You can go with how you feel about what you've done, but I suggest you read God's Word on the subject, ask Him how He feels about what you've done, then do what I did: go with what makes Jesus feel good, not your feelings."

Someone deceitful enough to masquerade as an angel of light (which is what the Bible says Satan does) can help you succeed and make you feel good while you do it. But all the while you feel good, that evil influence is causing you to sin against God and draw away from Him and what He has for you without your being consciously aware of what is really going on!

Afterwords

What's God's goal for each of us? Our best through Him. What's Satan's? The good instead of the best. From the *A* of acupuncture to the *Z* of Zen philosophy, we'd do well to apply the same principles this woman did to what we think, feel, believe, and hold dear—is it from God and is it His best, or is it something else? Something else, sooner or later, is going to bring us real problems.

Chapter 13

Manipulative Maneuverer

"Selfishness is always a terrible thing. But it is always at its very worst when we are not just selfish by ourselves but use another person in the fulfilling of our ends." —The Author

A Christian should not try to bend others to her will. She ought not manipulate others for selfish ends. But that's precisely what I did. If I'd known I was manipulative, I like to think I would have stopped, but I was unaware of what I was doing and oblivious to its disastrous effects on others.

Growing up in a dysfunctional family taught me an important lesson: getting close to others or letting them get close to me only led to pain. Survival then lay in keeping everyone at a distance. I saw only two ways of doing that: withdrawal and isolation or taking charge.

Withdrawal wasn't practical in my family. My relatives continually trespassed into my space. Manipulation was a more effective strategy and involved dictating to those younger and trying to please or placate those older, especially my parents, to get others where I wanted them and keep them there. So, I grew up alternating between those two extremes: raging shrew to the weaker and insinuating apple-polisher to the stronger (usually adults).

Needless to say, I developed a messed up personality. It may have bothered others, but my personality troubled me not at all, not until my son's fourth grade teacher complained about his abuse of her and most of the girls in his class. The principal and she required that we obtain counseling for him, or he wouldn't be allowed to remain in class and likely would not be promoted.

I was devastated! My pride was wounded. Virtually everyone in the public school system was saying, "Look at how that boy acts, and his parents call themselves Christians." I was also embarrassed because I had to slip off with my husband and son to consult with the Christian counselor I'd recommended to others, thinking all the while that they had problems we didn't. So much for smugness.

I went to that first counseling appointment thinking my son's abusive behavior could be traced back to my husband's easy-going nature. I was surprised to hear him explain his laid-back ways were a reaction to me! I was shocked at the anger behind what he said, and his conviction that our son was angry with me, too.

My husband said that before we married he'd been attracted to my spunk and drive and hoped it would be contagious, that it might help him to deal with his shyness, passivity, and general noninvolvement with people. It didn't work that way. I eclipsed him and he quit trying to bloom. He'd withdrawn, but all that time beneath that quiet exterior, he had burned with anger at me.

Realizing that both my husband and son were consumed with anger toward me overwhelmed me with grief and guilt. If God hadn't intervened, none of us would have been able to get beyond that sudden revelation. But God did intervene in that first appointment and turned my grief into real repentance.

I saw that I had been trying to usurp God's role in the lives of those whom I loved. How can anyone develop into the person God intends for him or her to be if the main influence in his or her life is another person, even a well-meaning Christian one? With tears I repented, and all three of us were reconciled.

During the next two sessions, we offered up healing prayers for the circumstances that had bred my desire to control and maneuver others. These prayers remarkably transformed me and those close to me. Perhaps another way of looking at it is to say that they created an environment where all of us could make necessary changes. My son behaved better in school, in the neighborhood, and in our company. My husband became the man I'd always wanted him to be, and that he didn't know he could be.

I became a woman for the first time. Not only had my manipulative ways prevented others from becoming themselves, but it had also held me back from being the woman God intended. I was too busy being what I thought He wanted me to be. What I'd become was not God's desire at all—it was only mine.

I thought my healing was complete, but my counselor suggested I attend a Christian conference where the speaker said that in life we have two basic choices: we either manipulate or we meditate. My spirit discerned the Holy Spirit saying, *"You've tried to manipulate Me just like you have others. You believed and felt that you were close to Me, but you're really no closer to Me than you were to others. You were far from them. It's one thing to stop manipulating, entirely another to meditate on Me and build a relationship with Me out of that meditation."*

I was devastated all over again. Once again I shed tears of real repentance. Then God worked a miraculous, wonderful change in my life again: He healed my relationship with Him. I fell in love with God all over again.

It is true that we either manipulate or meditate, but we have to add one caution here:

we must not meditate on just anything. Our meditation must be focused on God.

Transcendental meditation teaches that you can meditate your way into other emotional states. Biofeedback techniques assert that you can meditate from one psychological wave state to another. There are New Age techniques that insist you can meditate into another spiritual state. You name it and men have tried to manipulate and meditate on it.

Out of this endless variety of objects, which are really idols, I can see only one true object of meditation: God. When we give ourselves to the Lord, He doesn't take our free will. He helps us to voluntarily make our will subservient and secondary to His.

So we either manipulate or meditate on someone or something that eventually manipulates us. Or, we meditate on Christ. Meditation means to build a relationship. Jesus brings freedom to all who come to Him, the wonderful freedom to be who and what God intended.

Afterwords

Although I didn't counsel this family, their experience is common. I've seen many like them over the years, families where one, some, or all members try to control one another. Manipulation demeans both the controllers and the controlled. I've seen both men and women act as controllers. Many of these situations require more time and effort than this one did.

We chose to show how a Christian family, rather than a non-Christian, was healed to make this point: Christians suffer from these problems, too, and need to be honest and admit their need to be healed when they do.

Being a Christian means we are headed for and bound for heaven instead of hell, but it does not mean that we are immune from the ills and troubles the human race suffers in this life.

Two more points need to be made: First, the writer of this chapter succeeded partly because she assumed responsibility for her problems and stopped blaming her husband for her difficulties which he hadn't caused even though he bore responsibility in the marriage.

Secondly, in a country where the majority are uninterested in becoming Christians and when Christians live without revival, some self-help groups can be helpful. Where revival and its results are present, however, they're superfluous.

Chapter 14

Molested

"Nobody should approach a relative for sex. I am God!...Never have sex with your son or daughter." —Lev. 18:6, 10 (Author's paraphrase)

I suspect our father started molesting my two sisters and me when we were infants. We didn't know what he was doing with the other two, that we were all victims of incest, until I shared the "secret" one day with my best girlfriend when I was ten. She told our teacher who contacted child welfare authorities. They removed our father from our house before we went to bed that night.

Dad told me that the "secret" had to be kept or Mother would hit me harder than she did when she was drunk. He said that she would make him leave us forever which meant no money for food, rent, or toys. Having been hit often and hungry even more often, I believed him. I obeyed until the desire to be honest and open with my friend compelled me to reveal the truth.

You might think that telling the truth would have set us free. It didn't. Instead it brought down a holocaust on all our heads. I know that holocaust may seem like too strong a word to describe what befell us physically, mentally, and spiritually. When your earliest memories are a horrifying mixture of oral sex, foul breath, a raspy, evil voice, and lies from your father who threatens you with indescribable terrors if you ever "tell a living soul," then holocaust may not be strong enough.

Years before our caseworker explained incest to me, I knew deep inside that what Dad and I did was wrong. He assured me that it was something that all fathers and daughters did and kept secret. But I was deeply embarrassed and ashamed. Not only had my father tried to suppress my innate sense of right and wrong, but he had also perverted a healthy desire: a girl's desire to be close to her father.

The vague sense that what Dad was doing to me was wrong and the threat of my mother's anger was nothing compared to my shame, to that feeling that I was bad. After my father was picked up, my mother informed me that I was bad for costing my dad his freedom and depriving her of marriage and her children. My sisters, brother, and I went to foster homes because of mother's alcoholism.

I knew I was bad. My caseworker told me not to blame myself for what had happened. Nevertheless, when she explained incest to me and that other children had good fathers who didn't do those things to their children, it shattered what little self-esteem I had. In the midst of that ugly contact with Dad, some part of me felt some pleasure from it, so, I, too, felt evil because of that feeling of enjoyment.

Not even the best caseworker can heal a wounded spirit. Only another Spirit more powerful than others can heal our spiritual wounds. My spiritual scars urged me into a promiscuous adolescence. Feeling that I had long ago lost whatever purity other girls had, I participated in every sexual experience that came my way.

Every girl who has never experienced unconditional love from her father desperately seeks it. She also brings a volcano of anger and revenge at God and man for depriving her of that love.

When I married in my early twenties, I thought that the marital relationship would solve my problems. It only compounded them. My husband was kind and loving. He tried to make up for the evil that had happened to me, but I unloaded my rage on him for my father's abuse, for the boyfriends who'd used me, for my own self-loathing. I manipulated him— keeping him at arm's length, and, at the same time, provoking fight after fight.

You'd think my problems would have driven me to seek help. They didn't. Sexual dysfunction did.

Like many molested women, I was frigid in my marriage. Except during adolescent masturbation, I'd never had an orgasm. Although I fought like a banshee with my kind, loving husband, I couldn't bear being unable to have an orgasm with him—the ultimate in sexual pleasure and responsiveness, according to the magazines I read.

Deep inside I knew that my marriage wouldn't last if I didn't do something. I desperately wanted both marriage and children.

A sweet woman who worked in the same factory where my husband worked gave him a phone number with a comment: "This couple are counselors and have seen lots of women who have been through what your wife has."

Fear of divorce, frustration with my frigidity, and simple curiosity about what these people might have to say compelled me to phone them. My appointment ushered me to the most exciting experience of my life. It was the first time I'd found any life that was real.

Maybe guilt over incest and alcoholism and other sins kept my parents out of church. Whatever it was, it kept my sisters, brother, and me out, too. My first exposure to the spiritual realm was through the kind woman who'd given my husband the counselors' phone number. Before I went to see the Conners, she witnessed to us that Jesus Christ is still alive and can help people like me to deal with the injuries of the past.

During my first appointment, I asked the Conners if they believed in Christ. They, in turn asked me if I wanted to investigate who Christ is. I surprised myself by saying I did. It didn't take very long into the investigation for me to come to belief.

It's really more accurate to say that I "experienced" Jesus, who removed the evil and the effects of evil I had suffered from for so long. He took away the evil presence which had deceived me into feeling that I had enjoyed incest. For me, "counseling" and "removal" became synonymous.

When my caseworker helped me to express my feelings about my father's acts, I had felt some relief, but my anxiety and guilt actually increased. I experienced no complete relief. Bitter and unforgiving toward my father, I still felt utterly worthless and ugly until my husband and I knelt beside our coffee table and asked Jesus to remove our sins and the consequences of those sins, to come into our lives and make us whole. And He did! Repentance, not venting my feelings, healed my innermost wounds.

I can't share all the Lord did for me here, but I must mention two things. First, Jesus delivered me from the consequences of inherited sin (see Exodus 20:5-6). In the first chapter of Romans, Paul explains that obsession with the occult and perversion inevitably follow a turning away from God. When my father turned his back on God, my sister and I inherited the "fruits" of that spiritual defect: incest, a horrible perversion of the sexual instinct and of the wholesome, clean love God intended between parents and their children. What relief I felt when prayer broke that evil inheritance.

Second, Jesus restored what I had lost. In his first letter to the Corinthians, Paul discusses the notion of becoming one flesh with sexual partners. He talks about the price paid when sex is indulged in for sinful purposes.

The Conners prayed that God would restore to me that which my father had taken. It felt as if some missing part of my soul had been returned to me. I'm sure it was!

The Lord restored my marriage, too, to where I was able to respond to my husband's love with no other psychological agenda than the two of us and the present moment. No longer did I need to use his embraces to "atone" for the ugliness I had experienced with my father, nor experience sexual fulfillment as proof I was normal.

Jesus' healing brought me the capacity to live in the present, not the past, and to enjoy all God has given me in any given moment. I'm able now to give myself fully, in the manner the Lord intends for all who are his servants, and I am able to experience orgasm, as well as love, with my husband.

My healing from the effects of molestation was and remains to this day complete.

Afterwords

Although the woman in this story uses the word "restore" to describe her healing, she could have used the word "redeem." Redeem is a word that means to be completely bought back. This woman—her life—certainly was, and by The Only One who can buy lives back— The Author, The Creator, The Giver of life originally.

Chapter 15

New Age Convert

"*When they stopped glorifying God as God, they became fools and made simpletons of themselves.*" —Rom. 1:21-22 (Author's paraphrase)

My problems with the New Age began as a lark. My beer-drinking buddy of twenty years and I experimented with rolfing. The woman who rolfed us believed it when she said that real powers and energies were going to be unlocked in my body. What she believed didn't matter to me because I didn't believe any of it. She reminded me of the chiropractor I'd consulted: both were enthusiasts for their "thing."

Rolfing is a system of deep tissue massage that brings the human body into alignment with the force of gravity. My rolfed body felt better, but the knot in my stomach still troubled me, so my explorations continued through books, classes, and encounter groups on such things as psycho-cybernetics, biorhythms, biofeedback, relaxation techniques, hypnotherapy, yoga, and transcendental meditation—mantra

146

included. For the next ten years if it said "self-help" I laid my money down and tried it, but not only had all of it not helped me feel better, it had made me feel worse.

Trying desperately to find inner peace and release from tension, I found a new-age group which I believed would be my last hope. I paid my fifty dollars wanting to find out how to create and control my own reality and destiny.

To my surprise, I found myself listening to someone talk "religion" without turning me off. Not even vacation Bible school had turned me on when I was a kid, and I hadn't been in a church since then except for weddings and funerals. A man lectured about divine energy living in me and when my "god consciousness" developed sufficiently for me to tap into it, I'd start to develop my potential.

By the end of week four, I was trance channeling alone at home. I invited "helpers" to help me rise above this reality to create a new dimension and tap into inner and outer peace. I assumed these helpers were extra-terrestrials or unreincarnated spirits. Channeling is concentrating psychic or spiritual energies in such a way that spirit beings in the other world can be contacted and communicated with, making a channel for such interaction.

It didn't work. My thirty-year stomach knot remained and grew larger. I found no peace. I wasn't just disappointed or crushed: I was beside myself. Not even some beer on Saturday nights relaxed me. I was afraid I would snap.

I feared going to work. Fear affected my eating habits. A doctor prescribed nerve pills that loosened my stomach knot but didn't remove the fear that haunted me. I felt like I was being chased down a dark alley by someone or something ready to pounce on and annihilate me.

I returned to see the nurse at work and told her my medication wasn't doing enough. She didn't give me much sympathy. "I'm running a factory's part-time medical clinic," she said, "not a comprehensive mental health center for people who need more than tranquilizers."

She brusquely handed me a list of counselors. She explained that the list had been prepared by a Christian nurse who had preceded her, so they were "probably mostly religious-type counselors."

Desperate, I called the first one on the list. I resolved to keep calling names on that list until I found the one who would see me the soonest. Ever since that day I've been grateful for two things. First, the Conners' name begins with C, not Z. Because it does, I called them first. Second, the Conners keep open an hour on their appointment schedule every day for people as desperate as I was.

I told Clint right away that I needed a quick fix. He said he had one, and that it was free but would cost me the rest of my life. Of course, he meant that God's forgiveness was free provided I accepted Jesus Christ as my personal Savior.

If I could have walked out of that appointment at that point without paying, I would have. Hearing that I was a sinner who needed forgiveness through Someone else's blood, who needed to surrender his life to Another, made no sense and made me so angry I almost forgot the fear in my stomach.

But I stayed. I'm eternally grateful that I did. The Holy Spirit, through Clint, gave me a coherent and logical explanation of what had happened to me. I didn't buy it all right away, but it became the basis of my healing.

We went over each important event in my past, especially my rejection of church and the Bible as God's Word. He quoted a verse from Romans, chapter one, that talked about those who turned to occult and sexual sins after turning away from God. I knew that I had rejected Christianity as a boy but didn't equate that with a rejection of God. I told Clint I still believed in God.

He pointed out, however, that God, not man, defined what constitutes true belief in Him. God was merciful to me as a boy, but as I grew older I wandered into sexual encounters with various girlfriends and even prostitutes and the typical pornography circulating in factories. So Clint was right. No matter what I thought, I'd turned my back on God and was reaping the consequences of that rejection.

The rolfing and "self-help" New Agers I encountered obtained guidance from spirits other than God's. I didn't accept that. I told Clint that I didn't believe in demons or hell, and even if these things were real, I hadn't sought them deliberately. They couldn't be the cause of my troubles.

He replied, "Only gentlemen need to be invited. The enemies of all mortal souls are not gentlemen. They come into our lives when we've committed 'spiritual adultery' by going to spirits other than God's for spiritual experiences. We remove the protective grace and mercy of God from around our lives when we do. Sexual sins opened you up to what the Bible calls *unclean spirits,* and your occult involvement further opened you to a spiritual world devoid of God yet filled with religious spirits."

"Take rolfing, for example. It's the physical therapy of the New Age, but you got something spiritual from it, too. Many of its adherents are Hindus who believe in 'inner deities' that can be unlocked or released through rolfing. Rolfing doesn't release something from you. Instead, it brings a spirit—an evil spirit—into you. In sexual relations you gave your body to another. Beginning with the rolfing and what followed, you gave your spirit to another—a spirit, not God's."

"Let's talk about God for a minute. Certainly, God has both mind and energy, but He isn't mind, energy, matter or reality in the way you've been taught. The holistic therapies—most of which are New Age—are a modern reflection of an ancient heresy called monism, the belief that reality is one organic whole with no independent parts. When you were in high school, you bought the evolutionists' argument that 'good lies ahead' in that man is developing or evolving to a more perfect state. You mixed the idea that God is in this good to come and arrived at pantheism, the heresy that God is not outside creation but is within creation, that the sum total of the universe is God."

"All of this ties into a basic New Age belief—that all religions will eventually become one in the future. They contend that you may return then reincarnated. In your trance channeling during the last four weeks, all you managed to accomplish was to invite demonic spirits into your life without knowing it."

I interrupted Clint at this point. Although he spoke from love, his words brought spiritual conviction from God in a way I couldn't understand. It was logical, and I was unable to refute it, so I lost my temper and left without scheduling another appointment.

I decided to talk to a New Age lecturer and get answers to Clint's "put-down." I talked to a woman on the phone who suggested I sign up for another class. I gave her Clint's address to send material to him.

I had almost gotten over the whole episode except for one thing: I was back to square one. My stomach felt like a bag full of knotted ropes, and I was without a counselor.

Then Clint called to thank me for the material he had received. He had read it and now was asking what could convince me that the Christ of the New Testament was real instead of the "god consciousness" of the new world order that I believed in.

My stomach tightened, and I yelled over the phone that I would believe in whatever loosened my stomach for a while and that he could pray whatever he wanted after I hung up. I've never slammed a phone down harder.

Four days later I called back. I told him I hadn't had a knot in my stomach for over ninety-six hours. I knew it wasn't his prayer but who the prayer had been addressed to. I told him nobody but the true and living God could have done such a thing, and that I wanted to know Him.

Shortly afterwards, I returned to counseling. I gave God everything, not just the stomach He'd healed, but every part of me I could give: my spirit, soul, mind, sins, and those demon spirits which had tried to meld with me. Activities that filled me with revulsion before—church, fellowship with other believers,

Bible study, witnessing—all these things appealed to me as passionately as they turned me off before. I witnessed to my old high school drinking buddy and he converted to Christ, too. The signs and wonders he saw in my life influenced him.

A Christian friend described the change in my life this way: "For you, having God heal your stomach was as big a miracle as when Elisha saw the river stop flowing when he struck it with Elijah's coat. This miracle convinced him to go on with God. The miracle of a normal stomach convinced you to *start* with Him." I agreed.

All of us must make the choice I did: to go with the living God or to follow the false gods and spirits of the modern idolaters. The Lord liberated me from the New Age to Himself. May you make the same choice!

Afterwords

Counterfeits, whether of money or of the spiritual, regardless of how clever, only prove two things: (1) that there is the true of which (2) they are the false.

Chapter 16

Obsessive-Compulsive

It started harmlessly enough with an obedience to the same superstitious rituals my peers adhered to, such as "Don't step on a crack, or you'll break your mother's back." But it soon progressed to a slavish obedience not only to those innocent childhood rituals but to what seemed to become hundreds of ridiculous habits, none of which I could dare break.

Midway through life, I found myself still constantly eating all foods in a certain order, biting every fingernail to the quick (which I'd begun in first grade), and still having to have every part of my body covered before I could get to sleep no matter how hot the temperature. Also, despite being relatively satisfied sexually in my marriage, I still masturbated compulsively like I had done since adolescence.

To all those retained habits and compulsions from earlier years, I had added a whole series of new ones during adulthood. I would check every window lock in the house before going to bed, even in winter when the storm windows were in and I knew they hadn't been opened. After checking the windows, I checked each pilot light in the house (stove, water heater, and furnace) to be sure it was lit before I could bring myself to head upstairs to bed.

While my wife, children, and others around me lived in meaningful relationships and engaged in normal activities, I engaged in one compulsive ritual after another, meaningless rituals that I could not bring myself to give up even though they brought no release or satisfaction, let alone productive results.

After twenty-three years of marriage and forty-three years of life, it all seemed to come to a head with my wife saying she'd "had enough of my foolishness," and I could either see a counselor or she would see an attorney.

Within a two-year span, I had been to a psychologist who specialized in behavior modification therapy that didn't change mine, a stress-management group that left me more anxious, a hypnotist whose methods hadn't helped, and finally, a psychiatrist who told me my rituals were rage displacements (among other things) which didn't cure me either.

After two years and four attempts at counseling, I still had every compulsive act I had started with and wasn't any closer to an answer that would help me give them up than when I had started. And I still had a wife threatening me with: "Do something or we're through! I can't stand living with someone who pays more attention to a bunch of meaningless games than he does to me!" Worst of all, I had no idea where to go or what to do next.

Everybody needs to have some place they go, something they do, or somebody they see in an emergency when they're stuck or there's a crisis. I was no exception. I know everyone in America doesn't have an old Christian grandmother who prays for them, but those of us who do are indeed fortunate.

I treated her in a rather paternalistic fashion between times when I needed her. I would make perfunctory stops occasionally on my way home from work with superficial conversation, leaving my wife to stop with the kids on other occasions and remember holidays with presents.

But I always knew Grandma was there in a "deeper way" whenever we needed her to be there like that. And we had: a couple of times for money, for advice when the kids stymied us, and for prayers whenever there were problems we couldn't seem to solve.

Although we had told her a lot over the years, I had never shared my problems with compulsive behavior with her. She listened thoughtfully without interruption as she always had. When I finished, she said, "Clifford, (she was the only person I knew who didn't call me "Cliff") there is a lot I could say to you about your problem, but there is more to be said and done about it than I have to say. I suggest you get yourself a good Christian counselor and see if you don't get further than you did with all those others who weren't Christians. I know of one I can recommend and if you see him I'll help you with the fee."

Now I didn't mind having a Christian grandmother who prayed for me but I didn't want to hear advice about seeing a Christian counselor. I wasn't a Christian myself, didn't want to become one and felt reasonably certain any counselor who was would push me in that direction.

On the other hand, I desperately needed help, didn't know what else to do and just as desperately needed the financial help Grandma was offering.

I found myself calling Clint Conner, the counselor, not because I wanted to, but because I didn't know what else to do. Maybe, I reasoned, I could get the help I needed from him without having to endure much religion. Maybe, I hoped, I could take his help and leave his religion for a later day when I was old like Grandma without anything better to do than be religious. It wasn't that I was against religion. I just thought it was for little children or the elderly who faced dying but cumbersome and unnecessary for the years in between. I think my real fear was that I thought it would be just a whole new set of rituals its adherents had to obey. I was overwhelmed with more of those than I could handle already!

It took half an hour of that first appointment with Clint to tell about my compulsive behavior and another half hour to tell a story about an angry little boy—me—who had a very dominant mother and a very passive father.

When I finished, I expected to hear what I had heard in the psychiatrist's office: "Your hour is up, come back next week when I'll share my observations about what you've told me."

Instead, what I heard was: "If you have another twenty or thirty minutes I'd like to share some thoughts with you about what you've said."

I stayed and what followed (as I was to learn later) was how the Holy Spirit informs one person about what He wants a second person to be told about themselves, their problems and God.

That very significant half hour of my life began with Clint saying those who are controlled during childhood by a parent's manipulation for their own ends grow up with a desire to dominate as revenge for having been so dominated. Even when they are no longer manipulated by the original person, they remain dominated by somebody or something (rituals, in my case) because they have never forgiven what was done to them. They reap what they have sown. In other words, a secondary dominator becomes their lot because they have never forgiven the original one.

Clint allowed that underneath my overt "fear-born" adherence to the countless rules of a bossy and punitive mother was a silent, unconscious, yet real, defiant disobedience lodged in the midst of a will that had never been broken! What the psychiatrist had suggested to me had been true as far as it went: my rituals were lids for a brooding rage that smoldered beneath them.

Clint said he believed there was something else involved that the psychiatrist had not addressed. Defiant rage—even if unconscious—breeds an equally unconscious, but ever so real, guilty fear: the fear of punishment. Punishment for the rage and the desires for hurtful revenge that are its companions. Both the fear of expressing rage and the fear of punishment cause guilty fear to dominate and the rituals become not only lids for anger but magic atonement and gimmicks for short-circuiting guilt and preventing oneself from become overwhelmed with fear.

Clint went on to say that displacement never dispels, meaning that my methods (rituals) for dealing with anger, fear, and guilt only temporarily displaced and never permanently dispelled them. Therefore, what I ended up with was an ever-increasing bag full of rituals that brought ever-increasing bondage instead of pleasure and release. I had become as powerless to stop them as I was the anger and guilt in the relationship with my mother and the non-relationship with my father that birthed them.

He added that God often allowed a man's humanistic efforts to solve his problems to end without pleasure or success and in powerlessness to show him these efforts had come from within himself. Man's only real hope is to quit looking within where there is only human energy and to look without and up where there is only Power—God's—which is what all problems need applied to them to really solve them.

It took me awhile—six months actually—before I did that: look to God. In those months Clint helped me see that God wasn't going to deliver me from one set of rituals only to give me another—His. What He had for me instead were some things to adhere to that would bring me freedom instead of bondage and to do so from a motive of love for Him rather than a desire for personal freedom. Clint also helped me see that if I pursued freedom I would never find it, but if I pursued God, He would bring me freedom, freedom found in a Person, not rituals.

A few weeks after that realization, I found myself sitting in Grandma's trailer with her holding my hands while I prayed to give my life, including all my rage and rituals, to Jesus.

What happened after that was more than amazing. First, the Holy Spirit gave me the power to overcome all of my compulsions, one at a time, and not by substituting a different behavior in place of the old one. He didn't re-place or substitute ritual with ritual either. He did give me a temporary method or plan that helped me as I began to give each compulsive activity up.

He had me name ten people I wanted to see become Christians, designating each of my ten fingers for one of them. When I started to chew the nail on that hand, I stopped and prayed for that person instead. He gave me something that worked for each and every one, even the masturbation which seemed the hardest for me.

First He dispelled, then He replaced. And He didn't stop with the rituals that bothered me. He went on to clean the things out of my life that bothered Him. I found out that what I had called my values before I became a Chris-tian were mostly biases and prejudices that had to go as did what I called my convictions. These turned out to be trivial grudges. My in-telligence and knowledge turned out to be mostly pride that had to be replaced with humility. The process continues.

When my quest for an answer to my problems started, I was a man who knew vir-tually nothing of what was going on within him, a man running from himself and God. Now God helps me see what is there inside and shows me how to face it full on. I am no longer the brooding ritual-maker anymore. I am free because Jesus dispels those things when He comes—actually, when I come into His presence—and all freedom is found there. *"So if the Son sets you free, you will be free indeed!"* (John 8:36).

Afterwords

Cliff originally did not want to say a whole lot about his wife in this story because at the time of its writing she had not and still hasn't become a Christian. But the chapter seems incomplete without sharing the following.

Immediately after Cliff's conversion, she didn't like his being a Christian anymore than she had cared for him as a man riddled with what were to her silly habits she could no longer tolerate. However, when her teenage daughter also became a Christian, she began to feel differently. At this writing she attends church occasionally with Cliff and their daughter and is content to remain in the marriage.

Chapter 17

Panic Attacks

"There is no fear in love because perfect love casts fear out. The one who fears isn't perfected in giving or receiving love. Fear has to do with punishment [becoming like someone who has sinned and not been caught or punished for it yet]*."*   —1 John 4:18 (Author's paraphrase)

My first panic attack happened at a Bosses' Night Dinner during National Secretary's Week. I'd been pretty immoral my twenty-eight years of life up until that time—a lot immoral in fact. It is not surprising then that I wasn't feeling any guilt whatever as I sat half-listening to the after-dinner speaker extolling the virtues and wonders of secretaries and at the same time, fantasizing having an affair with him even though his wife was a good friend of mine. I'd deemed him the only real "hunk" in the room that evening.

Suddenly, right in the middle of my reverie it hit: I picked up my cup for a sip of coffee and my hand began to tremble, ever so slightly at first, then increasingly as I tried to control it. Finally it got to the point that when I tried to put the cup down it clattered noisily onto the saucer, spilling what coffee was left and attracting everybody's attention.

I could feel my face flush. I excused myself, claiming nausea. I let the other two girls who worked in my office help me to a lounge where I lay on a couch as my panicky feelings and embarrassment seemed only to increase rather than subside. I would never have believed it possible for any human being to feel what I was experiencing and try to contain it without exploding. Without warning, something beyond my control had suddenly hit me, causing me to understand the meaning of words like fear, panic, phobia, and dread in a way I never had before in my life.

I took the next day—Friday—off, feigning flu. I had no problems with trembling hands and spilled coffee as I padded about my apartment, enjoying the luxury of an extra day off to be alone and recover from what had happened the night before.

On Monday, when I had to hold a cup in the presence of others at coffee break, I began trembling again—worse than I had at the banquet! I managed to get the disposable cup still half-full of coffee thrown away before anyone noticed and left the break room to return to work with the excuse that coffee still wasn't tasting good after my bout with the flu.

At lunch, fearing the same thing would happen, I determined to order a soft drink with a straw to sip through. This would have worked fine and put me back in control again, except my trembling now spread to the use of knives, forks, and spoons. In a word, I was im-mobilized—immobilized with fear anytime I tried to eat in the presence of other people.

Eventually my fear expanded from the fear of trembling to include the fear of embar-rassment in front of others for almost anything that could possibly happen, even though nothing did. For some unknown reason, some-thing strange was happening to me for the first time in my life that was beyond my power to control. I had absolutely no clue about what to do to change it. It all seemed like a bad dream, but it wasn't. My life was turning into a living hell every time I was with someone. The more I attempted to stop what was happening inside me, the worse it seemed to get.

Life changed dramatically. I began turning down dates and other social engagements, es-pecially if eating were involved. I still had friends come over when I absolutely had to, but it wasn't long before those people you've always had for meals or even just something to drink begin to wonder why I never had any-thing, despite my excuses about a diet.

Frankly, I stopped caring about things like that when I found myself in a situation that was rapidly deteriorating from bad to worse to crisis! I was beginning to be scared about whether I could continue working. I was brown-bagging lunch and waiting to drink any liquids during the day only when others weren't around. Then I'd bolt down a glass of water and head for my typewriter where my fingers would fly across those keys without the first hint of a tremor. How could that be when they trembled so violently and uncontrollably in the presence of others, especially when eating was involved?

You can only live like I was for so long before you have to do something about it. The first thing I tried was reading everything I could get my hands on from magazines articles to library books about fear, anxiety, phobic conditions, and panic attacks. Depending on which author I chose to believe, I could conclude that I was either phobic, experiencing panic attacks, or had an anxiety disorder. But becoming better informed left me no different than before—irrationally fearful of something I had no business being fearful of and hadn't been before that fateful banquet.

Next, I opted for understanding my biorhythms and getting biofeedback training and counseling, which are basically self-calming techniques I had read about in my search to understand my panic disorder.

Sooner or later, regardless of which technique you choose, you have to attempt eating in front of others. When I attempted that—all the while concentrating on telling my emotions and body to stay calm—my anxiety level only increased. Invariably I had to put down the fork, glass, or whatever and flee the scene as soon as possible before I looked like an idiot dropping something. I soon ran out of excuses for not finishing meals or accepting social engagements that included them.

I could see only three other options: talk to a professional, confide in a friend, or explore the possibility of taking some kind of anti-anxiety medication. All three brought new fears of their own, but I decided on the second, making up my mind to tell a man I was dating what no other living soul knew about and ask for his help.

Tell him I did, but help he didn't. I was both devastated and furious at his simplistic "try harder" response and made three decisions as a result: never date him again, never tell another person what I was going through, and go see a doctor who didn't know me for medication. When I did, he only referred me to a psychiatrist who tried me on one prescription after another because of problems with side effects. When dosages ultimately reached levels that kept me from shaking, I was so medicated I could barely stay awake or function like I needed to mentally. Friends became seriously concerned that I either needed a drug treatment program or hospitalization for mental problems.

I felt like I was going to die if I didn't get some effective help and get it quickly. I had to have an answer if life were going to go on in any meaningful way. After all, I was neither a celibate nor a hermit, and my life's circumstances wouldn't permit me to continue living like one or the other just because I couldn't hold a cup or eat a meal in the presence of anyone else.

I decided in one last ditch effort at help to share my plight one more time, picking my best girlfriend to talk with in an effort to prevent a repeat of the kind of response I'd gotten from my boyfriend.

She was understanding, even sympathetic. Our conversation ended with her telling me she got nervous in front of others, too, and attended a group where attendees made speeches to each other at regular dinner meetings in an effort to get over their various forms of stage fright and nervousness. She suggested I attend one of the meetings with her.

I went, deciding I had nothing to lose and in the hope that it might help. Arriving after the meal so I wouldn't have to eat, I sat down next to other obviously fearful but otherwise friendly people, only to have a waitress set down in front of me an already-poured cup of fresh coffee. I let it set there until half-way through the meeting. I found myself thinking, "Why not try to pick up that cup?" With only the quickest of glances around the table to be sure others had their eyes on the speaker (and without a drop of medication in my body), I put that cup of coffee—ice-cold by then—to my lips and drank it down without the first hint of a tremble! My phobia or whatever it was had departed as suddenly as it had come! I was beyond ecstatic. Only being among strangers kept me from shouting exuberantly. I was sure I was cured. No more panic for me ever. I was back, back to where I had been before that banquet.

I stayed ecstatic until I went to lunch with friends on Monday, the first day not to brown-bag in months. I found myself luxuriating in a restaurant, anticipating nerves of steel and a steady spoon to consume the cup of chowder the waitress was about to set in front of me. The next thing I knew soup was spilling down the front of my blouse as my hand began trembling uncontrollably with the first spoonful. There was nothing I could do in front of my co-workers who were embarrassed for me but feign the "sudden illness" lie they knew to be totally untrue, pay my bill, and leave. I headed for the only place one can be alone in most workplaces: a restroom stall, where I cried silently until it was time to get to work.

Months passed without any change. I couldn't figure out why I had been fine when I'd tried the coffee only to be back to the shakes after that. From time to time, I would try to eat in relatively safe situations, only to fail and be worse than ever before. There was only one ray of hope on my horizon. It was the thought that if I had been normal again even that once, then wasn't being that way all the time still a possibility?

There was still one of my original three options I hadn't yet explored—counseling. I would not have known where to start looking if it hadn't been for a friend at work who offered the names of a counseling couple she knew. It seemed like my last hope even before I made the call. I had no place else to turn, no other options. I wasn't contemplating suicide at that point, but for the first time I was beginning to feel like life wasn't worth living anymore if I didn't get better. Counseling just had to be my answer.

The girlfriend who'd offered the counselor's name was a Christian. She had been concerned enough about my not being one that she shared what it meant to be a real Christian. She told me she would be praying things would happen in my life whereby I would desire to become one.

I hoped that what was happening to me wasn't some terrible answer to her prayer because God hated me. And I hoped just as fervently that I wouldn't get some "religion is your solution and only hope" when I told her I was ready for the counselors' name she had for me. I didn't. In fact, she told me she had gone to the couple a few times herself about a year before over struggles she was having being single and twenty-eight.

I also got a non-judgmental, listening ear when I shared the pain of what I'd been through. She warmly responded, "I'm truly sorry. If I'd only known I would have been praying more for you and certainly will be from now on." That coupled with an offer to talk with her anytime was exactly what I needed—the love and genuine concern of another human being.

As I sat in my first appointment with the Conners, I sensed they were the same kind of loving, caring people as my friend. They proved to be the kind my battered emotions and soul needed so desperately at the end of a time littered with unsuccessful efforts to solve what had become more than a problem. It seemed like a struggle between life and death.

At the end of our appointment, Bonnie Conner turned to me and said that although she knew I wasn't a Christian and respected the fact I had no intention of becoming one then, she still wanted to share a verse from the Bible with me if I'd allow her to do so. She believed it to be extremely applicable to my problem, both in terms of its cause and effect. That something in the Bible could speak to both cause and solution aroused my curiosity and longing for anything that could be an answer. I found myself listening attentively as she read 1 John 4:18, *"There is no fear in love.*

But perfect love drives out fear, because fear has to do with punishment. The one who fears is not made perfect in love."

After reading that, she looked me squarely in the eye saying, "When you let God love you and you love Him, others, and yourself like you should instead of like you now do, your fear will be gone. You can try to love on your own and achieve a measure of success, but sooner or later you'll find someone from the past or present that you can't love enough or in the right way without Jesus in your life loving them through you, planting and growing a love for them in your heart for them. And when you get to that place, you'll see that the Holy Spirit has allowed these 'shakes' as you call them to come into your life because He loves you and wants to come into your life in their place. He didn't cause them. They didn't come from Him. He just allowed them in order to get your attention."

I was confused. Why would a good God allow something terrible, something He really didn't want? He could have stopped it but didn't. I didn't understand. Bonnie helped me see it was me who had "forced God" to deal with me like He had because of the way I had been. I wasn't even sure there was a God, but I was sure if it turned out there was, He had gotten my attention! Nothing else had gotten my attention in the preceding months except me and my problem. For the first time in my life, something had my undivided attention, and I saw I needed Somebody beyond myself. I had run into something I couldn't control or change by my own plans and powers.

I postponed additional appointments for several more fear-filled months. Months with an empty social calendar and meals alone. I was hoping I could find a non-Christian counselor who could help me. I called several and settled on one who proved to be nice but unhelpful. Interviews reiterated probable causes for my problem, causes I was already familiar with from what I'd read and his solution for me was some of the self-help, desensitization/replacement techniques I had already tried. After a few months of doing everything he suggested religiously, none of it worked and I quit seeing him.

Bonnie Conner's words about love and the verse she'd read played over and over again in my mind. She and Clint had both made it clear becoming a Christian wasn't prerequisite to seeing them, so I decided to go back to them for whatever help I could get.

A few weeks later one cold, damp Monday morning, I found myself seated across from the Conners again saying, "I want your help. I just don't want to become a Christian."

Their response was, "Christy, the bottom line of what you believe is that if you let God into your life, He is going to be like Cinderella's stepmother: give you rags to wear, moldy bread to eat, work you to death, and never let you go anywhere that's fun. If God were really like what you're afraid He is, do you think any of us who have let Him in our lives would let Him stay? Why don't you ask God to show you what His real nature is so your decision to become a Christian or not is based on reality, not what you think or feel?"

These were thought-provoking questions, and that's exactly what they did to me: provoked me to think—and pray. Eighteen years is a long time to go without praying, but it had been that long since I had quit the "lay-me-down-to-sleep" prayers at around the age of nine or ten. One morning driving to work, I found myself saying aloud: "God, I think there is probably such a Being as You, and if You can hear me, please show me what You are really like so I won't be afraid to know You. Amen."

A simple prayer that didn't take long to say. But God heard it and didn't take long to answer it. He did so in a way that might not convince you that He is a loving God who wants to do us good, not evil, but it was the one thing in life above all others that would have—and did—convince me.

My Dad hadn't spoken to me or my brothers and sisters since childhood years when he'd divorced Mom and we went to live with her. As I emptied my mailbox one rainy Thursday night after a particularly hard day at work, my eyes fixed on an envelope's handwriting. I knew it was my Dad's even though it had been years since I had seen his writing. I didn't even know where he lived or how to get hold of him. I just knew before either of us died, I wanted to see him more than anything else in life but never would unless some miracle happened. Even my brother had lost touch with him after Dad remarried a third time and moved to the Southwest (or so we'd heard), breaking contact with everyone he'd known out of embarrassment at another marital failure.

It was as if God were saying to me, "Christy, I *am* loving and I've done this in response to your prayer, just to prove that to you. Why don't you let Me in your life so I can keep demonstrating My love for you in countless other ways like this?" I did just that. And you know, He's done exactly what He said He would do, love me in every way possible.

When I told Bonnie what I had done, she encouraged me to get to know all three Persons of the Godhead—God the Father, God the Son, and God the Holy Spirit. She shared similarly about them as my girlfriend at work had after I'd told her I'd let God into my life.

I gave my life to Jesus, too, driving to work one crisp, sunshiny morning. It was as if Jesus Himself came into that car just like the sun's rays did. He penetrated and warmed me inside, in places I sensed had been cold and almost dead before He came. By the time I pulled into the parking lot, I'd given myself as completely as I knew how to all three Persons of the Triune God who not only loved me, but whom I loved as well, and whose presence I could feel inside me.

I was a truly happy woman. Happy, that is, until I tried to eat with someone and found I was no better off than I'd been before becoming a Christian. I was devastated and stayed that way until I got in to see Bonnie in the midst of the worst panic I'd ever felt. If God Himself couldn't or wouldn't help me after I'd let Him into my life I had nowhere else to turn. I entered that appointment with a terrible sense of doom, along with all the fear I was carrying.

After listening to me relate what had happened, Bonnie reminded me of the verse she'd shared with me the first time we met, that talks about perfect love casting out fear. She believed the fear I had wouldn't go away until God had used it to fulfill all the purposes He had for it in my life. Most important of those was that fear had brought me to a redemptive relationship with Him, but there must be a further purpose or He would have removed it.

I knew she was right. I could see one further purpose right away. I had come to Christ primarily to solve a problem, not because I loved Him. I was the same way with people. Sure, I wanted to see my Dad, but not because I wanted to give him love. It was because I wanted him to love me like I felt he never had.

I didn't love myself in the right way either. From all the immorality in my life to the things I stole from the office and a hundred other things like those—all added together showed me I was trying to love myself in ways that would make up for the absence of love from others in my past. Nothing I tried worked. All the things I'd done to try to produce love had, instead, left me feeling like a pretty low-down woman instead of a loved one.

As Bonnie and I began to pray about how unloved I'd been and how loving I wasn't and why, all kinds of things started to get healed in my life. One was a lifelong mistrust of others—and even myself—that had caused me to become very controlling. Another, just as lifelong, that was healed was a deep, abiding feeling of inadequacy and inferiority.

Every time I prayed with the Conners, I was sure that whatever it was that we prayed about on that day would be the prayer that resulted in me being able to eat normally once again. But none of the prayers about what was broken in me healed my fear. It took a prayer that removed the idol of getting healed by putting Jesus where He had never been— ahead of my healing.

With the Conners' help, I'd seen that fear drives out faith as well as love. There's no faith where there's fear. Wherever Jesus and faith are, there is no overpowering fear because He is never afraid nor is anyone who is with Him and trusts Him. I came back to where I'd started, to a Person, asking Him for the gift of faith in Him and for His forgiveness for coming to Him more for what I could get—healing, rather than give—commitment of myself just because He is God.

Bonnie helped me see that faith is simultaneously a gift one receives and a choice one makes to receive it, not a feeling to be obtained. I asked for the gift, chose to receive it, and felt for the first time that I had the key to my problem. Part of loving God was having Him and the gift of faith He brought with Himself. Having that gift would perfect or round out my love for Him to the point that my healing could manifest.

The Conners and I prayed for God to give me an action I could accomplish. The Bible says without works (that means without our doing something as a demonstration of our faith), faith is dead or ineffective.

I felt my "act" was to do two things: first, go to the club of speakers, give them my testimony of receiving Christ, and tell them the truth about the tremors I'd hidden from them. The Bible says if you believe in your heart and confess Jesus as your Lord you'll be saved. I'd believed and told Christians about it but felt strongly in my heart that confession before these people was to be part of my "being saved." Salvation includes healing in its very meaning.

The second thing I was to do was go to my sorority's annual banquet without skipping the dinner as I had the previous year. I was to go without any pills in my body (or purse), and without any of the self-help techniques I'd learned. I was to eat the meal depending on the Holy Spirit alone to get me through it. He had already shown me that whenever a person has a problem with control, whether of themselves or others, they have a faith problem as well. Faith is God's being in control!

I went to the banquet. It was awful. Not only cups and glasses with coffee and water and plates with solid foods to manage, but the ultimate test—a bowl of soup. I didn't want to risk having a waiter or those I was with ask why I hadn't touched it, so I had a choice: I could eat it or run away like I'd been doing all those agonizing months.

When I plunged that soup spoon into the bowl, I was trembling so badly it nearly caused a "soup tidal wave!" But let me tell you, when I brought the spoon out of the bowl it was steady, and so was I—rock solid, not-even-the-slightest-tremor steady! I was healed!

It was all I could do to keep from dancing around the room. I wanted to shout, laugh, cry, and tell everyone there what had happened. I settled for telling one person, an old roommate sitting next to me who nearly went into a panic attack of her own because she didn't know what to do with what I was sharing with her.

Many meals with others have been eaten in the four-and-a-half years since that eventful evening. Almost all of them have been the same—no tremors, no panic attacks. Very occasionally I may start to have the slightest tremble which I see as God's loving warning sign and reminder to me: *"Christy, you needed Me to get healed and you'll always need Me to stay healed."* Or, *"You're not as close to Me right now as you need to be, take care of ____."* For me, staying close means letting Jesus have control every day and I do. I don't ever want to be in control again. Twenty-eight years of controlling my own life almost cost me my sanity.

I may not get my way all the time. Nobody does with God. But that's all right because His way is not only loving and brings healing with it, it is also best, bringing the happiness and peace we all want and look for in life. Ask Him to show you what He's like just as I did, and if you are suffering, in need of healing as I was, ask Him what stands in the way of getting the healing. He desires to give it to you as much as He wanted to heal me. He'll do it, and you'll be eternally thankful.

Afterwords

Some professionals would say Christy's story shouldn't be titled ***Panic Attacks*** because it lacks at least four of the criteria or symptoms to allow that diagnosis. They would say what she had was an anxiety disorder (or reaction), or phobic reaction, depending on their definition, or diagnose something else altogether. Notwithstanding these arguments over diagnosis, what's really important here are two things: whatever you want to call what she had, the fact is it's just that—something she had, not has, because God healed her!

Secondly, it was something pride and control-related that was totally and unequivocally beyond her ability to solve (heal). She needed saved from it and saved she got—in more ways than one, thankfully! When she came to Christ as Savior of her entire being—body, soul, and spirit—her sins were removed, fear and other emotions were brought under the control of the One who saved her, and even physical tremors all but disappeared with occasional ones serving as reminders to stay ever so close to Him.

Chapter 18

Pitfalls of Abortion

"For You created my inmost being; You knit me together in my mother's womb....My frame wasn't hidden from You when I was made in the secret place. When I was woven together...Your eyes saw my unformed body. All the days ordained for me were written in Your book before one of them came to be."

—Psalm 139:13,15-16

Stopping near the campus of the college, I had planned to attend before my pregnancy, I hurriedly bought a fake ID that said I was twenty-one. Then I drove to the counselor's office to meet my parents for what I was certain would be my first and last appointment with Bonnie Conner.

Although she had put her faith "on the back burner" after marrying my non-Christian father, my mother insisted that I meet with a Christian counselor. My father had no objections. Not only was Bonnie a Christian, but she had also spent many years counseling pregnant adolescents like me.

Neither Mom nor Dad would consider abortion. In their eyes abortion was murder. They hoped their only daughter would become a mother long enough to sign adoption papers.

But I had other plans! Even though I was only six months shy of being eighteen, when I could sign for an abortion myself, six months would be too late! That fake ID was my answer—the ticket to that abortion I was determined to have.

With all my defenses up and sounding like the sarcastic, know-it-all seventeen-year-old I was, I went through the motions of my appointment with Bonnie and managed to repeatedly embarrass Dad and Mom until they blew up in front of her. I had accomplished my goal.

I was determined to have that abortion and equally determined not to regret it. When Bonnie told me of the remorse other clients had felt, I vowed I would be the first not to experience regret and promised myself that I'd drop her a card after my abortion to tell her so. (Nobody knew it yet, but I was leaving town!)

My folks were just as determined, too, never budging once in their refusal to consent to an abortion. Their obstinacy called for drastic steps on my part.

After the interview we went our separate ways, physically and mentally. They went to work. I went home.

I called a used furniture dealer, an abortion clinic, and an airline in that order. I arranged for the furniture dealer to show up at our house at nine o'clock the next morning, after my parents would have gone to work. My abortion was scheduled for 11:30 AM, and I had a flight to Texas at 6 PM the same day.

When the furniture men showed up, I told them that my husband had been unexpectedly transferred to a new job and that we were selling just about everything but appliances and one bedroom set (my parents'). They looked like they didn't care whether my story was real or not as long as the furniture was.

Taking their check and grabbing the luggage, I had packed in the wee hours of the morning, I left a note on Mom's pillow telling her that I was getting an abortion, would finish my senior year in night school, and would be in touch again when enough time had passed for them to get over what I'd done. I apologized for selling their furniture and told them to replace it out of the savings account they had started years before for my college education.

If I were asked today to describe the people and my experiences at that abortion clinic an hour later, I would say "repulsive, horrid, and frightening." Then, however, I wanted that abortion so badly, I rationalized and minimized the impact of everything that happened to me there.

I "prayed" that no problems would cause them to transfer me to a hospital or keep me there past my flight time. They didn't. I ran out of the clinic with enough time to fill prescriptions for pain and other medicine on the way to the airport. I carried a piece of paper describing the abortion procedure for the doctor I promised to see, but had no intention of ever consulting for the rest of my life.

I was so "wired" to accomplish my aims that I felt nothing physically until I was on the plane bound for Texas. The medication helped, and I forced my thoughts to turn to the new life awaiting me there: an apartment to share with my best girlfriend's older sister and the assurance of a new job where she worked.

Emotionally I felt nothing for about a year. Then it started. Seeing a mother with her child triggered thoughts like "Would my baby have looked like that?" Interspersed were flashbacks to the abortion itself. Both thoughts and flashbacks were followed immediately by twinges of regret and remorse which, over time, grew into constant, obsessive guilt that would not go away. I found myself bursting into tears in a heartbeat.

One day I broke through the door of the break room at work and cried hysterically in front of a girl I barely knew. As she helped me calm down, I found myself, uncharacteristically, between sobs, telling her about the abortion and how it had come to haunt me.

To my amazement, she confessed to having had an abortion, too, and explained how she was recovering from it with the help of other women in her church who discovered from one another that each was a victim of the abortion experience. She wasn't pushy but simply invited me to attend the group with her.

Church hadn't been a word in my vocabulary, let alone a part of my life, since coming to Texas. Thanking her for her invitation and telling her I'd think about it, I had no intention of going anywhere near a church. My mom's faith and her attempts to foist it on Dad and me were still too memorable.

I spent the next several weeks avoiding this girl. She seemed genuinely concerned, and while I appreciated it, I just couldn't handle it emotionally, because her compassion reminded me of the abortion I was trying to forget. I had to avoid her because I was running out of excuses to give her for not attending the abortion victims group with her.

Several weeks later, however, a new variation of recurring flashbacks broke down my stubborn resolve and changed my mind. They began at night. I would instantly and suddenly awaken, sit bolt upright in bed, lucid, totally conscious, and vividly remember some sight, smell, sound, or experience from the abortion clinic. Each flashback was different, but the emotion they engendered was always the same—total, overwhelming, mouth-drying, heart-pounding **fear**!

Soon I was afraid to go to bed because I knew I'd have a flashback followed by what seemed like hours of panic. Then after a few hours of fitful sleep leaving me emotionally depleted and physically exhausted when the alarm went off, I had to face another day filled with deepening depression which seemed to be reaching from the core of my being into every facet of my life. Sheer desperation pushed me to attend that group meeting of recovering women.

Having never attended or participated in any group, let alone a Christian one, before, I was mildly surprised to find seven or eight women, all within ten years of my age, and two others, one in her forties, the other in her late fifties, sharing problems they were still struggling with about their abortions. Each one shared her thoughts which were followed by prayer for her and her specific problem before the next member shared. When time came for closing prayer, one of the co-leaders asked if she could pray for me.

I'd said nothing about myself or experiences, not even admitting that I'd had an abortion, but not wanting to sound rude and unable to think of a good excuse to say "I don't want you to pray for me because...," I consented. That consent led to the most significant event of my life.

Her prayer for me was simple. Quietly, she thanked Jesus for sending me and asked Him to bless whatever my circumstances and needs might be. When she uttered the word "needs," a dam of emotion burst inside me. My questions about my aborted baby were suddenly answered: in my mind I saw my child, a beautiful little girl in heaven with one hand held by the forefinger of Another I recognized as Jesus. Her other hand pointed directly at me—there in that circle of praying women.

I heard no words, not audibly anyway, but she seemed to say, "That one is my mommy." Jesus looked at me knowingly. When I looked into His eyes, it was as if He said, *"Because you took this child's life into your hands, she died before her time came. She wasn't something else before she became human. From her conception she was My conception, someone whose life was meant to be in My hands, along with every other facet of her life. Although you sinned against her and against Me, I want to forgive you. I will do so if you will come to Me and receive Me and My forgiveness."*

You'd think one desperately needing God and His forgiveness would run to Him after a "vision" like that. No so. Like many others who run in the opposite direction, I tore out of that meeting, ignoring my co-worker's pleas that I return, and took a cab to my apartment.

I never expected to sleep that night, but miraculously I did! It was my first night of uninterrupted sleep in months. I woke with the sense that God had worked this small miracle for me to prove that He would not only forgive but also help me with all my problems if I'd run to Him rather than away from Him.

Still, I resisted until one night a couple of weeks later when the Holy Spirit gave me a dream in which I saw Jesus leading an innumerable crowd of people from heaven, my daughter among them. As they approached earth, I saw myself and others looking upward. Some, like my girlfriend from work, looked joyfully, expectantly at His arrival. Suddenly, a sword in Jesus' hand turned into a white, laser-like flame. Some, like my girlfriend, rose toward Him on that light. Others began to be consumed by it. When it reached me I knew that I, too, would be consumed—judged, condemned by it.

I awoke to a beautiful Sunday morning in May and knew that I had seen a dream of the Second Coming, an event I'd heard My mom mention years before, but had not believed in. By itself, that dream did not make me a believer, but a prayer a few weeks later did. That dream, however, did ignite something inside me.

No, not fear. Jesus did not scare me into becoming a Christian. I simply woke from that dream with a sure sense that Jesus loved and wanted to save me much more than He wanted to judge me. I had an overwhelming desire to know Him—and get to know Him I did.

A few weeks later, I mustered enough courage to return to the PAS group and the members explained to me what a Christian really is, how to become one, and helped me to do just that through prayer.

I had intended to continue attending those meetings and receive the healing I needed from the abortion and other wounds in my life, but within a few days of my conversion, I sensed the Holy Spirit telling me to re-establish contact with my parents. It was an emotional phone call, not only because of what had preceded it but also because of the news I received that my father had terminal cancer.

By the time I'd given notice on my job and returned home, Dad was nearly comatose. I saw him three times after my return. Our first reunion was highly emotional, spoken heart-to-heart rather than words. In our second meeting his eyes filled with tears when I told him how Jesus had forgiven me for my sins and had become both Savior and Lord of my life. His home, half-Jewish, half-Gentile, had not been very religious. Even though his Jewish father had not practiced his faith, it was difficult for my father to hear that his only daughter had become a real Christian.

During our third meeting, I held his hand and watched him lapse into a full coma and die shortly thereafter. I don't know if my witness had any effect on him. It was the first time I witnessed, but I did my best and thank God that He allowed me to return in time to so do. As far as I know mine was the only Christian testimony he heard in life, excepting my mother's life and words over the span of their marriage.

Also, as you've probably guessed by now, I contacted Bonnie Conner, the Christian counselor again. We talked and prayed through the abortion and all the other childhood, adolescent, and adulthood hurts I had gathered in a lifetime without Christ.

It was a bittersweet experience. The sweet part is my life now. I am grateful for the blessings and happiness God has given me. The bitter part is my sorrow for the pain I caused people before I became a Christian, even though I have prayed for them to be healed from what I caused them.

Although I emerged with the same Holy Spirit baptism and healings described by other Christians in this book, I realized with each healing that had I simply become a Christian before the hurts happened, they wouldn't have occurred—or, at least, my reactions would not have produced additional pain and emotional grief for me and the others I inflicted it on through what I did.

My life is still a mixture of the bitter and the sweet. The sweet part is my marriage to a wonderful Christian man. But only eleven months after we were married, the bitter came again: I gave birth to our first-born child, a beautiful but multi-handicapped daughter. She was stillborn.

This drove me back to my counselor bearing with me an overwhelming mixture of grief and guilt over my abortion and a sense that the abortion was somehow responsible for my daughter's handicaps and her death.

God gave Bonnie a Scripture passage for me that removed my guilt after I received its words of truth into my heart. Found in the John's Gospel, this verse is Jesus' response to His disciples inquiry about a man blind from birth, when they asked, *"Master, who did sin, this man, or his parents, that he was born blind?"* assuming that such birth defects are God's judgment for sin. *"Jesus answered, 'Neither hath this man sinned, nor his parents: but that the works of God should be made manifest in him.'"* (John 9:2, 3).

Bonnie gave me comfort and hope in God's wisdom. She pointed out that God was ready for a child with multiple handicaps but my husband, new marriage, and I were not.

I've been married eleven years now. We have three healthy children who seem to consume most of my time. God has blessed me richly.

The death I caused left me hopelessly scarred until Jesus healed me. The death the Lord sovereignly allowed left me rejoicing in the knowledge that His purposes would be fulfilled. I look forward to a glorious future reunion with both of these children.

My life has not consisted of only bitter-sweet moments. Let me give you four "sweet only" gifts God has given me: the first is my marriage; second, my three children. The third was seeing my mother commit her life to Christ again just before she died of cancer last year. My special ministry as a volunteer in the PAS group our church sponsors and working in a community teen pregnancy program is fourth.

When I talk to pregnant girls about my experiences, I stress that I believed the abortion would never affect me afterward even though a counselor told me it affected everyone she'd ever met. I explain how my abortion affected me and point out that although not every girl suffering post-abortion syndrome may exhibit the same symptoms I had, all will suffer some whether conscious of them or not. One way or another we are alike.

Not all of the consequences of abortion, or any sin, are confined to the individual who commits it. Leviticus 18:21 and 24:25 explain that God will punish a people or nation who kill their children. Revelation talks of the blood and voices of martyred people crying out to God. When their number is complete, He will come to judge their murderers.

Among the groups of voices are those of martyred children killed in every nation. This world calls the slaughter of innocents "women's choice" and thinks the unborn body and soul are the mere "products of conception."

I tell these girls that if you are a party to a death, as I was, you'll never be able to erase all the consequences of that death. We affect the destinies of others. If you abort your child, he or she will die before his or her time, before he or she could live here on earth to God's glory.

I also give them the very good news that they can be forgiven completely for that death. and they can be healed from abortion's aftereffects. To those who are considering abortion, I simply say: "That child growing in your womb is not your baby. That life belongs to the One who created his or her soul, the only Maker of souls that exists. Only He has the right to choose the time and means to end that life."

Afterwords

Resurrection is bringing life out of death. God began it with Adam, Eve, and Cain, continued it in Jesus, and did it here with two babies and the mother responsible for one of their deaths. The reality of new spiritual life now, the promise of renewed physical life later, and forgiveness for taking a life—what more could we hope for?

Few of us stand in need of more forgiveness than we see God lovingly bestowing here in this and the other testimonies. These stories ought to have us saying, if He forgave them for what they did, then I know He'll also forgive me for _____.

Chapter 19

Pre-Menstrual Syndrome

It began with cramps while I was in high school and progressed to tears and the "blues" in college. By the time I was thirty-six, I had serious problems dealing with anger that led me to throw temper tantrums like a two-year-old child. I also suffered painful headaches. My doctor diagnosed "a full-blown case of PMS (Pre-Menstrual Syndrome)."

I tried everything from medications prescribed by my family doctor and a PMS specialist to suggestions from members of my PMS support group, such as inviting in "spiritual helpers" and contacting "tranquil energies."

The results were disappointing. It looked as though I were going to be left with a sentence to hell for a week to ten days (sometimes more) out of every month for the rest of my life. I lived in perpetual fear of the monthly ordeal I would have to suffer which ruined the "normal" days between periods and PMS episodes.

Otherwise I had everything a woman could want: a loving husband, three wonderful children, a beautiful home, enough money and friends. I couldn't enjoy those blessings, however, because I was coming unglued, both emotionally and physically, each month.

The PMS made my life look hopeless. Hopeless, that is, until a friend from my support group told me how at her church she had committed her life to Jesus Christ and, as a result, had met a couple who counseled her. Her PMS had actually been healed—physically—after she'd prayed with these two counselors. It didn't take me long to call for an appointment

I met with that couple, Clint and Bonnie Conner, and they prayed with me, too. Miracles happened when we did, real miracles.

The first and most significant one of all was when Jesus forgave my sins after I gave my life to Him just as my girlfriend had done. Next, I prayed for and was baptized with the Holy Spirit. Then came my healing from PMS. Unlike the prayers for salvation and the baptism with the Holy Spirit which were answered as soon as I asked and received what I had prayed for, this healing came progressively.

While counseling me, the Conners stressed the difference between cause and effect. I had thought that PMS was strictly a physical disorder. But the Conners helped me to see emotional and spiritual factors from my childhood were the causes of my condition. The PMS was the result—the effect, if you will.

We prayed over many problems: my mother's unwanted pregnancy preceding my birth, my father's preference for a boy during and after her pregnancy, the attitudes about womanhood both of my parents had inculcated in me. I saw in these things the reasons for the volcano of anger, and the fear and ambivalence I felt about being a woman.

I sought forgiveness from the Lord and forgave my parents for their conditional love and outright rejection! I was healed from the negative feelings and bad self-image I had carried all my life. I also found myself being healed from what boyfriends had done to me, and from the occult "healing" I had experimented with in that PMS support group I had attended.

As my healing proceeded, I found my anger, tensions, cramps, and headaches decrease noticeably from one menstrual period to the next. A process of specific, thorough prayer was releasing the bottled-up emotional pains I had carried all those years.

During my last session with the Conners, in my mind's eye I saw Jesus hold His hand out toward me. It felt as though all the wounds that had caused my PMS leaped out of my body and piled up, a mound on His outstretched hand. I heard no audible voice, but a still, small, inward voice said, *"I carried all your PMS to the cross and bore it there in My body when I died. When I returned from the dead, I brought back a resurrection for you, too—a resurrection from the physical pain created by the emotional pain you've suffered, a resurrection to a new life without physical or emotional pain."* As I reached toward Him to receive my resurrection, the PMS wounds in Jesus' hand seemed to disintegrate and blow away.

When my period came twelve days later, I realized the old moods, tensions, and pains with which I was so familiar had not preceded nor come with it. They never showed up. They had vanished. And they have remained completely gone every month for the last five years.

Afterwords

Many people seek healing in many ways: New Age, new wave, Scientology, mind control, hypnosis, etc. People go to many gods that they address as "God," but the only God is *Jehovah-Rophe*, which means *"God is my Healer."* This is more than a name. It is who He became for this woman and can be for anyone who asks, including you.

Chapter 20

Shattered Narcissist

"Friend," said the Spirit, "could you, only for one moment, fix your mind on something not yourself?" —C. S. Lewis, ***The Great Divorce***

Until I went for counseling five years ago, during the first twenty years of my marriage I always had a girlfriend—often more than one. Whether I was married, getting divorced, or between marriages, my wife or fiancee was not the only woman in my life. I was always seeing a girlfriend, too.

I had women, yes, but I never had love, not even from my parents who were not only cold to one another but also toward my sisters and me. They had one temperature, emotionally, below zero; one expression, a frown; one tone of voice, irritation; and only one hope, that my sisters and I would grow up and get out of their lives as soon as possible.

With that kind of frigid childhood environment, how can any child grow up with room in his heart for another? I never loved anyone or really allowed anyone to love me. I sought love, yes, but only up to a point.

I may have appeared to be depressed but actually I was numb inside, seemingly incapable of feeling sadness or most other emotions. I vacillated between indifference, especially toward criticism, and flitting from one person to the next, behavior more appropriate to changing one's shirts rather than relationships.

By the time I reached forty and was divorced for the third time, I realized that I'd never fulfilled the promise of the talents which, over the years, teachers, employers, and friends had professed to see in me. Bored by the criticism of others, I was ready for my next "relationship" with another woman when something happened that forever changed my destiny.

I met Shelly who was different than any other woman I'd ever known. She wouldn't date me. She'd have a cup of coffee with me when her shift as a waitress ended, but she wouldn't let me take her home or go anywhere else in my company. Her reason? She was a Christian. I wasn't.

Had I been a Christian, she explained, she still wouldn't date me until my last marriage ended "spiritually" as well as legally. In her eyes I wasn't free to date or remarry. She meant that because I had divorced last time without just cause my ex-wife would either have to die or remarry for me to be free to date her!

Shelly was the first Christian I had ever met, male or female. She was also the first woman I hadn't been able to seduce.

When I told her that I was attracted to her, not because she was a challenge but because I genuinely loved her, she was quick to puncture that balloon. "You 'love' every woman you meet," she said. "I don't think you know the meaning of love. If I ever did go out with you, you'd do to me what you've done to the other women in your life—begin by treating me like someone you're entitled to, then devalue me after sex from pure to prostitute. Then you'd leave me without a single thought about my future or what was wrong with you that caused the failure of our relationship."

With me still engrossed in trying to understand what she was saying, Shelly ended the conversation and our incipient relationship with an abrupt: "I've never met a man more completely and totally lacking the capacity for normal human empathy, let alone love. Since I found Jesus two years ago, I've learned the meaning of the word 'transcendence.'" (I later had to look it up. It means living life on the basis of more than material things and more than on the basis of your existence itself.)

Shelly went on with, "Our lives must be based on Christ. They must transcend, or go beyond, our desires and relationships. You don't know what transcendence means and until you do, it's pointless even to talk to me at all. You have some serious problems and need help—yes, counseling, like I had. Until you realize what I'm saying is true and do something about it, I'd prefer that we not talk beyond 'hi' and 'how are you doing?' "

I was floored! I couldn't believe it! Here I was, the great "gift" to women, shot down for the first time in my life. And by a woman!

Her words devastated me, not so much because she had rejected me, but because I had to consider the possibility that her analysis was right, that I had serious psychological problems and needed help. I didn't understand this then, but I would later discover that beneath my exaggerated sense of self-importance I was totally dependent on what others said about me and did for me for my sense of self- worth.

A few days later, I did something I'd not done since being forced to do it as a child. I apologized. I wrote Shelly a note saying I was sorry that I had offended her and asked her for the name of the counselor she had seen.

I wasn't put off when I discovered that the counselor was a Christian and that he supported Shelly's commitment to Christ. I fully expected that and planned to charm the man anyhow. With the exception of two of my ex-fathers-in-law, I had met no person I couldn't con. Even my ex-wives thought I was a great

guy despite having been a bad husband. I figured that I could persuade him that if I had
any problems, they were few and minor. And I
calculated that since I believed there probably
was a God, he'd report to Shelly that I wasn't
such a bad guy nor an atheist, and she could
consider dating and getting to know me.

I couldn't have been more wrong.

It wasn't that Clint was unsympathetic.
After listening to my life story, he looked me
squarely in the eye and said, "Your feelings of
'love' for Shelly are actually an envy that
comes from a lack—something missing—in
yourself. Put another way, subconsciously you
know that she has it together and you don't, so
you're drawn to her for that reason. Underneath your exaggerated sense of self-
importance is the total absence of self-love.

"You are dependent and hostile," he continued, "dependent on others for your self-
image and everything else emotionally because
you received little, if anything, from any relationship, starting with your parents and others
thereafter. This 'lack' gave birth to both your
dependency and hostility.

"Your love then is a disguise—a mask—
hiding a desire for revenge. Like a Don Juan,
you're attracted to Shelly because she has
something in her you have never known, even
though God put a place in you for it—His love.
Because she has God's love, she has the right
kind of self-love, and her needs have been met.

Yours haven't. Where she's at is foreign to you. You don't have that play in your playbook; you don't even have the page to put it on. Totally unaware of yourself, you are, paradoxically, totally filled and pre-occupied with yourself. Can you see that what you are doing is reducing God-created people to a demeaned existence, not unlike slavery or prostitution, to exist only for your gratification and use?"

What could I say? Clint was neither sermonizing nor lecturing. He gave me more to think about and to reflect on than any sermon. Intuitively, I knew he was right.

"The only hope for you is *real* love," Clint concluded. "This real love would be, of course, your first—and such a love would expel your disillusioned 'love' for yourself. Jesus Christ is the only One who can do that. Only He has the power to set you free from the tyranny of *yourself* and to give you the capacity to give and receive love in a relationship with a woman *He chooses* to love you and be loved by you."

I was shattered to learn the life I'd led had been unreal, but shattered was better than continuing the unreality of my narcissism.

Okay. So I became a Christian and married Shelly, right? No. That didn't happen. I spent six months in counseling, meeting every other week with Clint. I sounded and acted like what I was—angry, argumentative, denying, rationalizing like any other totally self-absorbed person.

Eventually, however, I became a Christian but not necessarily because I wanted to or because I thought it would give me a chance with Shelly. The evidences about God, Jesus, the Christian life that I found in the Bible and other places were overwhelmingly convincing. I became a Christian because I knew what I had read, heard, and seen was true.

Nevertheless, committing mind and heart to Jesus Christ is different than healing heart and soul from a lifetime absence of true love.

Even as I write these sentences, my life remains in the middle of the journey (if that far) toward complete healing, a journey I wish were already completed! The healings I have received are the result of hours of healing prayer about my parents, my years of self-centeredness and a whole host of other things. Although I can't feel joy yet and my capacity for caring isn't very deep, my "cold" is thawing. I'm emerging from my isolation from the cave of self, slowly but surely.

I wrote to my third ex-wife, who is living with another man, to request that she put in writing—for the record—that she has no desire for reconciliation with me. Her actions say this, of course, but having her put it into explicit language is a prerequisite for my spiritual freedom from that relationship.

As for Shelly, I'm doing nothing. She is seeing another Christian man, but I'm committed to two beliefs: first, God has the power to keep her for me *if* it is His will that we be married one day; and second, I'm spending a year giving myself to others with no expectation, or desire, of receiving from them in return. Why? I spent a lifetime exploiting and taking, and though I've had a lot, little of it was real. I believe God will be pleased and His will accomplished if I spend time giving, for His sake, without thought as to what I'll get because of it or what God has for my future. Only He can unlock the door to it and to real, holy giving and receiving.

Afterwords

Of the three eternals mentioned in 1 Corinthians 13, love is called the greatest. If it were a feeling, we might or might not be able to experience it. But in most sentences, love is a verb, something one does or gives. Anyone can do it. Its true measure is in what is given, not in what is received.

Chapter 21

Single Parenting

"There is a destiny that shapes our ends rough hew them though we may." —Shakespeare

"My times are in Your hand. Deliver me from my enemies." —Psalm 31:15 (Author's paraphrase)

I was a complete mess. After years of cheating on me, my husband Eddie deserted me and our three children. My two boys were then only thirteen and eleven and suffered problems and inner turmoil that I didn't know how to handle. My seven-year-old daughter cried herself to sleep each night because she wanted her daddy back no matter what he had done.

The fortunate among us have someone to call on when trouble strikes. For me, that person was my sister, Connie. Never close as children, similar experiences as adults had driven us closer. Her husband had been unfaithful and had left a few times, too. Connie had reacted to that as badly as I was, but she had joined a church and her life had changed. She was at peace with herself, and her husband eventually returned. His affairs seemed to have ended.

She listened intently on that cold morning when I unloaded all my problems with Eddie on her. When I finished, she said, "Doris, for years I looked for answers in groups and books and from anybody who would take the time to listen to me tell my troubles. I never found any lasting help until I went to church. There I found the only Friend who has any *real* answers—Jesus. I invited Him into my life and gave Him all my problems, including my marriage. He carries them for me. I have no other solutions."

Desperate to try anything, I accepted her invitation to go to church with her. I'd attended with her before, on special occasions, but this time I went hoping to find the peace I saw in Connie.

A couple of weeks later, I did. The couple who led Connie's care group helped me pray to commit my problems and whole life to Jesus. When I did, He gave me the peace I sought.

The next day I was served with Eddie's petition for divorce. Involved with a woman even more manipulative than he was, Eddie wanted to marry her. His bride-to-be was convinced that his marriage to me had kept him from becoming all that he could. She was equally convinced that marrying her would be his "solution."

So, although in less than ninety days I was divorced, I was still hoping desperately that Eddie would come to his senses and remarry me. However, he married his girlfriend ten days after our divorce became final.

I was devastated. I had expected not only peace from my commitment to the Lord, but also that He would restore my marriage, as He had done for my sister. I confessed my despair to my sister one night after my children were in bed.

God didn't give Connie the words I *wanted* to hear. Instead, He gave her what I *needed* to hear. "Doris, when you came to Christ and gave Him yourself and your problems, you gave Him the right to solve those problems as He sees fit. God doesn't have to conform to your solution which is for Eddie to compound his sin with another divorce to return to you. Eddie isn't bigger than God. You seem to think that God wasn't big or powerful enough to prevent Eddie's remarriage. God was, Doris, but He didn't. You have to accept His decision and go on with Him, or let what's happened mess up your relationship with Him before it's hardly begun. Decide what you're going to do—get some Christian counseling."

I pouted for a while and delayed seeing a counselor. Eventually, however, I took her advice. I realized I needed help from someone other than my sister, my pastor, or the church care group. Healing had come out of what God did for me through all of them. I became a new woman inside.

However, I still had a host of problems to deal with as a single parent. I had a daughter who still cried for her father to come home. My two boys weren't new or healed. They seemed to fight constantly with one another, me, peers, and their teachers. I also had to contend with my ex-husband and his new wife who told horrible lies about me and how I tried to care for my children.

Even an old friend reappeared, having heard that I had become a Christian. She told me I could never remarry until Eddie died. It seemed like there wasn't any area in my life where I wasn't having difficulty.

My counselors, the Conners, not only introduced me to healing prayer but gave me practical help with my problems. Clint showed me in the Scriptures where Jesus said that when there was a divorce and remarriage without just cause, the divorcing party was looked upon by God as guilty of adultery. Sexual infidelity is not at issue. If a non-Christian spouse no longer wants the marriage, then the other spouse is free to remarry (see Matthew 19:9 and 1 Corinthians 7:15).

Through further counseling the Conners explained to my children and me that the divorce and immediate remarriage had shocked us and happened so quickly that we had expressed our grief and anger in different forms of depression. We needed more than healing from our grief. Letting go of Eddie was one thing; facing that he would never return was another.

Forgiveness is relatively easy in prayer. It is harder to *do*, especially when Eddie's wife phoned to arrange visitation for my children to stay with Eddie and her and her children.

In time, the power of the Holy Spirit and my willingness to forgive (not necessarily right away) enabled my family to recover. I had to learn to deal with my own sense of inadequacy brought about by Eddie's rejection and his choosing another woman over me. My children were angry with their father, but they took out their anger on me, the parent they had, and on one another. Again, counseling provided practical answers as well as inner healing.

I came to understand that my children suffered guilt over the divorce. Mistakenly, they believed that if they had been better kids, their father wouldn't have left. They needed reassurance that simply wasn't true, and that I wouldn't desert them, too. Counseling gave them confidence that I would stay with them, although my boys would not admit that, at first. Counseling also helped me deal with their unruly behavior after visits with their father. He and his wife continually told lies about our marriage, our reasons for divorce, and me. Seven years have passed now, but problems continue to come up requiring solutions.

If you are just beginning as a single parent, don't try to make up for your absent spouse. Just be, with God's grace and power, the best parent you can be—a good father or good mother. I've learned you can't be both. When you try, you won't be able to do the job God intended for whichever you are.

Also, you simply cannot go it alone, even with the Lord and Christian counseling. I involved myself and my children in a Christian singles group. We had social gatherings and camp where my children met other "divorced" kids. These activities built a network of relationships with other single Christian parents like me.

My children, like all children, needed contact with a man so they'd have a clear picture or model of mature manhood. My pastor gave me a list of men in our church willing to be "big brothers" to children from broken or fatherless homes. If your church doesn't have a program like this, encourage it to develop one.

Don't give up on marriage or the hope of finding a Christian mate. Three years ago, the Lord gave me a wonderful Christian husband and my children the kind of fathering they'd never have had with Eddie.

God is a good God! It doesn't matter if you are destined to remarry as I did or to remain a single parent. You are *never* alone. The Lord does indeed restore the locust years (see Joel 2:25-27).

Afterwords

God does far more than restore lost years of the past. He always gives a new future. Usually that involves a new mate because few single parents find themselves with God putting a call on their lives to remain single. Whether it does or not, however, God is always both the Healer of the past and Giver of good futures.

Chapter 22

Sleep Disturbances

"It is vain for you to rise up early, to sit up late, to eat the bread of sorrows: for so he giveth his beloved sleep." —Psalm 127:2 (KJV)

Fear woke me. I would sleep only three or four hours of "normal" sleep, but then I would dream that I'd be paranoid when I finally woke. Then the fear would wake me, and the dream would be reality. I would be unable to move for several minutes. Monsters appeared in my room, randomly, clinging to the walls, ceiling, standing next to my bed, or hovering above it. These were not the laughable refugees from a grade B horror movie. They left me in total fear and would gradually vanish. Then I could move.

No change in sleeping habits affected them. They appeared whether I slept alone or with my boyfriend when he stayed. At his apartment or mine, whether I'd been drinking or not, whether I was tired, happy, or sad during the day, it was the same.

I averaged a night a month of fear and immobility, but every night was ruined. I never knew as I lay down to sleep if that night would be the night my monsters reappeared.

It began a year after I graduated from college. After suffering for a year or two, I sought help, and in the process saw two counselors, four different doctors in succession, joined a therapy group, and went to a sleep disorders clinic. I wasn't made better.

Then my boss suggested I see a counselor named Clint Conner. Two other counselors hadn't helped, and my first appointment with Conner made me furious. He told me that he had found healing prayer to be helpful with sleep disorders when more traditional methods had failed. How would I feel, he asked, about trying such an approach if I decided to meet with him a second time?

That made me angry. I told him I wasn't interested in any kind of prayer or returning for a second appointment.

A month passed before I cooled off. My boyfriend kept saying, "For crying out loud, Beth, what've you got to lose? Harry's told us he's helped others. Nothing else has worked. Go back, let him pray for you one time and see if it works. If it doesn't, I'll pay for it. Don't be such a bigot." So I called, asked for another appointment, and apologized for my anger.

I was deeply embarrassed to agree to Clint praying for me. "Christ died on the cross for everyone," he said before he prayed. "So as we pray, see Him on that cross with His hands reaching toward you, ready to take your fear in one hand and your paralysis in the other. Release both to Him."

It seemed silly. I had never prayed aloud before, not even in the worst of circumstances. I was embarrassed and would have been even more so if Clint had asked me if I believed in prayer. Looking back, I'm not sure I believed in God then, let alone in audible prayers for healing. How could anything work, I thought, if I didn't know whether I believed in it or not?

The truth is, I didn't like Clint, had no confidence in him, and had known him for less than two hours when he said, "Pray these words aloud after me: 'Jehovah God, I come to You through Jesus at the foot of whose cross I stand, and humbly place my fear in one hand and my feeling of paralysis in the other. I stand ready to hear or see anything You have to say or show me about them. Amen'." My face flushed hot with embarrassment as I repeated the words.

Then my embarrassment vanished at once. I was suddenly overwhelmed by an absolute certainty that there actually is a real, resurrected Jesus who received from my hands into His what I was placing in them. In my spirit— my mind's eye—I saw His blood-stained hands and His face, too. Tears flowed from His eyes.

His eyes looked through me. I didn't hear an audible voice. The eyes spoke volumes. I understood what the tears and His expression meant. They said: *"Beth, you want only to give Me your troubles, which I more desire to take than you do to give. What I really want along with your troubles is you. What will happen when you die if all you've given Me is your problems but not your soul, the real you? What then?"*

All I knew was that present moment. That *"what then"* struck terror in my heart—a fear worse than my night horrors. I didn't know about *"what then."*

In panic, I interrupted Clint, told him what I had just experienced. "I know there's a real Jesus," I said, "I know it for sure. Why has He scared me so badly if He really means to help me? Is He evil or good?"

I'll always be grateful to the Lord for granting me that spiritual experience. I'll also be forever thankful that during that experience, He provided a genuine Christian to help me in my confusion.

Clint said, "Don't you think God has gone to an awful lot of trouble and wasted an awful lot of time creating people if they're just going to die and return to non-being like they were before birth? Is it possible He's telling you that non-being after being is impossible? Maybe there's life after death, and you sense that something worse than your night terrors exists if you're not ready to face God in it. The Bible teaches that all men and women must account for their acceptance or rejection of Christ in this life. Your answer to the question—do you accept Christ or not?—determines your eternal destiny."

I instantly knew what he said was true. I also didn't know what to do with that truth. I practically begged Conner to tell me what to do next. I cried then, realizing the counselor's face looking at me didn't seem as real as the face of Jesus with His tears, a vision that still clung to my inner sight.

Clint advised me to put my entire self into Christ's hands, just as I'd placed my sleeping and dreaming troubles into His keeping. Christ had another life for me to live other than the life I'd been trying to live by and for myself.

I did. I prayed for the Lord's death to count for my sins and for Him to give me a new life—with the Lord inside me, showing me what to do and empowering me to do it. No longer could I try to empower myself, as another counselor suggested I do.

And He did! Many changes accompanied Christ into my life.

Further counseling showed me how my "monsters" appeared. I'd stuffed feelings and thoughts into my subconscious for a quarter of a century. My monsters weren't demons. They were angry feelings at myself and others, feelings I repressed when awake. My fears were guilt—for sleeping with one boyfriend after another, for example. Consciously, I didn't think my behavior was wrong. Nevertheless, I violated God's will and His laws concerning the proper use of sex. Deep inside, my heart knew what I was doing was wrong.

My boyfriend left me shortly after I became a Christian. He had no objection to prayer if it stilled my fear. He wanted no part of prayer, though, if it meant having a Christian for a girlfriend.

Having become a Christian, I thought my boss, a fellow Christian, would give me the promotion I wanted. He didn't. He gave it to a non-Christian because "she was more qualified and experienced." His reasoning was right, but I was still disappointed.

My point? Life has had its ups and downs since I became a Christian. The good news is that while my working life has its share of disappointments, my sleep is innocent and deep at night. No monsters and no paralysis have visited me since I received Christ.

I've seen Christ's face again—without His tears. His expression tells me someday I'll have a loving relationship, not a counterfeit one, with a Christian husband, and that other promotions will come at work, promotions I'll earn and deserve.

Best of all, I have no fears about where I'll spend eternity. The Lord has taken care of that, too.

Afterwords

Sleep is one of those necessities we value only in its absence. Having committed murder, Macbeth lamented his lack of sleep, describing "sleep, the innocent, gentle sleep that knits up the raveled sleeve of care."

More exotic sleep disorders than Beth's exist, sleep apnea or narcolepsy, for example. I chose Beth's story because it wonderfully illustrates how God has implanted an intuitive awareness of His right to sit on the throne of our lives. Christ always holds the key to a more abundant life. He can bring peace to troubled days and troubled nights, the only true rest for troubled hearts. *"I will lie down and sleep in peace; for you alone, O LORD, make me dwell in safety"* (Psalm 4:8).

Chapter 23

Tourette's Tyranny

Tic de Guinon is what the psychiatrist called it. The brochures the school nurse sent home said I had "Tourette's Syndrome." But "nutsy Betsy" is what the kids at school and in the neighborhood called me, only for me to dissolve in tears and run off screaming.

I rarely heard my name "Betsy" without "nutsy" in front of it until revenge stopped the tears and started my fists landing all over anyone who teased me. Fighting back may have stopped the verbal abuse, but the bizarre behavior that started their teasing never stopped until I was nineteen. I'm in my thirties now.

My behavior didn't start out bizarre. It began in my eyes, a blinking that became increasingly more frequent. It was "a lot more than any of the other kids ever had," according to my dad who measured each of us by a standard derived from combining all the behavior of all his children and applying that against whichever child he happened to mention. I was the sixth (and third girl) of seven children.

I don't even know when the blinking actually started. I know it was pretty bad by kindergarten, and by the next year, there was added a facial grimace which I can only describe as a combined wink, squint, and "snoot" that involved blinking, wrinkling my nose up so quickly one had to look fast to see it happen, and the movement of my cheek, all of which occurred involuntarily and habitually.

By the end of first grade, my head, neck, and arms also sometimes jerked uncontrollably, much like the experience of involuntary muscle twitches in your arms or legs as you fall asleep, or like the involuntary startle response that takes place when someone scares you.

I don't know why the swearing and obscenities didn't come until later, probably because I hadn't heard or learned those words yet in kindergarten or first grade, nor had I been made worse by teasing from outside my family until school years started.

Those words came with a vengeance! Very quickly, they seemed as involuntary and uncontrollable as the tics and twitches. They did not start out as swear words you could recognize, but more like a rhythmic, guttural, growling noise that eventually became dirty language.

The "growls," as Dad called them, were annoying enough to him and Mom to get me almost daily harangues and lectures about the fact he wasn't paying taxes for my education so I could "go from talking like every other six year old, to cussing and sounding like the dumbest blankety-blank dog he'd ever heard."

I'm sure his open sarcasm and Mom's less direct version of it were one of the main things that helped turn those wordless noises into obscenities which eventually reached the point where they would have caused a sailor's parrot to blush. I remember I used to actually feel their words were like missiles coming at me, but if I blinked as they were said, the missiles wouldn't hit me. I believe now my growls and obscenities were the missiles I fired back.

What I was actually trying to do with those blinks is much like what someone does when they see something so gruesome they cannot stand the sight of it: they close their eyes to keep from seeing it. I was shutting my eyes to keep sights, experiences, and even people from getting to where they hurt me.

It didn't work. I still heard the nagging and the sarcasm from both parents and still had to live through their harsh and inconsistent punishment and often open rejection of me. Like most kids, I felt the majority of what was unjust in our home happened to me instead of my brothers and sisters.

If anyone believed in God in our family, it was a well enough kept secret that I never remember God or any of His other Names mentioned unless someone was angry and cursing. As a result, I grew up without any conscious thoughts about God. As childhood transitioned into adolescence, only occasional references to God were heard coming from those outside our family. I concluded He was probably "somebody" who existed somewhere, but I had no reason to devote any attention to Him then.

All that changed very suddenly one warm autumn afternoon my first year out of high school. I was working full-time and had signed up to take a couple of courses at the local branch of one of our state universities.

The week before classes started, all new students were invited to attend orientation meetings to acquaint them with the various campus organizations and their representative members. I was browsing through display tables and literature, alone as usual for my life.

Tourette's had kept me from making any lasting friendships during high school, and I assumed college would be the same. I had become a loner without a whole lot of thought about it or bitterness at those who avoided me because of my behavior. I expected the rest of life to be like it had been until then—me going my way alone, doing whatever my "thing" was.

All that changed as I sauntered past a nondenominational organization's display and was handed a booklet with a title that Christianity wasn't a religion. The thoughts that title provoked were intriguing, but what the two members of that group did when they handed me the booklet intrigued me even more. They did something nobody had ever done in my entire life. They completely ignored my "growls" and tics and talked to me like I didn't have them— like I was normal! I couldn't get over it. I was confounded by the love and compassion I saw in their eyes. I made up my mind on the spot I had to check out a group with people like that in it even if it was religious.

I did, and began to attend meetings that consisted of Bible study, discussion groups, or outside speakers. These were Christians who were engaged in professions similar to those we were preparing for. They addressed questions I didn't even know I had: evidence for God's existence, proofs for Christ's claims, the validity of Christianity, and how it differs from other religions.

Each meeting seemed to water a place in my soul that I didn't know had been parched. I found myself thinking after the speaker concluded, That's right. Why haven't I thought about these things before? I need to respond to this and get my life together spiritually. Although I knew I needed to do something, I kept putting it off and probably would have gone on postponing if it had not been for my favorite part of the meeting.

After dismissal, there were refreshments and informal chatting with group members and others like myself who had come to investigate Christianity. Sometimes we went someplace else for coffee and conversation, or made arrangements to get together later in the week to talk. Members sometimes came to my room to talk, see how I was doing, offer a ride somewhere, study together, or do something social that had no religious overtones whatsoever.

They cared for me as a total person and not just a soul to convert. That these people without Tourette's treated me like I didn't have it and cared about me went further in proving to me there really was a Jesus than the evidence all the speakers could offer.

Midway through my first semester late one gray November day, as I lay flopped across my bed getting ready to study, I said a silent prayer to Jesus asking Him to make me the kind of Christian my new-found, first-ever friends were. He did just that! Without my asking or even understanding why, something else happened—my cursing stopped. The other noises and the tics did not cease then, but did diminish considerably. Later, even those vestiges of Tourette's stopped completely.

Here's how that happened. Late in the second semester following my conversion to Christ, one of the outside speakers at our weekly meeting was a counselor who talked about inner healing, a process whereby Jesus heals the problems of our soul. It made sense to me that if God were interested in the whole person, He wouldn't heal their physical body only to leave the mind messed up.

I called the counselor, Clint Conner, for an appointment and was given one with his wife, who was also a counselor. That dear woman saw me the rest of that spring and through the summer for the few dollars my part-time job allowed. Inner healing went from something theoretical to something I experienced as we prayed through a lifetime of events and relationships that helped cause my Tourette's.

Hurts and wounds caused by others' feelings, words, and other sins committed against me necessitated lots of forgiving prayer. I also needed to repent for my sinful reactions which were the Tourette's symptoms that allowed me to "get even" in a way that kept me out of trouble (behavior others excused) and subconsciously delighted me because of the further consternation of those who had hurt me.

The prayers for my healing that followed my repentance and forgiveness of others left me ready to begin my sophomore year with symptoms of Tourette's completely *gone* for the first time since preschool years, a time of my life I was barely able to recall.

The story doesn't end there. After college I married a Christian man I met while we were students. We should have lived happily ever after, but we didn't. I had our two sons in the first four years of marriage which were hectic but seemingly happy for both of us. Happy, that is, until my husband started letting the responsibilities of being a Christian, husband, father, and employer begin to affect him instead of giving his stress and worry to Jesus.

Perhaps I could have helped him more to get things worked out with God. Instead, I allowed what was getting to him to start getting to me. My heart felt like it jumped instantly into my throat late one night. As I looked into the bathroom mirror while washing my face, I saw my eyes blinking back at me like they had before God healed me!

The blinking wasn't as frequent as it had been before my healing so I tried to blame it on excessive tiredness and tell myself it was an isolated incident that probably would never happen again, especially if I stopped overdoing. But in the back of my mind I wondered if I was losing my healing. I didn't have to wonder long.

Two days before Thanksgiving I received a call from a woman who said she had been having an affair with my husband, had fallen hopelessly in love with him, and wanted me to give him a divorce. I was sure I'd be told I was a victim of a cruel, practical joke when I told my husband about the call. Instead, I heard a sorrowful confession followed by pleas for forgiveness and promises that it would never happen again, with the rest of our lives together spent in his making it up to me.

By Christmas he was again seeing this same woman. I was blinking and swearing (but not cursing) almost as badly as I had as a girl.

I would like to tell you there is a happy ending to that part of the story but there isn't.

As the months and years went by the only change was from one girlfriend to another as the affairs continued. During each episode my Tourette's was awful. Between them, however, the symptoms would diminish but never completely disappear as they once had.

Never, that is, until a couple of years ago. I decided I had to have some answers about my marriage and for myself. I had seen the Conners at a workshop they had given at my church and called them for an appointment.

I began with my sobbing account of how half my friends were telling me I had biblical grounds for divorce and ought to leave my husband, while the others nagged me to stay with him. I didn't know who to believe or what to do. When I finished, the Conners said that part of my confusion was caused by my listening to people *before* listening to God. I would ask God what to do, but then listen to others before hearing from Him.

The Conners said that although there are times when God guides us through others, they were secondary sources for guidance. His primary sources are His Word, His Spirit (the witness of what the Holy Spirit says to our spirits), and circumstances. When God is leading us in a particular direction, those three sources will always be in agreement.

The Conners acknowledged that biblically speaking, I could get a divorce, but added that it did not say I had to. They suggested I not only ask God what to do, but also fast for my marriage, *listening* for God's answer. I was to try not to address the turmoil I was in over the return of my Tourette's until I had resolved what I was going to do about my marriage.

I took their advice to heart and within days knew I wasn't to seek a divorce. It was so clear. I knew that I knew in no uncertain terms. God was faithful to make known *His* will for *me*!

I returned to counseling to address the Tourette's, hoping it would be resolved as quickly and easily as the knowledge of what to do with my marriage. It wasn't.

I've heard people say all Christians go through something that is the trying of their faith. You would think my trial would have been my husband's adultery, but it wasn't. Nothing has ever tempted me to give up on God and my faith in Him as much as the return of Tourette's, but nothing has strengthened my faith in Him as getting over it again.

It took nearly six painstaking months of counseling to get back the healing I'd lost; a healing that came the first time by God's grace without any effort on my part. This time the healing I got back was by the same grace but not without a major effort on my part.

I have no answer for why what was so easy the first time was so hard the second (or for many other things I could ask "why, God?" about). What I have learned, however, I will share. The first is I've learned to quit asking God "why" when He doesn't answer me, and to stop being angry at Him for not doing so.

I learned that blinking was an attempt to ward off hurts. The blink acted as a shield to keep something from touching me. But it still did, and the blinking didn't stop until I learned to accept the fact that something had hurt me (usually something my husband said or did). I had to give that hurt to God, forgive the one who inflicted it, pray about any ungodly reaction to it, and then simply receive healing for it. It was in the receiving that my faith grew.

When I did not follow that prescription for hurts, I could only react to them humanly—my swearing—which became personal revenge. I found that I not only had to give up my "rights" to get a divorce, but my "rights" to be hurt and to respond to that hurt in my own way. It wasn't easy. It still isn't.

As I write this, the Tourette's is virtually gone, but the symptoms are "just around the corner." It is imperative that I keep on forgiving and not hold on to or handle the hurts in life my own way. Usually I do, but I can always tell when I don't because I'll start to blink again. This has become my warning signal from the Holy Spirit that I am internally holding on to things I need to release to Him.

If you are feeling sorry for me, don't! In regaining my healing, I've received something I never had before—an understanding of my

Tourette's and a prescription for handling it that never runs out! I am totally committed to walk with the Lord and have peace about His plan for me whatever it is. I never had that before. I'm not glad for the effects, but without a husband loving me like he should, all I have had is the Lord and He's been more than enough. Yes, I had a walk with the Lord before my marriage fell apart, but I have a deeper, more mature commitment now. I know that my walk will continue whether I end up with God saying "stay" or "divorce."

Afterwords

Between the time this was written and published, God has honored this woman's dedication to Him and obedience to His word. Her husband, although still not completely rededicated in his relationship to God, has ceased all infidelity and begun to attend church with her again for the first time in years.

Why not stop and say a prayer for this marriage and the countless others just like it around the world where, whether Tourette's is present or not, deep hurts are being inflicted repeatedly on thousands of men, women, and children. These hurts will only be stopped by the prayers of God's people for the return of godly love and fidelity to the marriage covenants He has given people to steward.

Chapter 24

Tranquilizer Junkie

I didn't mean to get hooked. My doctor prescribed something for my nerves when my husband died, assuring me the medication wasn't addictive, and, from a physician's standpoint, I'm sure it wasn't. But the psychological dependency that resulted was as bad as if I had had a physical addiction.

What started out as a simple little pill to help me get through the first weeks following the funeral ended up becoming the hardest thing in life I had ever been faced with getting over. My husband's illness and eventual death were something that had finality—an end, even though his death left me with something to get over. But those pills and my addiction to them not only presented me with something I had not found a way out of, it increasingly became something I believed there would never be a way out of for me.

The crushing downward spiral and seriousness of what I had been doing came to a wrenching halt one sunny, spring afternoon when I was arrested in my own home! I was immediately taken downtown and booked on multiple charges, including forgery and obtaining prescription drugs illegally, all of which were connected to having stolen prescription pads from my doctor's office and forging his signature to prescriptions for the tranquilizers he had been prescribing for me for over a year before he finally said enough was enough and declined to do so any longer.

I did what I had done out of necessity. Ours was a small town and the few other available local doctors had refused me. Naive and drug-fogged, it had never occurred to me how amateurish my actions must have looked. It is a wonder I had not been arrested much sooner.

My doctor and seemingly everyone else in town called, full of apologies, when the story hit the local paper, which indicated I had been the one arrested. But underneath the seeming concern of some, I sensed a gloating that one from among the so-called upstanding citizens in their community had fallen and was now exposed.

I was told charges could not be dropped because of the amount of drugs I'd obtained from various pharmacies before my arrest, and that I would be going to trial. A guilty plea, the circumstances of my husband's death, my being in my fifties, and no prior criminal record added together got me a suspended sentence, a fine, and five years probation, along with a mandatory counseling referral.

When it was all over, I was a basket-case and a fish-out-of-water both at the same time. Without pills I was a nervous wreck. Being in a drug and alcohol counselor's caseload and counseling group with mostly hard-core, young adult abusers of "street drugs" didn't exactly put me in the best of circumstances either for getting what I needed to get better.

Unable to cope with the shame of my exposure and living without pills, I found myself thinking death would be better than what I had now. I began to contemplate suicide.

Those thoughts were coming with increasing frequency and power when one morning my back doorbell rang. I opened the door to my next-door neighbor with whom I had been friends for years. She handed me a freshly picked bouquet from one of her flower beds. I went through the motions of inviting her to sit down for a cup of tea, something we had started to do on a fairly regular basis when Harry became ill. It had been both comforting and enjoyable to just engage in conversation with another adult who genuinely cared.

After some general chit-chat and sensing the "dark cloud" that affected my countenance and ability to converse as I usually had with her, my friend asked what was *really* going on with me. I shared most of how I had been feeling, stopping short of the suicidal thoughts.

I did tell her I had been getting nowhere and was about to give up and let whatever happened happen. I just couldn't bring myself to share the internal scenario in my mind: my parole being revoked for quitting counseling after which there'd be another hearing and newspaper story and then, rather than go to jail, I'd kill myself, hoping that whatever afterlife there was would find me rejoined with my husband in it.

When she got up to leave, my friend pressed a piece of paper on which she had written a phone number into my hand. She said she had gotten it from her niece who went to a church that had a team of lay counselors who were supposed to be very good.

I'd probably never have done anything with that phone number if my neighbor's niece had not stopped by a week later. She was such a cheerful and enthusiastic young woman that I found myself accepting her invitation to attend church with her and be introduced to the woman who coordinated the counseling program.

I went the next Sunday, and Cheryl, the coordinator, proved to be as encouraging as my neighbor's niece. As I later passed away the hours of that same Sunday afternoon, I found myself thinking: "Why not give the thing a try? I couldn't end up any worse off than I already am, ready to give up and die. Even if I end up in the same place I am starting from, I would have tried something. Who knows, it might actually work and help me solve my problems." The first thing I did Monday morning was call Cheryl to arrange a time to meet with her to discuss my situation.

Later that week she listened thoughtfully as I told her my story. A story I'd recently told a lot of times: to my attorney, to a judge and jury, and to the drug counselor and group to which I'd been referred. I wouldn't say I hadn't felt some care and concern when I'd talked to those people, but with Cheryl I felt something I'd not felt in those other places with those other people—God's love and concern for me, instead of just the compassion of people.

My time with Cheryl ended with her saying she felt one of her volunteers could help me, and after thinking and praying about which one, she would be in touch to arrange a meeting for both of us. Two days later I found myself being introduced to Marie, a raven-haired wisp of a little thing whom I learned had a husband, two children and had worked successfully with a number of women my age in the past. Almost instantly she seemed to become everything to me: a friend who understood, the daughter I had never had, someone who really cared and took time for me and did things with me, and most importantly, someone who for the first time in my life, helped me find what I needed spiritually.

We got together about once a week in the beginning around simple things: talking over coffee after grocery shopping together, meeting for an early morning walk before her husband went to work, watching her children play in the park while the two of us talked. Marie all the time was making me feel normal yet special by weaving me into her everyday life.

Within a matter of weeks, although I'd decided not to kill myself, it was clear I was probably going to die anyhow (or do myself serious physical harm) from the "over the counter" nerve and sleep aids I'd been overdosing on ever since my arrest had made it impossible to continue getting prescription drugs. I moved in with Marie and her family for two months while they helped me wean myself from all drugs.

It was a hard but wonderful time, in which I had to make two all-important decisions: first, not to die, and secondly, instead to live. Deciding not to die, you see, only leaves one in a neutral limbo. Deciding to live is another matter entirely, requiring an additional decision.

The month before I stopped the drugs was horrendous, much worse really than when I actually did quit. Thinking about doing something you haven't done yet is somehow worse than beginning or doing it. Thinking about living without drugs proved for me to be worse than actually living without them.

Fall had come and gone when I moved back home with the promise to call Marie whenever I felt nervous *before* heading for a drug store to solve those feelings. And I did, more than a few times.

That fall is now three years behind me, as is my probation which was terminated sixteen months early because of my adjustment and model behavior. Let me tell you just a little of what happened in that three-year time period.

First, I discovered that fallen people, which includes all of us, always have dependency needs. That means we all will always need a crutch. Three years ago I decided to make my crutch Jesus instead of drugs. I have been *dependent* on Him ever since to do for me what I tried to get drugs to do even though they couldn't and didn't—get me through hard times and all the other ordinary days between the hard ones. And He has.

In talking and praying with Marie, I found out that the root of my drug dependency was a dislike of myself that started in my childhood, but had really gotten a hold of me in a marriage where I felt guilty for bossing a husband around from our honeymoon until he died. I think the reason Harry's death was so hard for me was because he died without my ever having stopped what I'd done to him, and because without Jesus or Harry, I had no one, no one to depend on, no one for anything! I must have subconsciously thought and hoped that if I just told Harry what to do long enough, some day he would wake up and take over. Then I could stop and be taken care of and everything would be all right. When he died before that happened, my guilt (and loneliness sent me into pills!

I have learned that 1 John 4:8, *"Whoever does not love does not know God, because God is love,"* applies to loving yourself as well as to loving God and others. I never loved myself because of my bossy ways until I trusted Jesus and began to depend on Him. When I made peace with Him, I was able to make peace with myself and what I had done in my life and marriage.

What a difference that has made! Now I'm a volunteer in the very same program that helped me. While tutoring slow learners in reading and English, I get to know them and their single-parent, working mothers, showing each of them the love of Jesus as it was shown to me through a woman and a program I was initially very skeptical about, but a person and a program God used to save and change my life.

When I told my drug counselor I was going to be matched with a volunteer in a church program, he, too, was skeptical. His feelings about Christian people and their programs were that they didn't know very much, helped people even less, and only wanted to get them on a church roll anyhow. Despite his lack of encouragement, however, he admitted that as long as I saw him, came to group meetings, and met the other conditions of my probation, there wasn't anything he could do about my having a volunteer.

Now his begrudged acceptance has turned to complete enthusiasm. He believes in the changes he sees in me and the program that helped accomplish them. He even openly recommends it to some of his other clients.

What he doesn't realize is that it isn't the program or even the people who staff it, it is The One behind it all who first led them to establish it and uses them in it to lead those who come to Himself. Once He becomes our first love, He leads us out of the mires and messes the world and we have created for ourselves by having a specific, unique, and individual plan for success that He will implement in the life of every person who cooperates with Him.

Afterwords

The plan may differ because each person is different, even when their problems are similar. The Giver of the plan is always *"the same yesterday and today and forever"* (Hebrews 13:8).

Chapter 25

Welfare Farewell

"All statements concerning welfare recipients in this chapter must not be construed as pejorative or negative comments about the poor. The Bible teaches that Christians have a moral responsibility to care for the poor, orphans, widows, and aliens (those from foreign countries). Too often Christians are ignorant of the plight of these people and ought to learn about them. Negative comments here apply to the welfare system as we know it today and that system exclusively, not the poor."
                                        —The Author

"A man can do nothing better than to eat and drink and find satisfaction in his work, This, too, I see, is from the hand of God, for without Him, who can eat or find employment?"
                                        —Ecclesiastes 2:24-25

I began life as the third generation of a family on welfare. My grandparents were on the dole. My father sought welfare when he managed to get himself fired or quit a job he didn't like. I started receiving benefits in my early twenties. I discovered no doctor could prove that your back didn't still hurt even if you had really recovered from an injury.

The system, I found, distributed benefits without requiring real proof of disability, and I was looking for a way off a loading dock where I worked. It was too cold in winter, too hot in summer, and no fun in any season.

Since high school I'd lost or quit sixteen jobs. Some were dead-ends. Others might have presented me with a good future, but my attitude was, "The world owes me a living, a top-of-the-ladder job, from the first day I go to work!" "Working your way up the ladder" had no meaning for me. I had no desire to earn any education to go along with a job. In short, I was irresponsible.

After I dropped out of high school, I continued to live with my mother. My brothers and sisters always fought, and it wasn't unusual for Mom to kick one or another of us out of the house after an argument turned violent. Ejected, we'd slither off to spend a few days with a "friend" or maybe a relative we could get to take our side in the dispute. Then we'd slink back home to roost in whatever bed or couch was available without making amends or apologizing.

This exile, however, was different. I was innocent this time, I felt. My brother started the brawl, but I was the one that got kicked out. I resolved not to return for a good, long time. I wanted Mom and my brother to apologize when I did return.

I miscalculated. I couldn't persuade anyone to give me free board and bed. I was between jobs and my "soft touches" were between jobs too, or out of luck.

"Okay, I've stayed in missions before. I can do it again," I told myself. This set up my big change.

At the mission the man who assigned beds said to me, "The easy thing for me to do is to give you some meal and bed tickets. You think this will help you. The harder thing is to assume responsibility for really helping you to do what you need to do to help yourself." What he said pierced me like a knife. I took the meal and bed ticket, and I thought long and hard about his words that night.

Before everyone had to leave the mission, ostensibly to look for work, I hunted for that man. I told him that he was the first human being in my life who'd offered to help me. I asked him to explain what he meant.

He described a rigorous farm-work program two states away. Occasionally, the mission referred men to that program. It sounded like a Christian version of boot camp. You rose early, ate breakfast, and had time for prayer and Bible study lessons with questions you were required to answer about life, problems, God, and yourself. After that you spent a day in meaningful work, followed by an evening of classes where you were taught and discussed relevant to life issues and how to resolve problems with the other people you lived and worked with—all things my parents had never taught me. Bedtime and lights out were followed by another day of the same routine. He said he doubted that I could take the discipline unless I became a Christian before I left.

He didn't mean that as a challenge. I took it that way, however, believing I could take the hard work, just as I was then. Also, I was simply too full of pride, at that point, to slink back to Mom's house, so I asked to be referred to the farm.

I left two days later. Clutching a suitcase of belongings the mission had given me, I said good-bye to the first person who ever truly cared for me. Unexpectedly, I had tears in my eyes.

I worked at that farm for seven months. There were eleven other men living there; most were my age. We were supervised by the couple who ran the farm.

I did become a Christian, in spite of my vow not to. About three months after I arrived, I sat on the porch on a warm, autumn evening. My muscles ached. I thought over what I'd heard in a mandatory church service the day before.

The people in that church didn't just preach or moralize to me. They prayed for me.

They had shown me real love in those three months. They could love me, even while I was unlovable, because the living Jesus had come into their lives, giving them each a new heart—the loving, compassionate heart of God the Father, who loved them and gave them the ability to love others such as me.

I invited the Lord into my heart as I swung gently on that porch. And come in He did! This was my spiritual rebirth, and it transformed my life forever.

But let me tell you about the practical as well as the spiritual lessons I learned on that farm. First, I learned to accept responsibility for myself. Up to that time, like my ancestors, I'd blamed everything and everybody else for my problems and my inability to solve them.

How did I learn responsibility? Not just through work, although we did work hard on that farm. We took classes, too, and answered questions in workbooks. These questions required us to think about why we'd failed in school, work, and relationships. They taught us how the Lord viewed work.

These questions compelled me to see that I was a malingerer, descended from a line of malingerers. God didn't see sloth as a minor sin or little mistake. He saw it as a major sin— like violence or sexual sin.

I see now that the welfare system itself had fostered and perpetuated that sloth, but I had to accept responsibility for my attitude that I really didn't want to get off the dole.

Second, I saw that I had been a sponge. That was an unpleasant fact to face, but it was the truth.

God changed me. He's still changing me. The farm gave me a biblical view of life, a Christian work ethic, and a new kind of independence and dependence. Once I was dependent on welfare. Now I depend on the Holy Spirit. I'm independent of my family and the false values of the system that had schooled me in infancy and youth. I've received Christian counseling since my return from the farm. God has liberated me from welfare.

Some of my old friends call my reliance on God as a crutch. My reply is: "Everybody has a crutch whether they admit it or not. I know I use one. God is the only good and healthy crutch. None others are reliable. Without my 'crutch,' I'd wind up back on welfare, in the syndrome of failure, where I was."

Afterwords

"We hear that some among you are idle. They are not busy; they are busybodies. Such people we command and urge in the Lord Jesus Christ to settle down and earn the bread they eat. And as for you, brothers, never tire of doing what is right." —2 Thessalonians 3:11-13

"For all have sinned and fall short of the glory of God, and are justified freely by His grace through the redemption that came by Christ Jesus."   —Romans 3:23-24

Viewed together, this chapter and the next, **Workaholic**, give us a significant revelation: work, when done to excess or for the wrong motives and non-work (i.e., not working at all) can both lead to the same sins of pride and selfishness, not to mention the others committed by the two men whose lives we learn of here.

Both the refusal to make a place for work and work as salvation lead to a place even beyond the sin itself to serious consequences. On the other hand, the antithesis of both (work from the biblical motive of glorifying God and making provision for others and self), while it may not lead to riches, will lead to spiritual success and material sufficiency.

Chapter 26

Workaholic

"Thou shalt have no other gods before Me."
—Exodus 20:3

"The human mind is a permanent factory of idols." —John Calvin, **Institutes of Religion**

G rowing up in an old-fashioned American home during World War II instilled in me values of moral character and hard work. I tried to throw off some of those values during my wild, rowdy adolescence, but as an adult I returned to them, thinking they would make me rich. I see now I was trying to deal with spiritual guilt by working out my own salvation—not *"with fear and trembling"* as Philippians 2:12 says we must—but by winning approval for and feeling good about what I had accomplished by work and achievement.

I liked my reputation for honesty and reliability. I felt real pride in what I did and pride in myself. That satisfaction and pride in accomplishment satisfied me more than the money and material goods my work had earned for me and my family. When I was with others, if I couldn't talk about my work, I didn't know what to say next. If I had no opportunity to talk about my work, I felt cheated.

Then I came home to find a letter from my wife, Mary. She had decided, it said, to leave me. Our children were grown and she had nothing to do except visit them, spend money on them or on herself, which is what I was always urging her do to. Tired of an empty life and our phony friends, she wrote that she had considered killing herself, but her faith in reincarnation wasn't strong enough to sustain that act. "I'm going to Ohio, to live with my sister," her letter read. "I'm going to find out about the religion she's converted to. Maybe she or her religion can help me. No love anymore, Mary."

Her widowed sister had become a Christian. Her behavior and personality had altered so much even I noted the transformation.

That letter unglued me. I flew to Columbus, Ohio, to my sister-in-law's, convinced that—super salesman that I was—I could convince Mary to return with me.

She wouldn't talk to me. She wouldn't even come out of the guest room so I could talk to her. I stood on the other side of that door and begged and promised to change, but I found myself alone in a motel room afterward without having prevailed upon her to see or listen to me.

Mary eventually agreed to see me only if I would accompany her to the counselor her sister, Edna, had counseled with. I dreaded that.

Counseling had helped to transform Edna from a weeping, wimpy widow to a strong, peaceful person, so I decided the counseling couldn't be all bad. I had lied to get out of work to retrieve Mary. I felt bad about that lie. It violated one of those old-fashioned values I'd taken pride in—telling the truth.

The counselor, Clint Conner, was direct and to the point. He saw clearly why I wanted Mary to come back home: to supervise the cleaning, laundry, cooking, bill paying, and to accompany me to social and business functions—dinner parties with customers and associates.

I wanted her to be available for sex every month or so when I found either time or interest for it. My wife and I had not enjoyed a normal sex life after the second or third year of our marriage, following our children's births.

Conner wondered why I was more concerned about Mary's absence and not being able to perform certain jobs than about Mary as a person. That question made me uncomfortable, made me feel like a troubled man instead of a success. I didn't like it, but I continued the counseling. What choice did I have? After several more weeks and several more counseling sessions, I was a broken man. I was broken by the guilt of my selfishness, but

at that point I couldn't see the deeper brokenness that was at the root of my selfishness. I
wasn't ready or willing to deal with myself and
my problems at that depth.

Conner warned me that I could never fix
my troubles with my own energy and will.
Only God could do that. He would have to live
inside me. I did not agree to that, even if my
refusal kept Mary from returning. I left our
fifth counseling session insulted and determined. I decided I didn't like Conner at all.
Who did he think he was, lecturing me about
God?

Like some of my acquaintances in com-
merce, I assumed that my expertise in business
made me an expert in other matters like religion, family, marriage, counselors and their
counseling. Mary's leaving me obviously
showed that I didn't know as much about
marriage as I had thought, but I was sincerely
sorry for what I had done. I'd apologized sincerely to her, and was determined to talk to
her more, pay her more attention as we flew
back to our home and the life we'd led. I didn't
understand the spiritual element true marriage requires for true happiness. I simply did
not believe, contrary to John 14:6, that I
needed Christ's forgiveness. I was determined
to do it my way, without God or His help.

After two months, I stopped doing what I
promised Mary I would never quit doing if
she'd only reconsider and come home. After

four months, I was separated again and on a plane headed back to Columbus. I carried with me another letter warning me not to follow her this time. She didn't trust me, would never believe me again, and said I'd be hearing from her attorney.

It was my fault. My business trips lasted longer because of my customer's demands. When I was home, new business and endless details kept me where I really wanted to be: long hours in my office and on the phone. When I was with Mary someone else was with us or we were on our way to and from somebody's house or office.

When I arrived in Columbus, I called Clint, knowing better than to call Mary, and humbly asked for another appointment. When we met, I admitted my failure and asked him to help me retrieve my wife one more time.

Clint asked me if I were ready to submit to the God who had mercifully allowed me to confront this problem which was bigger than I could handle with my own resources so I wouldn't continue living life without Him, eventually facing eternity without Him. What I wanted was for Clint to help me manipulate Mary into another reconciliation. He refused.

That made me angry. I caught the next plane for home without calling Mary. I returned to my real wife, my job.

Over the following week, I called Mary three times a day. On day eight, she came to the phone and gave me good and bad news. Conner had advised her to call off her attorney. That was the good news. No more "gold-covered baloney promises," she said. "Show me the change first, then I'll consider returning." That was the bad news—and sounded to me like some more of Conner's advice.

When I returned to work without Mary, I was embarrassed. My associates didn't like working with a fellow whose wife was unhappy. It didn't reflect well on the company. The unspoken philosophy was, "A man who can't manage his wife can't really handle business." Business troubles failed to impress Mary. When I phoned and explained to her that my career was on thin ice because of her absence, she still refused to come home.

Three months passed and the golden plum of my career arrived. If I could land a certain corporation's account, I'd become number two man on the board immediately, earning a hefty percentage beyond my usual commission, additional stock options, you name it. I landed that account. That weekend I was wined, dined, and congratulated by all of my friends.

I went to work Monday morning, expecting more accolades. Instead, what I heard was: "Your perks end in three months except for your secretary. She's finished in one month. You can have her type resumes or whatever, but call her from home. Don't come back here."

"We've found someone else who fits into our plans better than you. You'll get the money you've earned. Clear out your personal papers and hand in your keys to all files."

Just like that, I was history. Their promises had been incentives to land the big deal, nothing more. My replacement, a board member's son, was willing to work for three-fourths of my commission and had no marital problems.

At that time I was convinced Mary's absence was the reason I got the sack. Today, I'm not sure. Then, knowing all the reasons for my firing was all that mattered to me. Today, I don't care.

My job was me. It was my life, my identity, me. Underneath that persona, "I" didn't exist at all, which is why I had nothing to give to Mary or to anyone else. I was bankrupt as a person.

I realized that soon I'd be bankrupt financially, too. We had much, but little of it was paid for. I'd violated an old-fashioned thrift principle and lived way beyond my means: renting an office too expensive for me so I'd have the "right address" on my business cards, living in an expensive home to impress people I did business with, leasing expensive cars to be seen in, everything for the right appearance.

Everything disappeared, beginning with our vacation condo on the coast. No one helped. Many of my former associates snubbed me. They didn't want to sully their futures associating with a wash-out. I saw that those good, old-fashioned values I believed in did not motivate our "friends" to help us when there was no advantage in it for them.

My children had finished college, but they were in no position to help an unemployed—and apparently unemployable—ex-executive whose wife had left him. My resumes turned up nothing. My father and Mary's parents were dead. My mother was in a nursing home, having suffered a stroke. My brothers ignored our need.

Our property was gradually sold, until all that remained were a few household goods which I moved to a storage unit. No friends stood by me. Mary still wasn't there.

I was afraid that when I was finished liquidating the material goods of our life together, Mary might forget about Conner's advice not to seek a divorce. Then I'd be alone for life.

I called her to tell her that I'd sold her car—for less than the payoff—and she said, "John, there's something I have to tell you." Overwhelmed, expecting her to tell me that she would divorce me, I burst into tears. That was the first time in my life I could remember sobbing uncontrollably.

Then she said, "Shut up and listen. It's good news, not bad." After three months of watching my life flushed down the tubes, it was hard to believe there could be any good news left. She said, "I'm not the same Mary who left you. I'm different, completely new. I've talked with Conner's wife; I've gone to church with my sister and talked to her, too. I've become a true Christian. I'm not ready to take you back, but I'm willing to consider it and to move in that direction.

"You have nothing to hold you there anymore, so why not move here. Edna will let you move into her husband's room. She'll sleep in the guest bedroom with me. How can we work out our problems in two different places? We can see the same counselor and see what God can work out for us. We haven't done much for Him, so why not give Him a try? Nothing else has worked.

"You don't have to become a Christian like me. But you must change and stay changed. I'm ready to live in the same house with you and work out our problems but not share your bed. If you can accept those conditions, I'm ready to try."

When she finished, I cried again. But these tears were tears of joy and relief. And brokenness. Not brokenness an inch deep and a mile wide like before, but the beginnings of a real deep brokenness, the kind that leads to true repentance—the kind of brokenness that begins when someone gives a man another chance when the man could offer nothing in return, when all hope of what he thought he wanted is gone and he is ready for new and real goals.

There were tears of hope, too—hope that this time I might really change and stay changed, and save my marriage and whatever was left of my life. I used my last remaining credit card to buy a plane ticket and left for Columbus at sunrise.

Mary's eyes told me she had changed, too. No longer angry and piercing, they were like her voice—warm, soft and loving. "You have a chance now, John, because I'm going to obey Jesus and do what He says I should do in relation to you and our marriage, not what I want to do. He may tell me to begin a new life with you without your becoming a Christian. But John, if you do let Jesus do for you what He's done for me, I feel certain our life together would be more than what we had on our best day and better than what either of us could have with anyone else."

When I went to bed that evening, I opened the Bible on the nightstand. My eyes fell on these words: "[God] *who is able to do immeasurably more than all we ask or imagine*" (Ephesians 3:20).

Beyond regaining Mary, I hadn't given any thought to the future. I was too afraid. I wasn't sure that I had any future if I had to face life alone. I had begun to wonder if I'd end my own life. I fell asleep thinking about what Mary had said, and what that passage of Scripture might mean to me. Perhaps something real could be transacted between God and me?

My conversations with Clint, Mary, Edna, and her pastor over the following weeks convinced me that no one can cut a deal with Jesus—not like the kinds of deals companies and individuals in the marketplace transact. Salvation can neither be bought nor earned. You either let Jesus into your life or you keep Him out. Either He runs your life or you try to run it yourself, as I had been doing and making a mess of it. I was tired of that, but still I didn't yield to Christ.

Then, about a month after my return to Columbus, I dreamed about an old man who prayed over his food but never stopped praying to eat. Some of his food spoiled and a horde of mice carried off the rest, while he continued to pray. I heard my own voice angrily yell at him to wake up. My frustration at the old man wakened me.

I told my dream to Mary and she told it to Conner who said that he thought I was the man in the dream. Life was going on. I knew that becoming a Christian was my only hope for a permanent change, but I hadn't become one. If I continued to "pray" (wait) like the man in my dream, I'd lose what I needed in life, just as he lost his food and nourishment. I would be hungry all my life for the spiritual nourishment I needed, salvation.

When Mary related Conner's interpretation to me, I knew it was correct. That night I went for a long walk around the park across the street from Edna's. On my sixth circuit, I whispered this prayer: "I've tried to be my own man, my wife's man, my customer's man, everybody's man but Yours. I'm not sure what a man even is or whether I am one or not, so I'll just say whatever I am, I'm Yours, from this moment on. You can make me into whatever a man is, the kind You want me to be."

At supper I told Edna and Mary what I'd done. We joined hands and I prayed aloud for the first time in my life, confirming the prayer in the park.

On the next Sunday, my wife and I joined Edna's church and asked to be baptized together. A month after our baptism in water, we received the baptism with the Holy Spirit.

We continued to seek counseling with Conner. God continued to heal us from the pain of those years of being without Him and uninvolved with each other. Clint counseled us together. We talked about our parents and home lives. We were able to see what each had suffered. We were also able to say prayers that brought healing from our experiences to both of us.

I came to understand through counseling the subconscious self-hatred that lay behind my addiction to work. My mother gave impetus to it. Her favorite admonition had been,

"Shame on you, John." I never could become the man I thought I was supposed to be. All the material success in the world couldn't compensate for my underlying self-hate and shame.

God revealed to me in counseling how empty I'd been. I had many "values" but little, if any, love. I'd learned sales skills but few personal skills. I considered myself to be an effective communicator, but as I reflected on it in counseling, I realized that I'd said little of substance except in sales.

My healing might be compared to emotional birth. I had to grow from a state of emotional infancy to adulthood emotionally. My perfection and my business ambition grew from a man trying to compensate not only for self-hatred but also for emotional and relational inadequacies.

In the last three years, I have grown from a beginning of believing in the Lord's existence to really getting to know Him, in the only way anyone can, through Jesus Christ.

Mary and I have grown together. I've gotten to know her, too. We pray, talk afterward, and now I care about how she feels, not about what she can do for me. I do what I should about her feelings.

I have a new job with a new company, one just starting. They cannot pay me anything close to my old salary plus commissions, but I'm grateful for them, and they appreciate me and what I give them. The owner and his sons not only respect my business knowledge, they also respect my Christian faith. They care about me as a person, not a commodity, which is very rare in the cut-throat world of business.

My salary pays our bills. After my mother died, my share of her estate gave us enough for a down payment on a small, fifties' vintage house in a working-class neighborhood. No one there knows how much we once had. They relate to us for who we are.

We're having a ball, grateful to God for a second chance at life and with each other. We're older than the couples around us, but we feel young again. We have the Lord, each other, and our health. We take time to smell the flowers.

Our relationships are not built on the basis of what others can do for us and our business. They are built on caring for people.

God has filled us abundantly, just as that Bible verse I read that night so long ago said He wanted to do. Even if my company expands and earns more than all the companies I was once involved with, I will never have more than I do presently. Financially, I'm debt-free. Emotionally, I'm happy and satisfied. I am not driven, and my marriage is strong and filled with love. Most of all, Jesus is progressively filling me, changing me from the empty shell I used to be when I was a workaholic.

Afterwords

Only three possible states exist for man:

1. A man who thinks he's happy and is deceived.
2. A man who thinks he's happy and is mentally deranged.
3. A man who thinks he's happy and who is correct.

John found that only Jesus, not work nor possessions nor power could get him from being the first man to number three.

Chapter 27

So Many More

"Behold, I am the Lord, the God of all flesh: is there anything too hard for me?"
—Jeremiah 32:27 (KJV)

We could tell so many more stories, some about clients, some about people we met under other circumstances. All bear witness to the same testimony: Jesus intervened and healed hopeless problems, really and truly incurable by any other means, method, or person beside Himself.

I recall the couple from another state who were rearing a daughter hopelessly retarded from birth. Then they and their church realized that retardation wasn't different than other "untreatable" physical conditions God had already healed in their midst. As a congregation, they prayed for over two thousand hours until that precious child tested normally for intelligence and lost the abnormal facial traits that had accompanied her condition.

Consider the young man I met at a conference who had tested positively for HIV. Healed by God, he tests negatively today. The Lord has not only given him before and after tests to verify his healing, but an effective, strategic ministry to homosexuals as well.

Others suffered no fatal diseases or birth defects, but had been dealt such terrible blows by life that they'd tried to take their lives. An Air Force widow who couldn't overcome her depression and grief after the death of her husband in a military crash had overdosed so many times trying to kill herself that her friends and those treating her despaired of keeping her alive. But when she placed her grief in one of Jesus' bleeding hands and her depression in the other, not only did she receive healing but also a blessing in the form of a ministry to other bereaved widows whom she now counsels and prays for.

Others we've met were so shattered emotionally and spiritually that they seemed to be in comas of the soul. Having been ejected by a cult when his mental problems had so overwhelmed him he could no longer solicit money for "the cause," one man could barely think. He could only sit and tremble until the Spirit of God moved on the face of his madness, redeeming him from the counterfeit into the life of the Real. He smiles now. His life has purpose and meaning. His head is steady and precise as he draws house plans for his employer.

Consider the story of the dyslexic young woman who had failed her way through public schools. Her failures ate away her self-image as a person and a woman. Her parents only reinforced her negative picture of herself. Months of healing prayer with and for her produced not only a positive self-image but also a cure for her perceptual and learning handicaps.

We could share stories about men and women from every station and walk in life, suffering from every imaginable problem, who've received total healing from the Lord, not just better feelings for a day or two. These are not special people but people like you, created by a God who wanted to heal them from problems they'd given themselves or that others and/or Satan had given them, not God. These people came to Him for the salvation of their souls and the healing of their bodies and minds, just as you can. All you need to do is ask and receive.

Finally, one cannot write about those who were and are healed without addressing the legitimate question, What about those who are not healed? The short answer is that I don't know. I don't think anyone else knows either why some are healed and others aren't.

This much I can tell you. Those who are not healed on the outside, but who stand before God in their suffering without quitting, receive the same internal wholeness as those who are healed externally. They also receive the strength to stand as Jesus did until the answer comes, whether three days must pass, as it did for Him before He was resurrected, or not in time and space at all but in eternity. Whether now or later, I assure you that all will hear *"be made whole"* (Luke 8:50) if they continue to look to and on Jesus as they wait.

One thing all of us can do in the interim as we await these words is dispel the false reasons commonly given for the absence of healing now. Invariably, they include: someone wasn't healed because there is secret sin in his life, or, he just didn't have enough faith.

Like Job's counselors, those who use the first "reason" to explain healing's absence are seldom able to point to a confirmed word from God revealing the sin they allude to. They support their condemnation of another with what Jesus said isn't always the case (see John 9:1-3).

Giving reasons is serious business. One needs not only to be right, but certain as well that no judgment has crept in to his position.

The experience of many with those touting the second "reason"—a lack of faith—is often comparable: elements of judgment, an incorrect diagnosis, and sometimes the displacement onto others of a personal lack of all but intellectual faith—that is, a lack of God-given, real faith as referred to in Ephesians 2:8.

People who present these two explanations as well as all of the rest of us must be very careful to heed the caution pertaining to judgment: the measure with which we judge comes back to us. Thus, we better have a revelation of God's wisdom when we send it out to another.

Chapter 28

You're Already Cured, Too

"When spiritual intuition doesn't accompany analysis, emotional and intellectual paralysis are the result." —The Author

Beyond the simple facts of the stories contained in this book lies a fundamental question: What really happened to these people during counseling? This question, of course, provokes others: How were they actually healed? Specifically, how were their problems solved? Can I achieve the same?

Modern medicine uses the word "therapy" to mean many different methods and processes. In early Greek *therapeutikos* meant "to attend to," and a *therapon* was "an attendant or midwife who made way for the goddess Psyche's head." In a fuller definition, therapy means to stretch one's limbs or consciousness, opening oneself to giving birth as well as to healing. This joining of meanings—"to heal" and "to birth"—is implicit in healing or therapeutic prayers.

Prayer does not by itself heal or restore. Jesus does that. Prayer stands in the same relation to healing as the midwife does to the birth of a baby. In presenting these stories we aimed to show the wonderful results of such healing prayer. We want to encourage you, the reader, that it can produce similar results for you if you are open to Christ and to being born again into a relationship with Him.

Each of the people in these stories renounced and totally quit former ways of thinking, acting, and feeling. In some cases they were delivered of evil spirits. They asked Jesus to come into their lives, to forgive their sins, to be their personal Savior. Unlike many Christians who stop at redemption, they pressed on to what God intended salvation in Christ to be for each of us which is far, far more than just forgiveness and the assurance of eternal life in heaven. They found salvation in its completed sense. The Greek word *sozo*, which is translated in our English Bibles as "salvation," means "wholeness." How did they become whole?

First, someone had to inform them that there is more to salvation than what's taught in many churches. A convert can't seek more than forgiveness unless someone tells her or him there is more to be had.

Second, the Holy Spirit released a personal Pentecost in each of these lives. The Holy Spirit, of course, came into their lives at the instant they were saved. But having Another within is not to be equated with being saturated with that One. Bear in mind that the Holy Spirit is not any spirit but the Spirit of God, imbued with the same powers and attributes of God the Father and God the Son.

Jesus listed the signs by which believers could mark the presence of the Holy Spirit in the passage usually described as The Great Commission: *"Go ye into all the world and preach the gospel to every creature...And these signs shall follow them that believe. In My name shall they cast our devils; they shall speak with new tongues....they shall lay hands on the sick, and they shall recover"* (Mark 16:15-18 KJV).

In 1 Corinthians 14:4-5, Paul tells the early church, *"He that speaketh in an unknown tongue edifieth himself...I would that ye all spake with tongues, but rather that ye prohesied."* I take this to mean that tongues plus the interpretation equals prophecy. The twelfth chapter of First Corinthians discusses the public use of tongues and indicates that not everyone must do it in church. The fourteenth chapter of First Corinthians relates to the private, devotional use. Paul asserts that everyone should use them for that, and apparently, everyone did. The equation isn't that being baptized with the Spirit equals speaking in tongues. The latter is simply one of the manifestations of the former.

The strongest evidence or manifestation of the Spirit-filled life is good fruit that will be seen, known, and desired by others—the kind referred to in Galatians 5:22-23: *"love, joy, peace, patience, kindness, goodness, faithfulness, gentleness, and self-control."* Such fruit is not produced in a day, but when God's Spirit is in and overflowing a life, a person begins to feel, think, talk, and act more and more like Him.

Holy Spirit baptism for anyone including the people in this book, means they've entered into a real, functional, and balanced relationship with the Father, Son, and Holy Ghost. This is not a simple intellectual recognition that Jesus is divine and will forgive the sins of those who ask. Like first century Christians described in the New Testament, these people walk with God. The miraculous accompanies this walk as the norm, not the exception.

Third, these people have accepted the biblical principle that the fundamental ingredient of healing prayer is the forgiveness of sins. Now, while Jesus forgives our sins, we must likewise forgive those who've sinned against us. We must forgive and bless them and ask the Lord to forgive and bless them, too. Even if we rationalize our hatred and believe it is somehow justified, we still sin.

Taking this thought a step further, the folks in these stories realized that we all hold resentments against God and ourselves as well

271

as others. Not being a sinner, God certainly doesn't need forgiveness, but we need to be forgiven for what we've held against Him and blamed Him for. Someday we'll discover that although we blamed a lot on Him, He had little to do with our problems. Many of our troubles arise from misunderstanding that is a result of man's fall in the garden.

Without thorough self-forgiveness, healing will always be incomplete. Sometimes it is easier to forgive others than it is to forgive ourselves. Yet it is this failure to forgive ourselves that can make life as hopeless and needlessly fractured and fragmented as it is when we haven't forgiven others.

When we hate others, we suffer for it—emotionally and, in most cases, physically, too. When we harbor resentments and guilt feelings against ourselves, we suffer the same consequences. We don't own ourselves. We belong to our Creator, God. What we hold against ourselves brings us to the commission of the same sin as when we sin against others. When either Christian or non-Christian people dislike themselves, they become cut off from that disliked part not unlike the raccoon who becomes permanently crippled by chewing off its trapped foot. We become, to use biblical terms, double-minded or, in the modern jargon of psychology, self-alienated. The part of our self that is alienated "infects" other parts of our self, breeding guilt, depression, and an increasingly deteriorating self-image at minimum or serious mental and even physical health problems at the other end of the spectrum. No one can live with a divided self without lasting negative effects, if left unaddressed.

Salvation must be whole—addressing not just the mind, but also the heart. Yet in the Western church too often, believers come to Christ mentally initially, but if the conversion process ends there, they are left with yet another division within the self—one between head and heart. Seduced by the power of reason, too many Westerners believe their job is simply to know God, which is only partially true. God designed us not to just think, but to feel and to be as well.

Much of the frenetic doing we see in the West today is the result of thinly veiled guilt of those trying to atone for their sin and self-loathing. The people described in these pages gave birth to their true, whole selves through yielding both head and heart to Christ. They also found their true male and female selves.

Although God is neither male nor female as a spirit, all that is genuinely masculine and feminine resides in His Being. Recall, Genesis teaches that we were made in His image. Although we are fallen, residue of that basic nature remains and needs redemption, too. "*Redeemed*" means completely bought (and brought) back. Bought back from sin, bought back from living only in part of ourselves, brought back from hurts we inflict on ourselves and the hurts others have done to us. It also means being bought/brought back from false masculine and feminine identities to what God intended.

Western culture has experimented with many different models of male and female roles; most of them are caricatures of the reality God intended.

Genesis teaches that God created Adam, who, like his Creator, contained both the male and female principles. Seeing that man needed a helper, God divided Eve from Adam. "Helper" is the English translation of two Hebrew words *ezer* and *kenegdo,* meaning equal powers that are counterparts of each other.

Genesis 2:24 talks about man and woman becoming one again in a different way than they were one before their separation. That they should *"cleave"* to one another carries the meaning of being glued together after having been broken apart.

Without healing prayers the relations between men and women are fallen. Also, men and women develop a distorted view of what being a man and woman entails. This, in turn, distorts and hurts sexual and family relations.

Finally, the people in this book pursued and discovered a lost art that God longs for each of His children to develop—listening prayer. Using a prayer journal, they recorded God's words to them about their relationship to Him and others, the dreams He sent, the life goals He revealed for them.

I'm convinced that without a continuing, growing effort at listening prayer, few Christians will not "backslide" to some bent attitude or habit that puts to death the true self and resurrects the false. Although still spiritually saved, such a person is left no better off in earthly terms than they were before they came to Christ.

Salvation and restoration can be yours through the therapy of healing prayer. The purpose of this book is to render testimony of this reality.

As you have made your way through these pages I hope you've found a chapter that really "spoke" to you, one that has helped. Some won't have, and perhaps will be saying, "You didn't include my problem," or, "I don't have any problems." If you are one who doesn't think you have any problems—no fears, no worries, nothing that concerns you at the moment, may I suggest you do have one thing in common with the storytellers of each of these chapters. Sooner or later (even if it isn't until death itself), you'll run into a problem like they did that's unresolvable, that you can't get rid of regardless of the amount of human effort—yours or others'.

Whether it's when we hear, "I'm sorry, it's terminal," and we face the big "Something," or whether it is one of the several other "somethings" most of us go through before that one, sooner or later we all come to the same place: "I can't get out of this one no matter what I do."

When that time comes, our different surface responses to things get stripped away, leaving us with the same underneath response, the one that's common to every one of us when we are in an inescapable place.

We've seen or felt that response in ourselves as the car skidded out of control, for example; or, if not in ourselves, then in somebody, sometime. Occasionally, you can even see it in everybody at the same time. I did, twice, most recently when our country became involved in the 1991 Middle East War.

The first time was November, 1963, that fateful date when everyone then alive remembers what they were doing when the heard the news: President Kennedy, assassinated in Dallas!

I was taking a series of "El" (elevated) trains and busses from the south side of Chicago to the northwest side, wondering what Christian holiday or Saint's Day I'd forgotten that had people streaming into the few inner city churches which were still courageous enough to keep their doors unlocked on a weekday, and what could be going on that had more people than I had ever seen walking down the street crying, some kneeling as they sobbed. Nothing had been on the news that morning. No bombs were dropping. The city wasn't on fire again. No major gang violence or riots had erupted in any neighborhood.

Walking through the large lobby of my office building after the El ride, the strains of a familiar Christian hymn were heard coming from a group of employees standing together in front of a coffee machine. I remained more than puzzled until I reached my office, heard the fateful news, and learned that other counseling centers like mine around the city were as jammed as all the churches were with distraught people, just like those I'd seen weeping on the streets.

The people in Chicago weren't crying only because we had lost our President. It was more personal, closer to home. They feared that if a conspiracy were involved, New York City would get the first A-bomb and Chicago, the second, not to mention realistic fears of gang (and individual) anarchy, violence, and rioting. But they were crying for yet another closer-to-home reason.

Facing what they thought might be only hours to live, many who didn't know God were quickly and desperately trying to get acquainted with Him before they were killed and had to meet Him in a judgment setting. The tragedy was that few had a clue as to how to go about really finding God on their own.

As I talked to some of those people in the days immediately following that tragedy, I learned for the most part they were people who had lived all their lives in God's world with all the health, material benefits, and loved ones He'd given them. Yet, coming to a time when they thought they were facing death, they had never had more than occasional thoughts about Him or spoken more than token prayers to Him.

The panic each of them was experiencing then and what we, too, have felt is really a gift of mercy God puts in each of us to tell us we're not ready to meet Him and desperately need to do what is necessary in order to be ready before the actual time arrives. What is involved in that readying and how to go about it is found in this chapter.

If you are a reader who didn't find a story that applied to your situation, you may be saying, "What about me? I've had serious problems with _____, and you didn't say a thing about those of us with that!" From stories shared with me five days a week, five times a day, over the last thirty-five years, I'm sure I could find your story or a variation of it and your problem among them.

"All right," you say, "but this chapter: *You're Already Cured, Too*, doesn't apply to me. Tell me, how could I be cured already when I surely don't feel that way? Real cure is what I'm still looking for."

A fair question. I would answer it this way. What we call "The Lord's Prayer" in the Bible really isn't His, it's ours. The real Lord Jesus' prayer for us (and Himself) is found in chapter seventeen of John's Gospel. The Lord's Prayer of Matthew 6:9-13 is a prayer Jesus told us to use repeatedly when we pray for ourselves.

One of things we've been told to pray in it is: *"Thy will be done on earth as it has already been done in heaven."* Merely saying those words does not mean that what God wants to give you in your life here and now from heaven will just automatically float down into your life and solve all your problems. It does mean that if you say those words and then do something—what the Bible calls faith and works together—your Cure that's already been created by God's Spirit will come to you in time and space, in your here and now.

"What's the something I do?" you ask.

Let's look at the answer to that question first as it applies to your salvation. Jesus has already died for everyone and "sees" them all (agnostic, atheist, etc.) alike: as though they had already accepted Him and His death for their sins. Does this mean everyone is going to heaven when they die like some Universalists and New Agers tell us? Of course not. The acceptance of what Jesus did has to take place in the heart of each individual on earth before heaven can "happen" to them. Sadly, there has never been and never will be a time in history when everyone will receive that salvation provided for them on the cross. Therefore, those who don't are not sent to hell by Jesus. They send themselves there by refusing to choose not something but Someone who gets God's will done on earth as it is in heaven.

The same is true with your cure. That cure for healing you and your problem is for everyone. Nothing that's happened to you, for whatever reason or cause, is without cure.

You are, in fact, already cured by the Healer, the Wonderful Counselor, Jesus. In His eyes in heaven, you are already "fixed." But all things given in heaven—whether salvation, healing, peace, or another gift—have to be appropriated and received by you, here and now, or whatever you need will never become yours.

Your next question may be: "What do I need to appropriate in order to get my cure, and how do I do it?" The answer includes the steps or ingredients in healing found in the stories you've just read. So let's review the restatement of them from the chapters here.

1. These people first came from a position of no or only mental belief in or about Jesus Christ as Savior to establishing a personal relationship with Him. This happened by praying to the effect that they received His death as payment for their sins and received Him into their spirits to begin a relationship with Him as Redeemer (one who buys everything back). They entered into an exchanged life where they laid down theirs so He could live His through them.

One of my sons at age five succinctly, if not eloquently, expressed it this way: "Daddy," he began in the sincerest of tones I'd ever heard him use, "last night I asked Jesus to come live in the part of me that will be gone when I die. I asked for His death to count for my sins, and I told Him He could run my life from now on." He didn't know to call this first "ingredient" he had described salvation, atonement, or redemption, but this is what he had been given at that very moment of his life as he entered into a relationship with Christ—Christ in Him, he in Christ.

2. The second ingredient involves a relationship, too, one with the Holy Spirit. After receiving the Holy Spirit (the Spirit of God and Jesus) at their conversion, our storytellers asked for and received the fullness, empowering, and release of that same Holy Spirit in and through them, so they could grow fruit in their lives and give it back to Jesus and to their fellow human beings through His gifting to them.

3. Some experienced what is spoken about in The Lord's Prayer, the literal translation being: *"deliver us from the evil one(s)."* They found deliverance, freedom, and exorcism (meaning release from) oppressive spiritual forces in and upon their lives and sometimes through them upon the lives of others as well.

4. All experienced inner healing prayer (healing of the mind, thoughts, will, and "heart"—our emotions and deep places of the

soul), the step in the cure that involves several aspects of forgiveness. It is prayer to God in Jesus' name about a specific matter, involving specific people. The person who is praying asks forgiveness of his/her sins against others, forgives theirs against him, and asks Jesus to forgive them as well. Healing prayer includes forgiving ourselves, too.

When healing prayer occurs, you don't get a new past life, but the Holy Spirit heals what happened in it, redeems that which has been irretrievably lost (as far as your retrieving it by your own powers is concerned), and restores it to you, thereby making you as if whatever happened to you in the past didn't. The Bible calls it putting off the old person and putting on the new. Jesus makes those He has created new in their inner selves by healing them.

Without that cure and the forgiveness that is such an essential part of it, unforgiveness continues to be our portion to ourselves, to others, and from God. We continue to reap hurt and problems because we've not changed what we sowed previously.

The cure for us took place historically two thousand years ago: Jesus' death on a cross. But because Jesus, God the Son, is outside time (i.e., all time is now or present to Him), He is still on that cross, a cross we can come to, lifting up what needs to be cured in us into His bleeding hand that removes it from us. It is the cross from which the other bleeding hand reaches down to us, giving us what He has to replace what we've given Him to change, fix, remove, cure, and/or heal.

5. Healing *from* something is but a partial aspect of the cure. What each of these people also received was a healing *to* something—a healing to be, to become, to do, or all of the above. In the Genesis account of creation, it says God created both male and female (Adam and Eve) to be in His image before they "fell." God restored the masculine/feminine in each when He forgave them, sent them to a new place and told them to start over forgiven. They did, bearing a son who replaced the slain Abel. This son they named Seth which has the meaning "new creation, new beginning, second chance, fresh start."

God is still doing today what He did for Adam and Eve, making us new creatures (though the same people) in Christ, not people who are all necessarily called to do great exploits and mighty things for God, but people who when converted are called to and able for the first time really to *be* and to *become* like Him through the process of life. And as men and women of God in Christ, He lives out His life in us and does mighty (by His definition, not ours) works through us.

In a nutshell that's what happened in these stories, stories of people with messed up lives who started a new life with Another, a life they have kept on living with Him through prayer and study of the Bible on their own and with others who befriended them when they went to "alive" churches.

These people had one other thing: another person in their lives just before or at the beginning of their spiritual journey: a therapist or counselor. Everyone doesn't need a professional therapist, but we can all benefit from someone who is therapeutic. As we've previously noted, the Greek words from which we get therapy and therapist mean to attend like a midwife does; an attendant who helps one "stretch" themselves and their consciousness in such a way that it brings to birth or to healing.

We can benefit from such a therapeutic person most if they are Christians themselves before we seek them out as our therapeutic attendant. God-given wisdom and spiritual intuition ought to be a part of all counsel, for without it change is partial—often only external—and emotional, spiritual and intellectual paralyses remain within us.

As I write these words, I'm pained for the ones reading them who are saying, "But I've already been to a counselor, even a Christian one. I've read and re-read this chapter and followed all the steps but I'm no better. I'm still not cured. What's wrong with me?"

Answering questions for people is serious business. Questions like these from persons with broken, wounded hearts are especially serious and difficult to answer, particularly through a book where seeing, listening to, and praying with the one who asks is impossible.

I can say with confidence based both on the authority of Scripture and personal and professional experience: *don't give up*. Avail yourself of the suggestions and resources given on the *For Additional Help* section that follows this chapter. It wasn't until my third trip through the *Twelve-Steps: A Spiritual Journey* (a workbook based on Charles Wesley's steps for new Christians, later discovered and used by AA in their 12-step program), that I was personally cured of some things I missed completely the first two times. The translation of the Hebrew of Psalm 32 says David prayed about past things in his life over and over again until everything was revealed to God's satisfaction. God already knew all about it, so it wasn't that David had to do this for God. He needed to "keep on keeping on" for himself. Most of us have less to get over than David did, but even so, the process of healing over a span of time—in increments we can handle—is really a blessing of mercy.

Ask God to lead you to a spiritually-alive church and to Christian people—even just one—who will help you as an "attendant" or "midwife" until you discover through prayer and God-inspired counsel why things aren't working for you and to help you get past whatever it is that is blocking your healing.

Your cure already stands completed in heaven as you read these words. And the God of heaven (and earth and you and me) says nothing is too hard for Him, including the delivery of this healing to you.

The Wonderful Counselor is waiting to impart to you His comfort, peace, and love and to restore your life to the wholeness He earnestly desires for you. *Domine vobisium et cum spiritutia*: "May God be with you and with your spirit," as you begin (or begin again) to do all you need to make His healing presence a reality in your life now.

*"The Spirit of the Sovereign LORD is on me, because the LORD has anointed me to preach good news to the poor.
He has sent me to bind up the brokenhearted, to proclaim freedom for the captives and release from darkness for the prisoners."*
—Isaiah 61:1

*"He heals the brokenhearted and binds up their wounds—curing their pains
and their sorrows."*
—Psalms 147:3 AMP

For Additional Help

If you are interested in additional information on the subjects discussed, the following books, tapes, newsletters, pamphlets, and conferences are recommended:

Allender, Dr. Dan B., *The Wounded Heart, Bold Love, Cry of the Soul,* Navpress, Colorado Springs, CO.

Basham, Don, *A Handbook on Holy Spirit Baptism,* Whitaker House, Springdale, PA.

Carothers, Merlin. *Prison to Praise,* Merlin Carothers, Escondido, CA 92025.

Conner, Clint. Pamphlets available from 570 Morningside, Lancaster, OH 43130, 50 cents each, including postage/handling: "Steps in Inner Healing," "Steps in Healing Prayer," "Cults and the Occult: Old, New and New Age," "Deliverance from Non-Demonic Bondages," "Healing Panic Attacks, Phobias and Fears," "Healing for Grief and Depression," "Child's Play," "Healing for Sexual Hurts and Sins," "Healing Your Shame," "Why Christians Fail," "Marriage Isn't for Happiness," "How to Raise Whole Children in a Broken World."

——. *Father-To-Be,* 570 Morningside, Lancaster, OH 43130, $2.00 each, including postage/handling.

Dalby, Gordon. *Healing the Masculine Soul,* Word Books, Dallas, TX.

MacNutt, Francis. *Healing,* Ave Maria Press, Notre Dame, IN 46556.

Payne, Leanne. *The Healing Presence, Real Presence, The Broken Image, The Healing of the Homosexual, Restoring the Christian Soul Through Healing Prayer, Crisis in Masculinity*, Crossway Books, Westchester, IL, and Baker Book House, Ada, MI.

——. Tapes and videos on such topics as "Practicing the Presence of God," "Incarnational Reality," "Self-Acceptance," "True Imagination," "The Disease of Introspection," and "Misogyny" available from FTM, 1111 S. Pierce, Lakewood CO 80226 (tapes) and ER Productions, 2670 Billingsley Rd., Columbus, OH 43235 (videos).

——. Pastoral Care Ministries conferences & newsletter: contact PCM, Box 1313, Wheaton, IL 60189-1313.

Recovery. *The Twelve Steps—A Spiritual Journey*, Recovery Publications, San Diego, CA.

Sandford, John and Paula. *Transformation of the Inner Man, Healing the Wounded Spirit*, etc., Victory House, Tulsa, OK.

——. Tapes, newsletter, conference information available from Elijah House, Couer d'Alene, ID 83814.

Seamonds, David. *Putting Away Childish Things*, Victor Books, Wheaton, IL.

Those needing help beyond that offered in books, and not aware of competent Christian counselors in your area are encouraged to contact Focus on the Family, Colorado Springs, CO 80995. This organization, directed by psychologist/author Dr. James Dobson, maintains a listing of Christian counselors/counseling agencies located throughout the United States.